A HOME FOR WICKED THOUGHTS

DAVID T DASSAU

A HOME FOR WICKED THOUGHTS

CONTENTS

Acknowledgements

Putting this collection of short stories together over the past year has been a journey, and there's no way I could have done it alone. So, here's my heartfelt thanks to the people who helped make it happen.

First up, Ted White. Ted, you've been like my personal editor, bravely reading most of these stories and offering feedback when you could have easily told me to buzz off. I couldn't pay you, but that didn't stop you from helping. If I had to pick a best friend (which I hate doing), it'd be you.

Alex Jimenez, you've been my rock as a "constant editor," reading stories under extreme pressure (aka my begging) and always finding a way to say something kind. Not to mention, you hand-painted the incredible cover art! Mamacita, thank you.

Mack Elder, you're one of the coolest humans on the planet. As a screenwriter and master of words, your insights have been priceless. Having you read and critique these stories blew my mind.

A huge shoutout to J. Kasper Kramer. Your brutal honesty about the writing life pushed me to not only pursue this collection but keep going in general. Without your wisdom, I'd still be spinning my wheels. And readers—if you like YA fiction, go check out her work.

Thanks to every English teacher who cared enough to invest in me, especially Mr. Matt Puryear and Coach Robert Kent, who created a space for me to grow as a writer.

To my family—Mom, Dad, Ben, Josh, and Amy—thank you for your endless support and weird inspiration.

And finally, my wife Lindsay and kids, Charlie and Erin: you keep me grounded. Without you, I'd be adrift. Thank you for being my anchor.

To my wife, Lindsay
When I found you, I found me

"Hello. My name is Inigo Montoya. You killed my father. Prepare to die!"

— **INIGO MONTOYA,** *THE PRINCESS BRIDE* **(1987)**

CHAPTER 1

A Ghost in Crestwood

Part I: A Haunted Past

8:07 PM

Will's eyes fluttered open to a world of utter darkness, the kind that suffocated and stole the breath from his chest. He winced at the high-pitched ringing that threatened to split his skull in two. Like an Etch-A-Sketch, he shook his head in a feeble attempt to clear away the pain.

The possibility of a concussion crept slowly into his consciousness. He smelled old, rotting wood. The dank aroma of mildew hung heavy in the air, causing his stomach to churn.

Cold and terrified, Will *yearned* to call for help. But his scorched throat kept the words from escaping. He tried to wet his dry, cracked lips, but his tongue—brittle and dehydrated like jerky—stuck to the insides of his mouth like velcro.

A blindfold concealed his vision. When he tried to remove it, a prickling sensation shot through his arms. Bound behind his back, his hands were like phantom limbs. He flexed what little mobility he had in his fingers in a helpless attempt to resurrect blood flow.

As he struggled against his confines, the darkness enveloping him, he desperately recounted the day's events. Will recalled the unrelenting mid-August heat as it bore down on him and his teammates during football practice. Not only did he contend with carrying the team on his back for the Fall 2019 season, but also felt the pressure of the scouts from the college teams.

He remembered meeting his dad for lunch, where they discussed *more* football-related issues. The weight of his *entire* future rested like an anchor against his back. Even *now* he could feel that pressure, as numbness radiated in his limbs.

Stepping further through the day's timeline, he recalled going home to shower and play a few games of Madden. Everything *after* that suddenly became murky in the waters of his memory. He was *almost positive* that he'd sent a few texts to his girlfriend Maxine.

Perhaps he had even sent a text to his friend Ben. Or did he *receive* one? Another dim light bulb came to life in his brain, remembering that Ben was due back that week from his summer wilderness retreat. It *was* that week... *right*? The irony of misplacing *this* piece of the mental puzzle was the likelihood that Will had *already* forgotten when his best friend was set to return home.

His memory fast-forwarded to the end of the tape, where he recalled pulling up in front of a seemingly vacant, dilapidated house. After exiting his car, Will had compared the weathered numbers on the mailbox to those on his smartphone's GPS. The warm glow of the sunset cast an orange haze across the overgrown weeds and grass in the front yard. The paint on the shutters was chipped and faded.

Will had a sudden, *striking* urge to *leave*—to get back in his car and drive away. *Fast*. But before he could act on this unforeseen impulse, everything went *black*. And now, here he sat—bound helplessly to a chair with a splitting headache, *consumed* by darkness.

His heart raced at the sound of approaching footsteps. The floorboards creaked and groaned under each slow, methodical stride. Will *pulled* at his binds in a fruitless, last-ditch effort to free himself. But he stopped when the footsteps came to halt.

"Wh-who's there?" Will asked, his voice creaking like rusted hinges. When he was greeted with silence, he called out desperately once more. "What's going on? Can *someone* please answer me?"

The blindfold was suddenly pulled off, and one darkness was exchanged for another. Will looked around frantically, impatiently waiting for his eyes to adjust to his dimly lit surroundings. When his vision finally pulled focus, they were trained on a looming figure in front of him, shrouded in a murky haze. He wanted to assume this was all some horrible dream that he'd wake from any minute. It was a nice thought.

"Hello, *William*," said the shadow.

It then struck a match, bringing forth a burst of brilliant light. After squinting through the flame that lit a nearby candle, Will could *finally* make out the dark figure.

"*Ben*?" Will asked. "Wh- what's going on?"

"It's so good to see you, my friend," Ben replied, ignoring Will's desperate query. "It has *certainly* been a summer. Tell me, how have you been?"

Will's worried expression morphed into one of profound confusion. The moment of relief by having his blindfold removed was short-lived. He was unable to conceive of any reason why he'd be in this predicament—tied to a chair in an abandoned house, with his best friend *looming* over him.

"How have I *been*?" Will asked, incredulous. "Ben, please tell me what is going on here! Where are we, and why do you have me strapped to this chair?"

"In due time, William," Ben smirked. "*All* in due time."

Will felt a chill shoot down his spine as he registered Ben's furtive grin. His friend then turned on his heel, and walked to an adjacent room in the dark, abandoned house, tossing the blindfold to the floor.

Will took slow, unsteady breaths as his mind raced to make sense of the situation. What could Ben want with him, and why *here*, in this godforsaken *dump*? Ben would've been someone he'd call to get him *out* of this situation. So it defied logic that he would be the one *responsible* for Will's predicament.

He thought about the last time he had seen Ben—almost *three months* ago, the day before he shipped off to his wilderness retreat camp. Although his parents were ultimately the ones that made the decision to send him, Will had to assume *partial* responsibility. After all, enrolling Ben in the camp *was* his idea.

When Will brought the brochure to Ben's mom and dad, he pointed out how it would help their son become more decisive and confident. There *were* ulterior motives for getting Ben out of town for a few months, but Will had decided to keep those to himself.

Just as Will's vision had acclimated to the darkness, Ben returned to the abandoned living room, carrying a chair of his own. He placed it opposite to William, sat down, and nonchalantly crossed his legs.

Will gawked at his friend, too dumbfounded to speak. His lasting memory of that 17-year-old boy, scrawny and timid, was the antithesis of the *monster* that sat before him now. The *old* Ben would've toppled over if you brushed against him too hard. This *shapeshifter* that wore Ben's face looked like Steve Rogers, *after* he was injected with the Super-Soldier serum.

Ben didn't say anything at first; he only stared at Will with a fondness that made his skin crawl. He felt as if Ben was sizing him up, like they hadn't seen each other in *years* instead of months. There weren't many people that could make Will feel exposed like this. And he would've laughed you out of the room if you'd have told him three months ago that *Ben* of all people would shoot to the top of that list.

"*So*," Ben began, "I know you must have a *ton* of questions right now. 'Where are we?' 'What are we doing here?' 'Do you think it's appropriate to duct tape your best friend to a chair?' I *know* how this looks. But *trust me*, once we're all done here, I promise that all of your questions will be answered... and *then* some. Deal?"

Ben held out his hand for Will to shake, then let out a short laugh. "Oh, my bad. I *forgot*. Silly me!"

Will, failing to comprehend the humor, shot his friend a confused grimace. Was this Ben's idea of a *sick joke*? If so, when did his sense of humor become so... *twisted*?

"Alright, I'm going to throw a date out at you," Ben continued, "and I want to see if you can guess its significance."

"Um... *okay*?" Will replied. His feelings of panic and fear slowly dissolved into anxiety and frustration.

"Okay, *here it is*: September 18th, 2017."

Will reluctantly mulled the date over in his mind, but came up short. He had *no clue* what the significance of this arbitrary date might be. It wasn't *exactly* a surprise, however. The pounding in his head was still relentless, muddying the waters of his memory.

"I... I *don't know*, Ben," Will answered. "I give up."

"Eh, that's alright," Ben excused. "It was a *little* unfair of me to expect you to remember something from almost *two years* ago. Not to mention the fact that you *just* woke up from me knocking you out earlier. How *is* your head, by the way? I didn't mean for you to hit the ground that hard."

Will's eyes widened as anger quickly overtook him. "What the *fuck*, Ben?" he asked, enraged as he strained against his bonds. "Answer me *right now*, dammit! What the *hell* is going on? What are you *up to*?"

Ben continued, ignoring Will. "September 18th, 2017 was the day we became friends! Don't you remember, you introduced yourself to me after geometry class? I'll *never* forget it. Mr. Hardin was giving you shit for not paying attention. You were laughing at me because *I* wasn't paying attention either. But since *you* were the class clown, with the reputation of causing disturbances, *you* were the one he picked on."

Ben's face was *beaming* with nostalgia, his eyes distant as they recalled their plutonic meet-cute. For Will, the memories slowly began pouring in.

"At any rate," Ben went on, "you ran up to me after class and we made small talk about how boring math was. You know, people *really* don't give enough credit to the *power* of commiseration. That conversation was so innocuous, and yet so fundamentally important. It's what brought us together. I mean, *fuck*, I couldn't believe it! *Will White*, the guy who played football, made *everyone* laugh, and fucked the hottest girls in school... *that guy* was talking to *me*. And here's the kicker: You even walked me to my next class. I didn't even realize it was out of your way until we finally said our goodbyes, and you doubled back in a sprint in the opposite direction."

Will let out an impatient huff of air. Ben carried on, uninterested in his friend's irritation.

"Those first few months were *incredible*. Clichés aside, you were *literally* the brother I never had. Looking back, I think it was the idea of knowing that somebody *cared* what happened to me. And I never really had that in a friend until you came along.

"But there *were* downsides to having you as pretty much my only pal. It was difficult, learning to share you with others. And it *did* sting a little, knowing that you meant more to me than I did to you. Some of your teammates had known you for *years*. How was I going to compete with that!

"Hell, I remember this one Friday at lunch, you were sitting with a handful of your football buddies. You guys had a game that night, so I was mostly just a fly on the wall while y'all talked shit about the opposing team. In an awkward attempt to be a part of the conversation, I brought up that you and I were supposed to have a sleepover later that night. And then things got weird *real quick*, like I just dropped a giant turd in the punch bowl. But I'll hand it to your teammates, they *were* nice enough to not say anything mean to my face, so I was at least able to avoid the *public* humiliation."

"*Come on*, man," Will cut in, sounding exhausted. "Where are you *going* with all this?"

Ben raised a hand and shot him a courteous smile. "Trust me, I'm getting there. As I was saying, we *had* plans to hang out that night after your game." Ben leaned forward and narrowed his eyes on Will. "But that didn't happen. *Did it?*"

Will rolled his eyes and shook his head, annoyed with this *meaningless* trip down memory lane.

"*Did it?*" Ben repeated, his voice suddenly low and ominous.

"I *stood you up*, is *that* what you want me to say?" Will barked in frustration.

His words echoed off the rotten walls, cutting through the silence that permeated the damp, dark room. A sly grin began to grow across Ben's face.

"*Now* we're getting somewhere," Ben said, leaning back in his chair and retrieving a phone from his pants pocket.

November 3rd, 2017

Tim's Diner, perched on one of the most popular corners in town, was a staple of Crestwood. As one of the oldest businesses in town, it was considered an honorary historical landmark. Long after all other businesses around it shut down for the night, Tim's shone through the dark like a brilliant beacon.

The no-frills brick facade and red awning provided a warm welcome to the townies. It was the *ultimate* melting pot, guaranteeing a space for families, loners, couples, and the town drunks. The coffee was always fresh, and the burgers were the *perfect* kind of greasy. It was the *perfect* slice of wholesome, Rockwellian culture. But during the fall months, when high school football was in full swing, the diner took on a *whole new* vibe.

Since Crestwood High's record-breaking season in 2015, when the football team clinched the Regional Championship, Tim Reubens—Tim's Diner's owner and namesake—instituted a standing rule: Priority seating will be given to the players of the team each Friday during football season, with a free basket of steak fries if they *won* that evening's game. And on those nights, the atmosphere was *electric*.

The halls of Tim's Diner were like a living, breathing organism that November 3rd. It was one week away from the homecoming game, and securing a win that night was the confidence boost that the team—and the entire school—needed. The air inside the diner was rife with post-pubescent, hedonistic fury: Ball players laughed loudly and unencumbered, thirsty couples made out in booths, and food was enjoyed like the spoils after a battle victory. In one particular section, Will and a few of his teammates did their own celebrating.

"*Man*, Will, I still cannot *believe* how you stiff-armed that idiot when you scored," John—the team's quarterback—exclaimed, squirting ketchup onto his post-victory burger.

"Yeah, dude," Mark—the left tackle—chimed in, "I've been watching you play for *years*, and I'll never understand how you make the running back position look so *effortless*."

"Come on, guys, what do you expect?" Will proposed. "This is what you get when you put the best players on the field. You get *fucking results*."

"*Ok, ok*, let's hit pause on the game talk for just a second," John cut in. "Will, I *gotta ask... why* are you hanging out with this guy?"

"Who, *Ben*?" Will asked.

"Yeah, man," Mark said, stepping in to clarify, "*please* tell us that's some Make-A-Wish bullshit you're doing."

A unified burst of laughter erupted from the booth.

"Alright, I'll admit that Ben is a little... *odd*," Will confirmed, "but he's a funny guy. He just *seems* weird because he's not a meathead like us."

"*Nah* dude," said John, jamming a fry into his already full mouth, "I think it's *more* than that. My step-sister's got a kid that's autistic, and he says the *wildest* shit. Seriously, no filter at *all*."

"*Exactly*," Mark agreed, "Maybe he's got that Asperger's thing or whatever. Were y'all *really* supposed to have a sleepover tonight?"

"Psh, *hell* no," Will replied, letting out a nervous chuckle. "Here's the deal: Earlier this week I told him that if I was feeling up to it, *maybe* he could come over to my place after the game to hang out for a little bit."

"Ok, but doesn't he know that we *always* come here after games?" John pried.

"I don't know, *maybe*? It doesn't really matter either way, because I was gonna find some way out of it."

After another bout of laughter, Will spied an exchanged look of suspicion between Mark and John. He *fought* the urge to sink down in his seat as waves of anxiety began to pummel him.

"Maybe he's *gay*," Mark weighed in again. "You ever think of *that*, Will?"

"Yeah, dude," John chimed in, "he could secretly want your dick, and you just don't know it yet."

Will's narrowed eyes darted between Mark and John, his jaw clenched tightly. They were tiptoeing dangerously close to the edge, and he wasn't sure how much longer he could keep them from crossing it.

"Oh, *come on*, Will," Mark continued, "we ain't trying to be homophobic here. You know we don't care about gay dudes being gay. We're just trying to look out for ya, man."

"Yeah, I get it," Will sighed, shoveling the last bite of burger into his mouth.

An awkward silence fell over the table, as each of them grasped for what could be said next to possibly lighten the mood.

"Maybe he *is* gay," Will mentioned nonchalantly.

The silence was broken immediately with an eruption of laughter and a round of high-fives.

8:42 PM

A smartphone sat face-up in Ben's seat as he slowly paced the living room, letting the two-year-old voicemail play. It was one he had listened to *many* times, but was a revelation to Will. When it ended, Will stared blankly at the smartphone. Feelings of disbelief and horrific embarrassment made his skin crawl. The inability to shift uncomfortably in his seat made him feel vulnerable, like an exposed nerve.

"Pretty crazy, huh?" Ben asked, placing the phone back in his pocket, and returning to his seat in front of Ben. "Until that night, I didn't even *realize* you could accidentally butt-dial someone on a smartphone. You really *do* learn something new every day. Except *that* day, I got a two-for-one special."

"Is *that* what this is all about?" Will asked, a slight tremble in his voice. "*Two years ago*, I do some harmless shit-talking in front of my friends after blowing you off, and by *some miracle* it makes its way to you. *Christ*, Ben, we had been friends for *barely* a month at that point."

"Oh *please*, Will. Give me at least a *little* credit! As far as I'm concerned, what you said that night is water under the bridge. And to prove it, I'm not even going to make you apologize for it."

"Then what the *fuck* are we doing here, Ben? Why would you even bring that up if you've gotten over it?"

Ben looked down at Will with a look of sympathy.

"*Why*?" Ben asked. "I'll *tell* you why. For the last two years, you've been the best friend I've *ever* had. At a time when I wasn't looking to make friends—simply because I had *given up* on the idea—you showed up in my life in *fantastic* fashion. You took me under your wing, helped me come out of my shell, and showed me a world that I had been *sorely* missing."

A bulb in the overhead ceiling lamp suddenly began to flicker. After wincing in surprise, Will turned his gaze slowly upward. The bulb continued to flicker for a moment, before it settled on a stable albeit *dim* shine. When his eyes returned to Ben, he noticed an *eerie* smile had grown on his face.

"*However*," Ben continued, voice low, his grin uninviting, "since I've known you, you've also been the *shittiest* friend I've ever had, and proven yourself to be a truly *despicable* human being."

Will's jaw clenched and blood rushed like a tidal wave into his face. Ben's accusations were baseless, and—*almost literally*—added insult to injury. Will was so taken aback by what Ben had said that he had completely forgotten about the mysterious appearance of light above them.

"This... *this* is the thanks I get?" Will asked through gritted teeth. "You know, I could have just as easily ignored you that day after class. I could've gone on my merry way, onto my next period. I didn't have to say *shit* to you! But I *did*, because you were the new kid, and I felt bad for you. And suddenly, after *one* lousy butt-dial, you decide that I'm this *awful* friend. You are a *piece of shit*, you know that? And you *still* haven't told me why you've got me held captive here. I'm starting to think—"

Ben leaned in *uncomfortably* close to Will and put an index finger to his lips. Will felt his outrage deepen, his chest heaving with arduous breaths.

"*Shhh...* I *told* you, my friend," Ben whispered, "I will answer *all* of your questions in due time. As for what you're feeling right now—anger, betrayal, confusion—*all* are warranted. I *completely* understand. The realization of how poorly you have treated me was as much of a shock to me as I imagine it is to you."

Who the hell is this person? Will thought to himself.

The "old" Ben would have *never* spoken to him like this—treated him like the *shit* you'd pick off your shoe. The Ben that Will knew, he couldn't dream of kidnapping his best friend and holding him hostage. And for what? To work out some irrelevant trauma from his past?

Will decided to grit his teeth and bear his way through it. After all, what other choice did he have?

"I'd like to get back to where we were in our story," Ben continued. "That night, you blew me off to party with your teammates. *No problem.* Like I said, water under the bridge. And you even made it up to me! A few weeks later, your birthday rolls around and you invite me over. I show up to your house with your gift and my overnight bag, only to realize that there's no other party guests. Turns out that you *purposefully* arranged your birthday celebration to only include one person: *Me.* I *did* have plans to confront you about the voicemail, but the second I arrived it suddenly felt so... *insignificant.* And so it simply *drifted* out of my brain like a lost balloon."

Ben stood up from his chair and once more paced the dimly lit room. Everything that he currently embodied—the nonchalance, the playful apathy, the laissez-faire attitude—all of it irritated Will to no end. Visions danced across his mind of strangling Ben with his hands—once they were unbound, of course. The thought actually brought a weak smile to his face, sustaining his sanity for just a *little* longer.

"Out of curiosity," Ben began, "do you remember what we did that night? How we ended up celebrating your birthday?"

Will let out a slight sigh. "Yeah, you brought over a bunch of old crap. I think it all belonged to your dad. Some magazines, a couple board games, and a camcorder. I think."

"That's *right*, it *was* a bunch of old crap from my dad! I knew that you'd probably get a ton of cool *modern* gifts from your parents and other friends. So I thought it'd be fun to mix things up "analog style", you know? The magazines were a few Playboys and Hustlers. And *sure*, the spreads were pretty tame compared to the porn we have access to now, but I thought they'd be fun for us to look at.

"Then there were the board games. I mostly brought those along because Ouija was in there. I knew how much you loved your horror, so I figured you'd get a kick out of owning a vintage version of it.

"And of course there was the camcorder—another *useless* piece of technology, given everything that our phones are capable of now. My dad wanted me to take a stab at digitizing all of our old home movies, so he just gave it all to me."

Will felt his pulse rate start to rise again, his patience continuing to wear thin. He had *no idea* where Ben was going with all of this, but he was *stuck here* whether he liked it or not.

"You got a lot of really cool gifts for your birthday." Ben continued. "Nothing I could've ever given you could compare to what your rich parents got you. And to be honest, I would have been completely satisfied to watch you play Madden and Call of Duty all night long on your brand new Xbox. But you actually had an idea for something we could do that didn't involve *any* of your new gifts."

Part II: Will's Birthday

November 18th, 2017, 9:36 PM

"Dude, we should *totally* play this!" Will exclaimed, holding an old board game box.

"Are you *kidding* me?" Ben replied with a chuckle. "You just got a new Xbox from your parents. Do you *really* wanna spend your birthday playing with an old Ouija board?"

"Yeah, man, fuck them gifts. I can play Madden *anytime*. Besides, I got an idea..."

"Uh-oh, what did you have in mind?" Ben asked, noticing the sly smile creeping across his friend's face.

"Are the batteries on your dad's camcorder charged up?"

Ben's eyes shot wide open. "Yeah! I actually charged them this morning. Why do you ask?"

Will smoothed his hands over the vintage game box, admiring its tattered edges and other various imperfections. He actually appreciated Ben's gesture of gifting him something *old-school* like this. It was one of those birthday presents that he'd *never* ask for, himself. But he was *very* glad he received it.

Will looked up at Ben, who was fiddling with the camcorder and its batteries.

"Have you ever seen the movie *Paranormal Activity*?" Will asked.

The idea was to replicate a certain scene from Will's favorite found-footage horror movie, where the lead character believes their house is being haunted by spirits. At one point in the film, her boyfriend attempts to persuade her to use a Ouija board as a way to contact whatever might be haunting their home.

While Will went hunting through his parents garage to find a tripod for the camcorder, Ben opened up the game box and took inventory of its contents. As his eyes read over the words on the instructions card, he noticed a flurry of anxious butterflies in his stomach. Was he nervous about the idea or possibility of conjuring spirits from the afterlife? *No*, he didn't think so. He thought it could be deeper than that, like perhaps the circumstance as a whole.

Ben was after all Will's *sole invite* to his birthday party, which made him feel special. And now, instead of playing with all the cool gifts that Will got that day, they were going to play one of the dorky board games that he brought over. Ben struggled to find a time in recent history when someone made him feel liked and appreciated like this. It was like being hugged from the inside out, and he imagined it was a feeling he could get used to.

Ten minutes later, Will returned with a long, dusty carrying bag containing a tripod that had long since seen its last use. But, it did the trick. As Will took a moment to read over the game instructions himself, Ben connected the camcorder to the tripod, then ensured it had charged batteries and a blank tape.

"Alright, *my dude*, are you ready to summon demons?" Ben asked with a grin, snapping the tape cassette door shut.

"Fuck yeah, I am," Will confirmed, holding up both of his hands in the shape of devil horns.

"Then let's do this shit." Ben powered on the camcorder, pushed the red "RECORD" button, and joined his best friend to playfully communicate with the afterlife.

9:15 PM

Ben had reproduced his smartphone from his pants pocket, and was holding it at arm's length so Will could watch the video playing. He recognized it right away as footage recorded on Ben's camcorder that night. A pang of nostalgia shot through his veins that he had to actively fight against. It *was* a memory mutually cherished by both of them, but Will was in *no mood* for reminiscing.

He had *hoped* to meet Ben tonight so they could hang out for the first time since the start of the summer—*not* be physically assaulted and held captive by him. However, Will understood that he must *play along*, in order to get out of his predicament. He could deal with doling out the consequences later.

When the video concluded, Ben rose from his seat and put the phone back in his pocket. He then let out a sharp, painful sigh as something weighed on his mind. He was about to hand his friend a shovel, and ask him to help dig up the skeletons of their ugly, unremarked past.

"That was honestly a fun memory, Will," Ben said softly. "One of the true, *genuine* moments that you and I have shared together. Looking back, the night of your birthday really did set the tone for our friendship in so many ways."

The rose-tinted smile began to slowly fade from Ben's face, sending an unexpected chill down Will's spine. He was reminded of a time when he took a flight to see family on the other side of the country. Shortly after takeoff, when the plane reached cruising altitude, it *burst* through the clouds and he was suddenly surrounded by magnificent shades of blue. But when the plane descended hours later, it was through tumultuous rainclouds that playfully rocked him and the other passengers like they were merely leaves in the wind.

"Now comes the *real* test," Ben continued. "Do you remember what happened *later* that night?"

Will *didn't* remember. He guessed he had been conscious for at least an hour by that point, and had managed to regain most of his mental faculties and memory recall. And it was a *miracle* that he could remember what Ben had brought over to his birthday party. But he was at a loss for what happened after their Ouija game that night.

There was an odd prickle on the back of his neck. He knew that *something* took place afterward. The question was: Was it something he couldn't remember, or didn't *want* to remember?

"*Um...*" Will began, deciding to take a shot in the dark, "I *think* we just played Xbox for the rest of the night. We woke up the next morning, ate breakfast, and then my dad drove you home." He did his best to make it sound like a statement instead of a guess.

Ben let out an abrupt snort that startled Will; a snort that transitioned into a bout of fake laughter. Suddenly, Will's eyes widened, and fragments of memories in his mind began trickling down and piling up like sand at the bottom of an hourglass.

"Well, my friend," Ben started back, "you're not wrong. Most of that *did* happen, but there's a key moment that you left out. And considering we've never discussed it, I've had to make peace with the idea that you've either *repressed* this memory, or have chosen to *ignore* the fact that it even happened."

Ben reached into his pants pocket once more to fish out his smartphone, and Will gave him the slightest of eye rolls. Although he wore his impatience on his sleeve, he couldn't dismiss the uneasiness that had settled in his bones.

"On Sunday, a few hours after I returned home from your house, I decided to see what I could do about digitizing my family's home movies. But I didn't want to risk something happening to them, so I started with our Ouija video from the night before. And then I discovered something... *interesting* as I watched through the footage."

"Holy shit, did we *actually* summon demons?" Will mocked, a playful grin on his face.

"No, not *quite*," Ben chuckled.

"Ok, *what then*, Sam Raimi? What was so *compelling* about the footage?"

"There was *more* of it."

A devious and menacing smile spread across Ben's face. It was the look of a satiated lunatic. Will had *never* seen that kind of smile on Ben before. The way the low light of the overhead bulb cast shadows across his high cheekbones made Will feel uneasier than ever.

Had Ben *always* had these devilish features, and Will just hadn't noticed before? Perhaps it was a recent development, like when fat kids go into Army boot camp, and come out skinny on the other side. Whatever the case, Will was now willing to play along with whatever Ben wanted, as long as it meant he got to leave here. And *soon*.

Ben had pulled up a second video on his smartphone. He turned it around to face Will, tapped play, and all at once the lost memory—the one that Will had tried *so damn hard* to forget—came *rushing* back to him from that night. He shook his head with incredulous disbelief.

"That's... *impossible*," Will whispered to himself, only vaguely aware he had spoken out loud.

November 18th, 2017, 11:51 PM

"Are you sure... this is... ok?" Will asked, his whisper cutting through the silence of his dark bedroom.

"Y- *yeah*... it's... *ok*," Ben reassured him.

Ben was on his stomach, his boxer briefs around his ankles. His hands tightly clenched the sheets as he bit ferociously into one of the pillows on Will's bed. Behind him and fully erect, Will made awkward thrusting motions with his hips as he pushed himself into Ben. The pressure that he felt as Will entered him was a surreal blend of pain and pleasure. And although he too was hard—feeling his erection rub the bedsheets with every thrust from behind—Ben was ready to be *done* with this.

"*Al-almost... there...*" Will whispered in between huffs and grunts.

Ben said nothing; he merely nodded his head, as he felt his tears trickle onto the pillowcase. He cursed himself for agreeing to this act. The power of persuasion habitually had a hold on him in his life, but tonight it was a *death grip*. Ben wasn't even sure *why* this was happening; it all seemed to escalate *so quickly*.

One moment, the two of them were climbing into Will's king-sized bed after a night of video games and raucous laughter. And the next? Will was saddling up next to Ben, and slipping off his underwear. He could have said "no", but he didn't.

When they had climbed into Will's king-sized bed, their brains still buzzing with the energy of video games and raucous laughter, something *shifted* between them. They had said goodnight, and turned to face opposite directions. But just as Ben's heavy eyelids sealed shut, drifting closer to sleep, he felt Will's warm body pressing against his.

He *thought* it was a dream. But when Will's hand found its way inside his boxer shorts, a shiver working its way up his spine, he knew that this was *real*.

In his groggy state of mind, Ben didn't put up a fight when Will pulled down his underwear; he was somewhat *thrilled* that this was happening. Ben turned to face his friend, only to be *shoved* back around. The weight of Will's naked body against his own felt threatening and scary. It was also *exciting*.

The choice was there for Ben to refuse, but he couldn't bring himself to do it. A mixture of curiosity and uncertainty filled every inch of the room as they moved closer together, ready to explore this new territory. They were two bodies becoming one in a tangled mess of sheets and limbs, a moment to be etched in their memories forever.

With a few final grunts and moans, followed by seizure-like spasming, Will had finished. Ben breathed a gargantuan cry of relief, barely registering the sensation of his friend's semen shooting across the back of his thigh.

As Will retreated to the bathroom, Ben raised his head to notice the abundance of tears, sweat, and snot that saturated the pillowcase. He flipped the pillow over, and lay his head back down. It was the only movement he could manage. His entire body *ached* from the contractions of his muscles.

Moments later, Will emerged from the bathroom. He tossed Ben a small hand towel, and without a word he climbed back into bed, and fell asleep. Ben let out soft, muffled groans as he wiped himself off and pulled his underwear back on. Tears welled up in his eyes one more time as he *finally* drifted off to sleep.

And in a dark corner of the bedroom, where shadows go to die, a camcorder sat perched on a tripod, its red recording light shining solid like a wicked eye.

9:41 PM

The video ended, and Will sat in stunned, *horrified* silence. The forgotten memory of that night—now unlocked and clear as day—burned bright in his mind. Ben stood up from his chair and paced the room again, allowing the gravity of the situation to properly sink in for his captive friend.

"How the *fuck* do you have that?" Will asked, his trembling voice interrupting the room's *painful* silence.

"That's a *great* question," Ben replied, awkwardly rubbing the back of his neck, "I'm still a little confused by it, myself. According to all of my technical knowledge and research, both the tape and the battery should have given out by the time that was recorded. But sometimes... things happen that *defy* logic."

Will shook his head slowly, terror still *firmly* plastered across his face.

"*No...*" Will denied, "it's... *impossible*. We... we turned the camcorder *off* after the game."

Ben looked down at his friend sympathetically, watching as he desperately searched for rationale.

"Do you honestly expect me to believe that?" Will asked. "That the camcorder just happened to *still* be turned on and recording?" His chest began to heave with labored breaths, his face filling with fire. "It was *you*, Ben. You're the one that turned it back on. I don't know *when* or *how* you did it, but it's the only *logical* explanation."

Ben dropped his head and sighed. "Believe what you want, Will. As far-fetched as it is, the battery lasting that long, it *is* the truth. In fact, that's what this *whole night* is about: Honesty. So while I don't expect you to believe this, you *need* to know that I wouldn't lie to you."

"*Bullshit!*" Will screamed. "This is fucking *blackmail!*" The sound of his voice echoed loudly throughout the empty house.

Ben let out another deep sigh, feeling the weight of their conversation pressing down on him. Tensions were high; he could practically *taste* the bitterness and frustration in the air. They had only just *begun* to scratch the surface of what needed to be discussed that evening, and already it felt like an insurmountable task.

He glanced over at his friend, who sat with a furrowed brow and tight jaw, clearly processing the new information that Ben had just revealed. Deciding to give his friend some time to digest it all, Ben held his tongue for a few moments longer before continuing.

The warped hardwood floors creaked and groaned under the weight of Ben's heavy boots as he meandered about the living room. The single lightbulb overhead casted a dull shine; it flickered infrequently under its phantom power. Under soft glow, Will uttered incoherencies under his breath, his mind racing to rationalize the events from that night. He couldn't recall the last time he felt so many emotions at once: Anger, betrayal, confusion, *fear*.

"What's your plan here, Ben?" Will asked finally in a low voice.

He gripped his fists together tightly within the constraints of his bonds, summoning all of his strength to *not* lash out and shout at his best friend. Once had been enough, now was the time to start devising a plan to get the hell out of here, as far away from this psychopath as possible.

"My *plan*," Ben responded, his voice light with patience, "is that we are going to continue sitting here, so we can work this out."

"Come *on*, man! Do I *really* need to be duct-taped to this chair? Can't you at least cut me free, so we can work this out like adults?"

"*No*, Will, that *won't* work. I need you in a position where you can't run off, or worse, try to attack me." He narrowed his eyes at Will. "I *promise* you, we are getting to the heart of things. It won't be much longer now..."

Will shuddered, ice water running through his veins. *It won't be much longer now.* What was that supposed to mean? Ben's statement *seemed* reassuring, but there was also an underlying, *ominous* cadence to it. Was it possible that Ben had plans on *not* letting him leave when this was all over? The abundance of questions and lack of answers was driving him mad—worrying him, *scaring* him.

Ben plopped back down in his chair across from Will, letting out a quiet sigh.

"You know, Will," he began, "I used to think about that night a *lot*. I'd wonder if you ever thought about it, too, and if it was just going to be *our little secret*. More than anything, though, I'd lay awake at night and wonder... what *it* meant.

"I thought *for sure* it would bubble up to the surface *eventually*. And when it did, we could get it out in the open, clear the air, and come to some sort of mutual understanding."

Ben paused, chuckling lightly to himself. "Boy, was I fucking wrong about *that*! I remember trying to bring it up a few times, in the most *casual* of ways. But from that day on, any mention of your birthday was immediately shut down, and you'd quickly change the topic.

"I get it, though. It was probably one of those 'heat of the moment' kind of things, yeah? And that's the idea I had to make peace with. But no matter how hard I tried to push away those thoughts and feelings, they'd *always* come back. It was like shoving a beach ball under water in a pool: I could hold it down as long as I wanted, but at the end of the day, it would always come shooting back up to the surface. And now here we are, two years later, with the *perfect* opportunity for you and I to hash this out."

Will stared back at Ben defiantly, his jaw clenched, face beet red. What had happened on his birthday two years ago was *less* than a one-off. It never happened again. So why had Ben been so *obsessed* with it? Why did he feel the need to dissect it; go over it with a fine-tooth comb?

"You know what?" Ben said, breaking the awkward silence. "Just to show you I'm willing to be a team player here, I'll go *first*. I'll tell you how that night made me feel, and what it meant for *me*, and then I'll turn it over to you. Sound like a deal?"

A furtive smile grew on Will's face. "*Deal*," he responded. If Ben so *desperately* wanted the truth, he'd get it.

"*Excellent!*" Ben clapped his hands together in excitement. "So, there's one thing I'd like to clear up right away: I considered our *act* that night to be consensual. I mean, *technically speaking* there's probably some gray area in there. But the bottom line is, if I didn't want to do *that* with you, I would have told you 'no'. It's just impor-tant to me that you know that, in case you've accrued any guilt over it."

"Gee, *thanks*," Will muttered under his breath.

"Now," Ben continued, ignoring Will's sarcasm, "moving on to how it made me *feel*, and why I let you do it in the first place. I got a funny feeling you don't know this first-hand, so I'll fill you in... be-ing on the *receiving end* of anal sex is *wildly* uncomfortable."

Will snickered at this, reading it as something he should be *proud* of.

"However, it wasn't *without* its pleasures," Ben carried on. "I *let you* put your cock inside me for a few reasons. I mean *sure*, I was cu-rious about how it felt. I think *all* guys have that curiosity at some point in time—it's *nothing* to be ashamed of.

"But you wanna know the biggest reason why I agreed to it? Be-cause it was *you*, and as a friend I *trusted* you. I figured it was some-thing you just *had* to try out. And I'd be lying if I said I didn't have my *own* curiosities about having sex with a dude. *So...* I let you *fuck* me.

"But even though it was a *painful* experience, and left me a little upset, I was *still* glad we did it. I felt like it brought us closer together, you know? Gave us a shared experience that we probably wouldn't have with anyone else. And I got to see a side of you that none of your guy or girl friends had, which made me happy."

The sense of fondness and nostalgia that had built up in Ben suddenly began to drain away.

"But when the weeks rolled by, and you *refused* to talk about it, it *tore me up* inside. Because I didn't know what it *meant* for you. Was it a one-time, just for fun thing? Were you *also* curious about having sex with a guy? All of these questions and *more* rattled around in my brain, day in and day out, and it drove me *insane*. And I was only further infuriated by my own lack of confidence, for not *pushing you* to talk about it."

Will let out a breathy noise that was halfway between a scoff and a sarcastic laugh.

"You always *have* been such a fucking pussy," he shot back finally.

"Oh, I can *already* tell this is gonna be *good*," Ben goaded. He leaned forward eagerly in his seat, a smirk plastered across his face.

"I don't know *who* you think you are, now. Okay, so you came back from that *stupid* summer camp with some muscles and a bit of confidence. *Big whoop*. But guess what, dude? Nothing will *ever* change the way that I see you—the way I've *always* seen you. A lanky, *spineless* nobody. A soft, mushy ball of *nothing*."

Still grinning, Ben peered at Will through narrowed, satiated eyes. "Please, *continue*," he said softly.

"Going back to that voicemail from Tim's Diner," Will continued, "I *didn't* feel bad about what I'd said. Those guys I was with—my *teammates*—I've known them for *years*. You and I were *barely* friends by that time. And sure, as time rolled on and you and I became close, I started to feel a *little* guilty about the way I talked about you. But that night, when they insinuated that you were gay, it felt more like an attack on *me*.

"Those few weeks in between blowing you off and us hanging out for my birthday, it was *all* I could think about. It was like this seed of darkness that they implanted in my brain, and as it grew I could see my *entire world* crumble around me; my entire high school legacy, up in flames. So these weird bouts of anger and resentment for you started building, and building, and had nowhere to go. That is, until my birthday rolled around."

Will paused for a moment. A look of humor mixed with pensiveness crossed his face.

"You know, it's funny," he continued, his voice suddenly low. "You mentioned forgetting all about the voicemail once you arrived at my place. Well, it's the same for me with that pent-up anger I couldn't get rid of. Goofing around with that dumb Ouija board and playing video games, they took my mind off it. But later that night, when I was trying to fall asleep, what my friends had said about you—and the feelings that came with them—came cropping back up again."

Will felt a lump begin to form in his throat. He hadn't considered how difficult it'd be to discuss the truth behind this part of their friendship. Choosing to focus more on the anger and hatred he had for Ben in that moment, he pushed forward.

"I remember staring at my bedroom ceiling, with you next to me, and I started to feel like I was at some sort of impasse. Like there was only room for one 'Will', and a decision *had* to be made. This *brand new* path was full of potentially terrifying and exciting possibilities. The other path was one I knew *all too well*: The one where I was a rude asshole, who occasionally said problematic and insensitive shit but didn't care, and hung out with friends who did the same.

"And *guess what*, Ben? I chose to be the asshole, which you've *probably* figured out by now. After I made that decision, I secretly hoped that our relationship would somehow just peter out, that you'd find someone else to latch onto. I know it probably sucks right now for you to hear all of this, but you wanted the truth, so I'm *giving* it to you."

Ben shifted in his seat as he looked thoughtfully at Will. It was the first time that evening when he appeared to be uncomfortable. This made Will's triumphant smile grow even wider.

"So... what was the sex to you, Will?" Ben asked, his voice soft and melancholic.

Will, looking like the Joker, took a moment to compose his thoughts. He was readying himself, because now it was *really* time to let Ben have it.

"It was *punishment*," Will stated. "It was... *irony*. I wanted to put you in your place. I wanted to bring you pain. And I wanted you to suffer for the torment you caused me. Because I *hated* feeling soft. Before you wandered into my life, my entire existence was hardness, strengthening, and building my mind *and* body into an impenetrable, ironclad temple. I didn't share or talk about my feelings or practice sensitivity toward others. I was the *asshole*, the bully. But you know what? *I got shit done.* And I wanted to split you in two for making me into someone I no longer recognized. *That's* why I fucked you, Ben."

Filled to the brim with rage, Will felt his last few words come out hot, spitting like snake venom. He envisioned his skin turning to fire, burning through the binds that held him down so he could leap on top of Ben. And with hands around his throat, he would squeeze and squeeze, and laugh while he watched the light slowly fade from his eyes. Finally, when he stood over Ben's limp, lifeless body, he would spit on him and curse the day they met.

Ben raised his hands and performed a slow clap, interrupting Will's fantasy of strangling him to death.

"That's *it*!" he exclaimed. His index finger was pointed enthusiastically at Will, a satisfied grin growing across his face. "That is *exactly* what I've been looking for! One hundred percent absolute, *brutal honesty*."

Ben shot up out of his chair and began pacing the room in a frenzy. To Will, he looked like a cocaine junkie who just did four rails off a stripper's ass. He watched in stunned amazement as Ben pumped his fists in the air triumphantly.

"You have *no idea* how much I've desperately longed for this moment, Will!" Ben exclaimed. "I always assumed that, even if I *did* manage to get to this point, where I could get you to spill your guts, that in the end it wouldn't be *nearly* as satisfying as I'd hoped. But, brother, this was cathartic *as fuck*."

"That's great, man, I'm *so* glad," Will said with heavy sarcasm, "now, will you please kindly GET ME THE FUCK OUT OF HERE!"

His screams of frustration reverberated off the walls of the old house, piercing the quiet night with bellowing echoes. Will's anger, however, was only met with roaring laughter from Ben.

"*Nah ah!*" Ben said, wagging his index finger. "We still have one more thing to discuss. *Then* you'll be free to go."

Coming down from his high, Ben meandered aimlessly, appearing to take stock of the empty room. He moved about with hands on hips, his face nostalgic.

"Do you recognize this house?" Ben asked nonchalantly.

Will, still seething with anger, refused to answer.

"I wouldn't imagine you'd recognize the inside," Ben continued, "but the outside *should've* rung a bell, provided you got a good look before I knocked you out. Of course it's a little run-down and dilap-idated, now."

Will reflexively balled his hands into fists again. He still could not understand how Ben, who *barely* pushed 155 pounds soaking wet, somehow managed a sneak attack on him *and* knocked him uncon-scious. But regarding the house, he admittedly did have vague recol-lections of the house, though couldn't place it *exactly*.

"It was Trent Goldstein's house," Ben confirmed. "You remem-ber him, *yeah*?"

More silence from Will.

"He was a sophomore last year, and even shared a couple of our classes. I remember him sticking out like a sore thumb, being two years younger than everyone else. Anyway, last Halloween you texted me with an address and told me to meet you at that location around 10 PM. You were waiting for me when I arrived, with a bunch of eggs, toilet paper, and a few of your football buddies.

"As a 'fun' little way of welcoming him to our high school, you guys wanted to egg and TP Trent's house—something that I was *wildly* uncomfortable with. Knowing what I do now, I think you were keenly aware that I'd be too chickenshit to participate, but would probably succumb to peer pressure. I also think it was a way to prove to your friends that I wasn't the *square* they thought I was."

Ben took a deep breath and sighed, processing memories from what seemed like a lifetime ago.

"Then a few months later, with *no warning*, Trent and his family were *gone*. I often wondered what happened to them, and why they left so abruptly. I can't imagine that *you guys* gave it much thought, however. His existence was merely a blip on your radar, and egging their house that night was just a disposable round of fun."

Ben turned back to face Will, who was angrily flexing against his restraints.

"Which is why I thought it would be *fitting* to do this thing here. When I returned from my wilderness retreat, I went for a drive just to be with my thoughts, and wound up here somehow—right outside of Trent's house. I don't know why—it was like something had pulled me here; like something *wanted* me here. And when I noticed the 'For Sale' sign out front, I decided to poke around a little bit, and came to discover that this house has been empty since that family left."

Ben solemnly returned to his seat across from Will, and leaned in with his elbows propped on his knees.

"Let me tell you, buddy," Ben said quietly, "it was like finding the missing piece of the puzzle underneath the coffee table. Because all at once, everything in my head—all the thoughts, like tangled-up twine—suddenly made sense, and I knew what I needed to do."

Will glared at his captor with confusion and anger in his eyes.

"Let me get this straight," Will began, "you returned home from your wilderness retreat, and had some sort of weird revelation... that involved *kidnapping* me and holding me hostage?"

"Close!" Ben responded with excitement. "I'm holding you *captive*, not hostage. But broad-strokes, yes. I understand that my motives are still a little unclear, so I'd like an opportunity to discuss this final chapter with you... *unencumbered*."

"Meaning *what*, exactly?"

"Meaning... that I will cut you loose, *if* you are willing to sit here with me for a little while longer so we can hash this out."

Will's gaze lingered on Ben, trying to decipher the true nature of his intentions. He couldn't escape the guilt that weighed heavily on him for neglecting their friendship over the past two years. Was it worth risking everything to make amends now? With the idea of his restraints finally removed, he felt a surge of conflicting emotions—the desire for physical confrontation mixed with the fear of what could happen if he acted impulsively.

With a final sigh and nod of his head, Will said softly, "Sure, let's do that."

Part III: Maxine

10:20 PM

Will rubbed his wrists where the tape had been as he paced the living room. After two hours of being tied down to a chair, it was a relief to experience proper blood flow again. As the tingling subsided, and rational thinking took hold, he considered how often he might've taken for granted his bodily autonomy.

He had spent so much of his life sculpting and perfecting his temple, always assuming he'd have complete control over it. It was never even a possibility before now that he'd be *robbed* of that freedom. And yet, *here he was*, recently released from Ben's bondage.

Fresh in his mind, Will recounted the events of his birthday all those years ago, and what he'd done to his friend. There was no lie in what he had told Ben earlier—his motives for advancing on him that night. But there was an itch in his brain that he just couldn't scratch. Sure, he had been truthful to Ben. But what about *himself*?

And where *did* those memories go? Had he repressed them? Decided that they didn't even *happen*? That night, he wanted to show Ben who was in charge, and it was the only way he could think of to express that sentiment. But now, as those memories burned brighter than ever in his memory, he was suddenly second-guessing himself.

"Here, drink this," Ben said, interrupting Will's train of thought.

Ben had re-entered the living room, and was extending a bottle of water toward him—an *olive branch*. Will glanced down at it with weary and untrusting eyes, then back up to meet Ben's.

"Don't worry, it's sealed," Ben reassured him with a kind smile.

Will accepted the water reluctantly, inspecting it for good measure before twisting the top and taking a long swallow. After replacing the cap, he looked around the room, suspicious of some unknown element lurking about. Something was *different*. He could sense it, but couldn't quite place it.

He glanced back at Ben and his face seemed to be a bit more illuminated. Could that be it? Was it getting *brighter* in here? Earlier, a single overhead bulb crackled to life completely unprompted. Were there *other* lights coming on now?

When he was tied to the chair, it was dark, he was dehydrated, and his head felt like it was splitting down the middle. Back then, he lacked the proper faculties to take a proper inventory of the rundown living—*hostage*—room. But now that he had water and his mobility back, and his headache was beginning to subside, he was now free to clock the things around him.

There *were* other lamps, set atop small TV trays and folding tables. They had steadily buzzed to life without him knowing. and now cast long, dark shadows against the peeling wallpaper. He grimaced at the sight of dark stains and green mold that grew unchecked.

"I know you're probably not too eager to sit again," Ben started, "so feel free to stand if that's more comfortable, but we *should* get back to it."

"Yeah, right, ok," Will responded with a notable eye roll. He leaned against the corner of the fireplace mantle as he watched Ben return to his chair. "So, uh, what's this last thing you needed to discuss?"

"Do you remember that one Saturday, back in February?" Ben asked. "At Tim's Diner, with—"

"*Maxine*," Will finished, nodding his head. "Yeah, I remember..."

February 9th, 2019

Outside Tim's Diner, cold winter winds blew a light dusting of snow flurries across the sidewalks and streets. Crestwood townies walked hurriedly about the square, desperate to seek shelter from the relentless southeastern chill. Inside the diner, patrons were offered a warm refuge. The air hung heavy with maple syrup and fresh-brewed coffee, accompanied by the roar of cheerful chatter.

On this particular Saturday, nestled into a secluded corner booth, sat two teenagers in the throes of young love. They giggled playfully as they poured over the menu, their fingers interlaced with the other's under the table. Each time the bell chimed from the diner's entrance, the boy would jerk his head in that direction, then shift anxiously in his seat.

"So, are you *nervous*?" Maxine teased.

"Nervous about you meeting Will for the first time?" Ben asked, rubbing his sweaty palms together.

"*Yes*, silly. You're all *jittery*! I was curious if you were maybe a little nervous about introducing me to him. You've definitely *waited* long enough."

Curling her fingers through his hair, she gave him a reassuring smile that helped steady his racing heart.

"You think so?" Ben asked, dancing around the question.

"Two months? Yeah, I think that's enough time to keep this thing a secret. I mean, I've met your *parents* for fuck's sake, there's no reason to keep me from your *best friend*."

"*Whoa there*, sailor," Ben chuckled. "You've met my parents because we all go to the same church. I've *chosen* to keep this a secret from Will because I wanted it to be 'our thing' for as long as possible. It's not that I don't trust him, or didn't want him to know."

"*Alright*... if you *say so*," Maxine teased.

Their hands reunited, and he gave hers an abrupt, firm squeeze. He breathed a sharp, panicky gasp as he watched the diner's front door fly open.

"Well, here he is," Ben muttered, butterflies scurrying in his stomach.

From the front entrance, Will scanned the occupied tables and booths, searching for his friend. He found him—*and a girl*—tucked away in one of the isolated corner booths. Standing statue-still, his feet planted to the diner's tiled floor, he glared at them with a confused expression.

That *is* Ben, isn't it? It certainly *looks* like Ben, and he *is* waving him over to their table. But who is this *girl*? They *are* sitting awfully close to each other. And are they... *holding hands*?

Will felt his body begin to move slowly in their direction. His heart raced in his chest as he tried piecing together all the possible scenarios. There was, however, only *one* logical synopsis; one single conclusion that made sense, but *didn't* make sense.

"Hey *dude*!" Ben exclaimed with a slight tremble to his voice. He reached his arm around the girl's shoulder and squeezed it gently. "I'd like you to meet Maxine."

She reached her hand out to Will as he took a seat across from them. He shook it with some reserve, his eyes darting back and forth between the couple, his look of uncertainty transforming into a sly grin.

"It's... very nice to meet you, *Maxine*." Will said in a polite tone, his mind still racing to piece all of this new information together.

"It's so nice to meet *you*! And *please*, call me Max. Ben has told me *a lot* about you, so it's great to finally put a face to the name!"

"So, I take it you're a *friend* of Ben's?"

Ben and Max looked at each other as they let out a synchronized spat of nervous laughter.

"You *could* say we're friends," Max replied, "but I'd like to think we're a *little more* than that."

"You mean like... friends with benefits?" Will teased dryly.

Letting out another quick chuckle, she replied, "Ah, *there's* that quick wit that Ben *also* mentioned." Max moved to place her hand over Ben's and gripped it softly. "I guess if you wanted to go by Facebook standards, our status would say 'In a Relationship'."

"*Although*," Ben interjected, "we haven't made it 'Facebook official' just yet. We wanted to wait a while before we told anyone."

"Right!" Max agreed, jumping back in. "Up until *now*, only our parents have known about us dating, but that's only because we all go to the same church. It's kind of hard to avoid parish gossip, so we didn't really bother to try and hide it."

Will continued to smile and nod, his head and heart *swimming* with conflicted feelings.

"So... how long have you two been... *dating*?" he asked.

"About... two months, I guess?" Max replied, giving Ben's hand a squeeze.

She and Ben shared a few facial expressions, seeming to communicate in their own special language. Eventually Ben gave her a look as if to say "go ahead".

"Our parents *firmly* encouraged us to participate in the teen ministry program," Max began. "That's how we met for the first time. But it was our *lack* of enthusiasm for the program that really drew us together. Neither of us really wanted to be there, so it kinda became a 'misery loves company' thing."

The two shared a mutual chuckle at the recounting of their meet-cute. They gazed dreamily into each other's eyes as their hands, like magnets, once again locked together in a tight grasp.

This was *normally* the kind of vomit-inducing behavior that Will despised—overt public displays of affection. He never understood the need to *prove* your infatuation by shoving it down other people's throats. It was never enough to just say "I like you" or "I *love* you" when you're alone. *No.* It had to be performed *publicly* as well, in front of an audience, so *everyone* knew that you were together.

But *this*? Will had no clue what to make of this *anomaly* in front of him. In the year-and-a-half they'd known each other, Ben had never even been out on a date with a girl, let alone been in a relationship. It was a facet of their friendship that Will rather enjoyed. He couldn't quite place it, but there was a distinct pleasure he felt in being Ben's main companion.

What sat before him now spat in the face of everything he had grown comfortable with. He had come to Tim's today to meet Ben for their usual lunch, talk about movies, and other random nonsense. Instead, he was *ambushed* by a meet-and-greet with Ben's new squeeze.

And more than that, Max was *hot*. Ben wasn't an ugly dude, per se, but she was *way* out of his league. With her strawberry blonde hair, fair skin, and petite frame, Max was more of a girl that *Will* would date.

A fire burned in the pit of his stomach as he watched her lush lips connect with Ben's. Will was positively *incensed*. He felt like upending the booth table and storming out, and became further enraged knowing he had to feign happiness for his friend who had found love.

"That's uh... that's *so great* to hear," Will finally responded, forcing his best fake smile. "So have you guys ordered yet?"

"Nope, not yet," Ben replied, slightly taken aback by his friend's abrupt change in topic. "We've been waiting for you."

10:45 PM

"I'll never forget the look on your face when you walked into the diner and saw us that day," Ben said. "I was *so nervous* about finally telling you about Maxine, *and* the fact that we had been dating for two months. But once I saw your face, all of those anxious feelings just *drifted away*. You wanna know why?"

"Why's that?" Will asked. He continued inspecting his wrists, refusing eye contact with Ben.

"Because I *had* something," Ben said with passion. "I finally had something that *you* didn't. Right under your nose, while you weren't paying any fucking attention, something *amazing* happened to me. And for whatever reason, in that messed up brain of yours, that didn't sit right with you."

Will let out a disapproving scoff, and shook his head with a sly grin.

"Oh, I am sure you had some *positive* feelings as well," Ben continued. "I know deep down, you were at least a *little* happy for me. Max was the total package: Beautiful, smart, kind. And as corny as it is to say, she really *did* bring out the best in me."

Ben's breathing was suddenly more labored. Quiet little huffs of air blew out of his nostrils.

"And then *you* walked in." Ben spat. His tone carried heavy doses of disdain, anger, and rage. "Tell me, Will, at what point did you start scheming to take her away from me?"

With all fondness and elation drained from his face, Ben narrowed his eyes on Will. And for the first time since being cut loose, Will met his eye line and stared back.

With a wide roll of his eyes, Will responded, "Oh my god, do you *really* want to do this, Ben?"

"Yes, *Will*, I *do*. Because for all the hell that you've put me through over these last two years, I think I deserve to hear the *truth*. So right fucking now, you tell me *exactly* what happened that day in that fucked up little brain of yours."

As if on cue, all of the lights that had steadily come on the past few minutes began to flicker, threatening to burn out again. Will's arms unfolded and he glanced around curiously, goosebumps prickling his skin. It was becoming more difficult to reconcile these strange abnormalities with the lighting. As much as he wanted to brush it off as some cheap parlor trick, he just couldn't ignore the eeriness of it.

"The second I saw the two of you," Will admitted, swallowing past the lump in his throat.

"So, you knew in that moment that you wanted to take her from me?"

"*Yes*." Will's confidence was stern and unwavering.

"That's so fucked up," Ben said, shaking his head. His face curled into a half grin.

Will shrugged his shoulders, and countered Ben's grin with his own. A moment of mutual reflection passed between them, each friend carrying their own unique weight.

"Okay," Ben said, breaking the silence, "let's fast forward a little bit. Less than a month later, Max breaks up with me. Naturally, I am *heartbroken*. Cue me wallowing in self-pity and despair for nearly a week straight. I really had my parents worried, as you are already *well aware*. Their little boy just had his heart broken for the first time."

Will could visualize the connective tissue that fuzed together their interlocking experiences with Maxine. He was *well aware* of everything that took place after that day in February. Taking another swig of water, he once again became agitated at this rehashing of history.

"When I didn't show up to our lunch that week, you came to visit me," Ben continued. "Which I thought was kinda sweet—until you dropped the bomb that decimated my entire world. Not only had Max broken up with me, but she did it so *you two* could date! I couldn't *fucking* believe it. It was like all at once everything good in my life had gone up in smoke."

"Oh come *on*, man!" Will exclaimed, balling his fists. "It's over and *done with*. You need to move on, and find someone *new*."

"That's fucking rich, coming from you."

"What's *that* supposed to mean?"

"It means that last February, you walked into that diner and came to the stark realization that your days of pushing me around—of keeping me as your pet just to make yourself look and feel better—were fucking *numbered*. I had Maxine, and you had pretty much any girl of your choosing. You saw her as a threat to your rank and status in my life, and you weren't about to let someone take that from you, or let *me* have something for once. So, you pulled the old 'one two' punch combo: You convince Max to break up with me and date you instead. *Then*, you come to me when I'm at my weakest, and make it look like it was all an accident, like things just happened, and *boom*, you two were dating."

"Ok, so what do you *want* from me, Ben? Do you want me to get on my knees, hat in hand, and give you a big heartfelt apology? Because you can just fucking *forget it*. I made my choices, and so did Max. End of story. There's nothing you can do to change what happened."

Ben sat stoically, watching as Will screamed in his face. He had reached his tipping point. Exhausted and filled with spite, he turned and walked toward the front door of the abandoned house. Ben waited until he reached for the door knob before speaking up.

"I wouldn't do that if I were you," Ben called out, checking his wristwatch, his legs stretched out in front of him.

"Oh, yeah, why's that?" Will asked, not turning around.

He had the front door open, and could smell the fresh night air as it wafted in his face. It was a sweet relief to the putrid stink of the mold-infested house.

"If you walk out that door," Ben replied, "before we have a chance to finish our chat, our entire school will find out *exactly* who you are."

Will stood frozen with his hand on the knob. He then turned slowly to look at Ben from over his shoulder.

"What the *hell* are you talking about?" Will asked, his voice low and trembling.

Ben's face was still curled into a grin, his hands shoved into his pockets, legs crossed at the ankles. His relaxed posture and nonchalant attitude made Will's blood boil all over again.

"Do you remember Rivers Johnson?" Ben asked casually. "You *might* not. But you *did* have a brief run-in with his girlfriend Jenny a while back."

Will's eyes widened and his jaw went slack.

"Jenny was at a house party last year," Ben continued. "She was dancing alone because Rivers was working late. He was on the yearbook staff and had a deadline to meet. So, you decided to lend yourself as a dance partner. After a few drinks and dances, she needed a little break. She *had* to rest because someone *slipped* something in her drink." Ben squinted his eyes and pointed his index finger directly at Will. "*You* drugged and raped Jenny that night."

"How do you know about that?" Will asked. His hands were clenched into white-knuckled fists at his sides, his teeth gnashed together in a *furious* snarl. "I never told *anyone* about that night. So, tell me, *seriously*, how the *fuck* do you know about that?"

"It doesn't matter how I know," Ben replied, rising to meet his friend. "What *does* matter is that I know. And Rivers, who happens to have the comprehensive student body contact manifest, he knows too. And tonight at midnight, that video from your birthday—as well as the information between you and Jenny—will be automatically sent to every single student at our high school. That is... unless you come sit back down, and we finish our talk."

Will had stopped dead in his tracks. His heart chugged like a locomotive, pumping boiling-hot blood through his veins. The entire world around him had gone red, and in an instant he saw his entire future go up in smoke. Everything that he had worked and fought for his entire life could be gone by the following morning, all at the hands of this wimpy piece of shit standing in front of him.

He could not understand how all this had happened, no matter *how hard* he tried. For *two years* he managed to keep Ben on a leash, to be used as a prop. But somewhere along the way, there had been a *disruption* to the natural order. Something had happened to Ben on his wilderness retreat. This was *more* than just an increase in confidence and a bit of muscle tone—this was something *sinister*.

It was time for all of this to end. Will understood what needed to be done. It was simply a matter of allowing himself to cool down, and figuring out how he was going to kill his friend Ben.

Part IV: The Camp & The Ritual

June 1st, 2019, 1:00 AM

A discreet, flat black SUV crept to a stop in front of 4999 Chatham Way. The tinted windows hid two large men in the front driver and passenger's seats. It was perfectly quiet in the respective

Crestwood neighborhood, save for the usual ambient sounds that come perfectly packaged with an early June morning in suburban Tennessee. A nearby dog barked, cicadas chirped from the trees that lined the streets and front yards, and the occasional exhaust as cars roared by.

The house's porch light flicked on suddenly, and the two men glanced at each other and nodded.

"Few more minutes," said the driver. He double-checked his wristwatch, then cut the engine.

The passenger kept watch over the house as his partner in the driver's seat took one last opportunity to flip through the client's file. All of the preliminary information was typed neatly inside, with a small wallet-sized photo of a high school aged male paper-clipped to the top of the page. Under "Name: Last, First" the file read "Nolan, Ben".

"You think we'll get much resistance on this one?" the passenger asked, maintaining his visual over the subject's home.

"Hmm, I don't think so," the driver replied, leafing through the file. "The boss mentioned this wouldn't be our typical teenage delinquent round-up. I don't see anything in his file that would indicate potential violence."

"Still. You *never know*."

"Nope, never do."

"Keep an eye out. I'll get the gear ready."

Passing off watch duty to the driver, the passenger opened up the glove compartment to reveal two long-range tasers and a single 9mm handgun. He considered the unloaded and safetied handgun for a moment, before ultimately exchanging it for the two tasers. He clipped one of them to his utility belt. handed the other to his partner, then closed the glove compartment's lid.

"Any activity?" the passenger asked, glancing back at the house.

"Nope. I saw a set of eyes peer out through the blinds of what appears to be the living room. Pretty sure it was one of the parents, though."

The driver took one final look at his wristwatch, then glanced over at his partner.

"Ready?"

"Ready."

The large, black-clad figures exited the SUV in tandem and made their way up the walkway to the front door. Discretion was the name of the game, here. That meant no knocking, no bell-ringing, and no shouting. To successfully acquire their targets, it was crucial that they remain unaware of the situation until it was too late.

As the time adjusted to 1:15 AM on the driver's wristwatch, the front door opened slowly with a quiet creak. In the foyer stood a man and woman, approximately mid-40s, presumably the target's parents. They stared back at the men, their faces contorted with fear, eyes misty from concern. The mother motioned the two large men inside, who flashed their identification quickly with a nod of thanks.

The door closed quietly behind them, and the two men turned to face the parents. The husband had reached his arm around his partner's shoulders, pulling her into a tight embrace. Small tears drizzled down her red, puffy cheeks.

"It's going to be alright, ma'am," the driver whispered, making eye contact with first the mother and then the father.

"Which room is—" the passenger began.

"Mom, dad? Wh- what's going on?"

Ben stood rubbing his eyes from a doorway at the hall's end. The two men looked at each other, then slowly reached for their tasers.

11:10 PM

Ben and Will were once again seated to face one another. Will wore a blood-thirsty scowl, his arms crossed tightly against his chest. Ben maintained his leisurely position of crossed legs and hands in his lap.

"So, Will," Ben began, "I'd like to cover a few things real quick, just so we can get them out of the way and prepare for our main event."

Ben took a deep breath, then let it out while holding up his index finger, as if to begin counting items.

"After you started dating Max, you secretly consult with my parents about sending me to the wilderness retreat camp. Because the camp was primarily targeted for 'at risk' youth—a demographic that I couldn't be *further* from—I'm going to assume mom and dad were initially resistant to the idea.

"But then you insisted that it was for *any* teen boy that could stand to gain confidence and leadership skills. This was probably your *main* selling point, and my parents eventually bought it. And since you wanted to take things to the next level with Max, getting me out of town would allow you to make your moves on her guilt-free. How am I doing so far, am I close to the mark?"

Will, still with arms crossed, staring daggers at Ben, remained motionless and quiet.

"I'll take it from your silence that that's a 'Yes'." Ben held up his middle finger next to his index finger to count the next item. "In the early hours of June 1st, I wake up to two large men standing in the foyer of my house, unclipping tasers from their belts. Ten minutes later, I'm in the back seat of their SUV, driving off to a destination unknown, tears streaming down my face. I remember thinking how I had heard of these camps, and how they were by and large reserved for troubled youth. So it made *no sense* to me why my parents seemed so complicit in sending me to one. But by the end of the three-hour drive to the middle of nowhere, I had pieced everything together.

"They led me to the barracks, and showed me to my bunk. I remember laying there that night, staring up at the ceiling, and all I could think about was you and Max together. I couldn't *believe* how wild of a turn my life had taken in only a few months, going from some of my happiest days to literally the worst ones. Most of all, though, I could not get over how *brilliant* your plan was. I fucking *hated* you for what you had done, to the point where I couldn't think straight. But I had to hand it to you."

An underhanded grin grew across Will's face. So far, his friend had been on point with everything he'd guessed at. He also thought it was quite ironic that now, at the end of their friendship, was when he felt the *proudest* to be Ben's friend. To know he had finally grown a backbone.

"Luckily for me," Ben continued, "when camp began, there wasn't much time for any of us to think about our personal lives. Because for the two and a half months that I was there, I endured the most strenuous physical—and mental—abuse of my life. These 'camp counselors', they broke us down, Will. I mean sure, the three-a-day physical fitness routines were exhausting, but were nothing compared to the psychological mind games. They utilized tactics that would even make *you* blush!"

Will let out an impatient scoff. "Are we nearing the *point*?" he asked, tilting his head up and rolling his eyes.

"As a matter of fact, we are." Ben shifted in his chair, switching his crossed legs. "One night, about a month after arriving, I was lying awake in my bunk, my muscles screaming in agony. Suddenly I felt a tapping on my shoulder, so I turn to see what it was. Three campers stood motionless in the dark at my bedside."

Will shifted in his seat, unexpectedly intrigued by the story's turn of events.

"The only light in the barracks was the moon," Ben continued, "but it was full, so I was able to make out who they were. I didn't know their names, but recognized their faces. They told me about a natural hot spring nearby, and that they were going to take a quick dip to help with the soreness. Sean, the one who tapped me on the shoulder, invited me to tag along with them. Immediately I was confused, because there were at least 30 other campers and I didn't understand why they'd pick *me*. And if I wasn't in so much pain, I might've thought clearer and understood that it was just a ruse. But that wasn't the case, and you of all people know how gullible I can be, so I went along with them."

"And let me guess... there *was no* hot spring?"

"Oh, there *was*," Ben confirmed. "At the time I wasn't aware of it, but I found out later that one did actually exist. But that wasn't where they wanted to take me.

"Sean and his friends led me to a couple acres of wooded area back behind the main campsite. Once we were deep enough into the woods, where there were no more security cameras, the three of them flanked me on all sides."

A smile appeared on Will's face. "Did you get your ass kicked? *Please* tell me you got your ass kicked!"

For the first time that night, Will sounded happy; *excited* even. Like he *wanted* to be there, and was genuinely interested in what came next in Ben's story.

"I didn't *just* get my ass kicked, Will," Ben said, lowering his tone and leaning in. "They were trying to fucking *kill* me. You see, this wilderness retreat camp has this sort of... *ritual*. I doubt that it was in the pamphlet you gave my parents. This ritual, and what it entails, only gets passed around by word of mouth and is only spoken of by the campers—*never* the counselors. But the gist is this: A few of the 'alpha' campers will single out the weakest in the herd, and lure them to a fate that's akin to death."

"And *you* became the unfortunate soul that took part in this ritual, yeah?"

"*Correct*. They first took turns pushing me around this triangle they had formed. Shoves became fists. And you know me, Will, I don't know how to fight or defend myself to save my life. *Literally*. I did have one chance to get away, but I blew it.

"When I was down on the ground and the guys had taken to kicking me, I managed to grab someone's foot and trip them. That gave me a chance to get up and run back to the barracks, but because my muscles were so sore—and I had just gotten the crap beat out of me—I didn't make it very far before they caught up to me.

"Again, they pushed me to the ground and took turns beating the ever-living piss out of me. So I decided to play opossum, covering up the most vital parts of me as best I could, and hope that this didn't actually end with my death. But since I only have two hands and arms, I couldn't protect *everything*.

"All told, they cracked three ribs—which punctured one of my lungs—broke my left ankle and several bones in each foot, and caused a hemorrhage in my brain."

A small part of Will's smile began to fade. After all of the torment he had endured here tonight, he was *elated* to hear of the bad things that happened to Ben over the summer. But based on the description of Ben's injuries, he was curious as to how exactly he had *survived* this attack; things just *didn't* add up.

Assuming all of this was true—the broken bones and the brain hemorrhage—Ben would likely not *be here* right now. If he *was* lucky to be alive, he would have been flown by helicopter to the nearest hospital. He would have several casts on, and most likely be bedridden. His story simply did not track, which meant he was lying about something or had left out details.

"I can tell by the look on your face that you're not buying it," Ben said, seeming to read Will's thoughts. "That's perfectly fair. It doesn't make sense for anyone to come that close to death, and then come out on the other side unscathed, like none of it even happened. But if you look close enough…"

Ben leaned forward closer to Will, and flipped his hair up to reveal a gnarly horizontal scar at the base of his hairline.

"That's the scar from where they cracked my skull open," he said, allowing Will to get a decent look in the dim light of the room. "I don't have much proof of the broken bones, so you'll have to just take me at my word on that. And speaking of suspending your disbelief, I'm going to have to ask you to do a bit more of that for this next part."

Shaking his head with a sarcastic smile, Will said, "Sure, why not?"

July 3rd, 2019, 2:19 AM

The forest behind the campgrounds was docile, with the sounds of insects and nocturnal animals penetrating the night air. Through a clearing in the trees came a trio of stout teenage boys, quietly bumping fists as they made their way discreetly back to the barracks. Further back through the clearing, whimpers and cries reverberated softly through the thick fog that began to settle.

Ben lay curled up on the ground, consumed by the excruciating pain that radiated throughout his body. He was terrified to move, knowing he could have a concussion, internal bleeding, a broken ankle, or even *all three*. Every breath he took was agony. Each passing second was torture. And through all that pain, he felt darkness begin to set in—a cruel reality that these could be his last moments of life.

Gone were the optimistic days of assuming he'd die old, his life partner at his bedside holding his hand in hers. Instead they were replaced by flashes of events yet to happen, where his mother and father were beside his casket, burdened with the horrible reality of having to bury their only child.

Through the thudding and pulsing in his brain, Ben was able to make out a faint rustling of leaves nearby. Then came steady footsteps on the grass. As they neared, he tried to maneuver his body so he could see where the steps were coming from. Was this the end for him? Could this be Sean, or one of his two friends, returning to finish the job? Crippled with fear that this was the end of the line—that this was how his conclusion was determined—he closed his eyes and reluctantly welcomed death.

"It looks to me as though you've seen better days, brother." A strange, gravelly voice spoke up, piercing the night air.

"Wh- who's there?" Ben managed, his voice cracking from the pain. He felt blood trickling down his forehead, slowly streaming its way to his brow.

He managed to roll himself onto his back, where he saw a shadowy figure emerge from the unknown. The figure approached Ben's side, and as it knelt down, letting each get a better look at the other.

"Well, hello there," said the shadow figure, his face slowly coming into Ben's focus. "Just who might *you* be?"

There was an odd amorality to his southern drawl, that Ben found somehow worrisome *and* comforting.

"B-B-Ben." It was a painful struggle just to state his name aloud. "Wh-who are *you*?"

Ben's eyes had adjusted well enough to recognize that this person was not Sean, or anyone else from the camp. In fact, Ben had never seen this guy before tonight. Now almost in complete focus, Ben noticed he was dressed in all black, a *true* figure of the night. He wore a shirt and tie, his hair slicked back in a style that reminded him of Elvis. Ben could literally *see himself* in the shine of his dress boots. Based off all this, he could be the world's sexiest snake oil salesman.

"I, my friend..." the figure began, pausing for dramatic effect, "am *salvation*."

Inching closer, the man extended his arm toward Ben. He placed his hand on Ben's and as he gently caressed it, a sudden jolt—as cold as ice—shot through his entire body, followed by a warm, tingling sensation. This felt like a transformation, a *reanimation*. It felt as if he was coming back to life.

The darkness that blurred his vision began to subside, and the pain from his cracked and broken bones miraculously reversed their shattered state. In a brilliant climax, Ben's chest filled with oxygen and he let out a bellowing gasp that pierced the night air. He coughed and sat up on the forest floor, instinctively backing away from the man in black. Holding up his hands in a universal "I come in peace" gesture, he smiled and allowed Ben his required space.

"I understand this is a bit disconcerting," he said calmly, "but what I've gleaned from prior experiences is that you should be feeling a *lot* better right about now. What do you think?"

Breathing heavily, Ben inspected himself, paying mind to all the parts of him that only moments ago had been brutally mangled and broken.

"How... how the *fuck* did you do that? Did... did you just *heal* me?"

The strange figure let out a chuckle as he cautiously inched his way back to Ben.

"I'd like to think of it as... 'taking the edge off'." The stranger pointed to his forehead. "Where those three guys cracked your skull, you'll have a small scar. It'll be permanent, but you got a good head of hair, so I imagine you could get creative with a hairstyle that would help cover it up. The other injuries, like your broken bones and punctured lung, you'll feel the effects of those for the next few days. But you're a strong pup, I'd imagine you'll be feeling right as rain by the weekend."

Ben glared at this dark, guardian angel with bewildered amazement. His "fight or flight" response was screaming at him to run. But how dangerous could the guy be, if he *magically* healed Ben's wounds? Has he earned a fair shake because he had literally brought him back from the brink of death?

"The name's Kenneth, but you, sir, can call me Ken," the man in black stated.

He'd made his way over to sit next to Ben. When he held his hand out, Ben took a cautious look at it before eventually shaking it.

"I'm... Ben."

"It's so nice to make your acquaintance, Ben." Ken's voice was full of warmth, helping to put Ben more at ease. "Now, by the look on your face I can tell you have a *lot* of questions."

Ben let out a nervous chuckle as he nodded.

"*Yessir*," Ken said, matching Ben's laughter, "that is *understandable*. By the way, I am *so* sorry that you had to be a part of this ugly ritual. It's an unfortunate piece of history that comes with this campsite."

"*You're* sorry?" Ben asked, confused. "I would probably be *dead* if it wasn't for you. You *saved* me! How the hell did you do that, by the way? Wait, am I having some kind of weird, messed up dream right now?"

"*No*, Ben." Ken let out another quick chuckle. "This most certainly is *not* a dream. But I do have to be honest with you, in a way it really *is* my fault that you fell into this predicament. Those three assholes could have picked *anyone* in this camp to kick the crap out of.

So, while I didn't have much to do with them choosing *you* as their victim, still I must take some responsibility."

The expression on Ben's face turned to confusion. Setting aside all the oddities that had occurred since Ken had showed up, he was unsure of what this stranger was referring to.

"Tell me, Ben, how much do you know about this horrible ritual that you fell victim to?"

"Um, not *much*. Just that it *is* a ritual, like a hazing sort of thing. About a week into my time here, my bunkmate James and I were cleaning the mess hall and he filled me in on it. His brother had been through the camp a few years prior, so I guess he told him as a kind of 'heads up'."

"Mm-hmm. And did James give you any specifics?"

"Not really," Ben replied, shaking his head. "Would've been nice, though. I probably wouldn't have gotten out of bed tonight if I knew."

Ken let out a playful chuckle. "No, I can't imagine you would. Now, tell me this Ben... do you know *why* this ritual exists?"

"Because some people fucking suck?" Ben responded, shrugging his shoulders.

A bellow of laughter erupted from Ken. He leaned back, cackling into the night sky, then patted Ben on the knee.

"Oh, man, how right you are, good sir," Ken chortled. "Sometimes, people do in fact *fucking suck*."

"So... I take it there's a little more to the history of all this?" Ben asked.

"That's right, Ben, there is a history here. But it's not just *a* history... it's *my* history."

The look of confusion on Ben's face deepened.

"About 60 years ago, this camp opened up for the first time," Ken began. "A few weeks after the first batch of troubled teens arrive, the ritual materializes out of *thin air*. It was almost like a natural pecking order *demanded* it to exist. And barely a month after the gates are open!

"So, one night, not unlike *this evening*, the ritual claims its first victim. Now, I don't want to belittle the pain and agony *you* went through earlier, because I could *feel* the extent of the damage that was done to you. But this guy... he *really* took one for the team, as they say. A few of the other campers lured him out into these very woods, and beat him senseless."

"*Wow*," Ben whispered in a stunned haze.

"Yessir, '*wow*' is right! But here's the thing, Ben, he didn't have someone like me to come to his aid at the 11th hour, and do for him what I did for you."

A pang of guilt shot through Ben. Feeling his head grow heavy suddenly, he shifted his gaze to the damp grass beneath his feet.

"So... what happened to him?" Ben asked, noticing his bloodied shirt.

"Well, you know how it goes, Ben," Ken began, "these things *usually* start out as harmless fun for the bullies—which us little guys understand is complete horseshit." He gave Ben a quick wink. "But the ass-kicking escalated, and those bullies were suddenly filled with a kind of primal rage that dates back to the beginning of time. They realized, more than ever before, how *powerful* it felt to break someone down physically—to have that kind of control over a lesser, *weaker* man.

"So, they beat this kid harder, and faster. Suddenly he began foaming at the mouth, his body convulsing violently. What those bullies didn't realize was that they caused that kid to have a seizure. They didn't lead him out to the woods with the *intention* of killing him, but that is exactly what happened, Ben."

"When they saw that foam, like a rabid dog, and the convulsions, like he was possessed by some demon, they ran away. They left him for dead. Maybe there was something that could've been done to save this poor kid, or maybe not. But the truth is, a stone's throw from where we sit right now, he *died* that night."

Ben's mouth hung open, his eyes wide and transfixed by his savior. There was an unease deep within Ben's guts, knowing that Ken's story so closely mirrored his own. He sensed the clouds of confusion beginning to part, felt his brain starting to piece details together. The conclusion he came to was beyond belief, and disregarded all logic that resided within his practical world. And yet, moments earlier he had been brought back from death's door by a mysterious and unknown figure who seemingly materialized out of nowhere.

"That kid," Ben asked, swallowing hard through the lump in his throat, "he was *you*... wasn't he?"

"I'm afraid so," Ken responded.

It was the first time that Ben could recall seeing a frown on his face. He felt awful, like somehow all of this was *his* fault, despite that being the furthest from the truth.

"So, does that mean you're... a *ghost*?" Ben asked, feeling ludicrous as he did so.

Ken's face transformed back into a smile.

"I'd like to think of myself as more of a *spirit*; or a 'ghost of vengeance past,' if you will."

Ken rose to his feet, and extended his hand to Ben to join him. As he accepted the assistance, he winced in preparation for a world of hurt, but was only met with a slight cramp.

"Each time one of these poor souls gets lured out from the rest of the pack to be brutally beaten by others that are stronger, it becomes a sort of... tentative invitation for me. The deal is, though, I can only offer my assistance if death is on the line."

Ben straightened up, feeling his blood go cold.

"*Wait*, does that mean I was about to *die*?" Ben asked.

With a sigh and a nod, Ken responded, "Yessir. You were about *four minutes* from death's door."

"And you— you *saved* me."

"I was *avenging* you. Simply put, I was only doing for you what I could *not* do for myself all those years ago." Ken put a hand on Ben's shoulder, and looked him in the eyes. "Listen, Ben, the time we have left together is limited, so why don't you tell me a little bit about why you're here at the camp. I may be a ghost, but I'm not some omnipotent, all-knowing entity."

11:31 PM

Silence had fallen on the empty living room once again. With his arms still crossed, Will peered at Ben through narrowed eyes, gobsmacked. This look slowly transformed into a grin, and then a toothy smile. Finally, Will erupted into raucous laughter.

"Holy *shit*, Ben!" he said through bouts of laughter. "Fucking *ghosts*? I mean, clearly this camp helped you gain a bit of confidence, there's no denying that. But *ghosts*? Seriously, are you sure your parents didn't accidentally send you to the fucking circus? Because that is hilarious!"

Ben stared back at Will with an empathetic smile. He understood that the recounting of his near-death experience—and subsequent introduction to Ken—would be met with skepticism, so he was willing to lend a certain amount of patience toward Will.

"Ok, Ben," Will began again, regaining his composure, "let's be honest here, you were *probably* hallucinating from being kicked in the head. I'm not a doctor, but that seems like a probable conclusion. But for the sake of argument, let's assume you *did* see and talk to a ghost that night.

"So, when this apparition finally asked you why you were there at the camp, did you rat me out? I bet you sang like a fucking bird. You probably couldn't *wait* to tell him that I was the mastermind behind all this. But what good did it do you, huh? Did your invisible friend help you out when you once again refused to take responsibility for your actions?"

"As a matter of fact, he did."

July 3rd, 2019, 3:47 AM

Ken listened without interruption as Ben told an abbreviated version of his friendship with Will, including the bit involving Maxine. Occasionally Ken would nod his head in understanding, but did not once look as if he was surprised by the horrific actions of Ben's best friend.

When Ben finished his recounting of the last two years, Ken took a long, deep sigh.

"Ok, here's the deal, Ben," he began. "You have two choices. And keep in mind there is no right or wrong choice, but whatever path you *do* decide to go down will echo throughout the rest of your life. I know that this will be a lot to let sink in, and in such a short amount of time, but that's simply the circumstances we're dealing with."

"Oh-okay?" Ben had butterflies in his stomach. This had already been the weirdest night, and now, despite his uncertainty that this was real, he needed to brace himself for *more* weirdness?

"The healing that I did for you," Ken continued, "that was a gift. You deserved it; you earned it. And from here, you can go back to the barracks, wake up tomorrow and move on with the rest of your life. However, you will forget me and everything else that's happened here tonight between us. That's option number one."

Ben nodded his head in understanding.

"Here's option two: You take your healing with you, and exact your revenge on those guys that kicked the shit out of you. Flip the script, and make them very, *very* sorry they decided to fuck with you."

"Are you *crazy*?" Ben exclaimed. "What makes you think I won't get my ass kicked again? They could *really* kill me! Obviously, I don't know all the details of this whole 'ghost-saving' business, but I gotta imagine it's a one-and-done kind of thing."

Ken let out a quick chuckle. "If you choose the second option, you *won't* be alone—you'll have *me* with you. Well, you'll have a *piece* of me."

"Wait... what does that mean exactly?" Ben asked, more confused than ever.

"Let's just say that you'll have certain... *abilities*. And once you exact your revenge, you'll go forward with these for the rest of your life."

"*Abilities*?" Ben asked, his heart racing inside his chest. "What kind of abilities?"

11:42

Ben had once more produced his phone from his pocket. He navigated to the final video he needed Will to see, then handed the smartphone to his friend.

"About six weeks into the camp program," Ben began, "certain privileges were extended to the campers that demonstrated appropriate behavior and showed growth. One of those privileges was an hour of phone time each week, and we were allowed to do whatever we wanted on them. Most guys used that hour to call their parents or girlfriends back home, others would spend the whole time watching porn.

"So, one week during our allotted phone time, I was lying in my bunk, just twirling my smartphone in my hand. There was no one that I wanted to talk to, and porn was the furthest thing from my mind. You know who *was* on my mind, however?"

Will shrugged his shoulders apathetically.

"I was thinking about *Sean*. Ever since the night of... *you know*, I had been racking my brain on how I was going to get even with this motherfucker. And like a flash of lightning, it *hit me*.

"So, I hopped off my bunk and started talking to my bunkmate, James. I promised him my dinner rations that night if he was willing to help me out. All he had to do was take my phone, discretely head into the latrine, and begin filming once I met him in there."

Will shot Ben another impatient glare. "Are ya done? Can I play the video now?"

Ben's lips curled into a devious grin. "Go right ahead. I think you're *really* gonna like this one, being a fan of found-footage horror."

With one last suspicious look to Ben, Will tapped the play button. With all this talk of ghosts and raising from the dead, he wasn't sure what to expect.

The shaky camera footage began with a wide angle shot of someone—unmistakably Ben—running into a large restroom, soon followed by a much *larger* person, wearing nothing except boxer shorts. Ben was holding a phone in his hand—presumably the giant's—and was taunting him with it.

"Come on, Sean!" Ben said in the video. "You want your phone back? Come and get it, big boy!"

"You dumb son of a bitch!" Sean in the video yelled. "I should've kicked you in the head harder. I cannot believe we let you live!"

Another smile crept across Will's face. Sean the giant looked as if he belonged on the football field alongside Will, and he did *not* look pleased with having his phone time interrupted by Ben. The large camper descended on Ben with an unmistakable look of rage in his eyes. James had to dart out of the way to keep filming the video clearly.

Sean swung his monstrous fist with the intention of making crippling contact with Ben's face. With lightning-fast reflexes, Ben juked to the side, narrowly avoiding being hit. The anger on Sean's face intensified as he squared up, swung, and again missed contact with his skinny underling.

The giant took a few steps back to rethink his strategy. He then put both his fists up and narrowed his eyes at Ben, letting him know in no uncertain terms that playtime was officially over. Ben slid Sean's phone into his pocket, and then mockingly also put his fists up into the boxing position.

The third and final time the giant advanced, Ben effortlessly grabbed the meaty fist, and in the blink of an eye twisted his arm clockwise. There was an audible snapping sound, as well as an off-camera gasp. The videographer cautiously moved in closer to the two subjects, then panned around to show the giant's arm twisted in an unnatural position, with one of the bones forcefully jutting out through the skin. With a final swift motion, Ben delivered a chop to the giant's throat, just in time to render him incapable of screaming in pain for help.

Will was *mesmerized* by what he was seeing. So much so that he almost forgot he was watching a smartphone video, and *not* some clip from a found-footage film.

Back in the video, Ben released the oversized fist, and Sean fell to the floor with a thud. What had just unfolded—*was unfolding*—was a literal "David and Goliath" story. It was all Will could do to *not* stare slack-jawed at the shaky camera footage.

The final scene that played out left Will even *more* stupefied. Ben straddled his defeated giant, knelt down, and placed both hands around his throat. Unprompted, the cameraman moved in closer. The giant flailed his legs and one good arm in an attempt to wiggle free, but the pressure that Ben was dealing had been too great. His face turned bright red, and then purple, his limbs flopping like fish out of water. And then all at once, it was *done*. There was no more life left in the giant.

Will let the phone drop to his side, his brain racing to make sense of what he just witnessed. The idea that his friend Ben was capable of doing something like this defied all logic. He had *killed* someone. And not just any someone, but a guy twice his size!

"He didn't make it, *obviously*." Ben said, breaking the silence. "I was supposed to die the night that Sean and his goons attacked me. But I was saved by the spirit of a dead man. He didn't just save me, though. He helped me realize my true potential.

"You know, in the end I'm *glad* you convinced my parents to send me to that camp. If it wasn't for you, I wouldn't have been granted the opportunity to not only knock on heaven's door, but live to tell the tale of who answers. I needed the confidence to stand toe to toe with you, look you in the eye, and demand your respect. And it would be fine if you weren't willing to give it, because then I'd finally learn that you are not worth my *fucking time*."

Ben's phone suddenly began to ring, and without looking at the caller ID, Will passed it back to him. Ben glanced at who was calling.

"Sorry, Will, I need to take this."

Ben strode into the adjacent room to accept the call in private. As Will heard the distant sounds of a one-way phone conversation, he took advantage of the opportunity to refine his own plan. An hour ago, he had one foot out the front door and could smell the sweetness of the fresh late-summer air. And then Ben had dropped the *bombshell* that coerced him into sticking around.

It was probable that Ben had been lying about some or all of the details involving his blackmailing scheme, but he wasn't willing to risk finding out the hard way. No, it would be much easier to take care of things here and now while the opportunity was rearing its ugly face.

Up until this evening, Will had never considered himself to be a potential murderer. Then again, he couldn't fathom Ben to be one, either, though only moments ago Will had seen hard proof that he was.

Will paced nonchalantly and scanned the living room, looking for anything that could be used as a weapon. The only things that could be considered weapons and that weren't nailed down were the two chairs and a few small lamps. There *was* a fireplace along the longest wall of the room, but it appeared to be empty and clean.

Will glanced into the adjacent room to ensure the coast was clear, then walked slowly toward the brick-lined mantle. He stooped to a crouched position, and felt along the inside of the dark hole that was the fireplace, hoping to stumble across something—*anything*—that he could use to ensure that he would be the only person walking out of this house alive. Huffing quietly to himself, he arose empty-handed.

"Looking for the fireplace poker?"

Ben had quietly made his way back into the room, causing Will to jump out of his skin as he asked the obvious question. The poker *would* have been an excellent tool to take care of the job.

"If you are, don't worry, there *isn't* one," Ben confirmed. "I scoured the place pretty thoroughly before I set this all in motion. Knowing you'd be pretty angry by the end of the night, I didn't want you to get any bright ideas about retribution."

"Yeah, that would've been a *shame*, wouldn't it?" Will sneered, turning to face Ben.

"Oh, by the way, here's your phone back."

Ben reached into a front pocket of his jeans and handed Will a smartphone that was unmistakably his. After accepting it from Ben, he looked at it in amazement, unable to believe he had gone this entire night without noticing his phone was missing.

An avalanche of new ideas began pummeling Will's brain, now that he was reunited with his phone. A slew of notifications displayed on the screen, from missed calls to unanswered texts. Without any thought, he navigated to the group chat with Mark, John, and a few other teammates.

Will *hated* the idea of sending out an SOS message to his buddies. He wanted—*needed*—to take care of this situation himself. But the walls were slowly closing in on him. He was running out of time and options.

The idea was to stick this thing out with Ben and work through their issues. And for better or worse, they had done that. Ben was apparently convinced they could both walk out of here tonight, as if none of this had even happened. Will, however, had other plans. He had no intention of letting Ben leave this house tonight alive. No. In Will's mind, this night only had *one* ending: Him—and him alone—walking out the front door, after *killing* Ben with his bare hands.

In the group chat, Will tapped the message box to bring up the keyboard. He dropped a location pin, then began typing his message.

> Hey dudes, I can't talk right now but this is VERY important. If you can, I need you to meet me here ASAP. You were right about Ben. But he's more than a nutcase. He's fucking dangerous, and needs to be dealt with.

Will tapped the send button, then breathed a sigh of relief as the "Delivered" notification displayed under his message.

"So, who was on the phone?" Will asked casually as he scrolled through the rest of his notifications.

"Oh, that was just Maxine." Ben answered casually. "We're supposed to meet up tomorrow. It sounds like she missed me a *lot* this summer, and wants to talk about patching things up between us."

Will chuckled behind the light of his smartphone. "You're so full of *shit*."

The first reply came through in the group chat. A message from John, saying he was on the way. Almost immediately after, Mark and the others followed suit. The calvary was *officially* on their way.

"I just talked to Max earlier this afternoon," Will continued. "Your name *did* come up, but there was *zero* indication she's taking your sorry ass back. Sorry, brother."

Ben chuckled, shoving his hands in his pockets. "Yeah, I guess I don't really have any hard proof of that, unfortunately." He paused for dramatic effect, watching Will's smile widen. "But if I'm not mistaken, I believe that *you* do." He nodded to Will's phone. "Perhaps... a *voicemail*?"

Will's suspicious eyes met Ben's for a moment, then dropped back down to his smartphone. The muscles in his face tightened. He navigated away from the group chat to the phone app, noticing he *did* have one new voicemail. It was from *Maxine*. His thumb hovered over the play button for several moments before finally tapping it. He glared at Ben as he raised his trembling hand with the phone to his ear.

Over the course of the next 90 seconds, Will's smug and self-assured countenance slowly transitioned into one of disbelief and unadulterated rage. A mere 12 hours ago, he had a firm grip on almost every aspect of his life. He was the star athlete of *two* different sports teams for his high school, and a shoo-in for multiple athletic scholarships next fall.

Will had Ben under his complete control, like a well-trained dog. He could treat him however he pleased. Any girl at school would jump at the chance to be with Will, but for fun, he chose to steal Maxine from Ben instead. It had become second nature, siphoning off his friend's pain to fuel his pleasure. It was all pure *entertainment* for him.

"You flew too close to the sun, my friend," Ben spoke up, disrupting Will's downward spiral. "Oh, *my bad*. You 'took your eye off the ball'. Sorry about that, it was *insensitive* of me to use a metaphor that'd fly over your head."

Will stared back at him with profound hatred that burned red in his eyes. "Oh, so this is *funny* to you, then?" he asked, his voice low and trembling.

"Sometimes... you fuck around and *find out*. And *you*, my friend, have been fucking around for a *long* time. But now it's *my turn* to take what's rightfully mine."

"Max doesn't *belong* to you! She's not some piece of property that you can just *take*!"

Ben's lips curled into a grin. "And yet, that's *exactly* how you treated her."

Another moment of silence passed between them. Will's heavy breathing filled the quiet of the living room.

"You must be *awfully* proud of yourself," Will replied through gritted teeth. Without realizing, he began taking small steps toward the old friend that meant to ruin his life. "Do you feel like the *big man* now? Are you everything you ever wanted to be, now that I'm about to have nothing?"

Ben dropped his head in disappointment. "Will, if you haven't figured out by now the *true* purpose of you being here, there is nothing else I can do for you. I never wanted to be the 'big man', I only wanted your *respect*. I need you to know that I honestly did all this as an attempt to even out the scales between us, if you were going to *insist* on keeping one boot firmly on my neck. But I can tell that you're *never* going to see it that way. You'll always see it as an attack on *you*, and that you'll never have anything to apologize for, despite all the terrible shit you've done to me. And since that's the case, I—"

Will charged at Ben, seizing the opportunity of digression to physically enact his revenge. He wasn't afforded the time to properly sort out his plan for taking Ben down, so he knew he had to rely on his relentless strength and conditioning discipline to take care of this—*fast and dirty*.

Ben fell to the floor with a thud, a victim of Will's spear tackle. Grunting and breathing heavily, Will climbed on top of Ben and began to pummel his fists into the face of his victim. Burning red filled his vision as he unleashed his fury. Ben held up his forearms to protect his face, absorbing most of the blows. At the sight of blood beginning to pour from Ben's nose, a devilish smile grew on Will's face as he continued his quest of becoming the grim reaper to this pour, misguided soul.

Will paused his punching, taking a split second to consider his next move: To pick Ben up by his shirt and toss him across the room. He envisioned him sailing across the room like a rag doll. He could *hear* the sound of Ben's bones breaking.

But a second of respite was all it took for Ben to uncover his face, and head-butt Will hard enough to cause his own nosebleed. Will stumbled backward as he instinctively grabbed his nose, allowing Ben the opportunity to rise to his feet.

"You really shouldn't have done that," Ben said, panting and wiping his nose. "I gave you an out! You could have just left!"

"Not while we have unfinished business." Will swiped at his own nose to clear the blood, then once more balled his hands into fists.

Suddenly, all of the lights in the living room began to flicker, but Will remained locked in eye contact with Ben.

"I'm done with your cheap fucking parlor tricks," Will spat, "It's time for you to be a man, and take your medicine."

Ben slowly began to relax his stance, then looked longingly at his best friend one last time. His deep blue eyes under the flashing lights were distant and sorrowful.

"I'm sorry it had to be like this, Will."

The flickering of the lights ceased, and complete darkness consumed the room. Will could hear his heart racing over the incredible silence that had fallen over them. Arrested by the twilight, he could only tell that Ben wasn't directly in front of him. But he *was* here. *Somewhere.* Will spun around the room, fists raised, waiting to catch a glimpse of this *magician* that needed to accept his fate.

"Come out and fight me like a man!" Will screamed and beat his chest in anger. "It's time for you to—"

All of the lights in the living room came back on in a brilliant flash, temporarily blinding Will. His eyes adjusted just in time to see Ben, only inches away from him.

"Goodbye, my friend." These words, spoken in Ben's voice with immobile lips, echoed in Will's mind as the last reception it would receive.

With inhuman and supernatural speed, Ben took Will's head in his hands, and in one swift motion, twisted it around 180 degrees. A loud crack echoed throughout the entire house. Bones unnaturally protruded from Will's neck, threatening to break skin, as Ben held the head attached to his friend's lifeless body. He let go, and the corpse fell to the floor with a thud.

With a hard and thoughtful sigh, Ben bowed his head and closed his eyes. Memories that he and Will had shared flickered like a slideshow in his mind. His chest felt heavy with sobs that wanted to erupt and break. But the broken man at his feet reminded him of how little his tears were truly worth. And so his mournful thoughts began to dissipate just as quickly as they had came.

A chime rang out from the smartphone in his pocket—a notification from Rivers.

"It's done." was all the message read. The time in the top right corner of his smartphone read "12:01 AM".

Ben texted back the "thumbs up" emoji, placed the phone back in his pocket, then headed toward the foyer. Halfway out the front door, Ben looked back one last time at Will's limp, lifeless body. A smile crept across his face as he turned back to head into the warm summer night. He closed the door, then let the lights in the living room go out for the last time.

"I must not fear. Fear is the mind-killer. Fear is the little-death that brings total obliteration. I will face my fear. I will permit it to pass over me and through me. And when it has gone past I will turn the inner eye to see its path. Where the fear has gone there will be nothing. Only I will remain."

— **FRANK HERBERT,** *DUNE* **(1965)**

CHAPTER 2

The Last Stall on the Left

Part I

Ever since Tim was a little boy, he absolutely loathed using public restrooms. Of course, back then he was known as "Timmy," yet another aspect of his life that he despised. The need to extend and infantilize his birth name was one he never quite understood. His childhood friends like Bill and Tom never had to suffer the unnecessary elongation of their names. But, even more than his childish sounding name, he hated using the public facilities.

The cold, sterile smell of disinfectant never quite covered up the pungent stench of urine and sweat that seemed to linger in every public bathroom. The harsh fluorescent lighting always seemed to dim the moment he walked in, leaving him squinting and disoriented. The porcelain sinks were always cracked and stained; the faucets dripping incessantly. And worst of all were the stalls, with their grimy doors and toilet paper that felt like sandpaper against his delicate skin.

Tim shuddered at the mere thought of having to use one of these abominations. He would hold it in for hours, waiting until he was home or in a private, clean restroom. It was a small price to pay for his comfort and peace of mind.

All of these vivid details—as revolting as they were—came secondary to Tim's *true* fear surrounding the use of public restrooms: The "Toilet Monster". Tim was no stranger to all of the absurd rumors that were passed around on the playground, at the back of the school bus, and anywhere else that provided a safe haven for illicit subject matter. These included such classics as "If you swallow a watermelon seed, one is going to grow in your stomach," and the always popular "You get a girl pregnant by giving her a kiss." Then there were the rumors falsely spread by parents, like "If the ice cream truck was playing music, it was out of ice cream," and "If you keep making that expression, your face is going to stay that way."

Young Tim—*not* Timmy—could spot the flaws in all of these preposterous tall-tales *except* for the Toilet Monster. Like many cautionary folk tales, the Toilet Monster story made its rounds through adults and kids alike. And although its distinct appearance would change depending on *who* was telling the story, the general consensus was that the creature was an amorphous and floating black cloud, with red beady eyes and long fingers. If the story was told by adults, it was typically a deterrent—not unlike the boogeyman—such as "don't forget to wash your hands, or the Toilet Monster will get you." But if it were kids telling the story, they would exaggerate the sinister intentions of the monster and the gory repercussions for violating its rules.

Along the beam of life, Tim *had* found ways to avoid public facilities—*and* the Toilet Monster. There had been an unfortunate incident in second grade, when another boy looked over Tim's shoulder as he was at the urinal and proceeded to point and laugh at his wiener. The "nail in the coffin" came in the form of that same boy yelling out to Tim as he left the restroom "Hey Tim, don't let the Toilet Monster get you!" After this altercation, Tim lucked into the teachers allowing him to use the faculty restrooms. These first-class facilities came equipped with a single toilet and a door that locked.

He had trouble rationalizing *why* the toilet monster was only prevalent in public restrooms, and not the private ones; it was simply one of those things that only made sense in his mind. Perhaps it was the *fear* of it all.

One of Tim's most prized possessions was one of his own making: A pocket-sized spiral notebook, with every single business and location within a 20-mile radius of his home and school that offered a private restroom. Years later, when Tim's parents gifted him his first smartphone, the very first app he downloaded was called "Bathroom Buddy". Although excited about the upgrade, Tim was somewhat morose to no longer require his long-lived analog companion. It had truly become a "buddy" to him over the many years he carried it around, dutifully logging entries. But the app *too* was helpful, and offered more features and better organization tools than simple pen and paper could provide.

Tim had desperately hoped that his strange bathroom phobia was just another childhood phase, and that at a certain age he'd simply grow out of it. Many nights he would pray that in the morning he would wake up and suddenly no longer be terrified of peeing next to another boy. This, however, was *not* the case.

As Tim entered his teenage years, his fear of public restrooms remained as strong as ever. It had become an integral part of his identity, a constant weight on his shoulders that he carried with resignation and determination. He knew it was irrational, knew that the Toilet Monster was nothing more than an urban legend concocted by the fearful minds of children. But that knowledge didn't make the fear any less real.

His friends and family didn't understand his phobia, often dismissing it as a silly quirk or an exaggerated excuse to avoid uncomfortable situations. They would laugh and tease him, thinking it was all a joke. But Tim's fear cut deeper than their understanding allowed. He could always feel the long, phantom fingers of the Toilet Monster gripping him like icy tendrils, leaving him trembling at the mere thought of entering a public restroom.

Around the time when Tim started college, he experienced the cold realization that his days of outsmarting his phobia—and the Toilet Monster—were numbered. He had grown tired of letting his fear control him, and longed to be free from the shackles that bound him to this irrational terror. And so, he decided to seek professional help for his unique aversion. In his first session with Doctor Simmons, Tim had tiptoed around the topic of what had ultimately brought him to the couch, foolishly afraid of the judgment that the therapist would pass. When he finally broached the subject, he lingered on every word as if telling a spooky campfire story. His therapist gave a slight, innocent chuckle at the final reveal of what had been eating at Tim for so long. Infuriated, he stormed out of his session with 30 minutes left on the clock, and decided right then and there to never return.

When his attempt at therapy went belly-up, Tim turned to the internet to see how other grown adults went about handling their phobias of public toilets. He was both shocked and relieved to learn that so many others his age suffer from the same problem. It was equally frustrating, however, to learn that there were so many different "cures" that existed. One user claimed that it took them *years* of trial and error to figure out the winning formula for urinating freely. Another user—an older gentleman in his 80s—stated that he was *still* looking for the right treatment plan. An angry and defeated Tim slammed the lid of his laptop closed, then reluctantly accepted that he'd simply carry on the rest of his life like this, forever doomed to shit in the comfort of his home.

Part II

As he reached his mid-twenties, Tim's fear of bathrooms had become more tolerable, thanks to his forced nonchalance. He still couldn't fully shake off the dread, but at least he could use the "private" public restrooms without having a panic attack. Tim had become skilled in finding alternative solutions to his bathroom needs, whether it was strategically planning his outings to ensure he was always near a private restroom, or utilizing the buddy system with trusted friends who would stand guard outside the stall. Tim had even developed a peculiar talent for holding it in for seemingly unreasonable lengths of time, much to the amazement and disbelief of those around him. He became known as "the guy who can hold his pee forever" among his coworkers and acquaintances.

Tim's luck, however, didn't hold out forever, and the incidents and accidents started to pile up like dominoes. One particular case was the college graduation party he and his roommates threw. After a long night of drinking, Tim awoke to use the shared bathroom, safe in the assumption that he wouldn't be bothered. As he stood at the toilet, hungover and bracing himself against the wall, he breathed a sigh of relief as the flow of urine began. Suddenly, to Tim's horror, the shower curtain next to him began to rustle.

This is it, he thought to himself, *this is how it ends. The Toilet Monster's gonna get me while I'm simultaneously drunk and hungover.*

A hand curled around the curtain and slowly pulled it aside. But it wasn't a darkened hand with long, bony fingers; it was much more delicate, tanned, and boldly showed off freshly manicured fingernails. The curtain then abruptly tore open to reveal a girl who had passed out in the bathtub. In a similar drunken haze, she appeared to not be immediately alarmed by Tim's intrusion, but the same could not be said for Tim. He shrieked in terror when he instinc-

tively turned toward the intruder, and accidentally urinated all over
her. From that day forward, Tim added "look behind the shower
curtain" to his checklist for every bathroom he visited, a precaution-
ary act he couldn't believe he wasn't already performing.

Deep down, Tim knew that this was not a sustainable solution,
going about life as if he could avoid public toilets forever. He
couldn't continue living in fear, constantly on edge whenever nature
called. There had to be a way to conquer this phobia once and for all.
And so, with newfound determination, Tim embarked on a silent
quest to face his fears head-on.

When Tim approached his late twenties, he met Cynthia—his
future wife. They met at a Starbucks—coincidentally a location
with "private" public restrooms—and they fell deeply in love with
one another, getting married soon after. A few weeks before their
wedding, Tim pulled his fiancée aside and said he had something
important to tell her. Cynthia was initially confused and worried,
thinking that Tim was getting cold feet. He took in a deep breath,
then proceeded to tell her all about his long-lived terror of using
public restrooms. Cynthia had to stifle her laughter as her fiancé presented this, truly thinking that it was some sort of joke. But when
she realized that Tim was *deadly* serious about his phobia, she did
her best to assure him that it wasn't a big deal—even though she still
found it a *little* humorous.

"Tim," Cynthia began, taking his trembling hands in her own, "I
want you to know that I love you no matter what. Your fear doesn't
define you, and it *certainly* doesn't change how I feel about you. We
will face this *together*."

Tim's heart swelled with gratitude as he listened to Cynthia's
words of reassurance. He knew he had found someone special in her,
someone who would support him unconditionally. With Cynthia

by his side, Tim felt a renewed sense of determination to conquer his phobia.

Together, they researched methods and therapies to help Tim overcome his fear of public restrooms. They attended support groups where Tim met others who shared his struggle, finding solace in their stories and encouragement. Cynthia even came up with a code word they could use whenever they were in public and Tim needed to use the restroom: "Banana".

Six months before his 30th birthday, Tim told himself and his wife that if he was still suffering from his toilet phobia when he blew out the candles on his birthday cake, he would once again seek professional help. And sure enough, Tim's 30th trip around the sun came and went, but his fear of peeing in front of other people remained. He even secretly wished his phobia away before he blew out his candles, just as he'd prayed for its end as a child. Tim had hoped to turn over a new leaf, but instead was met with an overturned stone, revealing a still-terrifying mental image of the Toilet Monster.

And so began Tim's second attempt at therapy. His new therapist, Doctor Maya Nguyen, had specialized in psychological disorders, and unlike his previous doctor, didn't laugh at Tim when he brought up the reason for his therapy.

"So, Tim, why do you think you're unable to use public restrooms?" his therapist asked curiously.

"Um, isn't that what *you're* here for?" Tim responded, buying himself some time.

Tim understood the nuance of his therapist's opening question, but found himself automatically resistant to answering it. The act of attending therapy and verbalizing his irrational phobia would in turn make it as real as it had ever been, and there would be no chance of putting *that* ship back in the bottle.

"It very much is, Tim," she said reassuringly, despite her honest chuckle. "However, at this point I am more interested in learning what *you* think the cause might be. After all, this is an issue you've lived with for a long time. Certainly you must have given some thought as to why you have an aversion to public restrooms."

Tim rubbed his sweaty palms together and took in a deep breath. His face felt clammy, and his mouth was as dry as the Sahara, but he understood that his opportunity to banish this fear was now or never.

"I'm afraid of the Toilet Monster," Tim said, his head hung low and heavy.

Doctor Nguyen stared back at Tim with narrowed eyes, her head tilted to the side.

"I'm... sorry, the *what*?"

"The *Toilet Monster*," Tim reiterated slowly.

Doctor Nguyen took a moment to carefully consider her response. The "Toilet Monster" was a new one for her.

"*Okay...*" she replied cautiously. "Why don't you tell me a little bit about this... *Toilet Monster*?"

Tim looked up at Dr. Nguyen, a mix of apprehension and hope lingering in his eyes. He had rehearsed this moment in his mind countless times, but somehow the words still felt foreign on his tongue.

"The Toilet Monster," Tim began, his voice trembling, "is supposedly this... *hideous* creature that lurks within every public restroom. It's a grotesque, otherworldly being, with long, gnarled fingers and piercing red eyes. And it's always there, waiting for me to let my guard down."

Dr. Nguyen leaned forward, her eyes locked on Tim's face. She reached out and clasped her hands together in a gesture of support and understanding. Before continuing, Tim clocked his therapist's expression and was almost taken aback by her calm, docile face and sympathetic smile.

"It's not *just* the Toilet Monster," Tim continued, his voice growing more animated. "It's the feeling I get when I'm near a public restroom. A sense of dread washes over me, like I'm being taunted by something sinister. I'll catch myself standing outside the men's room, completely transfixed on the door as it opens and closes. And sometimes... sometimes I *swear* I hear whispers coming from the toilets."

Tim felt absolutely ridiculous, recounting the childhood folktale that had influenced so much of his life. Doctor Nguyen's demeanor, however, was calm and compassionate, like somehow she *herself* was well-acquainted with the concept of this evil bathroom dweller.

"So, Tim, do you *still* believe in the Toilet Monster?" his therapist asked.

Tim looked at her with a baffled expression. "Wh- what do you mean?" he asked, rubbing his hands together.

"Do you think," Doctor Nguyen began, shifting her weight and considering her clarifying words, "that this prowler of public restrooms is a *literal* entity that is taunting and waiting for you?"

Tim's confused expression deepened. "As opposed to... what, exactly? Are you trying to say that this monster is just some physical form I assigned to my deep-seated fear of public restrooms?"

Doctor Nguyen's face curled into a proud grin. "So you *have* given this some thought."

She and Tim shared a bout of light laughter, releasing a small amount of tension from the room.

"Look, I *know* how ridiculous this all sounds, being afraid of some childish tall-tale," Tim said. "And maybe it is, or maybe it isn't the *actual* Toilet Monster I'm terrified of. But the fear I experience every time I walk by a public restroom is very real."

"Tim, it's completely understandable that this phobia has such a hold on you," Doctor Nguyen said gently. "Fear is a powerful emotion, and it can manifest itself in ways that seem irrational or even foolish to others. But I believe that with the right tools, you can overcome this fear and regain control over your life."

Tim breathed a sigh of relief as his entire body unclenched, feeling the weight of decades of trauma lifted off of him. The confidence that his therapist exhibited regarding the "curing" of his phobia made him feel like overcoming this would *actually* be possible.

At the end of their session, Doctor Nguyen took several moments to scribble down notes on a pad of paper. She then tore it away, folded it in half, and handed it to Tim.

"What's this?" he asked.

"Homework," Doctor Nguyen replied with a wink.

The very next day, Tim began the first steps of his "exposure therapy", where he would gradually work his way up to urinating just as freely and unencumbered in public as he would in the comfort of his own home. For one week, he was to inform his wife Cynthia every time he needed to use the restroom. This act alone was intended to acclimate his mind to the idea of other people knowing that he was relieving himself. And because Tim was already relatively comfortable with his partner's understanding of his bathroom routine, this turned out to be a quick and easy win for him.

The second week built upon the first, and involved Cynthia standing outside of their bathroom door each time that Tim had to urinate. This step proved to be slightly more difficult than the first, but he managed to breeze through it in the seven days that he and Doctor Nguyen allotted.

The real challenge began on step three, where Cynthia was required to be present in the bathroom while Tim urinated. It wasn't a prerequisite that she actually bear witness to her husband relieving himself, just that she was there when it happened. Tim stood at the toilet for more than 15 minutes on the first day, waiting for the flow. As it turned out, there was a *major* difference between his wife being on one side of their bathroom door versus the other. In the end, Cynthia had been the true MVP of week three, coming up with the idea of telling her husband jokes and citing fond memories they had shared, which ultimately aided Tim in relaxing and letting go.

The couple repeated this technique, and by Thursday of that week Tim was able to urinate freely within 20 seconds or less. And by the end of the week, Tim had become such a pro that he might as well have been peeing by himself. That Sunday afternoon, Cynthia threw her husband a small congratulatory party, where she bought him a "toilet humor" joke book and baked a cake with the letters "ICUP" written in frosting.

That night while lying awake in bed, Cynthia fast asleep next to him, Tim considered the potential outcomes of the next steps of his treatment plan. Cautious optimism had been the prevalent emotion flooding his brain. There had been challenges throughout his first three weeks of treatment, but he had both emotional and physical support systems in place. Once he was out in the real world, stepping up to a *public* urinal, it would be him and him alone. And maybe, the Toilet Monster...

Part III

The time had finally come for Tim to graduate to a public restroom, although he still had numerous steps to complete before he was ready to use the urinal. For the first week of his treatment out in the real world, Tim would be required to visit the public facilities at every opportunity, but was only expected to use the handwashing station. And although this step was simple in theory, Tim still experienced waves of anxiety since he hadn't even been inside a public restroom since he was a kid—not even to wash his hands.

Tim had been at the grocery store with Cynthia when he was forced into the deep end of his treatment. As he approached the restroom door, his heart thudded fiercely, and his palms were cool and clammy. The nauseating combination of cleaning chemicals and urine wafted through the opening, making his stomach churn. He took a deep breath and pushed it open, stepping inside.

The fluorescent lights flickered overhead, casting an unsettling glow on the grimy walls and floors. He scanned the empty stalls, thankful that no one else was around. The smell intensified as he walked to the sink area, and he wrinkled his nose at the pungent odor of stale urine mixed with disinfectant. He paused for a moment, trying to steady himself before reaching out to turn on the tap. The cool water splashed against his hands, shocking him slightly from his anxious daze. Slowly, he lathered up some soap on his hands and breathed steadily—through his mouth—doing his best to remain calm.

As he toweled his hands dry, a steady drip from one of the sinks echoed off the walls. The exaggerated "plinking" sound conjured an ominous feeling in his guts. A creaking and groaning sound stirred from one of the toilet stalls, and Tim stood frozen, his heart beating rapidly in his chest. When the creaking came to a stop, the auto-flush feature on the toilet activated, and he let out a burst of nervous laughter.

Those damn faulty motion sensors, he thought to himself.

Tim tossed the paper towel in the trash can, and had one hand on the restroom door handle when he heard the whispers of a disembodied voice.

"Timmmmmm. I see you, Tim!"

Its words were low and ominous, and Tim immediately felt his blood run cold. Although frozen in terror, he knew exactly who—or *what*—had called out for him. The voice came from the direction of one of the stalls. One, Tim noticed, had its door closed, despite him being the only person in the restroom. Suddenly, the door of the stall began trembling in its loose hinges, begging to be opened.

Tim desperately wanted to leave, to push his way out of that tile and porcelain hell hole and never come back. He was, however, hypnotized by the violent rattling of the door, his feet mysteriously rooted to the floor.

"I know you're there, Timmmmm... I can see you, and I can smell you!"

The voice had become a siren's song and Tim's grip loosened on the restroom door handle. His feet dislodged from the cracked tile and carried him a single step toward the closed stall. The thudding of his heart was loud within his ears. It mixed with the sounds coming from the stall, creating a macabre cacophony that only intensified his nausea.

Tim was about to take another step toward the force that called for him when he was jerked from his transfixed state. A store employee with a handful of toilet paper had pushed the men's room door open from the other side, causing Tim to let out an audible yelp. Before either could apologize, Tim had taken off from the restroom as fast as he could, his heart thudding inside his chest.

In a stupor, Tim managed to locate Cynthia in the frozen food section of the grocery store. She could tell immediately that he was shaken.

"Oh, my *god*, baby, are you okay?" Cynthia asked with wide, sympathetic eyes.

She grabbed a bag of frozen vegetables from the cart, and placed it on his forehead.

"I'm, uh... yeah, I'm okay," Tim replied, one hand on the cart to steady his balance.

Cynthia studied him for a moment, noting his pale complexion and physical instability. "What *happened* in there?" she asked, her voice warm with compassion.

Tim stood with the frozen broccoli on his face, thankful for reality seeping back into place. "I'm fine, honey," he said after a moment. "I just... freaked myself out a little bit."

Cynthia flashed him his favorite pouty face and rubbed his back. Tim gave her a halfhearted grin, and they continued their shopping without further mention of his incident in the restroom.

At his following session with Doctor Nguyen, Tim anxiously recounted his first experience in a public restroom.

"Well, it's a bit of a 'good news, bad news' situation," he began, noticing a confident smile and nod from Doctor Nguyen. "I *did* manage to make it through step four, but not without a... *minor* incident."

Tim paused for a moment, taking a deep breath to better ready himself.

"I- I *think* I heard a voice," he continued. "When I was drying my hands, *something* called my name from one of the stalls, like it was reaching out for me. It felt sinister, *evil*."

Doctor Nguyen took a moment to consider her patient's confession. She firmly believed that this was all in Tim's mind, that there truly was no such thing as a "Toilet Monster". But, she thought, outright telling a patient that what they perceived to be real was in fact *not* real, was typically deemed counterproductive. The key was to isolate the truth of the matter, and spin it in a way that was relatable for them.

"Have you ever read *The Tell-Tale Heart* by Edgar Allan Poe?" she asked finally.

"Um, yeah, like a long time ago," Tim replied with a look of confusion. "I think we may have read it in one of my high school Literature classes. I'm... not too big on the horror genre."

"Oh, me, either!" Nguyen responded quickly with a reaffirming smile. "But I think we can draw a line from it to your experience this past week, if you're willing to entertain it."

Tim gave his therapist a subtle nod.

"So, in the short story, the main character murders his roommate, citing only the uneasiness he felt by the old man's pale blue 'vulture-eye'. Soon thereafter, our narrator believes he hears the heartbeat of the deceased old man, thudding through the floorboards in which it was buried."

Tim was unsure of the point his therapist was attempting to make, but he had to admit that he was certainly intrigued.

"When the police arrive at the narrator's apartment to investigate, he is able to reassure them that the old man is out of the country. However, when he begins to hear the sounds of a heartbeat, he's somehow convinced that it belongs to his dead roommate. The police's decision to 'ignore' the beating heart drives our narrator *mad*, which leads to him pulling up the floorboards in his bout of insanity, and ultimately confessing to the murder."

The confused look on Tim's face had only deepened. He sat motionless, confused as to whether he'd have to piece this all together himself. And had she *really* just compared him to a psychopath who killed their roommate?

"Okay, so... what are you saying exactly?" he asked, a hint of frustration lining his tone.

"Do you think, Tim, that it was the *old man's* heartbeat our narrator was hearing? Assuming, of course, that there is no supernatural element to this story, and it's all grounded in reality."

"Um, probably not..." Tim said, still unsure of the connection. "But I still don't see what—"

His voice broke off when he noticed his therapist looking at him over the bridge of her glasses. It was one of those classic "I've given you the puzzle pieces, now it's up to *you* to put them together" looks.

"So, you're trying to tell me that it was all in my *head*?" Tim clarified. "The whispering voices, the rattling stall door. Those were all just symptoms of an... overactive imagination?"

"Well, it's a rather reductive and dismissive diagnosis, and one that does not lend you the credit you well deserve. But broad-strokes purposes, yes. You may not have killed a man and buried him underneath your house, leaving you riddled with guilt. But remember, Tim, you are contending with a fear you have lived with your whole life, so naturally the road to overcoming that fear won't always be freshly paved."

Tim considered his therapist's sage reassurance. And although it made sense in theory, it did little to put him at ease. *If* there truly was no Toilet Monster, and it was just his heightened sense of awareness, then it truly meant he was just a thirty-year-old man who was afraid of peeing alongside other people.

"So... what do you suggest I do now?" he asked morosely.

"You carry on with your treatment plan, Tim. Just as we discussed. And the next time you walk into a restroom, and you start to feel anxious, just remember... there's no heartbeat underneath those floorboards, and there's *no* Toilet Monster, either."

Part IV

Although Doctor Nguyen's words had been reassuring enough to get Tim back into public restrooms, he still *felt* the looming presence of an intangible haunt. He had little doubt that he'd be able to continue on with his treatment plan, but was yet to be convinced that his therapist's words should be treated as gospel. Nguyen could very well be right, that there was no evil entity lurking in the men's room. The undying question of "what if", however, seemed to unfairly plague Tim's mind relentlessly.

Regardless, Tim marched forward with his "pee plan" with as much confidence as he could muster. He elected to repeat the fourth step for another week, to ensure he truly was ready to move on to the next. And when that time had come, the faith he had for himself was that much stronger. As Tim approached the sixth week of his plan, he was washing his hands like some sort of professional hand-washer. He felt only a small amount of anxiety when he initially pushed his way through the restroom door, and was able to wash and dry without hearing any voices whatsoever.

In the penultimate step of Tim's treatment plan, he would begin with a restroom stall—as opposed to a urinal—to allow for a proper amount of privacy. The goal of this step wasn't necessarily for him to achieve a flow at the toilet; he was only obligated to enter the stall, unzip, and let it hang. What separated this step from the others in his plan was the timeframe, in that it would only *officially* start once he was able to successfully relieve himself for the first time. After that, as long as he could continue that way without issue for a full week, he would move on to the urinal.

While Tim and Cynthia were at the mall one day that week, he had that familiar urge creep up in his bladder, and anxiously excused himself to take care of business. As he walked down the seemingly endless corridor that led to the restrooms, he came across his old friend—the single-stall "family" restroom. Tim stared at it longingly for a moment, remembering how it had been there for him so many times throughout his life.

How was I ever able to justify a "Toilet Monster" that exists only in multi-person restrooms? he thought to himself.

Having made it this far into his treatment journey, the very idea of such a creature sounded more asinine than ever. Still, that ever-present desire to abandon all hope remained in his mind, knowing how easy it would be to simply fall back into his familiar pattern. Instead, Tim forced a look of disgust upon that private sanctuary, and walked into the public men's room.

Tim's mental images of what he expected the restroom to look like were a stark contrast to reality. A small wave of relief washed over him as he discovered only a few other occupants, as well as the facility's general cleanliness and aroma. He thoughtfully selected the final stall in the row, gently nudged the door open, and closed and locked it once he stepped inside.

Performing the breathing techniques that Doctor Nguyen had taught him, Tim unbuckled his pants, unzipped his fly, and pulled it out. He took a slow and steady inhale for seven seconds, then let it out for seven seconds, and repeated this several times over. As he performed these breathing exercises, wafts of cleaning chemicals and urine permeated his sense of smell, doing little to relieve his anxiety.

Tim became attuned to the deafening quiet that had fallen over the restroom, and surmised that he was most likely all alone. A soft plinking of dripping water in one of the nearby sinks conjured up recent memories of his last session with his therapist. She had cleverly equated Tim's fear and heightened sense of awareness to what the narrator had experienced in *The Tell-Tale Heart*. The idea of an evil monster—one with long fingers and red eyes, who haunts public restrooms—happened to be right on par with the same level of insanity as a dead man's heart beating beneath the floorboards of a bedroom. This somewhat humorous thought had brought a smile to Tim's face, and without even realizing it, he began peeing into the toilet.

When the sound of his urine splashing into the bowl disrupted his meditative state, his smile widened and he began laughing to himself out of pure joy. He had done it; he was officially underway with the second-to-last step in his treatment plan.

Tim exited the stall and walked over to the sink with swagger in his step, whistling to himself as he began washing his hands. He couldn't wait to run out and tell Cynthia the good news. It was such a simple thing to be excited about, peeing in a public place. But Tim counted himself incredibly lucky to have a loving, supportive partner who took his unique phobia seriously.

It wasn't until Tim turned the water off that he noticed a faint static-like noise emanating from everywhere, and nowhere. He could only liken it to a white noise machine, only one that's intended use was to cause overwhelming fright and increasing mental anguish. Just then, a whispering voice rose up above the white noise, causing Tim's heart to sink.

"It was good to see you again, Tim", the voice said. Its words radiated menace, and were slow and calculated.

Tim stopped dead, his heart pounding as he tried to catch his breath.

"H- hello?" Tim's words reverberated off the walls of the empty restroom. "Wh- who's there?" His voice trembled as he forced the words out.

"Why, it's me! Your old pal, the Toilet Monster! I'll be seeing you again... real sooooon!"

With clenched fists and his eyes tightly shut, Tim silently pleaded for this moment to be over. Better yet, he held out hope that all of this was exactly what Doctor Nguyen declared it to be—a projection of his fears, manifesting into a literal form.

"You... are not... *real*..." Tim whispered through clenched teeth.

A strong sense of will and determination began to creep up through the terror that had left him frozen. Not two minutes ago, he had made his most notable stride in *decades* toward overcoming his long-lived phobia, and he was not about to let his *own brain* rain on his parade.

Tim softened his balled-up fists and gripped the sides of the sink, its porcelain cool under his fingers, and began counting backwards from five.

"Five..."

The white noise grew louder in his head.

"Four..."

He heard faint cackles of horrendous laughter.

"Three..."

The crackling of the white noise was almost ear-splitting.

"Two..."

"Hey man, are you ok?"

A voice broke through the ominous static that had been haunting Tim, and all at once reality came crashing back into view. He spun around to witness a stranger, who had placed their hand on his shoulder.

"Wh- what?"

Tim's eyes blinked rapidly as he looked upon this stranger, desperately assuring himself this was all real. His shirt had become saturated with his sweat, and his words felt like sandpaper as they made their way out of his mouth.

"Your, um... your wife, she wanted me to check on you," the person continued. "Do I need to go—"

"No, no, I'm fine," Tim said hurriedly. "Um... thank you, I guess."

Tim gave the guy a halfhearted smile and moved for the restroom door. He felt the cold steel of the door handle, and as he pulled it toward him he *swore* that he could hear the sound of retreating laughter.

It had been a significant victory for Tim, crossing the threshold of the penultimate step in his treatment plan. The fact that he was able to relax enough to urinate inside of a toilet stall—on his first attempt, no less—had reached far beyond his own expectations. He took it all as a win, despite his chance encounter with the Toilet Monster—a potentially real *or* imaginary entity that haunted public restrooms.

Ultimately, it took Tim slightly longer to move on to the final step than he originally anticipated. The goal that he set for himself was two weeks, starting with the day at the mall. And by the end of that 14-day period, he would have ideally been ready for the ultimate challenge. This proved, however, *not* to be the case.

Tim discovered, subconsciously, that he had fallen back into familiar patterns. He would make up excuses to *not* leave the house, so as to avoid the possibility of needing to use public facilities. And since it was an off-week for his therapy, it was Cynthia that had called him out on it.

"Tim, have you noticed anything... *unusual* lately?" she asked from the opposite side of their living room couch.

"I... don't think so?" he responded, confused.

Cynthia's bewildered look toward him intensified, as if she were *willing* him to read her mind. Tim, citing ignorance, could only manage a shrug.

"Tim, *honey*, you haven't been out of the house in *days*. Don't you think it's time you get back out there? How are we supposed to kick that Toilet Monster's ass if we don't show him what we've got?"

Tim breathed out a puff of air, put down his smartphone, and looked over to his wife.

"Darlin', I- I don't think I can do this…" he said, his voice trembling.

"Why not?" Cynthia crossed her arms over her chest. Her demeanor, her expression, her body language, they had all shifted *dramatically*. She was more than willing to remain the supportive wife that Tim needed, but had decided that it was time for her husband to receive some "tough love".

"Because…" Tim began timidly, noting the sudden change in Cynthia. "I'm not *strong* enough."

"That's *bullshit*. You *are* strong enough! Just look at all of the progress you've made so far! So what, you've had a few setbacks. That's why you have me and Doctor Nguyen. We're here to support you, and that's exactly what I'm doing right now."

Tim felt the faintest of smiles creep across his face. Despite her sudden shift that had taken him by surprise, he secretly loved it when Cynthia showed her affection for him in odd ways like these. The determination and the faith she was willing to put in him had always been an affirmation of her love.

Tim took in another long breath and exhaled slowly. "Okay, Cynthia. Let's… take a trip to the grocery store."

"Great!" she said with a smile. "We need almond milk, anyways."

With the combined support of his wife and therapist, Tim rediscovered the courage that was necessary to get back into the stalls of public restrooms. And while it wasn't without its challenges, he felt confident enough by the end of the week to move on to the final step.

Tim found himself so anxious to begin the final step in his treatment plan, that he actually drank the rest of the orange juice in the refrigerator, just so he had an excuse to run to the store. And because he guzzled close to a half-gallon of OJ, he was more than ready to pee once he pulled into the parking lot. With his head held high, Tim could hear angels singing choir hymns as he opened the door to the men's room and stepped inside. All signs pointed to a successful attempt at using the urinal.

Tim proudly considered how far he'd come, and in such a short period of time. Only *months* ago the lingering smell of cleaning chemicals, paired with all the other "natural" aromas of an average restroom, would've sent him for the hills, vomiting along the way. And yet here he was, a grown man, getting ready to urinate in front of God and anyone else that might be using the grocery store men's room.

Tim *did* clock only one other person in the restroom as he entered, who was already zipping up and flushing by the time he himself reached the urinal. When he stepped up to the urinal, he unzipped, pulled it out, and the flow began almost immediately. Tim stood triumphantly with his hands on his hips, feeling a single tear roll down his cheek. He was incredibly fond of himself for all that he'd accomplished, and thankful for the support system that provided the necessary foundation to make it this far. Tim felt grateful most of all for Cynthia, because without her, it was likely that he'd still be following in the same cowardly patterns he had for his entire life.

As the last trickle of urine came out, the lights in the restroom began to flicker, and a chill blew through the air. His skin prickled with gooseflesh as he immediately began rationalizing.

Hmm. Probably a power surge, or something, he thought to himself.

And yet, he stood motionless, waiting for something else to happen. Suddenly, the lock on the bathroom door clicked shut on its own, and the lights flickered once more. An ambient static of white noise—not unlike what he heard in the mall restroom a few weeks prior—began to swoosh in and fill his head.

The flashing of the overhead fluorescents evolved into a steady dimness, as if the darkness had come up to swallow them whole. And then he heard *it*: The *voice*.

"Hellooooo Timmmmm", whispered the harsh, obtrusive voice. *"I always knew you could do it..."*

Tim had literally been caught with his dick in his hand. His breathing was shallow and his blood ran cold as he stood frozen at the urinal, still unzipped. He squeezed his eyes shut and shook his head, trying to erase this supernatural phenomenon from existence. He told himself that once he opened his eyes, things would once again be normal. He'd still be at the urinal, but the lights would be on, the door would be unlocked, and it wouldn't sound like he was in the middle of a hurricane.

"I'm not afraid of you!" Tim yelled out.

"Then why do you have your eyes closed, Tim?" asked the sinister voice.

Tim remembered his breathing exercises and began practicing them immediately. His first attempted inhale, however, was soured by his tight, restricted chest. It was as if some invisible force was gripping his lungs, with no intention of letting go.

Come on, Tim, this is stupid, he tried to calm himself. *You're just imagining things. There is no such thing as—*

"The Toilet Monster?" The voice finished.

Tim was clenching and unclenching his free hand into a white-knuckled fist, his palm greased with sweat. His blood turned to ice water, immobilizing his extremities. The arctic sensation made it even more difficult for him to breathe, and he wondered when the time might finally come when he'd begin his final gasps of air.

The icy cold coursed its way through him like an IV drip. It slithered its way toward his groin where it felt like a wet, lifeless snake started to curl itself around his penis. Thoughts of confusion swirled in his mind, joining the fear and anxiety perfectly like old friends. Tim felt violated by whatever had crept up from the depths of nothingness, and suddenly it was anger that joined the cornucopia of emotions that were bubbling inside of him.

Visions of a madman, desperately pulling up bedroom floorboards, arose to the surface of his mind's eye; flashes of a narrator who'd gone insane, plagued by the guilt of his own misdeeds. For it was not the beating of a dead man's heart that pulsed within his eardrums, but his own. And this, *this* had been what his therapist had warned him of: Projections of his own fear, manifesting itself into otherworldly albeit literal beings.

Tim knew that he *must* open his eyes. He had to witness for himself that this all was just a horrible conjuring of his mind's own doing. And because of that, he *must* open his eyes and face it down where it stood. There would be no other way to cross the threshold into *true* living, unless he could corner what had plagued him since he was just a little boy known as "Timmy".

Tim's breathing was shallower than ever, with his mouth hot and dry, and a cold, alien-like grip that remained attached to his penis. And he knew that the time was now. It was now, or never.

Ok, Tim, you can do this, he pleaded to himself. *Here we go, we're gonna count down from five. Are you ready? Five... Four... Three... Two... One...*

Tim's eyes shot open, but it was not the tiled restroom wall that was in front of him. Instead, he stared into two red eyes that glared back at him as they floated among a cloud of black and gray smoke. A hideous and evil laugh emitted from the thing in front of him, causing Tim's heart to leap into his throat. His wide eyes scanned the dark, amorphous plume, and discovered an absurd arm protruding from the cloud. He traced the misshapen appendage from its source to where the hand had grasped below his belt line.

It sputtered and hissed as it drew even closer to him, its unblinking eyes peering into his soul. Then, a makeshift hole began to form in the center of the black cloud, and it flapped up and down like some perverted iteration of a mouth as it spoke.

"Be sure, Timmy... to wash your hands..."

"It's forced conforming. That's what's killing the kids. That's the real monster."

— **EDDIE MUNSON,** *STRANGER THINGS*
(SEASON 4, 2022)

CHAPTER 3

I Fucking Hate Cannibals

I spin around at the sound of approaching growls, just in time to witness a rabid, flesh-hungry cannibal charging toward me at full clip. I only have a moment to register the face beyond the crazy eyes and blood-stained teeth—it's Mrs. Prichard. A lifelong middle school teacher, beloved by all. Also, a virulent racist, but hey, nobody's perfect. I'm not ready to deflect her mad descent—luckily, Maddie is.

She materializes out of nowhere—not unlike the tenured teacher herself—and thrusts out her forearm like a clothesline. Maddie contacts Prichard's flabby, turkey-like neck and her head flies backwards. The rest of her body follows in a limp, backwards somersault. Even over the angry mob's roar we hear the crack that Prichard's skull makes as it hits the pavement.

"Close one," Maddie says.

"Yeah, no shit," I chuckle. "That preacher wasn't kidding about sending the entire town after us. I thought maybe a few—look out!"

Maddie drops to the pavement, and the clumsy Millhaven resident who tried to wrestle her into a bear hug comes up empty. Getting ambushed by half your town is serious business, but I can't help but laugh at this blundering idiot. He suddenly turns his sights to me, eyes black as night, and I curse my inappropriate sense of humor. Hoisted by my own petard.

I swing my Louisville Slugger like a golf club, uppercutting his jaw. He bites clean through his tongue, and his teeth chip as the top and bottom rows make contact.

Maddie springs back to her feet and looks at me wide-eyed. "Well that was nuts."

"Now we're even?" I propose.

She flashes me that award-winning smirk. "We'll see..."

Ok, I know what you're thinking: Brainwashed cannibals? Demon priests? Gratuitous violence? Now, *that's* a lot to process. But if you told me three days ago that my best friend and I would be orchestrating an all-out brawl between the Bible-thumpers and us, the tainted youth of small-town America—well, friend, I'd probably assume you had some first class weed.

It's a headbanger, for sure. But I'm gonna do my best to walk you through it. Maybe by the time we circle back around, this will all make a little more sense...

Hey there, all you night owls and headbangers.
*This is the **Midnight Metal Mayhem Show**,*
Where the hair is big, the riffs are loud, and the spandex is tight.
I'm your host, Ronnie "Riffmaster" Rockwell,
Bringing you the hardest rock and heaviest metal... to melt your face off.

I'm gonna need all you sexy sadists out there—
Grab those acid wash jeans,
Apply that eyeliner, comb out that beautiful mullet.
Know why?
'Cause tonight,
We've got a lineup hotter than a Van Halen guitar solo.

Mötley Crüe...
Guns N' Roses...
Def Leppard...
The bands that make you wanna throw up those devil horns and head-bang
till your chiropractor begs you to stop.

Now listen...
I know we're living in some contentious times right now.
The battle rages on between us—the so-called "tainted youth"—and the Man.
But hey... we ain't getting too serious tonight.
Life's too short to worry about anything other than the next killer riff.
Ya dig?

So go ahead...
Grab that air guitar, crank the volume up to eleven.
We're making this a night for the ages.

Whether you're cruising down the highway...
Or chilling in your mom's basement,
*The **Midnight Metal Mayhem Show** is your ticket*
To the rockin' good time that the Man doesn't want you to have.

Keep that dial right where it is.
More face-melting tunes are on the way.
And remember...
Raise those devil horns high.

Riffmaster out.

Part I

Let me tell you, my fellow Rock-and-Roll Warriors, we are living in some wild times. The days of big hair and heavy metal come all too easy, but also at a cost. I mean, so what if you're bad-mouthed by a parent for wearing black lipstick, or your gym teacher calls you a no-good degenerate. Fuck that. Those idiots don't know shit anyways. First of all, I am a degenerate. So that I can live with, and I know you can too.

But you know what really chaps my ass? When these assholes go out of their way to make our lives a living hell, like they're on some fucked-up mission from God. And they're determined to rid the world of those who just want to turn it up to eleven and rip the knob off.

Living the life you want often comes at a higher cost, requiring sacrifice. But that's just part of life: accepting the trade-offs for living on your own terms. If you want to rock hard, you have to work hard. Simple as that.

This was a lesson they tried to teach us when we were younger, but we didn't want to hear it. Of course, it doesn't help that it came in the form of your step-dad yelling in your face, telling you "turn down the Metallica and do something constructive with your life." But even if your old man or lady was nice about it, I don't think we'd want to hear it. It's every new generation's responsibility to throw up those middle fingers to the status quo, and demand more out of life. Your mom might see a lazy sack of shit sitting around and doing nothing. I see someone who's waiting patiently for the right time to strike and make their mark. It's all about perspective, baby.

The thing is, it can be tough as hell when it feels like the devil himself has got you by the shoulders, pushing you face-first into the dirt. And the complexity of this problem is only compounded if you live in a small town like Millhaven. This is the type of place where the head librarian—Evelyn Hayes—holds a seat on the town counsel, and a bank manager—Leonard Blackwell—is a well-respected public figure. They told us growing up that these people deserve our reverence, like it was owed whether it was earned or not.

So, you'll have to forgive me if I don't fall in line with the rest. Respect ain't automatic. It's earned. And I'm going to insist on rocking to the beat of my own wild drummer. Because I never wanted much out of life except some tasty tunes, my electric guitar, and my best friend Maddie to share it all with. But I'm learning that sometimes, life doesn't give a shit about what you want.

"*Alright*, good evening to all you Millhaven metal-heads! The time is 12:01 AM, September 7th, 1989, and you've got your dial tuned to the Midnight Metal Mayhem Show. I cannot *wait* to kick off this block of non-stop rock, but first... we're going to take a few calls. According to producer Maddie 'Mayhem' Mason, we've got a live one who is just *itching* to spill the beans on a delicious secret he's been holding onto. Caller, you are on the air!"

"Uh, yes, *hi*... um, am I on the air?"

"That's what I said, airhead," I chuckled, rolling my eyes. "What's going down in your neck of Millhaven this fine evening?"

"Ok, so I've seen some *strange* stuff go down lately," the caller said. A tiny bit of confidence had crept into his voice. "I don't mean to alarm your listeners, but there's a good chance there are dark figures in hooded robes, moving about in the night."

I swiveled in my chair to lock eyes with Maddie. She was busting a gut, about to fall out of her seat from laughing so hard. I rolled my eyes, then shimmied back to the mic.

"It sounds like *someone's* been enjoying a little too much of the 'Devil's Lettuce' tonight," I said to the anonymous caller, a giant smirk on my face.

"*Look*," the caller continued, "I *know* how crazy this sounds. People have been laughing at me my entire life for believing in crazy conspiracies. But I swear, this one is true!"

The voice sounded familiar when I first took the call. But his rhetoric was almost a dead giveaway.

"Wait a sec... am I talking to Curtis Layhew right now?"

There was a beat of silence on the other end before the voice spoke up once more.

"N- *no*," he declared. "I don't know who that is. But I *do* know that the folks of Millhaven should heed these warnings!"

"Curtis, that *is* you! How've you been, man? It's been a minute since high school!"

There was another beat of awkward silence, followed by a click and dial tone.

"Awe, *come on*, Curt!" I said playfully. "I was just joking around. Please, call back anytime. But on that note, we're gonna kick off that solid block of tasty tunes for you night owls. As always, the requests lines *are* open so if there's something you just *gotta* hear, give my girl Maddie Mayhem a holler!"

I dropped the needle on the title track of Metallica's Metallica's Master of Puppets and music burst through the radio airwaves like thunder and lightning. The sound booth door clicked open behind me and in waltzed Maddie. She plopped herself into the torn black leather chair in the corner and put her feet up on the cluttered counter. Maddie's always been a total spaz, unable to sit still for a minute. So, anytime we had a long block of music, she'd join me in the booth to shoot the shit.

"Man, I forgot how much of a *weirdo* that guy is," Maddie chuckled, folding her hands behind her head.

"Well ain't *that* the pot calling the kettle black," I responded, twirling in my seat to face her.

"Hey, I don't need your *sass!*" Maddie shot back as she kicked the legs of my chair. "I get plenty of that on the request lines. In fact, you should be *thanking* me for fielding your phone calls from the crazies."

"Alright, *alright*, fair enough." I laughed and threw my hands up in an *I surrender* gesture. "Man, I haven't thought about Curtis in *forever*. I always felt kinda *bad* for him, back in high school. He'd badger anyone who'd listen to his crazy conspiracy theories."

"That's *right!*" Maddie exclaimed, slapping her thigh. "He was always going on about UFOs in New Mexico, or Mothman, or the Jersey Devil."

A wide grin grew across my face as the memories came flooding back.

"*Yep*," I agreed. "And then even *after* we all graduated, I saw him at the library trying to get people to sign some petition. He was waving it around wildly, shoving it in people's faces. This was right after Geraldo Rivera said all that bullshit about Satanic cults and how Dungeons & Dragons was corrupting today's youth."

"Man, I *love* D&D," Maddie said nonchalantly, plucking a stick of gum from her black jean jacket pocket. "My Barbarian just got to level 15."

Normally, obnoxious mouth noises—like smacking gum—are like nails on a chalkboard for me. But because of the way Maddie does it, with her trademark air of nonchalance, I somehow find it endearing.

The phone rang in Maddie's booth, and she let out a disapproving scoff.

"Welp, *that's* my cue," she said, springing up out of her seat. "Talk to ya in a bit."

We bumped fists, and I began gathering records from the shelves to add to the queue. My brain went on autopilot as I sifted through our collection of modern-day classics. There was always a method to the madness when it came to curating the "Midnight Metal Mayhem Show". Each block of music was *carefully* planned out from beginning to end. I'm not a dummy—I *know* that our show didn't have thousands of listeners, but I take music *very* seriously.

However, Curtis's call had me doing 80 in a 45 down memory lane, and my curating prowess for once took a back seat. It's funny what just a *little bit* of time will do for you and your past. I've never been a big believer in rose-tinted glasses. But sometimes, nostalgia can shine bright enough to blind your ass. And suddenly, you're thankful for the good times *and* the bad.

As it turned out, I didn't have to wait long to hear from Curtis again. We were nearing the end of another long stretch of tunes the following night. I was up out of my seat playing air guitar and head-banging to Slayer, when suddenly Maddie chimed into my headphones.

"Hey Ronnie, you'll *never* guess who I got on the line."

I look over to see Mayhem grinning like the Cheshire Cat, and I don't have to ask *any* follow-up questions.

"Alright," I said to her, plopping down in my seat, "as soon as this one's over, patch him through. I'll take it on-air."

As the final notes ring out from the track, I welcome our audience back and take the call.

"Alright, welcome back listeners! I hope you all enjoyed that *sick slate* of headbangers. We got another caller on the line. Hey caller, you're on with Ron!"

"*Bro*, they're at it *again!*"

It was Curtis, alright. But he sounded *way more* worked up than he did the night before.

"Wait, they *are?*" I replied, feigning enthusiasm. I pivoted to look at Maddie, who was cackling in her booth. "What are they up to now, buddy?"

"Ok, I *know* this is going to sound crazy, but—"

"Brother, this is the *graveyard shift*. 'Crazy' is our middle name."

"Yeah, ok... but I *did* see another cloaked figure last night, *right after* I called you! They were in the alley behind my house, dragging something into the bed of their truck. I... I think it was a *body.*"

My face contorted into a look of amused confusion.

"Okay, *Curt*, how do you know it wasn't like a bag of trash or something?"

I realized I sounded like a parent, trying to convince their kid that there *wasn't* a boogeyman living in their closet.

"*Ronnie*, when was the last time *you* saw a bag of garbage that had legs?"

"The last time I looked in the mirror, baby!" I laughed heartily at my own joke. Maddie was shaking her head.

"Come *on*, man, I'm being serious! You need to—"

"Curt, if this *is* serious, then why don't you call the police?"

Curtis let out a sarcastic cackle.

"Are you *kidding* me? Chief Harper and his goons are as useful as tits on a bull. I wouldn't trust them to run animal control."

"So, *instead*, you decided to call me. Again."

In my headphones, Mayhem's voice was telling me 30 seconds to commercial break.

"Look, Curt," I said, "we gotta go to commercial, but why don't you hang on the line and we'll keep chatting."

Before he had a chance to respond, I put the line on hold and started our reel of adverts. However, when I went to pick up the line again, Curtis was gone. An unexpected wave of goosebumps crawled across my skin as the trilling of the dead line rang in my ear. I wasn't yet willing to put stock into Curtis's claims. But off the record? My curiosity was officially piqued.

"Curt hang up on you?"

I jumped at the sound of Maddie's voice, not even hearing her come in.

"Y-yeah. So *weird*," I responded, taking off my headphones.

I envisioned Curtis huddled in a darkened corner of his house, squinting out his back window as some shadowy figure hauls a body into the back of a pickup truck.

"Do you think he's telling the truth?" I asked Maddie.

"*Man*," she began, "Curtis told me one time that I should build a bomb shelter in case *skin-walkers* show up in Millhaven."

"So I take that as a 'no'?"

"*Fuck* no," Maddie laughed. "Look, the guy knows how to construct a narrative, I'll give him that. But that's *all* it is, Ronnie. He needs to get out of his house more."

Maddie rose from her seat and began plucking records from the shelves.

"Yeah, you're probably right," I said. "Maybe we should invite him to hang out one night."

"Alright, let's not get ahead of ourselves."

After a moment of pacing the booth, Maddie placed a stack of albums next to the turntable. I gave her a suspicious look before considering her picks.

"I thought *I* was the DJ, here?" I said with a smirk.

"Shut up," Maddie shot back, punching me in the arm, "you know just as well as I do that we share a hive mind. Now, say *'thank you'* for helping you do your job."

With one hand on the doorknob, Maddie gave me a smirk I know all too well. Her heavily shadowed eyes glistened under the harsh overhead lights.

"Thank you, Ms. Mayhem," I said with a courteous nod. "Now, get the hell out of my sound booth."

"You got it, boss."

I lined up the next non-stop block of metal tunes, my mind still preoccupied with my latest exchange with Curtis. Again, I saw flashes of darkened figures, shrouded by moonlight, loading a body into a truck as if it were cargo.

"Ronnie, when was the last time you saw a bag of garbage that had legs?"

I cracked a joke as a response to his question. I *should* have taken him more seriously.

Part II

Saturday night rolled around, and the struggle *continued* for ridding my mind of the brief—albeit *effective*—picture that Curtis painted for me the day before. The harder I tried to push out the thoughts of secret shadow figures moving stealthily through the night, the more their heels dug into the recesses of my mind's eye.

I decided to head out to the garage, to crank out some tunes on my Ibanez electric guitar. Music has *always* been my savior, whether I'm in my captain's chair at the radio station, cruising the streets of Millhaven, or just chilling at home. I felt like when I listened, *it* listened back. And I know that *might* sound corny, but music has never failed to clear my head, and help put things in perspective.

With the garage door open and my fingers dancing across the fretboard, the cacophony of sounds from my amplifier cut through the night air. Shadows danced across the garage as the lone lightbulb above my head flickers and buzzes. A battle raged within me, as the music my two hands produced did their best to force out the negative thoughts. My long black hair—held back by my *lucky* red bandana—bobbed around my face as I banged my head to the rhythm.

Before I get to this next part, there's something you should know about the town of Millhaven, Tennessee. There's been an indisputable shift in the tone of our small town over the last several years; one that almost felt *irresponsible* to ignore. And yet, it was as if the elite members of our small town had zero concerns about it. Several years ago, a bunch of idiot talking heads on TV started spouting nonsense about child molesters and the dangers of D&D. And being a small town, the leaders and citizens of Millhaven were just as worried about the *manufactured* "Satanic Panic". But mysteriously, like a fart in the wind, most of that apprehension and anxiety seemed to disappear without a trace only months later.

It wasn't long after that when the fliers of missing teenagers started popping up. Millhaven's numbers were nowhere near that of Derry, Maine, but they were high enough to notice. And it always seemed to follow the same cycle: Some kid goes missing, the fliers would litter the streets for a week, and then suddenly the interest would drop off.

Furthermore, there was a distinct through-line with every single disappearance: They all looked like me. You know the type—long hair, Metallica t-shirts, black makeup. The "Dungeons & Dragons" types. The "metal-head" types. In other words, *not* someone you'd expect to see at Sunday church service. Boiled down to a single word: Disposable.

There was little *soul* in my hands that night in the garage. My feeble attempt to shake off the demons with loud, fast rock had failed. I stood from my old, tattered chair reserved *specifically* for jamming, placed my axe back on its stand, and walked to the mini fridge to grab a beer. When I heard the familiar rumbling of a Chevelle pulling into my driveway, its headlights illuminating the garage, I knew right away to grab *two* beers.

When I kicked the fridge door closed with my heel, I half-expected to turn and see Maddie already crossing the threshold of the garage. However, she was still by her Chevelle, leaning against the driver's side door, a lit cigarette between her fingers.

Uh-oh, she's got a story for me, I thought to myself.

She accepted the beer without invitation, twisted the cap off, and took a long swig. Her face was contorted into a frustrated grimace that I knew all too well.

"Rough night?" I asked.

I leaned against the car next to her, and twisted the cap off my own soldier. Maddie stared forward, taking a hard drag off her cigarette, her dark lipstick staining the butt end of it.

"Ronnie, how long have we known each other?"

This was not an opening line I expected to hear from her. But then again, you never know with Maddie.

"Um..." I began hesitantly, "since like, sophomore year I think? Why you ask?"

"So you *know* what I hate more than *anything* else in this world, yeah?"

Something was clearly bothering her.

"Well, I know you hate being *wrong*," I replied.

Maddie spun on her heel to face me and pointed her fingers in my face, the cigarette clasped tightly between them.

"*Exactly!*" She exclaimed with wide, insane eyes.

"*Whoa*, OK, Maddie, you're kind of freaking me out, here. Why don't you start from the beginning, and—"

The sound of banging from the Chevelle's trunk cut me off.

"*Let. Me. Out of here!*" cried a muffled voice.

Maddie's eyes remained locked onto mine as the banging continued.

"Maddie..." I began cautiously. "Do you have something in your trunk that you need to show me?"

Without saying a word, Maddie grabbed the keys from the ignition, and I followed her to the back of the car. She produced her brass knuckles from the inside pocket of her jean jacket, and guided them onto her fingers. A cold chill shot down my spine as she took one last look at me before popping the trunk.

"Oh, and you *might* wanna take a step back," Maddie added.

I followed her orders, and she popped the lid. A dark figure immediately moved to leap out and escape, but Maddie was ready and delivered a single blow to the figure's head.

"Gah, *fuck!*" the unknown captive screamed. He fell back into the Chevelle, moaning in pain.

"Maddie, what the *fuck?*" I yelled, backing away from the car.

"Do you still have Rufus's old dog crate?" she asked, ignoring my panicked state.

"W-*what*?"

"Your old dog cage, do you still have it?"

"Yeah, I think so. But—"

"Great, go get it and set it up in the garage."

Less than an hour earlier, Maddie was at her house, listening to Def Leppard and doing laundry. Maddie likes to listen to her music *really* loud, and also tends to forget to lock her back door. This made it relatively easy for this cloaked figure to sneak in unannounced. The bad news for *him* was that Maddie's house is like a fortress of hidden weapons.

Now, Maddie has *plenty* of guns. In fact, when this guy finally decided to make himself known, she was within arms reach of her favorite revolver. But Maddie has *always* been a knife girl, especially when it comes to dudes that try to fuck with her. And boy, did she let this guy have it.

When Maddie and I dragged this dude out of her trunk, the first thing I noticed were the two knife wounds, one in each leg. They were executed perfectly, too; deep enough to immobilize him, but not serious enough for him to bleed out right away.

"So as it turns out," Maddie began, lighting another cigarette, "our friend Curt was *right*."

She took a drag then passed it to me, as we stared down at the hooded figure trapped inside of my dog's old cage. It was none other than Frank Steiner, our high school algebra teacher. Also known as one of the biggest assholes in the known universe.

Maddie grabbed the Louisville Slugger that I had mounted on the wall in the garage, and beat the top of the cage with it. The loud clunks echoed in the dead of night.

"Hey, *asshole*!" Maddie yelled, "You mind telling me exactly what you were doing in my fucking house?"

The hood of his cloak fell from his head as Steiner looked up slowly. His mouth spread wide in a devilish grin, bearing blood-soaked teeth.

"I'm... *so sorry* about that, Ms. Mason," Steiner hissed, his tone low and ominous. "It wasn't my intention to..."

"Get *caught*?" Maddie finished.

Steiner's smile *widened*.

"*Precisely*," he replied. "I assumed that I had *confiscated* all of your knives back in my class."

"Well, you *assumed wrong*, dickhead!"

I *thought* about chiming in. I had fantasized for *years* about beating the shit out Frank Steiner, but in the end, he never seemed worth the trouble. Besides, this was Maddie's show, anyway.

Maddie knelt down so she was at eye level with Steiner.

"I'm gonna ask you one more time," she began in a surprisingly calm voice, "why were you in my house? Are you some kind of sick pervert? You get off on watching girls do their laundry?"

"Oh, don't *flatter* yourself, Ms. Mason," Steiner mocked. "I'm not interested in *anything* you have to offer."

"What then, huh? Out with it! If you tell me what you were up to, I *might* consider calling the cops and having you arrested."

Steiner let out a hideous cackle that actually sent a chill down my spine. I couldn't help but think of how much he sounded like a Batman villain in that moment.

"That won't do you any good, *either*," Steiner added.

I turned my back to him and whispered in Maddie's ear.

"Look, Maddie," I began, "I don't think we can trust *anything* that this guy says. I'm pretty sure he's just fucking with us."

"Yeah, no shit," she replied in a hushed tone, "but we *need* to figure out why he was after me. And we need to—"

Maddie stopped short and a sly grin grew across her face. It was an expression I was all too familiar with; it said she had a *delicious* idea.

She reached into her outside jacket pocket and showed me a ring of keys I didn't recognize.

"The keys to *Castle Steiner*," she whispered, jingling them in front of my face.

My face curled into its own furtive smile.

"Time to go straight to the source?" I proposed.

"Lock the garage," she said with a wink. "We want our prisoner sealed up nice and tight for when we get back."

We turned back around to face Steiner. Maddie held out his key ring and jingled it again. Steiner's face slowly shifted from an evil smirk to a grimace of outrage.

"Don't go anywhere, Steiner," Maddie taunted. "We have to make a quick house call, but we'll be *right back*."

Steiner's screams and swearing became muffled as I closed the garage door. In that moment I was glad that I had soundproofed the interior.

We hopped in Maddie's Chevelle and made our way to Steiner's house. We were silent on the drive over, our minds racing with the possibilities and implications of what *this* could all mean. It *definitely* meant that Curtis wasn't as crazy as we thought. And if Frank Steiner was involved, it also meant things were merging into the "personal" territory *very* quickly.

I was hard-pressed to think of someone that *hadn't* had an unfavorable run-in with him. But perhaps Maddie and the rest of the young women of Millhaven had the *largest* personal stake in this discovery. He was a total dick to all of his students, but he had a personal vendetta against the girls. So, in retrospect, I thought Steiner should've been grateful that Maddie only stabbed him in the thighs.

With everything she'd been through in her life, things could've gone way worse for him.

Maddie's parents separated when she was five, and when her mom passed away a few years later, her dad stepped up and took her in full-time. Tom raised Maddie in his own way. Most 12-year-old girls got dolls and Easy-Bake Ovens for Christmas. Maddie received a lock-picking set and a television black-box from her old man. This kind of fatherly love is what shaped her into the "Maddie Mayhem" that I know and love.

Maddie would spend her Saturday nights listening to Black Sabbath records and playing Atari, with the muffled sounds of raucous laughter coming from the living room, as Tom and his friends played poker. The turntable that played Maddie's music and the gaming console were gifts, courtesy of Tom's friend Jim—a package courier, who had an unusually large number of packages "fall off his truck".

One particular poker night, Tom's friend Jeff got up to get another beer and somehow "got lost," finding his way into Maddie's room. But long story short, Jeff decided to get handsy with young Maddie.

Once she found the courage to confide in her dad what had happened, he hugged her real tight and kissed her on the forehead. Then, he stabbed Jeff repeatedly with a butterfly knife. The irony, of course, was that Tom spent more time in the clink than Jeff did.

Through certain channels, Jeff kept tabs on Maddie. And when she was 16 and living with her aunt, she received a surprise visit from him, having been recently released from prison. His plan was to seek her out, and finish what he'd started four years prior. What he *hadn't* counted on, however, was Madding becoming proficient in numerous forms of self-defense, including the handling of knives.

Frank sat in his beat-up old truck several houses down, watching and waiting for Maddie's aunt to leave. When she finally did, he snuck inside and surprised Maddie in her bedroom—right where he wanted her. Twenty minutes later, the police and paramedics arrived to witness Maddie smoking a cigarette on the front porch, her white t-shirt caked in coagulated blood.

"He's inside," she said, breathing out a plume of smoke, "last bedroom on the right."

As the paramedic bandaged her up, the police stared at Maddie as if she were an alien life form. She told them the truth of what happened, even *if* it was stranger than fiction. Frank burst through her bedroom and advanced toward her, the giant hulk of a man that he was. He pinned her up against the wall, his meaty hand gripped around her throat. Too excited about watching the life leave her eyes, he didn't even notice the knife she held in her hand.

Seconds later, Frank received multiple stab wounds from a *second* member of the Mason family. He released his grip on her neck and she slid to the floor. When her vision returned, Maddie climbed on top of Frank and smiled down at him. He *tried* to call her a "crazy bitch" but blood was bubbling out of his mouth, slurring his speech. She brought her daddy's knife down repeatedly into his chest.

I'll never forget the word she used to describe how she felt in that moment, the first time she told me this story: "Exquisite". She wasn't *looking* for blood, but she wanted to be ready if—or *when*—it found *her*. She did, however, have a fun time explaining to the police *why* it was necessary to perform the coup de grâce by stabbing him in the dick.

"*What?*" she asked them quizzically, a sly grin on her face. "Did they not teach you about Hammurabi in cadet training?"

Maddie and dad Tom were eventually reunited, and as a "welcome home" gift she presented him with his pair of butterfly knives, freshly sharpened. The proud father he was, he told her to keep them for a job well-done.

The summer leading up to our sophomore year—only months before we would meet for the first time—she attended a wilderness retreat summer camp. Maddie hit it off with her bunkmate Trish, who helped Maddie discover the reason why she lacked a fondness for boys.

Their relationship extended well beyond high school graduation, and they even spent a year living together. However, one night they got into an argument, and Trish stormed out of the house with an overnight bag slung over her shoulder. That was the last time Maddie saw her girlfriend, before she disappeared.

Trish mentioned on her way out the door that she was going to stay with a mutual friend of theirs. But when Maddie called for her the following day, hoping to make amends, she learned that Trish had never arrived. It wasn't long before Trish became just another number in Millhaven's "missing teenagers" statistics.

For weeks, Maddie was inconsolable. I pulled double-duty at the radio station—acting as both producer *and* host—while she lay in bed crying her eyes out, wondering what happened to her partner and friend. I had *seen* Maddie upset before, and angry, and enraged. And I had learned over the years how to best comfort her when she needed it. But as it turns out, alleviating your best friend's pain when their girlfriend drops off the face of the earth is no easy task.

Weeks poured into months. And when *years* had separated her and Trish, Maddie slowly transformed into the new version of herself. She was, as she put it, a "refurbished Metallica record that sounded good as new, but skipped on a track or two". She'd always been rough around the edges, which was just how I liked her. But the shit that life had thrown at Maddie had *hardened* her. It shaped her into a black diamond. A fucking *tank*. It's what *made* her *Ms. Mayhem*.

A short 15-minute drive had us pulling into Frank Steiner's driveway, the Chevelle's headlights illuminating the property's dark exterior. I had never been to Steiner's house, but somehow it was exactly as I pictured it. The lawn was meticulously manicured, paired with modest landscaping. The house itself was painted an uptight and sensible light gray, and the blinds in every single window were pulled down tight, perfectly isolating the inside from whatever lay beyond its front door.

The house's interior was even more bland and neurotic. Every piece of furniture and decor was perfectly positioned, as if it were part of an exhibition for boring assholes. If Steiner wanted to, he could put his home on the market the following day and wouldn't have to do a thing.

"I'm gonna search upstairs," Maddie began in a whisper. "You stay down here and see if you can find anything."

I nodded my head in agreement, and watched Maddie ascend the stairs, taking each step with a cautious tiptoe. When I turned around, it *finally* struck me that I had *no clue* what we were looking for.

I flicked on the flashlight I had grabbed back at my place, and began cluelessly searching the kitchen. I pulled out drawers, opened cupboards, and looked under the sink. Other than some household rat poison, there was nothing even *remotely* nefarious about what I'd uncovered so far.

When I transitioned from the kitchen to the living room area, I was *immediately* drawn to the fireplace mantle. For someone that I *never* took as the sentimental type, Frank Steiner *loved* his framed photographs. There were several, and they appeared to be arranged in some sort of strange hierarchy.

Starting on the far left of the mantle, Steiner was grinning and holding up a signed copy of "A Documented History of Millhaven" as he posed next to Evelyn Hayes—Millhaven's head librarian. The next frame down, Steiner was at Millhaven Financial, shaking hands with the bank manager, Leonard Blackwell. Leonard made another appearance in the next photograph, as he and Steiner stood on either side of Marjorie Caldwell, as she cut the ribbon to her brand-new general store.

Next was a candid-style photo of him and our chief of police Winston Harper, sharing a carafe of coffee at the Pancake Palace. The penultimate picture had him standing next to Geraldine Mitchell, Millhaven's mayor. They were both sporting giant "I Voted!" buttons on the lapels of their shirts.

At the very end of the mantle, sticking out like a sore thumb, was a *much* older photograph. It was yellowed and weathered by time, like one you'd see in your mom's family photo album. There were two men in the portrait, one of whom was *undoubtedly* Frank Steiner, but he looked almost as young as I did. He was standing next to a thin man with wiry glasses, who wore a white button-down shirt with short sleeves, and a black tie around his collar. His left arm pinned a thick black bible to his side, with the other arm draped around the young Steiner next to him.

I felt a wave of worried confusion as I stepped back from the mantle. I could *sense* a purpose to this monumental shrine, but I struggled to see the bigger picture. Regardless, I couldn't keep my eyes from returning to that fifth photograph. It *bothered* me that I knew everyone on that mantle *except* for that last guy.

"Who's that?" Maddie's voice asked from behind me.

I felt my heart leap into my throat, and muttered *fuck* under my breath.

"I... have no *fucking clue*," I replied.

Maddie gave a thoughtful "Hm" as she carefully scanned the rest of the photographs on the mantle.

"What about you?" I asked. "Find anything?"

"Absolutely *jack shit*," she replied, surveying each framed photo with narrowed eyes.

"Yeah, same here. *This* is the closest I could come to any sort of intel."

Maddie spun around, her hands thrown up emphatically.

"I don't *fucking* get it!" she exclaimed. "How is there *nothing* here that we could pin to this asshole?"

"Well," I started, "it makes sense, once you think about it. I mean, just *look* at this fucking place. It's *spotless*. Not one single thing is out of place. If there were any contraband around, it would be—"

Maddie cut me off with an enormous gasp, and she turned to me, eyes wide.

"It would be *hidden*!" she said, finishing my sentence.

Maddie performed another quick scan of the room, as if she were blocking out movements for a one-woman play. I suddenly felt like the "Watson" to her "Sherlock", and decided to let her do her thing. For a moment she stood motionless, her eyes darting to every corner of the living room. Then, she began slowly crossing over to the threshold into the kitchen.

"Occasionally," Maddie began, "my dad's friend Rob would host poker night, and I'd get to tag along. And he had the *exact* same floor plan as this."

Maddie was gesturing wildly, getting caught up in the excitement of her revelation. Then, she suddenly pivoted to the refrigerator, which stood adjacent to the main row of cabinets and the long stretch of countertop.

"But *this*," she continued, "*this* is all *wrong*."

"Wh- what do you mean?" I asked, my face scrunched in confusion.

Maddie didn't answer, only took a small step toward the fridge. She approached it the same way a lion tamer would their cat during a theatrical circus performance.

I had to admit, the placement of it did seem odd, as it stood alone like an island with only a wall behind it. Maddie walked over to the refrigerator and began nudging it from the side with both hands. I ran over to help her, still not fully comprehending *why* we were moving the fridge. That is, until it was completely removed from the rectangular space it usually sat.

"Holy. *Fuck*." I said unbelievingly.

Hidden behind the fridge was a brown door with a gold knob, with a padlock as a safeguard, and cobwebs decorating its frame. Maddie, too, stood dumbfounded by her own discovery.

"What do you think the chances are that he's got a key to that lock on his ring?" I asked.

Maddie jumped as if struck by lightning. She frantically fished for the key ring in her jacket pocket, and studied each key closely, eliminating certain possibilities. Eventually she decided on a brass key, and it slid into the padlock with a satisfying *clink*. As we held our breath in anticipation, the sound of the lock clicking open punched through the stiff air like a wild disruption in the night.

The hinges of the door screeched like banshees as they opened with the door. Maddie pulled on the overhead light switch cable, casting a warm glow on a set of basement stairs. She turned around slowly to face me, her face wider than ever.

"Jackpot, *motherfucker*!" She said, her mouth curling into a wide, furtive grin.

Maddie had led the way down the flight of stairs, into the unknown abyss that was Frank Steiner's basement. Many homes in Millhaven had basements, so it wasn't any revelation that we had found one in our old algebra teacher's house. However, there were two things that put us on our toes. The first and *glaringly* obvious was that he didn't want anyone to find it. The second was what we found when we reached the basement proper.

More than three-quarters of the basement's square footage was taken up by a giant walk-in freezer. It too had a padlock over the latch. I felt somehow outside of my own body as I watched Maddie, clearly shaken, fumble with sliding the proper key into the padlock. Only moments prior, she was a glorious female warrior, all too prepared to tackle whatever could be waiting for us at the bottom of the stairs. But *nothing* could have prepared us for an enormous walk-in freezer. And we *never* could've guessed what would be waiting for us inside.

We were blasted by a rush of ice-cold air as Maddie lifted the heavy-duty metal handle and tugged open the large, heavy door. The inside was no bigger than your average "his and hers" walk-in closet, but it was stacked floor to ceiling with air-sealed bags of meat. The *rational* side of my brain immediately jumped into action, forming thoughts such as "Steiner is a wild game hunter" and "Frank likes to buy in bulk". But those thoughts were immediately squashed once both of us realized *what* was inside those bags.

The left wall contained internal organs; bags labeled like "Roberts, Joann / Liver / 06-03-1978", and "Thompson, Greg / Heart / 02-14-1982". The racks on the right wall held preserved body parts, with bags labeled "Smith, Kelly / Right Leg / 10-24-1984" and "Lancaster, Vincent / Left and Right Buttocks / 12-02-1983".

"What... *the fuck*," Maddie muttered.

Her voice was low, and it trembled in a way that I had never heard before in my life. It scared the shit out of me, to hear her speak like that, because *nothing* scared Maddie "Mayhem" Mason. But that fear didn't hold a candle to what surrounded us, neatly packaged and stored, as if all of this was completely normal.

"We, um..." I began, swallowing hard past the lump that had formed in my throat, "we need to get the fuck out of here. Now."

Maddie didn't reply. She only looked at me, wide-eyed and shaken, and nodded her head. I was reaching for the interior door handle when Maddie spoke up again.

"Wait!" She exclaimed in a harsh whisper. "What... what the hell is *that*?"

I turned to see what she was referring to. She had her flashlight pointed to the back wall of the freezer, where a stand-alone rack stood with a gray tarp draped over it, completely concealing its contents. Maddie took two unsteady steps forward, and slowly reached out for a corner of the tarp. It was like watching that pivotal scene in a horror movie, where the final girl *had* to pull back the curtain or open the closet door, so they could be *absolutely sure* that the boogeyman *wasn't* hiding on the other side.

She gave the tarp a swift tug and it fell to the floor in a crinkling heap. Maddie and I stood side by side, staring in resolute *horror* at the makeshift shrine of decapitated heads that neatly lined each row of the multi-tiered storage rack. Each of the heads had their natural eyes removed, and were replaced with black, soulless beads that seemed to drain every inch of hope from my body.

"Maddie..." I said in a breathless whisper. "We need to leave..."

I stood statue-still, holding my breath as Maddie reached her hands up to one of the shelves. Her entire body trembled and shook like a dead leaf. And as she pulled the head closer to her face, she began convulsing with tremendous sobs.

Maddie brushed the hair away from the face that she held in her quivering hands.

"Oh... *Trish*," Maddie wept, "Trish.... I am... so *fucking sorry*..."

With her long-lost girlfriend's decapitated head clutched tightly to her chest, Maddie fell to the floor of the freezer, and dissolved into primal, uncontrollable sobbing.

Part III

When I was finally able to coax Maddie off the floor of the walk-in freezer—when the tears had come to a temporary halt—she had an unrecognizable fire in her eyes. And in those flickering flames, I saw *everything*.

I saw the day her and Trish first met, all those years ago at summer camp. I could visualize the transformation that Maddie experienced as she *finally* crossed the threshold into her own sexual identity. I saw her and Trish, holding hands and making plans together, imagining all the exciting possibilities that their lives would offer.

And in a single moment I saw all of that *ripped away* like some cruel, *fucked up* joke. In my bones, I could *feel* the senselessness of her loss. It broke my heart. It made me want to weep for—*and with*—Maddie. But above all else, I felt white-hot rage.

The night air blew through the interior of the Chevelle like a turbine as we raced back to my house in complete silence. Talking wasn't necessary, because we both knew that Steiner needed to die; that he *deserved* to die. The only question left was *how*.

"You listen to me, and you listen good... *you motherfucker*. You have *one* chance to come clean about that meat locker of horrors in your basement, and why my girlfriend's *severed head* was in there."

Maddie was crouched down, face-to-face with the still-imprisoned Frank Steiner. Her face was *beet red*. Her teeth clenched in an unnatural snarl as she stared daggers into the face of the man that was cowered before her; the *shitheel* who was *undoubtedly* responsible for the disappearance of her girlfriend. He stared back at her un-blinking and motionless, his face void of all expression.

It didn't come as a surprise when Steiner insisted on silence. He huddled inside the dog crate, his knees pulled up to his chest, com-pletely placid. The look on his face blatantly said "*Your move*".

"What do you wanna do?" I asked Maddie, pulling her aside. "This shit is so *fucked*. And I hate to say this, but I gotta imagine he's willing to take this to his grave."

She let out a frustrated sigh, and clenched her fists at her sides.

"I want this motherfucker to *talk*," Maddie replied through grit-ted teeth. "I want him to tell me *why* he did that to Trish, and all the others. I want *answers*. And most of all, I want him *dead*."

We stood in silence for a moment, mulling over our limited op-tions. My mind flashed back to one of the photographs on Steiner's mantle, where he shook hands with the branch manager of Mill-haven Financial. From there, I drew a line to a newspaper article I read not too long ago, about he and several others investing in a brand-new housing development on the edge of town.

At first, I struggled to understand *why* my brain was making these odd connections. But then it clicked. Where they had just bro-ken ground for the new development was isolated. And we still had several hours of night left. There was *plenty* of time to drive Steiner out there, and introduce him to his final resting place.

"You're right," I said, breaking the silence between us, "Steiner deserves to *die* for what he's done. And if he ain't gonna talk, there's only one thing left to do."

Maddie's eyebrow arched in curiosity as she asked, "What did you have in mind?"

We threw Steiner back into the trunk of the Chevelle, then made a quick pit stop at Maddie's for a few supplies. The bellowing night winds were our soundtrack as we swerved through the dark and winding roads toward the edge of town.

We eventually came to stop at a gravel driveway, the headlights shining brightly on the gate of a long, galvanized fence, a "Private Property Keep Out" sign reflecting from the glare. Beyond the fence lay the large plot of undeveloped land, earmarked for the construction of the new neighborhood.

As Maddie severed the lock and chain of the gate with a set of bolt cutters, I popped the trunk and yanked Steiner out and onto his feet. I guided him to the freshly opened gate with my Louisville Slugger shoved in his face, just in case he decided to try anything. There was nothing but satisfied greed and contempt saturated within his devilish grin. The gravel crunched loudly under our feet as I marched him through the gate and toward the center of the abandoned, dimly lit lot.

Maddie met us with a bag of items slung over her shoulder, a pair of red cans of gasoline in her hands. The two metal containers made an abrupt *thunk* sound as she dropped them to the gravel. Maddie crossed her arms and shifted her weight to one side. She peered at Steiner with narrowed, judgmental eyes. He stared back with a blank expression, as if he didn't have a care in the world.

I circled behind him, raised my Slugger, and swung it hard and sharp like a battle axe, connecting between his shoulder blades. The unmistakable sound of bones cracking rang out in the dead night air, and Steiner dropped to his knees, howling in excruciating pain. With his mouth agape, Maddie—like a magician—quickly produced a stick of M-80 dynamite from her bag and crammed it in his mouth. She balled her hand into a fist and punched the stick farther into his pie-hole. As she wrapped duct tape around his head—creating a makeshift gag—I swung my Slugger twice more, connecting powerfully with his left and right ankles. I backed away from Steiner and looked to Maddie, who gave an approving nod.

His pained cries were only a faint, muffled vibration in the otherwise peaceful early Sunday morning. Maddie crouched down in front of him one last time. She pulled a pack of cigarettes from her jean jacket, lit one up, and after taking a long drag, blew the smoke into Steiner's face. Although his eyes were red from the tears, he peered at Maddie with contempt, as his chest puffed in and out from his heavy, labored breathing.

"You know," Maddie began, "back in your algebra class, you *loved* giving everyone shit. But the burnouts, the metal-heads, the punks, the degenerates? It's like you had a special mission to make our lives a living *hell*. And goddamnit, did your hand of justice have an *exceedingly* long reach, even *after* graduation."

Maddie took another long drag on her cigarette.

"Like a fucking *wrecking ball* of hate, you *ruined* my life," she continued. "Next to Ronnie, here, Trish was the *only* person I gave a shit about."

Tears welled in her eyes, and she gritted her teeth.

"And you... *took her from me*!" Maddie's screams echoed all around us. She rose to her feet and stared down at Frank Steiner one last time. "For that, and everything else that you've done, you deserve a fate *worse* than death," she muttered, her voice dry and hoarse. She reached down and uncorked the first can of gasoline. "But this? *This* is a *good start*."

I grabbed the second can, removed the cap, and in unison we stepped backward, pouring the pungent liquid into a long, skinny trail. We stopped and set the cans down when we reached a safe distance. Over the horizon, beautiful streaks of orange and pink light stretched low in the sky, ushering in the first signs of daylight.

"I *love you*, Trish..." Maddie whispered. "This... this is for you."

She took one final drag off her cigarette, then flicked it to the gravel below our feet. The wet streak that led from us to Frank Steiner ignited in a brilliant ball of blue and yellow light. He squirmed frantically as the fire raced toward him with a vengeance. With broken ankles, he could barely *crawl* away, and I *swore* I heard the softest of giggles from Maddie.

Steiner's dark robes became engulfed in magnificent flames. He burned like a bright beacon of light. And when the fire finally reached the wick of the M-80, a loud, thunderous crack erupted out of the early morning, putting an end to his muffled screams. Together we watched as our horrible, no-good, *cannibal fuck* of an algebra teacher exploded into a million pieces. It was horrifying. It was glorious. And I couldn't think of a more deserving fate.

Maddie produced two more cigarettes from the pack, lit them both, and handed one to me. In the far-off distance were the sounds of sirens.

"We should probably get out of here," Maddie mentioned carelessly.

"Totally," I replied. "But first, I believe we owe someone a house call."

"And... an *apology*," Maddie said, rolling her eyes.

The two of us were exhausted and mentally taxed. But before we could call it a day, we had a pit-stop to make, as well as some crow to eat. The silver lining was we could knock both out at one location.

Curtis Layhew peered at us with narrowed eyes through the screen door, as we stood on his front stoop, hats in hands. His thick arms were crossed over his meaty chest. He wore a stained sweatshirt that had the "Millhaven Hogs" logo on it. We watched him with uncertainty as his gaze bounced back and forth between Maddie and I. Finally, his eyes settled on me for what seemed like forever, before speaking.

"You made fun of me on *live radio*, for the *entire* town to hear," Curtis said, his voice low and disapproving. "Why the *hell* should I talk to you two, let alone allow you inside my sanctuary?"

"Curt, we weren't trying to make fun of you," I replied, "we were just... goofing around! I'm a third-shift radio DJ. Sometimes we get a little... silly."

"Yeah," Maddie chimed in softly, "and we're here to apologize. Because we need your help."

"You don't *sound* very apologetic," Curt snapped back.

I could *feel* Maddie tense up immediately, and I reached my arm out in front of her in a preventative measure.

"Dude, we *are* sorry," I continued. "But I cannot stress *enough* how badly we need to talk to you right now. And every second spent on this front porch is a second *wasted*."

"If you guys need to speak to me so badly, why don't you *prove* it?" Curt said, somehow crossing his arms even *tighter* over his chest.

Just then, two police cars and a fire engine sped by Curtis's home, sirens violently blaring through the early morning silence. In a town such as Millhaven, with an embarrassingly tiny population, three government vehicles barreling toward a single destination was a *big deal*. Curtis looked at us suspiciously when he noticed that Maddie nor I seemed concerned. Then, Maddie dug in her pockets and pulled out Frank Steiner's key ring.

"Those cloaked figures you mentioned the other night?" Maddie began. "Mr. Steiner—our old algebra teacher—*he* was one of them."

Curtis's expression shifted to one of mild curiosity.

"He broke into Maddie's house," I added, "*with* the intention of kidnapping her. That didn't pan out so well for him."

"*Okay*..." Curtis began, his tone full of suspicion, "so... where is he now?"

Maddie and I shared a look, then both of our mouths curled into grins.

"He's... all over the place," I said, and Maddie burst into laughter.

It was the first time I had heard her laugh in several days. In that moment it was like a glass of cool water after a 40-day trek in the desert. Curtis's face cringed into a mix of curiosity, confusion, and suspicion. His eyes then looked past us again, as if to follow the sounds of sirens. It suddenly seemed like everything clicked for him, and he unlocked the several bolts and latches and led us inside his house.

Curtis lived in one of the oldest neighborhoods in Millhaven. He took over the deed when his mom passed a few years after graduation, and turned it into his own "conspiracy bunker". Curt's name rarely came up in conversation between Maddie and I, but when it did we would theorize about all the ways he might've transformed his mother's old house into the "tin foil hat's" paradise.

However, *nothing* could've prepared us for what would *really* be inside his home.

Newspapers and magazines were collected in giant heaps where you'd expect to see living room furniture. Across the long wall in the family room, where you might find an enlarged family portrait, Curt had an enormous map of Millhaven with pins of different colors stuck into various spots.

Curtis returned from the kitchen with three beers, then led us into his den where Maddie and I recounted the events of our last several hours. We spilled the beans about Maddie apprehending Steiner and imprisoning him in my garage. Maddie let me take the reins on explaining what we had discovered at Steiner's house, confessing to his walk-in freezer of horrors and all that we found inside. We finished with Steiner's brutal end on the other side of town.

The only point at which Curtis seemed mildly surprised was when Maddie went into ghastly details about setting our old algebra teacher on fire, and then watching him erupt like an exploding volcano. Throughout the *rest* of our tale, however, he wore a look of righteous vindication.

Curt shot up out of his seat and rapidly paced the length of the den, madly mumbling incoherencies to himself. Maddie and I shared a look, then shrugged our shoulders as if this was what we expected all along.

"You guys *know* what this means, right?" Curtis exclaimed, taking Maddie and I by surprise.

"Curt, we have no fucking clue what *any* of this means," I shot back. "That's why we're here!"

Curtis power-walked to a framed photo of he and his late mother, and removed it to reveal a wall safe. After unlocking it, he produced a large leather-bound folder, set it on the coffee table in front of us, and began violently pulling out its contents.

"Several years back," Curtis began, organizing the photographs and written documents into piles in front of us, "Evelyn Hayes published that *ridiculous* excuse for a town history on Millhaven. I mean, *sure*, for the sake of argument I'll admit she captured the *thousand-foot view* of our history. But she *conveniently* glossed over a few key details. Things that she and the other 'Millhaven Elites' *wanted* left out, and buried deep within the catacombs where no one could find them. Luckily, Millhaven has *me* to thank for picking up the slack. *Someone's* gotta dig through the muck and detritus that nobody wants to hear *or* talk about."

Maddie gave me a side-eye look that was full of impatience.

"Hey, Curt?" I began. "Less than an hour ago, we uncovered a psychopath's deep-freezer, and then killed him dead. Do you think maybe we can just hit the highlights here?"

"Oh, of course," Curtis said, waving his hands emphatically. "Sorry, it's just that you two are pretty much the first people to ever put stock in any of this." He motioned around the room to the stacks of documentation that seemed to tower over us.

"It's ok, dude," I said, chuckling lightly. "But we need to combine our efforts, and *fast*. Because if we can't make a case for us, then—"

"That's just it though, Ronnie," Curt interrupted, "there *is* no case to be made. Because no one of importance in Millhaven is going to be stoked about us bringing them all of this."

"And why's that?" Maddie asked.

"Because," Curt replied, his tone dropping low and slow, "they are *all* in on it. Every *single* one of them."

Another puzzle piece fell into place. Suddenly, the odd assortment of individuals on Steiner's mantle wasn't as baffling as it originally was.

"*Curtis...*" I began slowly, rising to my feet, "are you saying that Steiner, Hayes, Winston Harper... they're all part of some... *cult?*"

Maddie also rose to her feet, clapping her hands together once in a profound "eureka" moment.

"*Now* it makes sense, all those fucking pictures on his *mantle!*" she exclaimed, her eyes wide open.

"Yes!" I shot back. "*All of them* must be tied up in this together. Whatever... *this* is."

"Wait, what the hell are you two talking about?" Curtis asked.

"At Steiner's house," I began, turning to face him, "he had this... *shrine* of photographs—all Millhaven bureaucrats. Steiner was in all of them, posed with Harper, Hayes, and several others. Except..."

I trailed off as my brain recalled that last photograph, of a young Steiner with the lanky pastor and his black bible. I looked up to find Maddie and Curtis glaring at me, impatiently waiting for me to finish.

"Curt," I said, "do you know anything about a priest, or a pastor from a long time ago?"

He considered this in silence for a moment before experiencing his own "eureka" moment. His face lit up and he began madly shuffling through the stack of photographs on the coffee table.

"Ah ha!" he exclaimed, shaking one photo in particular and shoving it in front of my face. "Is *this* the guy you're talking about?"

I took the photograph from Curtis, and Maddie leaned over to study it with me. After considering the photo for a moment, we looked at each other, wide-eyed.

"That's him..." Maddie confirmed.

"*That* fucker is the most *mysterious* out of the bunch," Curt began. "He was almost like a 'new' founding father of Millhaven, when the charter was rewritten several decades ago. Throughout *all* my years of digging through the lost annals of history, that guy has been the *most* elusive. It's like he went out of his way to ensure his footprint on this town was as *minimal* as possible."

"Okay, so what does it all *mean*?" Maddie asked.

Curtis shrugged and started pacing again, his expression stern and serious.

"It means..." he hesitated, forcing out the words, "we're dealing with something *much worse* than just a cult. They've been pulling strings from the shadows, and for *who* knows how long."

I shook my head incredulously. The thought that Millhaven's high society was not only corrupt, but actively plotting some dark machinations was too ludicrous to comprehend. But after what we had witnessed that night... well, *anything* seemed possible.

"As much as it pains me to say this..." Curtis continued, "I *think* our information is drying up. We need to—"

"Infiltrate the cult," Maddie declared. "Steiner had *nothing* but silence for us when we gouged him for intel. Maybe it'll be different with these other fucks. We'll need a plan, though. Other than who they are, we don't really know anything about them, like when or where they meet."

Between murdering our old algebra teacher and discovering our town had a secret underground cult, I forgot that I *took* something from Steiner's house. As I was guiding a weeping Maddie out of the walk-in freezer, I noticed something hanging on the back of the door. At first I thought it was just an inventory of the meat locker's contents. And although I had little interest in discovering more about that, I decided to take it with us, *just in case.*

As Maddie and Curtis went back and forth, trading feeble ideas, I reached into my jacket pocket and pulled out the folded-up pieces of stapled together paper. After quickly flipping over the inventory page, my eyes widened at what I discovered next. It was a calendar, marked with dates, times, and addresses.

"Guys..." I said slowly, rising to my feet once more.

When they finally stopped talking long enough to acknowledge what I held in front of them, they suddenly became interested. Maddie took it from my hand and studied it closely, her eyes widening as she realized what it was.

"Wait..." Maddie began hesitantly, "is this their fucking *schedule*? Where the *hell* did you find this?"

"It was hanging on the back of the walk-in freezer door," I said. "I didn't get a good look at it, until *now* that is. Take a look at today's date."

As Maddie and Curtis narrowed on Sunday, their eyes grew wider than I previously thought possible. Then, we all glared at each other in silence, as if we were attempting to read each other's thoughts. Except, that wasn't necessary in this instance.

"Well, guys..." Curtis said, breaking the silence, "I *believe* we have our heading."

Hey there, night prowlers...
And rebels of the midnight hour.
*You've tuned in to the **Midnight Metal Mayhem Show**,*
where the shadows speak louder than words... and the secrets of the
night come alive.
I'm your guide through the twilight,
Ronnie "Riffmaster" Rockwell,
And tonight, we're diving deep into the darkness.

Now, I know we're all about the rock 'n' roll rebellion,
And trust me, I'm all for breaking the rules.
But I gotta drop some knowledge on you, my nocturnal comrades—
Beware of the strangers lurking in the night.
Those shadows may be hiding more than just mystery,
If you catch my drift.
Keep those eyes peeled...
And remember, not every leather jacket conceals a friend.

You see...
Life in the nocturnal realm can be like a twisted Alice Cooper song—
Full of surprises and danger around every corner.
So, whether you're rocking out in the neon-lit alleys...
Or cruising down the moonlit highways,
Stay sharp... stay smart...
And stay true to the rebel in your soul.

Now...
I've got a message for those elusive night creatures
who think they can play games in the dark.
You know who you are,
Lurking in the shadows with your secret

handshakes and hidden agendas.
Well, guess what?
DJ Ronnie is onto you,
And I've got a playlist of justice that's
about to drop like a thunderbolt.

To the secret cult that thinks they can
dance in the shadows without being seen—
Consider this your warning.
*The **Midnight Metal Mayhem Show** is*
rolling into your secret lair,
And I'm bringing the rock 'n' roll truth with me.
Your dark days are numbered, my friends.

So, to all you night warriors out there...
Keep rocking, keep rebelling,
But don't let the darkness swallow you whole.
*The **Midnight Metal Mayhem Show** is just getting started,*
And there's a reckoning on the horizon.

Stay tuned...
Stay vigilant...
And remember—
DJ Ronnie sees all.
The shadows may be deep...
But they can't hide from the light of rock 'n' roll justice.

Until next time...
Keep the flame alive.
DJ Ronnie, signing off.

Part IV

It was fully dark outside by the time Maddie picked me up to hurdle toward Curtis's house. I remember feeling a sense of peace as the cool night air circulated through the Chevelle. And I wanted to hold onto that feeling as best I could; *savor it*. This was, after all, the calm before the storm.

Our first setback came in the form of Curtis's disappearance. Considering how jazzed he was earlier that morning, I half-expected him to be waiting for us outside, bag packed and ready to go. But as we hustled up the porch and knocked on his front door, it opened slowly with a creak. The inside of his house was pitch black. I took a small step forward, then stopped.

Something felt *off*. The hairs on the back of my neck stood on end, and I called out his name.

"Curt, you there?" Silence greeted me in return. "Maddie, this ain't right. He wouldn't just take off without..." My voice trailed off as she pushed past me and flipped the light switch. And that's when we saw it; all over the walls, scrawled in blood like some twisted children's handwriting, were the words: "SACRIFICES MUST BE MADE."

By this point, if Maddie and I weren't already terrified enough, this *could be* the final nail in the coffin.

"What the fuck are we gonna do now, man?" Maddie asked from the driver's seat. "Curt was our lifeline for all this shit, and now he's just *gone!*"

"Look, Maddie," I replied, doing my best to remain chill, "we *need* to keep our heads cool right now. Focus on the things that we know for certain. We *know* that this cult is going to be at the community center tonight. So, let's stick to the original plan, and then—"

"And what? Just *hope* that Curtis shows up somewhere along the way?"

I gave Maddie an uneasy shrug from the passenger seat. I hated sounding blasé in that moment, *especially* toward someone who we considered a friend. But we were staring down the barrel of something sinister. Something *wildly* unknown. And we needed to remain militant.

Maddie gripped the steering wheel tightly as she let out a long, exhausted sigh. We drove the rest of the way to the Millhaven Community Center in silence, drinking in the last sip of the calm before the storm.

We parked a few blocks from the town square to avoid being noticed, opting to hoof it the rest of the way to the center. Maddie and I walked with determination toward the square, trying to push aside the negative thoughts that had been plaguing us for the past day. The discovery of Steiner's gruesome meat locker from hell and Curt's sudden disappearance weighed heavily on our minds as we approached our destination.

My heart began to race as the community center came into view. From our perspective, it was completely void of life. Save for the street lights that lined the square, total darkness encompassed the area. This was all typical of a Sunday night in Millhaven, and it *should* have put my mind at rest. But it didn't change the fact that we were about to walk into the lion's den, wildly unprepared for what was inside.

We approached the community center from the rear, and while Maddie worked on getting us inside, I kept a lookout for any signs of activity. It wasn't a *complete* shock to us that the back door was locked, and that none of Steiner's keys fit the deadbolt. Luckily, we had a backup plan.

After crouching down and analyzing the lock on the door, Maddie reached into her bag and pulled out a black rectangular box. The lock-picking set—a Christmas gift from daddy, *many* years ago—had come in handy on a few occasions. Although, I could sense that using the tools as a means to infiltrate a dangerous cult managed to eclipse all those previous instances.

Less than a minute later, we were inside the community center, and my heart beat even faster as we began our search for answers. The interior was dark and silent, its halls stretching out like an endless maze. The only source of light came from the faint glow of the moon through a nearby window. The soft patter of our boots on the slick floor cut through the almost deafening silence, and I became all too aware of the horrible taste in my mouth as it dried up.

It was excruciating, the tug of war between needing to hurry and needing to be quiet and patient. Every passing second where we *didn't* find the cult—*or Curtis*—meant precious time wasted. And yet, we were all too aware of how incredibly cautious we had to be.

When it came to navigating the complicated labyrinth that was the community center, our saving grace was the deeply-cemented muscle memory we had of its layout. We took ample time to clear each individual room and alcove we passed, but our primary focus was dedicated to the main auditorium at the back of the building. These sick fucks could've been hiding in *any* dark corner of this maze, but the twisted feeling in my gut told me we'd find them in the main hall.

The distinct smell of incense wafted through the air as we drew closer to our final destination. A few steps further, and we could hear a single voice speaking over incoherent and ominous chants. Maddie and I hugged the wall tightly as we tiptoed closer to the double doors. Even without a clear view of what lay beyond the opposite side of the hallway, we both knew that this was where we needed to be.

When we reached the double doors of the auditorium, Maddie and I took turns rising from our crouched positions to peer through the skinny glass windows. My brain *struggled* to comprehend what I was looking at.

The single voice we'd heard rang out from the auditorium's PA system. It was a pastor's voice, preaching words of hate and ignorance, disguised as ones of salvation and redemption. Five anonymous figures, shrouded by dark robes, formed a circle in the middle of the hall. In the middle of the circle was *Curtis*, blindfolded and bound to a chair. He was twisting and writhing in the seat, his cries for help muffled by a gag around his mouth, as the cloaked figures chanted and circulated ceremoniously around him.

"Holy *fuck*..." I muttered in a disbelieving whisper.

"Well, at *least* we found Curtis," Maddie whispered back. "So what are we supposed to do now?"

I slung my backpack off my shoulder and propped it against the wall. The blunt end of my Slugger stuck out the top. I began digging through the various pockets, eventually producing a cassette tape. I held it up triumphantly to Maddie with a smirk.

"It's time to break up this party," I told her.

"Fuck, yes," she replied. "Let's go get Curt back."

Maddie hung back and readied our slew of melee weapons while I took the back stairwell up to the control room on the second floor. I opened the door to find the room dark and empty. Quickly, I scanned the control board, looking for the source of audio that played forth the disgusting words of the disembodied voice.

...And so I say unto thee, go forth and clean thine self of impurities. I say to you, cleanse your soul, so that you may be fit to cleanse the souls of your fellow man. You, my children, will eat the flesh of the unclean, so that those that have lost themselves may finally be found. You, my children, will drink the blood of the lambs of Millhaven that choose not to lead a life of purity. Do this in my name, so you may wash clean their souls, so they may be fit to wander this world...

I finally stumbled on a digital readout screen that read "2:01" and was counting backwards. There was another sinking feeling in my stomach as more dots connected in my head. The impending sense of urgency caused my hands to shake as I plucked my own cassette tape from my jacket pocket.

"Billy Idol," I spoke to myself in a prayer, "*please* be our guide as we deliver the souls of these *fucking assholes* from their limp-dick bodies."

I planted a quick kiss on the cassette, then popped it into the second slot of the tape deck. With "1:25" on the readout, I quickly configured the deck to play my tape as soon as the current one ended. Before exiting the sound booth, I took one last look down on the main floor, where the cult continued to circle Curtis.

"We're coming, buddy," I whispered.

I fled the booth, and traversed the stairwell as fast as my legs would carry me.

When I reached the first floor and returned to the double doors, there stood Maddie with her smorgasbord of weaponry. She picked up my Louisville Slugger and handed it to me.

"I hope you don't mind," she said softly, bearing a furtive grin, "I made a *slight* alteration."

She pointed to a spot right above the grip tape, where the curvature of the baseball bat began. In black marker read the words: "I FUCKING HATE CANNIBALS".

I feigned sentimental tears and pulled the Slugger close to my chest in an embrace.

"Awe, you *shouldn't* have!" I teased, before she punched me in the shoulder.

"You got Billy queued up?" she asked.

I gave her a silent nod and a wink, and we turned our attention back to the huddled cult in the convention hall. In an act of perfect timing, the preacher's sermon came to a halt and one by one the cultists removed their hoods, finally showing their true identities.

My blood boiled as the cult members bore a direct reflection of those who lined the mantle of Steiner's fireplace. This revelation was *not* a surprise. In fact, it was something the three of us were *counting* on. But seeing is believing, as they say. And we now had no other choice but to accept the fact that the most powerful and elite public figures of Millhaven were evil, murdering *pieces of shit*.

Just as the five cloaked figures began to slowly descend upon Curtis, the intro to "White Wedding" began playing loud and proud on the PA system.

"That's our cue," Maddie said with a grin, lighting a handful of firecrackers she held in her hand.

I readied my Slugger as Maddie kicked the double doors in, tossing the firecrackers toward the group of cultists. They only had enough time to turn around and register our presence, before the fireworks blew up in theirs. Four of them scattered like roaches while one of the cultists—Leonard Blackwell, the bank manager—screamed in pain as exploding debris peppered his face.

I was tempted to make a mad dash to spring Curtis free, but the remaining cult members reappeared like living dead from the dissipating fog of the fireworks. Winston Harper—the lawman of Millhaven—charged at me like a linebacker, his giant gut bouncing ridiculously underneath his cloak. For a moment I was almost impressed with his speed and agility, until the business end of my Slugger met his chin, snapping his head backward. Even over the wailing guitars, I could hear his neck crack right before his body hit the hall floor with a thud. He only had a moment to scream out in pain before I brought the bat down on him again, rearranging the contents of his face.

Evelyn Hayes—the head librarian—materialized behind me like a haunting ghost. She dug her long, talon-like fingernails into my cheeks and I felt fresh, warm blood trickle down my face and neck. I gritted my teeth as the natural want to scream out in pain rushed into my chest.

Hayes continued digging into my flesh and I could feel her hands pulling outward, as if she wanted to peel my face skin right off my skull. I choked up on the baseball bat and forced it backwards like a battering ram, connecting with Evelyn's ribcage.

Relief and adrenaline flooded my veins as her grip on my face loosened. I turned to face her, then drove the butt end of the Slugger into her face. She let out a blood-curdling scream as it sank into the socket of her right eye with a wet crunch.

With both Harper and Hayes out of commission, I scanned the room quickly to locate Maddie. I found her double-teaming Marjorie Caldwell and Geraldine Mitchell. And by the looks of how her fight was going, I didn't know whether to lend a hand or pull up a chair and watch.

I sauntered over to their three-way grappling session, just in time for Maddie to disappear under the mangled mess of arms. Using my Slugger like a broom, I swept Caldwell's legs out from under her and she fell to the floor with a hard thud. I don't think I'll *ever* forget the look she gave me—that disapproving sneer of confusion and contempt.

I was so caught up in the moment that I *almost* forgot our plan: to leave a few of them *alive*. Maddie had regained the upper hand, and had her knee pressed in between Geraldine's shoulder blades. She zip-tied her hands together with lightning speed. I dropped my Slugger and pulled a few zip ties out of my jacket pocket, then bound Caldwell's wrists and feet together in a similar fashion.

Maddie kept an eye on the two women as I finally made my way over to Curtis, to free him from his restraints.

"Holy *shit*, guys, that was awesome!" Curtis exclaimed. He reminded me of an eight-year-old who'd just witnessed their favorite wrestler perform their finishing move.

I laughed, but instantly regretted it as fresh blood streamed down my face from the puncture wounds. I removed the red bandanna wrapped around my forehead, and dabbed at my cheeks, wondering if I needed stitches, and if I could even *trust* the doctors in Millhaven at that point.

"Th-thanks for coming to my rescue," Curtis continued, wobbling as he rose from his prisoner's chair.

As I kept one hand tended to my facial wounds, I gave Curt a playful slap on the shoulder.

I gave Curtis a playful slap on the shoulder with one hand, the other pressed tightly against my facial wounds. "Don't mention it, brother," I said, my face throbbing from the pain. "We're just glad you're okay."

Just then, Maddie made her way over and slapped Curtis on his opposite shoulder.

"Yeah," she said, chiming in, "glad you're not dead, man."

I leaned in close to Curtis, as if to tell him a secret, but the whisper was loud enough for Maddie to hear.

"Maddie's not much into showing affection, so you should take that as high praise."

I could tell that she wanted to punch me for that one, but refrained from doing so, taking pity on me and my injury.

"I hate to break up the reunion," Maddie began, "but we have some business to tend to."

Between supplies that we brought with us, and things we found in the community center, we managed to bind and hog-tie Marjorie

Caldwell and Geraldine Mitchell together. They glared at the three of us with white-hot rage in their eyes.

Maddie bent down to be face to face with both of them, studying them through narrowed eyes. "Ok," she began, "who wants to talk first?"

They responded with silence, staring *daggers* back at Maddie, as if it were all *her* fault that they had to be in a cult to begin with.

"We *were* discussing a way for you two to live through this," I added. "But you guys have to play ball. Know what I'm saying?" I tapped my Slugger in my palm a few times, so they'd get the picture.

After a solid minute of silence, Maddie clicked her tongue in disappointment, then reached into her backpack for her famed pair of brass knuckles. She almost slipped them over her fingers, but then reconsidered, looking over at Curtis. She extended them to him, but he shook her off.

"Be my guest," Curtis said with a grin.

Maddie slipped the brass knuckles over her right hand, stood up, and delivered a bone-crunching blow to Mitchell's face. She cried out in ear-splitting pain, cursing Maddie's name, then spat a wad of blood out onto the hardwood floor.

"You idiots have *no* idea what you've done," she hissed, her eyes darting between the three of us.

"Oh, I think we got a *pretty* good idea," I said, casually cartwheeling my Slugger like a medieval weapon, "but now that we got the ball rolling, why don't you two sick fucks start filling in the blanks for us."

"Without the elders, Millhaven is *doomed*," Caldwell said through gritted teeth. "You three think you've done this town a favor?" She threw her head back, letting out a bird-like cackle.

"You all have *no clue* the lengths we've gone to, just to keep this town *safe*," Mitchell added, blood dribbling down her chin. "For *decades*, Millhaven has been the *ideal* place to live. To raise a family. A *wholesome* family."

"The small sacrifices we've made," Caldwell continued, "are a drop in the bucket, compared to the alternative."

I pointed my bat to the limp, lifeless bodies of the other cult members lying about the auditorium.

"If you two don't start making sense *real* soon," I began in a low, firm tone, "we're going to add your bodies to the pile."

"The fabric of this town was stitched and held together by the elders," Mitchell spoke. "We made *small* sacrifices, so that Millhaven and its residents could live in peace. *So what* if a few kids go missing each year? Do you think that anyone would *truly* mourn the loss of societal leeches such as yourselves?"

I had to physically restrain Maddie as she lunged toward Geraldine, butterfly knife in hand.

"You killed and dismembered my girlfriend, you sick fuck!" Maddie screamed.

Geraldine let out a cackle, showing her blood-soaked teeth.

"Oh, *honey*," she began, almost innocently, "*we* never hurt *anyone*. No, that was Frank Steiner's job."

"Yeah, we *found* his meat locker," I shot back. "And if there *is* a Hell, he's certainly there now."

The smile faded from Geraldine's face. "Frank was a *good* man, and a *loyal* foot-soldier," she continued. "His job was to butcher the sacrifices for us. Cut their bodies up into pieces, and store them. And then... *we* would consume their flesh."

A deathly quiet fell over the auditorium. The three of us looked at each other, our eyes growing wide. A crucial puzzle piece had just fallen into place, but we had no idea what to make of it.

All I could think about was Trish, and Maddie, and what might be going through her mind in that moment. It crushed my soul in that moment to learn what had ultimately become of her girlfriend. I couldn't begin to imagine the hurt that Maddie herself felt.

"It was all done in the name of Reverend Ezekiel Stone," Mitchell said, finally interrupting the silence.

"This Reverend," I began, steadying the tremble in my voice, "I'm assuming he was the ignorant asshole on that cassette tape you guys were listening to?"

"How *dare* you speak of him like that!" Mitchell hissed. "He is our *savior*! And he is yours as well. You just didn't *know it* until now. You three should be on your knees, *thanking* us!"

"*Thanking* you?" Curtis exclaimed. "You fuckwads kidnapped me! You were going to sacrifice me to... whatever the hell *this* is! And for what? So you can 'keep Millhaven safe'?"

"Safety *always* comes with a price tag," Geraldine replied with an air of confidence. She then shifted her eyes to Maddie. "*You* of all people should understand that."

"What the fuck is *that* supposed to mean?" Maddie asked incredulously, taking a small step forward.

Geraldine's face curled into an uneven, sinister grin; one that made my blood run cold. It was as if the devil himself had taken over her body, and was working his demon magic to manipulate our feelings and emotions.

"Oh, I think you know *exactly* what it means," Geraldine answered. "Would you like to know how your *girlfriend* tasted?"

I turned my head slowly to look at Maddie. Her face had become *beet red*, hands balled into white-knuckle fists at her sides, chest heaving with labored breaths. I couldn't tell if she was trying to quell the rage inside her, or if she was surrendering to it.

She unclenched her fists and slipped off the brass knuckles, tucking them into her back pocket. She was trading them for the butterfly knife, and I knew in that moment it would all be over soon.

"You know," Maddie began softly, taking another small step toward the bound women, "you've got a lot of balls to talk about Trish that way, being tied up and your lives hanging in the balance."

"Trish was... *delicious*," Geraldine continued, indifferent to Maddie's intimidation. "When this all started, I myself wasn't a fan of human flesh. I *detested* the act of eating it—the *taste* of it. *But...* over time, I learned to tolerate it. And by the time your little *girlfriend* wound up in our clutches, I quite *enjoyed* the taste of—"

Maddie quickly descended upon Geraldine and cut her throat with a lightning-fast flick of her knife. She then moved over to Caldwell and began stabbing her repeatedly in the torso.

"*Fuck you, fuck you, fuck you!*" Maddie's screams echoed through the silence of the auditorium.

Both of their bodies spasmed as blood shot out like geysers from their wounds. Maddie stood over them, her breaths rapid and heavy. Curtis and I only exchanged a wide-eyed glance. We stood silent and stoic, waiting for the writhing of their bodies to cease.

Night dwellers...
And survivors of the unknown...
*You're back with the **Midnight Metal Mayhem Show,***
where the air is thick with uncertainty... and the echoes of the past still
linger.
I'm your host, Ronnie "Riffmaster" Rockwell,
Joined by my partner in crime... the indomitable Maddie "Mayhem."
We've returned to the airwaves... but not without a heavy heart and a
tale to tell.

So, here's the deal, my friends...
We thought we'd vanquished the shadows, defeated the cult,
And brought light back to the midnight airwaves.
But sometimes...
When you stare into the abyss,
The abyss stares right back.
Maddie and I... we might've inadvertently opened Pandora's rock 'n'
roll box,
And what's escaped... well...
It's something far worse than any devilish riff we've ever played.

You see...
The battle against the cult was just the beginning.
The airwaves are crackling with a new kind of energy...
An unsettling vibe that sends shivers down our spines.
It's like we've traded one darkness for another...
And now, the danger isn't hiding in the shadows—
It's lurking in the notes of every power chord.

So, here's our late-night PSA to all you night owls out there...
Tread carefully, my friends.
The night may be alive with the sound of guitars and drums,

But there's a melody of malevolence weaving through the airwaves.
Keep your guard up...
Check under your leather jackets...
And don't trust a power ballad that feels too good to be true.

Part V

The following night, Maddie and I were back on the airwaves cranking out sick metal tunes for our loyal listeners. The two of us were riding a very particular kind of high that evening. What should have felt like a victory strangely felt like the furthest from it. In a single weekend, we discovered a secret cannibal cult, then *disbanded* said cult by relieving the souls from their bodies. It was a satisfying act of revenge, of course. But it came at a hefty price. And little did we know that we'd soon find ourselves in debt.

During one of our first long blocks of music, Maddie trudged in and flopped herself into her favorite seat. She wasn't her usual chatty self. In fact, she hadn't said much of anything since the night before. I couldn't fault her for her reservations though. Over the last 48 hours, we'd all been through some fucked-up shit. But what Curtis and I would have to live with didn't hold a candle to what Maddie will have to carry with her for the rest of her life.

As the final chords of "School's Out" by Alice Cooper rang out, Maddie finally broke the silence.

"I know this is gonna sound fucked up," she began, soft and low, "but I'm kinda glad we found Trish. I mean... I'm not happy with *how* we found her. *Obviously.* And it breaks my fucking heart to finally know exactly what happened. But... *at least* I finally get to have some closure."

I didn't say anything in response. I only nodded. I remember feeling so fucking hollow at that point, like the way you feel at a funeral when you've got nothing useful to say to the bereaved except the typical bullshit. "She's in a better place". "I know he's up there right now, looking down and smiling on all of us". I felt like a fucking heel for coming up speechless, but anything more than that felt like a farce.

My old man dipped out of our lives when I was only a kid, so my mom was stuck raising me all by herself. And she did the best she could, under the circumstances. I was always such a little shit, growing up. I never made things easy for her. After a few particular incidents—one of which resulted in me doing a few months in juvie—I found some perspective, and ended up being *less* of a heathen. Just in time to watch mom die of cancer.

That was the bad news. The good news—if you could call it that—was that it was late-stage, so she didn't have to suffer for very long. When she passed, my aunts drove into Millhaven to help with the memorial and all that. Afterward we had a wake at our house—which was suddenly *mine*—and later that night when all the visitors went back to their lives, my aunts stayed with me. Until the early morning hours, we sat at our little kitchen table, trading stories about mom. My aunts would bring up funny or heartwarming memories from when they were younger. When it was my turn to share my *own* stories of mom, I felt like dogshit all over again; I was only reminded of the sheer *hell* I put my old lady through.

I eventually dug deep enough to find a memory worth sharing. There was a time when I was 11 years old, and got picked on relentlessly for my interests in the macabre. While most kids in Millhaven were watching wholesome classics like "The Andy Griffith Show", I was watching shit like "The Twilight Zone" and "Alfred Hitchcock Presents". My mom could have *easily* told me to "get in line" and stop reading so much Stephen King. But instead, she showed an active interest in it.

The first time she sat down with me to watch reruns of "The Twilight Zone", I assumed she wanted to *monitor* the garbage that I couldn't get enough of, and then ultimately tell me I'd had enough and turn off the television set. As it turned out, she just wanted to be involved in my interests, as bizarre and messed up as they were. She wanted to at least *try* to understand why I was so fascinated by all things dark and twisted.

"Remember that time," I said to Maddie, "when you and Trish convinced me to ditch last period so we could go to the movies?"

Maddie continued to stare blankly at the stained carpet in the sound booth, hands in her jacket pockets, but the faintest smile began to blossom on her face.

"Wasn't that the time where we snuck into a bar afterward, and Trish tried to get you laid?"

Maddie looked up slowly just in time to see me nod, grinning ear to ear.

"That's the one," I confirmed. "We still didn't know each other very well, and that was her idea of getting to know me better. She would walk up to random girls and hit on them for me. And she'd have a different backstory for me with each new girl."

Maddie slapped her thigh so hard it actually made me jump in my seat.

"Oh my god, that's right!" she exclaimed. "Your backstory would get crazier and crazier *every time*."

"She told one girl I was a *dentist*. Do I look like someone you'd let near your teeth? I'm not really sure why she insisted on that tactic."

"It was because she liked you."

Maddie said this so matter-of-factly that it gave me pause. She chuckled at the slightly confused look on my face.

"You *know* Millhaven, Ronnie," she said softly, but with a stern voice. "I mean, even *before* all this... cultist *bullshit*, you know how... *two-faced* our town is. The people here can be unkind to our kind. They don't like those who don't fall in line, or dance to their own rhythm. And *gay* people? Fucking *forget* about it."

Maddie rose from her seat and began pacing around the tiny sound booth.

"Being a boy who likes boys, or a girl who likes girls... it's *never* been easy for us," Maddie continued. "In fact, sometimes it can be fucking *dangerous*. But Trish? She *saw* you, Ronnie. She noticed how protective you were of me. And instead of perceiving you as some sort of threat, she embraced you as a cornerstone of my life. She took comfort in the fact that, when she wasn't around, I had *you* to fall back on."

The trilling of the phone in the producer's booth broke up our Hallmark moment. And Maddie Mayhem—tough-as-nails and harder than the hammer that hits them—wiped a single tear from her cheek and left to answer the call. After the shit-fuck of a weekend we shared, I wanted to bask in the glorious nostalgia and good feelings all night long. But there was music to be played, calls to answer, and work to be done.

I began prepping the mixing deck for the next set of tunes due to come after the commercial break, when I heard Maddie's voice chime into my headphones.

"Um... *Ronnie?*" Her voice was low, and laced with caution and anxiety.

"Yeah, what's up?" I asked, trying to sound positive.

"There's... some *guy* on the phone. He says he wants to talk to you. On air."

Maddie was clearly shaken, so I understood right away that who-ever it was—and whatever they wanted to discuss with me—wasn't good.

"It's your call, dude," she continued. "I can try to tell him to fuck off if you—"

"No, that's OK, put him through," I interjected.

After all we'd experienced over the last couple of days, I didn't know what to expect when I took the call.

"Alright, welcome back, night owls! I hope you enjoyed that rock-solid block of metal tunes, because I got some bad news for ya, we have to go to commercial so we can pay our bills! But don't worry, we'll be back with another long stretch of face-melters for that ass. Before we pay our bills, though, we got a caller on the line who *apparently* has some pressing matters to discuss. Caller, you're on the air with the Midnight Metal May—"

"Hello... *Ronnie*. It's a pleasure to finally make your acquain-tance."

The voice that came through my headphones sounded both fa-miliar and inherently evil. It had a southern twang to it that was un-characteristic for our radio show, but would fit right in at a Baptist revival sermon.

"Heh, alright, guy, good to meet you too," I said, trying to laugh him off. "Is there something I can play for ya, or did you just—"

"You know, I *do* admire your courage," he said, cutting me off again. "Both you *and* that little harlot of yours did quite a number on my friends last night."

I spun in my chair to look at Maddie, who was glaring at me wide-eyed.

"Well, you know that's how the Riffmaster likes to roll, my man." I replied, my voice on the verge of cracking under the pressure.

"Tell me, *Riffmaster*," the anonymous caller continued, "I bet you'd like to think you've done this town some good, yes? Kept the good folks of Millhaven safe and sound, and free from the worries of the outside world?"

I recognized the fucker's voice right about the time I realized he wasn't calling for a friendly chat, or to request a tasty jam. And in my bones I knew that things were about to get *ugly*.

"Alright, listen, *dude*," I snapped back, "I think we've heard enough nonsense for tonight. Call back when you've got something important to say. Or feel free to not call back at all, since I'm not into wasting my own time."

My trembling finger hovered above the call-end button, ready to hang up on the fucker at a second's notice.

"Oh, that's just *fine*," the voice affirmed with its *obnoxious* southern drawl. "I actually *do* have something important to say, if you don't mind. I just wanted to say a quick *thank you* to the man responsible for seeing to a... *delicate* end to my legacy."

"Oh, you mean the legacy where you kill kids you don't like, and *eat* them in order to keep Millhaven 'safe'?" The words shot out of my mouth like flash bangs before I even had a chance to consider them.

"Oh, *come now*, Ronnie, don't be like that. We can have a civilized conversation, can't we?"

I belted out a chorus of sarcastic laughter. "I think we are *way* past civilized, thanks to you, *Reverend*."

There was silence on his end for a moment, before he let out a chuckle of his own. "So you *do* know who I am."

"Yeah, contrary to what you might believe, I'm not a total idiot, Ezekiel Stone."

My heart was pounding like a kick drum inside my chest. Little white stars began to form in the corners of my eyes as red flooded the rest of my vision.

"Well, then," Stone continued, annoyingly cordial, "I suppose we can skip right to it. You see, Ronnie, I've had my *eye* on you, and that little harlot producer of yours. Even that big goofball who thinks he knows everything—Curtis, if I'm not mistaken. And I really do think you all made a *big mistake* last night, cutting their throats and all."

"Oh yeah? And why's that?"

By this point I was up out of my chair, staring down at the microphone like I was staring into the eyes of this sick fuck on the other line.

"*Because*, dummy," the Reverend snickered, "now *all of you* must face the consequences. Every single degenerate sinner of Millhaven will be subject to God's wrath. *Tonight*. You think you've won? Boy, I'm afraid the war has just begun. And as soon as I hang up this phone here, the wonderful *God-fearing* citizens of Millhaven will be under my control. And they will descend upon you and yours with that swift, almighty hammer of justice. I pray for your sake that they'll be quick to put you out of your misery. Except... I think we *both* know that won't be the case. *Do we?*"

Wide-eyed, I look over to Maddie. She was glaring back at me, seemingly frozen in both space and time. I remember thinking about that old saying "no good deed goes unpunished", and how it never made more sense as it did in *that* moment.

"Hello, *Riffmaster*? Did we lose our connection?" Stone's deceitful voice snapped me back to reality.

"Look," I began through gritted teeth, "I don't know who the *fuck* you think you are, coming onto *my* radio show and making threats. But I can promise you that you're gonna be sorry you did. So bring on the fucking *world*, man. We'll be waiting for ya."

I punched the call-end button harder than I ever had in my life, leaving us and our listeners with dead air. I didn't know what would be more responsible in that moment, addressing our listeners and apologizing for the rude caller, or quickly cutting to commercial. Ultimately, I opted for the latter.

Maddie came bursting through the studio door, the poster-child of stress and anxiety. She was no longer the cool-under-pressure, tough-as-nails Maddie Mayhem I knew and loved. She looked exactly how I felt: Scared shitless.

"Dude..." Maddie began, her voice quavering, a palm to her forehead, "what in the ever-loving *fuck* have we done?"

I could only shake my head. In that moment I felt paralyzed of both mind and body. What *had* we done? We *thought* we were doing the right thing. We *thought* we were "surgeons of the night", seeking out cancers and plucking them out, leaving Millhaven better than it was before. But wasn't that exactly what this cult thought they were doing? I began to not only question every decision we had made over the last 48 hours, but every single choice I'd ever made leading up to that moment.

We only wanted to be better than those that sought to actively oppress us. We didn't want to exact revenge. Evening the score was only meant to be our attempt at a fair shot in life. We just wanted to be treated fairly. To not be chastised and criticized for looking different. And now, I thought, were we no better than those who literally made a deal with the devil.

"Ronnie? Earth to Ronnie!" Maddie was shaking me by the shoulders, driving me out of my hypnotized state. "Dude, what are we gonna do?"

I slumped back into my chair, my chest feeling thick and heavy. "I... I don't know, Maddie. We could take on a handful of old geezers, no problem. But more than half of Millhaven?"

Maddie fell back into her own chair and placed her face in her hands. I looked over to the control board to see we only had 90 seconds left of our commercial break. Ezekiel Stone's sinister voice reverberated in my head like an evil tuning fork. And that's exactly what he was: *Evil.* I knew that he—*and* the cult he rode in on—were wicked. *Black-hearted.* I don't know how the truth managed to rear its head in that moment for me, but it did.

"I'll tell you what we're going to do," I said determinately, "we're gonna do our jobs."

Maddie sat up in her seat at the sound of a possible plan.

"You're gonna go back to the producer's booth," I continued, "and I'm gonna go live in 45 seconds. This *fight,* Maddie? It's *not* over."

Maddie shot up from her chair, her face molded into the stern expression of a glorious female warrior. She held out her fist and I bumped it back.

"Fuck their shit up, Ronnie." She turned and ran back to her booth, and went into action mode.

"Alright, night owls, welcome back to the Midnight Metal Mayhem Show. Whether you're *just* tuning in, or you had the *pleasure* of listening to our last caller, it's important for you all to know something..."

I took a deep breath, and readied myself for a responsibility that I was ill-equipped to handle.

"Over the weekend, Maddie Mayhem and I made a *shitty* discovery about Millhaven. That guy who called into the station before commercial? His name is—*was*—Revered Ezekiel Stone, and he used to be a pastor here. A long time ago, he, along with five other elite members of our community, made a... 'deal' in order to ensure protection over our town. For *years*, they have been hunting us down. *That's* the reason why so many of us go missing every year. They hunt us, kill us, and *eat* us. It's all part of their fucked up ritual that guarantees safety for the citizens of Millhaven."

I paused for a moment, considering my next words. An unbelieving smirk came across my face.

"But that's not really true, is it?" I continued. "Their idea of safety comes at a great cost. And that cost is *our lives*. The lives of me, and Maddie, and all of you listening out there. There's a good chance that many of you have had someone you love just up and disappear from your life. And while it pains me to be the one to deliver this news, I *have* to do it. They didn't run away or abandon you. They were probably captured by these sick fucks, killed, and consumed.

"Now, if you heard Stone on the radio, you *know* what's about to happen. Even right now, there are probably 'God-fearing' bigots out there that are now under the mind-control of that guy, and are mobilizing as we speak. And I... I shouldn't have to ask this of you amazing listeners. I *should* be telling you all to seek shelter, and hope that everything turns out ok. But I cannot in good conscience make that request."

I looked over to Maddie in the producer's booth. She was standing at attention, a determined expression on her face, and giving me a thumbs up.

"This, my friends, is a *call to arms*," I said. "If you are of sound mind *and* body, we are *pleading* with you. Rise up with us tonight. *Fight back* with us. Let us wage war against those that have sought to oppress us. To isolate us. To make us feel inferior, like the *other*. If we stand tall, and stand together, we might just live to see another day.

And if we do, maybe we can rebuild Millhaven, the way it *should* be. And for those about to rock? We *salute* you."

While Maddie went to work on fortifying the station's interior, I took inventory of our supplies that I'd brought in from the Chevelle.

We had a few leftover fireworks from the night before, as well as my Slugger and *all* of Maddie's knives. She also found the station owner's handgun and shotgun that he kept lying around—*just in case*.

While Maddie sharpened her blades, I modified my Slugger with random materials I found around the station. It was no longer just a baseball bat. It was now a tool for bloody disruption. With nails and razor blades hammered into the blunt end, it was twice as effective in relieving souls from bodies.

"Any word on Curtis?" I asked Maddie, as I proudly surveyed my Frankenstein-esque abomination.

"*Nothing*," she replied coldly. "I called his house several times. No answer."

"*Fuck.*"

I couldn't decide if Curt not answering was good or bad, so I put the entire notion out of my mind.

A few minutes later, the phone began to ring. Then, the second line lit up. And the third. Suddenly I'm helping Maddie answer calls. They were our listeners, our *fans*, giving us updates.

An angry, brainwashed mob was barreling toward the radio station. And although we thanked each of our loyal fans for calling, I didn't have the heart to ask if they'd decided to fight back. *Once was enough.* I put up the Bat-signal for aid, but ultimately it was Maddie and I who brought this upon Millhaven. We couldn't fault *anyone* who decided to take shelter in their homes, away from the calamity that was about to ensue.

When the last of the calls petered out, we estimated the growing mob to be only 10 minutes away from the station. There was nothing left for us to do but sit and wait.

Posted up in the station's lobby, Maddie and I sat quiet, smoking what could've been our final cigarettes. I *should* have been anxious and terrified. But my final transmission to our radio listeners had me jazzed up, so I was hopeful that not all was lost.

"Do you remember the day we first met?" Maddie asked, interrupting the reflective silence between us.

"I think so?" I answered. "One day at lunch, you randomly sat across from me and—*completely unprompted*—asked me to list my top five metal albums."

Maddie nodded and let out a laugh, blowing out cigarette smoke. "*Close.* That was more like the day we *became friends*. But the day we *met*? *That's* a different story."

She was right, it *was* different. My mind had solidly attached to that one memory—of us going on and on about Metallica and Def Leppard, as if we'd be friends for *years*. And in doing so, I'd *completely* forgot that us meeting and becoming friends weren't one in the same.

"The day we first met was about a month earlier," Maddie continued. "I had jimmied into Carrie Pinkerton's locker, and sprayed shaving cream inside it. It was *payback* for calling me the 'degenerate daughter of a convict'. The title *fit*, but that's beside the point. Then later that day, I was walking home and Carrie and her friends started following me. They were giving me shit for being a lesbian. *And* the shaving cream."

"*Fuck*, I *totally* forgot about that." I said, the memory slowly coming back to me. "They tried to kick the crap out of you, didn't they?"

"They *would* have, if you hadn't shown up. To this day, I *still* have no clue where you came from. It was like you and your Camaro materialized out of thin air. Carrie and her stupid friends only got as far as kicking me with their stupid fucking pink heels, before we all heard the squeal of your tires as you pulled a U-turn."

A smile tugged at the corners of Maddie's mouth as she recalled the memory. But then her expression turned grave and her eyes glazed over as she delved into deep thought, lost in introspection.

"I remember *hating* the fact that I needed rescuing," she continued. "*Especially* after all I had been through, with my dad and Jeff. But seeing you chase those bitches down the sidewalk, with your Slugger raised over your head like a *battle axe*... it made it *all* worth it."

"Yeah well, that skank had it coming," I said warmly.

"I don't know how they found out I was gay. I mean, *I* barely knew. But the way you threatened to cripple them if they outed me... *that* was something else. It took me a while to work through my shit, and find out who I truly was. Trish definitely helped. But when I did, you were my first stop. That's why I came to see you at lunch that day."

Maddie turned toward me, then leaned in and gave me a peck on the cheek. Even after all we'd been through, she continued to struggle with showing signs of affection. So the idea of her giving me a *kiss* kind of blew my mind.

Another beat of silence passed between us, before she spoke up again. "If we die tonight, I'll die happy, knowing that—besides my pops—you're the only man I've ever loved."

"Oh my god, you are *so* gay!" I teased, right before she gave me a playful jab to the ribs.

"And don't you forget it, motherfucker!" She said with a playful cackle.

"Seriously, though," I said, my smile beginning to fade, "if tonight *is* our last night on this dumb planet... I'm glad I got you next to me, when we go down swinging."

The sound of shattering glass from the back of the station forced us to our feet.

"*Fuck*, they're here..." Maddie said, her wide eyes darting between me and the direction of the breaking glass.

"I guess it's just you and me, Mayhem," I replied, springing for our weapons.

Flashlight beams cut through the closed-off blinds. My heart thudded inside my chest as the roar from the mob outside grew louder. I kept my eyes trained on the dancing shadows while my trembling hand reached for my modified Slugger.

Meanwhile, Maddie tucked the handgun into the waist of her jeans, and began loading shells into the double-barrel shotgun.

Another loud *CRASH* of shattering glass made us go rigid. We spun around, once again facing the front of the station. A wild mass of arms were reaching through one of the windows. They writhed like the snakes of Medusa, wiggling and pleading to reach us.

"This isn't going to hold them forever," Maddie said, racking the shotgun, her voice trembling.

"I suppose we'll just have to get—Maddie, *behind you!*"

Heavy footsteps in the darkness gave way to a hobbling, brain-washed citizen of Millhaven—*the first of many*. From the looks of it, he'd broken his ankle while climbing in through the back window. His teeth bore down in a snarl, eyes glazed over as if stricken by late-stage glaucoma.

Maddie gave me a side-eye and an arched eyebrow, then lowered the shotgun to her side. "You're up, *Babe Ruth*," she said. "No use wasting ammo on *this* fucker."

I reared back my bat, then *swung* for the fences, connecting with his forehead. He fell to the floor with a hollow *thunk*, and his snarling was replaced with groans of pain.

More glass shattered from all around us. Windows and doors buckled from the pressures of the growing mob. It felt like we were in *Dawn of the Dead*, but instead of zombies, we were being corralled by mindless townies under the control of Ezekiel Stone.

The radio station's exterior began to *shake*, further threatening the integrity of our fortress. We slowly surveyed our surroundings, wide-eyed, our knees bent as if readying ourselves for an earthquake.

I readjusted my grip on the Slugger's handle, and swallowed past the lump in my throat, my mouth dry as *sandpaper*.

"We are so *fucked*," I muttered, my voice shaking.

A shotgun blast erupted, and I turned to see Maddie had gunned down another intruder that came in through the back.

"Here, help me barricade this back hallway," she said hurriedly. "It might be too late, but we can at least try to keep them contained to the back of the station."

I set down my Slugger and helped Maddie build a wall that sealed off the back hallway. It *wasn't* pretty, and it wouldn't hold them for long, but it was *something*.

Moments later, Maddie and I stood back to back—weapons at the ready—prepping ourselves for action at a moment's notice. Our heads were telling us this was the end, that it would soon be all over. But our hearts—thudding hard but steadfast—were telling us a different story.

The herd of brainwashed grew so large that it blotted out the street lamps outside. Maddie and I were *shrouded* in darkness. Sweat trickled down my forehead. I could *feel* the blood coursing through my veins at breakneck speed.

"Well, we *tried*, right?" Maddie said, her voice trembling.

Over the thunderous banging against the station, I whispered, "We sure *as fuck* did."

Suddenly, seemingly *thousands* of floodlights, as bright as the sun, illuminated the station's interior. The thunderous banging and rattling against the radio station's exterior facade came to a stop. The Metallica album that I set on a loop on our radio station played *triumphantly* outside, louder than life itself. Maddie and I turned to each other, wide-eyed.

With our weapons lowered, our hands naturally found themselves and clasped tightly. We took slow, cautious steps toward the lobby entrance. The volume of the flesh-hungry mob outside had dulled enough for us to hear the racing riffs of "Master of Puppets". And as we rounded the corner, finally able to peer outside, our hearts and hopes were simultaneously restored.

As our boots crunched over the front door's shattered glass, we glimpsed a figure standing in the floodlights' glare. It was Curtis, megaphone in hand and surrounded by an army of misfits—punks with spiked hair, metalheads in leather jackets, and everything in between. All of the deplorable, no-good, societal rejects of our small town had banded together.

"We're taking back Millhaven!" he roared over the din of Hetfield's shredding guitar, and my heart soared with an adrenaline only a call to arms can summon.

Our desperate plea for aid had been answered. The degenerates of Millhaven had shown up, ready to defend their town against the oppressive tyranny that threatened their lives. The brainwashed mob stood frozen in the street, a hundred plus deer in headlights.

"They came," Maddie said, barely audible. "I... can't believe it." A wide smile grew across her face as she looked to me, restored hope in her eyes.

"I guess it pays to have friends in low places," I whispered in her ear, smiling back at her.

"What do you think?" she asked. "You up for one more fight?"

I raised my Slugger at the ready, the nails and razor blades glistening from the barrage of headlights. Maddie gripped her knives, one for each hand.

"For Millhaven."

"For Trish."

"For *us*."

"There is love in me the likes of which you've never seen. There is rage in me the likes of which should never escape. If I am not satisfied in the one, I will indulge the other."

— MARY SHELLEY, *FRANKENSTEIN* (1818)

CHAPTER 4

I've Created a Monster

Part I

There he is: A flash of thick, dark hair, perfectly tousled as if by the hands of a god. His teeth glint in the sunlight, straight and pristine like polished pearls. Full and luscious lips adorn his well-defined face, surrounded by just the right amount of stubble that adds a touch of rugged masculinity. My eyes, curious and hungry for more, travel down to his chiseled, shirtless upper body. Sweat glistens on his beautiful bronze skin, tracing a path down his sculpted chest like tiny sparkling diamonds. Every muscle is defined and toned, making my knees weak with desire. But as I continue my gaze south to his waistline, I can't help but notice the v-lines that lead tantalizingly toward what's waiting for me below. Like a moth drawn to a flame, I am practically begging for more as I anxiously wait for my mind's eye to reveal the *full* extent of his perfection—his fabulously long—

"Excuse me, ma'am? Here's your receipt. Hope you have a nice day!"

My daytime fantasy falls and shatters at my feet like safety glass. The peppy girl behind the register hands me the mile-long strip of paper, bearing an obnoxiously youthful smile. I accept it with a perfunctory smirk. Meanwhile, my inner horndog is screaming *fuck you* for interrupting my reverie of the man outside the grocery store.

As penance, I wanted to tell her to savor that vivacious hope; hold onto it as long as possible. Because just like my daydream she so *rudely* interrupted, all of this is fleeting. Her breasts that perch perfectly on her chest, they would eventually begin to sag—if her future breastfeeding babies wouldn't get the job done, Father Time certainly would. That luscious chestnut hair that cascaded in waves down her toned shoulders? One day it'd begin to show strands of silver, and would only grow like weeds if she plucked them out. Even her *smile* would create unattractive wrinkles at the corners of her eyes. Absolutely *nothing* goes unpunished.

Alas, here I go again, placing blame and projecting my issues onto others. *Classic Angela.* It's not the cashier's fault I let myself slip into another one of my sexual fantasies—this time with the hot piece of ass that's outside the store, passing out fliers. This just means I now have an excuse to talk to him, instead of waving him away like I had planned on. Besides, *someone's* got to talk to this poor bastard. All of these ungrateful housewives, too busy to show him the time of day.

I push my shopping cart to the side of his marketing tent. He smiles wide, a look of genuine surprise on his face at someone making a point to stop and speak with him.

"Hey there! I'm Brad."

"Hi Brad, I'm Angela." I shake his outstretched hand, wondering what his fingers might feel like inside me. "So what's a guy like you doing outside a health food store on a day like this? You should be at the beach!"

Alright, reel it in, Angela. You thirsty bitch.

Luckily he laughs it off as another dime-a-dozen joke, then hands me one of his many glossy adverts. The images on the flier depict gods and goddesses working out, sipping protein shakes, and flashing staged smiles.

"You're right, Angela, it is a *gorgeous* day." He gives me a wink as he says the word *gorgeous*, and my knees weaken. "Luckily I get to enjoy it by talking to lovely people such as yourself."

I let out a playful giggle, performing a not-so-subtle flirtatious hair flip.

"Speaking of," Brad continues, "have you heard of our health club, New You? We just opened up across the street."

He pivots and points to a multi-level health mecca, its windows brightly reflecting the light of the afternoon sun.

"I *have*, as a matter of fact," I reply. "New You must be where the rich, unattainable idols go to see and be seen exercising."

Brad lets out another charming laugh, showing off his pearly whites. "Well, Angela, I can safely say that you'd fit right in with the rest of us. Would you consider spoiling yourself and giving us a try?"

I'd rather give you a try.

"That's very, um, *kind* of you to say. I mostly just stick to my pilates. We converted our bonus room into a little workout area, and I just sweat alongside some YouTube videos. The power of the Internet, you know!"

"Ah, *very* cool! Speaking of the Internet, we do have high-speed Wi-Fi- at the club. We also have state-of-the-art workout..."

My mind goes on autopilot as Brad drones on about various perks and amenities at New You. It's a generic and superficial sales pitch that any upper-middle-class housewife might fall victim to. The joke's on him though, because I'm a mom, and I can multitask like a *motherfucker*. So go ahead, Brad, *gab away*. I'll just keep envisioning you naked.

He eventually nears the end of his rehearsed monologue. Arching his eyebrows and tilting his head, Brad says, "So, what do you think, Angela? Are you ready to meet the *New You*?"

Holy shit, is this guy serious? Also, I am soaked.

"I'm *so* sorry, Brad, I'm just... not that interested. Plus, with our two girls in private school, our budget's already stretched thin."

Brad's expression shifts, knowing he's reached the end of the road with *this* potential gym rat. "It's not a problem, Angela," he says with one last warm smile. He taps a spot on the flier in my hand just as I turn to leave. "One last thing. We *are* running a special for new members. Maybe you can talk it over with your husband, see what he thinks."

I look down at the flier, noticing bold words in a brightly colored starburst:

"Want to turn your partner into the man or woman of your dreams? Give them a gift certificate!"

I thank Brad for talking to me about his *ridiculous* health club, then push my cart toward the parking lot—not before getting one last mental snapshot for the ole "spank bank". A tiny seedling of an idea sprouts in my mind as I load bags of overpriced groceries into the back of my SUV. A notion just out of reach, like that awful feeling when a word is *right* on the tip of your tongue. I suppose it'll come to me later.

Part II

I'm in the kitchen, enjoying a glass of white wine, when Doug arrives home from work. Both girls are eager to greet him and spring off the couch as if it were a trampoline, tackling him with open arms in the doorway. I used to watch this happen day in and day out with tiny hearts in my eyes like some silly cartoon character. Now it just pisses me off.

It's so nice that at least one of the parents gets a nice welcome-home greeting.

For a moment I pretend that it's *not* Doug walking through the door and into our kitchen. It's *actually* Brad from the grocery store, in a Speedo, handing me a fruity mixed drink as I lay by a beach cabana. I'm wearing one of those wide-brimmed sun hats and a pair of those larger-than-life sunglasses. Brad's hands begin to rub suntan lotion all over me, making sure to get *all* of those hard-to-reach places. And what's this? It's time for him to pull me into a kiss, and he—

"Hey hon, how was your day?"

Reality pulls back into focus and Doug's standing in front of me, offering his typical peck on the cheek.

"It was... *fine*," I sigh.

"Just fine?"

"Yeah, it was *fine*, Doug. You know, just your typical day in paradise!"

I'm projecting again. I let myself get caught up in one of my fantasies, and get mad at my loving husband when I eventually have to come back down to earth.

"I'm sorry, honey," I apologize, "it's just been a... *weird* day."

Doug circles behind me and massages my shoulders, knowing full well that this is where the "how's your day" small-talk stops. Say what you will about the boring marriage life, but there's something to be said for understanding your partner on *this* level; knowing when to press on, and when to *shut the fuck up* and touch me.

Doug goes to grab a beer from the fridge, and the bald spot on his head stares back at me like a cycloptic eye. For some reason it's more noticeable today. He turns around and twists the top off, taking a long swig, and my eyes fall to the buttons on his shirt. They're holding tight as the seam spreads, threatening to burst open from his protruding gut. I can't tell if I want to laugh or feel sad.

I actually looked forward to this day when I was younger. Not this day *specifically*, of course. Just the phase of our lives, our marriage, where we'd look around one day and discover the monotonous glory of adulthood. We would *embrace* each other's imperfections, unlike those other unhappy fools out there. You know the ones. Those obnoxious couples that share a Facebook account, and use it to post pictures of nothing but *amazing* times their family had shared together. Nope, not Doug and I.

Some of what we had planned out for ourselves *did* in fact materialize. I got pregnant with Samantha when I was 28—just in time for me to finish my bachelor's degree. Her conception was both a gift and a temporary setback—nine months to a year, and I'd be out in the workforce once more! And then I got pregnant *again*, this time with Rebecca. And while Doug was busy working and climbing that corporate ladder, I busied myself with raising the girls, and cleaning the house, and doing the laundry, and the shopping, and...

I somehow found the time to keep up with my pilates—I *think* it was the unrelenting societal pressures. I busted my ass after each baby, endless crunches to battle the stretch marks, pushups to combat the sagging boobs. Doug meanwhile, he got to sit on his fat ass, reaping praise for doing the bare minimum as a husband and father. Just where in the hell were the societal pressures for him? For *all* fathers? Shouldn't they be held accountable for more than just "bringing home the bacon"?

I know it's not fair of me to be this resentful toward him. After all, he only fell victim to the culture that holds the bar so much lower for men. *Right?*

"What's this, a new gym?" Doug's voice brings me back to reality, and I see him scanning the health club advert.

"Oh, it's just a flier that someone gave me as I was leaving the grocery store today."

"Thinking about joining a gym, babe?" He asks.

Do I detect genuine curiosity in his voice?

"Oh- no..." I respond, giggling. "I think I got *all* I can handle with my pilates."

Doug studies the card for another moment before he sets it down and retreats to the living room. I'm a little tipsy as I start on dinner, not at all sorry for creating a racket by banging the pots and pans around. I slip in one of my AirPods and listen to music while I cook. It's a good distraction from the passive-aggressive rage that's currently at a low boil.

No, that's alright Doug. I didn't want any help at all with preparing supper. You go right ahead. Relax on the couch with your feet up and a hand down your pants.

I give the girls their bath when we're done eating, and I hear Doug playing one of his video games. He's swearing and having a one-way conversation, wearing one of those goofy headsets with the attached microphone.

That's totally fine, honey! Play your silly video game! I am "Super-Mom", who will single-handedly take care of everything!

Rebecca yelps when I brush the knots from her hair a little *too* hard, and I've once again let my anger get the best of me. I apologize and give her a smooch on the head. More swearing and aggressive button-mashing from Doug. I think about the awful shade of purple his face might change to, as I straddle his waist and suffocate him with his own headset cord.

Try playing Call of Duty and talking shit with your friends now, you ungrateful asshole.

Both girls are in bed, and I can *finally* change out of my wet clothes that got soaked from the bathwater. I'm down to my bra and panties when a familiar embrace approaches me from behind. This is a trick I am *all too* familiar with—Doug's half-assed version of intimacy, thinly-veiled by his desire to fuck.

I try to imagine that it's actually *Brad's* hands that are wrapped around me. Closing my eyes, I can still see that award-winning smile of his, that perfectly tanned skin and chiseled jawline. The fantasy dissolves when I feel Doug fumbling with the clasp of my bra. When he finally unhooks it, I sling it off my shoulders and toss it aside. He massages my breasts, still from behind, and I can feel his erection through his pleated khakis.

It's not long before his butterfingers are fishing down the front of my underwear, and I widen my stance a bit so that he can (hopefully) improve his reach. I attempt—*and fail*—to sort through my mental inventory of sex gods I've collected like trading cards. All images fade when his fingers begin fondling my vagina like a clueless teenager on prom night.

I allow his thick, blundering hands to finish undressing me, and we retreat to our bed to complete our typical half-assed version of foreplay. I yank his boxers down and suck him just long enough to get him hard. Then I climb on top of him out of habit, and guide him inside of me.

Doug and I used to have *several* positions in rotation—the sky's the limit when you're young and limber. Nowadays, we have one position: Me on top. *Super* exciting stuff. It's never been directly addressed why we've restricted ourselves to this one-and-done position. I suppose it isn't necessary, though. Doug has gained *so* much weight over the years that he would practically *crush* me if he were on top.

I don't make a habit out of tooting my own horn, but I'll admit I've gotten pretty good at it. Through trial and error I've learned how to buck my hips and grind against him in just a way that makes him come quick. I employ these techniques when I'm not looking to make things last long, which happens to be most of the time.

Except tonight, because I would *really* love an orgasm. I'm massaging my clit as I bounce on top of Doug, desperately striving for climax. I can see the light at the end of the tunnel—it's a pinhole, but it's there. Then Doug lets out a distracting moan of pleasure and I'm thrown off my rhythm by the violent jerking of his body. I'm *almost* there when I feel his limp penis unfolding out of me. And it's all over, just as abruptly as it began.

I excuse myself without ceremony and retreat to the shower. After washing away the ick of the day, I let the removable shower head pick up the slack from my husband's underwhelming performance. And just as well, because now I can *properly* fantasize without interruptions or distractions.

Doug is already fast asleep when I step back into the bedroom. I crawl into bed next to him and his snores rock me to sleep, concluding another day in the life of a bored, horny housewife.

Part III

Two weeks have gone by since my little meet-cute with Brad outside the grocery store. And during that time he's practically been the branch manager of my spank bank. He's not wearing a suit from Brooks Brothers, mind you. He's actually wearing swim trunks that are too short and show off his perfectly toned ass. When he turns side-profile, silhouetted by the setting sun, it looks like he's smuggling a python in the front of his shorts.

It's peculiar, though. I have a pretty solid rotation of eye candy to fantasize about, and yet I'm still hung up on this handsome lunk. I take pride in my ability to use up and then toss aside these men

I've saved away for those intimate moments for one. I think it comes from being married too long.

Speaking of which, I've decided on what to get Doug for his birthday this year. That weird feeling I got as I was loading the groceries into my car that day two weeks ago—the itch I just couldn't scratch—I *think* I figured out the cause of it. I was tossing out a bunch of junk mail, but held onto the New You flier. I turned it over and over in my hand, eyeing it suspiciously, asking myself *why* I hadn't thrown it in the garbage.

It finally clicked when something that Brad had said echoed in my mind: *"We're running a special for new members. Maybe you can talk it over with your husband, see what he thinks."*

And then the bright starburst, which stated:

"Want to turn your partner into the man or woman of your dreams? Give them a gift certificate!"

An innocent chuckle escapes me as I mull the idea over. A plan begins to form, puzzle pieces falling into place, and suddenly I'm cackling with maniacal laughter. It's so good. It's *too* good, this idea of mine. There's margin for error, but it's minimal, and if I can pull it off it'll be the greatest birthday gift ever.

I normally don't pick up the girls until 2 PM, but I leave an hour early so I can pay a visit to the pretentious health club for rich assholes. I pull into the parking lot and again I'm wincing from the sun's reflection off the building's polarized windows. All these really attractive people are walking in and out, all with ridiculous smiles on their faces, and I start to feel nauseous. I'm second-guessing whether this is actually a good idea or not. Is it maybe *too* cruel of a joke? And who the hell is this happy about exercising?

I ultimately say *fuck it* and walk inside, the flier folded in my hand. When I approach the front desk I unfold it and show it to the receptionist. She smiles when I mention Brad, and I can't tell if it's because she recognizes the name or if he just has that effect on women.

The receptionist is obnoxiously perky as she hands me a clipboard with some paperwork to fill out. I occasionally glance up, craning my neck to look for Brad. The health club is teeming with beautiful, sweaty bodies that glisten under the fluorescent lights, but unfortunately Brad isn't one of them.

Ten minutes later I emerge from New You with my husband's 42nd birthday gift. The rest of my day is on autopilot—picking up the girls, making dinner, cleaning, folding the mountain of laundry—all so I can plan out Doug's big day. It has to be *perfect*, from start to finish. If I truly want to savor the moment, if I'm going to stick the landing, everything needs to be carefully executed.

It's Doug's birthday, and I'm pretty sure I'm more excited about it than he is. I spanked his butt as he was leaving for work this morning, and he gave me this coy look. In that moment I reconsidered my entire plan. The look on his face was just so... innocent. He has no clue what's coming, and I'm wondering if it's perhaps too much—if it's too mean. But I stick to the plan, because I've sunk a lot of time, energy, and money into it.

I pick up Samantha and Rebecca from school and drop them off at my parents' house for the night. The entire car ride they trade giggles and looks of amused suspicion. They're a little too perceptive and know something's up. Doug and I, we haven't broached the sex talk with either of them yet, and *still* they seem to have an idea of why their parents are celebrating *alone* tonight.

We'll see if Doug is still "in the mood" once he opens his gift.

We have a nice, romantic dinner at his favorite restaurant, and all night long I'm lending obscure hints for what I got him. It feels a little like playing with fire because he *could* guess exactly right, and I'm not sure I have the poker face to call his bluff. As dinner winds down, so do the hints and we drive back to our house.

Doug hasn't been home since this morning, so he's completely surprised by the decorations. On the kitchen table he finds a "man basket" that I made for him, complete with his favorite whiskey, a set of golf balls, and the new Stephen King novel. He confuses it for his *real* gift and I let out a small chuckle. When he asks what's funny I point to the hallway where I have red rose petals leading to the bedroom. His mouth drops open and he sets the basket back down on the kitchen table. I take him by the hand and lead the way.

My heart is thudding hard inside my chest, and I can't remember the last time I felt so anxious and excited while holding Doug's hand. I sit him on the bed and give him a seductive look over my shoulder as I pretend to rummage through my lingerie drawer. It's not sexy underwear that I pull out, but a dark blue envelope.

The butterflies and giddiness are in full force as he tears into it. The card is a tasteless "dude humor" joke, something Doug would definitely appreciate, and a perfect way to soften the blow.

He gives the gift certificate a quizzical look as it falls into his lap. After picking it up he studies it closely, reading the front and then the back, and then the front again.

The corners of his mouth curl upward to form a weak smile. "Thanks, hon," he says, finally looking at me.

"What's the matter, babe? Don't you like it?" I ask, donning my preconceived expression of profound confusion. I've been practicing this to the bathroom mirror for the last several days. I was counting on this exact reaction, and I wanted my tone to present the perfect blend of *genuine* and *underhanded*.

"I...I *love* it. Thank you." he says, but I know better.

I gasp. "You *do*? It's just... you *really* seemed interested when you were looking at the flier a few weeks ago. I knew you'd like the basket, but I felt like it wasn't enough. So I wanted to give you a little something extra, to show my appreciation for everything you do."

I had to practice this last line a *lot*. I knew it would take some strength and reserve to not crack up laughing.

"No, it's perfect," he continues. "I've been meaning to do something about this big ole gut anyways."

We share a laugh—a *genuine giggle* at his self-deprecating humor—then he excuses himself to play video games. I fight back the urge to feel even an *ounce* of guilt over my purchase. Doug *does* have a clever way of carrying himself when mining for sympathy. Objectively speaking, I suppose experiencing *some* level of guilt would be apropos. This gift certificate was basically the equivalent of a man gifting his wife a vacuum cleaner—a present that said "Why yes, I considered it *just* enough to get you this thing that will make your *job* easier!".

But this was the opportunity of a lifetime, and one that I just couldn't pass up. I mean, it was a *total* win-win situation. I found a unique birthday gift for my husband, *and* it came with that look of surprise on his face after tearing into the card. That *priceless* look of realization that I called him fat without even opening my mouth.

The cherry on top had been my discovery of "New You's" money-back guarantee. The receptionist had filled me in on the club's unique promise of results, stating that my husband could cancel the 12-month contract—*with a full refund*—if he didn't drop at least 10 pounds in the first four weeks. I handed that overeager receptionist my Mastercard so fast that it startled her. It was almost a gag gift. Fuck, it *transcended* gag gifts. Doug would attend the health club a handful of times, give it up, and I'd have my vindication that my husband is a big, fat loser.

This isn't *just* about having a laugh at his expense. I wanted Doug to have a taste of his own medicine. He needs to know what it feels like to be constantly surrounded by, and compared to, the unattainable. And the club members of New You are the perfect candidates to take care of that for me. Yes, I have successfully outsourced my revenge. And when he finally decides to throw in the towel, I'll be there to pick it up and wipe up the mess with a smirk on my face.

The television and a glass of wine are keeping me company when Doug arrives home from his first session. I hold back a giggle as I notice the drained look on his face and the hobble in his step.

"Hey babe, how'd it go?" I ask, springing up from the couch. He moans in pain when I give him a tight hug.

"I feel like death," he mumbles, eyes half-open.

"Awe, it's ok, babe. It'll get better! Plus, tomorrow's Saturday so at least you get to sleep in!"

Doug replies with another grunt as he pushes past me, shuffling toward the kitchen like a zombie.

The following morning, I'm sneaking into the girls' bedroom to prompt them with yet *another* golden idea I came up with. They burst out of bed with excitement and begin jumping on Doug who is fast asleep, begging him to make pancakes. I stifle another laugh as he moves at a glacial pace toward the kitchen, groaning and holding his sore muscles along the way.

Now this is the gift that keeps on giving.

After breakfast I offer to rub ointment on his aching muscles. Perhaps I feel a *little* guilty, but those accusatory feelings are easily eclipsed by the years of inequity in our marriage. Lately, I have come to the realization of how much people walk all over me. Maybe I'm being a bit dramatic by trying to make Doug's life difficult, but I have to look at it as an investment. One day, my husband will understand just how good he's had it, and then maybe I will finally get the recognition I deserve.

Four short weeks fly by, and just as promised, Doug has dropped his first 10 pounds. I patronize him to the point of it bordering on hyperbole, citing how proud the girls and I are. But in the secret underground bunker of my psyche, I'm counting down the days until he gives up. Despite his impressive achievements, there were still *plenty* of days when he'd come home white as a ghost because his trainer had kicked his ass. He'd then saunter off to bed prematurely, unable to keep his eyes open, while the girls and I laughed and watched movies.

Now, if I'm being honest? Beneath that secret underground bunker, lies another level of feelings that Doug had unknowingly conjured up. Sure, I've spent a lot of time making sure that each of my compliments toward him were subtly backhanded. Deep down, though, I *am* proud of Doug. At the end of the day, he is still my husband, and it's my responsibility to support him. But there's nothing that says I can't have a little fun while doing so.

And come to think of it, I *have* noticed a few other changes besides his minor drop in weight. He's been slightly more considerate with the things he does—or *doesn't* do—around the house. Doug has always been the first one up and out the door in the mornings, leaving me solely responsible for getting the girls dressed and ready for school. Now I wake to their clothes neatly laid out and lunches made, all ready and waiting on the kitchen counter.

The first time it happened I stared at the spread dumbfounded, my morning cup of coffee cradled in my hands. His minor act of service took me completely by surprise and suddenly my brain began to spiral. Was he on to me? Had he finally seen through my clever ruse? Was this his *own* backhanded way of evening the score between us?

Once the coffee had kicked in, I remembered who I was thinking about. This was *Doug*, after all. Not some conspiratorial mastermind. So I took his kindness at face value and appreciated it for what it was. I sent him a text, thanking him for what he'd done, and he replied with a few sappy love emojis.

This subtle metamorphosis in Doug is igniting something in me, a flickering desire I hadn't felt in years. And I am finding the change to be as satisfying as it is uncanny.

Part IV

I am *astounded* by the progress Doug's made, thanks to his training at New You. Three months to the day have gone by since he started, and with each passing day he leaves me nearly speechless with his transformation. There have been genuine moments when I've asked myself "Who is this man?". I bet you didn't see that one coming, did you? Yeah, neither did I.

I'm sitting on the living room couch, anxiously anticipating Doug's return from his three-month fitness report. Samantha and Rebecca are lounging on the carpet in front of the TV, watching one of their *obnoxiously* loud Netflix shows. And all throughout the day I've been thinking of sympathetic nothings to greet my husband with as he lumbers through the front door. The manufactured condolences have played on a loop in my head. I suspect that today is the milestone that does him in, despite all evidence pointing to the contrary. In order for this hilarious long-con to succeed, I need to have faith in it.

The sound of Doug's car pulling into the driveway pulls me back to reality. I prop myself up on the couch, overflowing with nervous excitement, and force the biggest smile onto my face. The second he walks through the door—the smile, the rehearsed backhanded sympathies, my optimism—they all disappear like a fart in the wind. Because he doesn't just look good, or great. He looks *amazing*; like the day we were married.

"Good news, everyone!" Doug exclaims, dropping his gym bag to the floor. "I'm officially a *gigantic* loser!"

I let out a confused chuckle, eyeing this strange man in my foyer. Meanwhile, Samantha and Rebecca are literally rolling on the floor, laughing. Doug runs over to scoop them up—one under each arm—with the speed and agility of a man *half* his age. He spins in circles in our living room, his daughters like makeshift helicopter blades. Several newfound muscle groups flex as he effortlessly performs this maneuver. His biceps are like pythons. His calves bulge like swollen grapefruits.

Who the fuck is this man?

I mean, sure, he still has a bit of a gut, and lumbers around with the posture of a bridge troll. But the man—*my* man—had officially seen my challenge, and rose up to meet it.

I'm feeling dizzy and lightheaded, confused as to how all this panned out the way it did. Absolutely *no part* of my "win-win" plan involved *this* much success on Doug's part. And now sharp pangs of guilt are shooting through my nerves as I cower on the couch.

"Alright girls, today's dad's cheat day," Doug says, setting both girls back down safely, "who wants *pizza* for dinner?"

Samantha and Rebecca squeal in excitement. Doug lets out a corny chuckle in response, then asks them to go play outside, whispering something about "needing to talk to mommy". My muddled thoughts have me so far removed that I barely notice him looming over me. When he leans over, I'm expecting his usual peck on the cheek. Instead, his muscular arms scoop me off the couch and into a bridal carry.

"Now, it's *your* turn, mom," Doug whispers softly, cradling me close.

A giggle escapes me as I'm lifted unexpectedly from the couch, and suddenly I'm peering deeply into his baby blues.

Have his eyes changed?

"What, now you're gonna spin *me* around like a helicopter?"

"That's not *exactly* what I had in mind," he replies, arching his eyebrows.

He marches me into the bedroom, kicking the door closed with a flick of his heel, and tosses me onto our bed. I let out a surprised laugh as I bounce gently, landing in a sea of decorative pillows. I roll over just in time to see him lock the door and shoot me a seductive look. It's a glare of passion, of sexual hunger, and I can't remember the last time I've seen him like this.

"What are you doing, babe?" I ask. "Shouldn't we be ordering the pizza?"

He's slowly making his way toward me, a predator lurking toward its prey, and my giddiness fades away.

"You and the girls can have pizza," he says, standing over me like a giant. "There's only *one thing* I'm interested in eating tonight."

Before I can say another word, both of his hands are around my ankles and he jerks me toward him. I let out another surprised gasp and Doug is now dropping to his knees. With finesse his nimble fingers unbutton my jeans and unzip the fly, slipping them off my body with ease. Butterflies scurry wildly in my stomach as he slides off my panties, and I feel a distinct, almost foreign vulnerability.

His fingertips glide softly against the inside of my thighs as he lowers himself between my legs. I can't remember a time when his touch was this soft, this sensual, this generous. I know for a fact that it's Doug who's caressing me, who's loving me tenderly, but it all just feels so *new*.

My skin prickles in goosebumps as he forces my legs apart. I glare at him in wide-eyed amazement. I'm watching him as he watches me, my face folding into ecstasy as his tongue traces the slit of my vagina. My arms go weak, wobbling from propping myself up. They soon give out and I fall back onto our pillow-top mattress, heart racing in my chest.

I writhe against our satin sheets, soft moans escaping me as Doug takes his time. His tongue flitters gently against my clit as two fingers massage the lips of my vagina, teasing the inevitable. The pleasure is so intense, so consuming, that I'm barely thinking about how this isn't Doug. My husband isn't this generous, or delicate, or sensual. But right now none of that matters.

I am absolutely *soaked* when his fingers push into me and another gasp escapes my throat. He giggles when I finally catch my breath, moaning loud enough that I cover my face with a pillow. His soft lips suckle at my sensitive clit while his fingers curl up, expertly massaging the elusive spot deep inside me that sends shivers down my spine.

I thread my fingers through his hair as he continues to work me, and briefly I wonder if his hair is somehow *thicker*. The fleeting thought is lost when I feel another finger plunge into me, and now I'm bucking my hips uncontrollably, pressing his face harder against my pussy.

How the hell did Doug get so good at this? And when did he become so generous?

I feel the pressure building inside of me, a pent-up pleasure that is *begging* to be released. I'm a tinderbox, ready to explode. My back is arched, hips thrust upward, and my entire body lets loose in a fit of uncontrollable spasms. And Doug—my *new and improved* husband—brings me to orgasm in a way that he hadn't since before we were married.

I close my eyes and instantly, a spectacular fireworks show explodes in my mind. Every single synapse in my brain ignites, creating a kaleidoscope of vibrant colors and electrifying sensations. My entire body is consumed by waves of euphoria, muscles tensing and releasing, dancing to the symphony of pleasure. Each burst of sparks colors my thoughts with a vast spectrum of vibrant sensations, leaving me in a state of euphoric agony.

When my reality pulls back into focus, Doug is leaning over me, a warm smile on his face. Those *brand new* eyes, full of passion, stare deep into my soul. I take a breath and let it out in a satisfactory sigh, resting my palm against his face. And now I'm waiting for that all-too-familiar line: *My turn.*

But it doesn't come. Doug remains fully clothed, and he playfully bats my hand away when I reach for the button on his jeans.

Planting a soft kiss on my lips, he says, "Why don't you take a nice, long bath. I'll go order that pizza."

Doug's bouts of altruism—those sexual in nature and otherwise—steadily increase throughout his third month of training. They are the perfect antithesis to his weight loss, and I embrace *all* of these changes. It feels like I've traveled back in time, to when Doug and I were first dating and he pulled out *all* of the stops in order to impress me. Back when we *made love*—not *had sex.* When we lived to impress each other—*not* get on the other's nerves.

But there is something... *off* about him. I'll find myself staring at him, baffled, like he's the last piece of a jigsaw puzzle but doesn't fit into place. I try to rationalize it, saying it's only Doug reverting back to the mindset of his younger self—*before* he had a wife and two girls. I tell myself that it's *normal,* that as his body becomes more sculpted with each passing day, he's apt to change *other* things about himself, too.

When I *do* try to quantify the changes I witness in Doug, I end up sounding like a complete *lunatic*. A few nights ago we were laying in bed and I was doom-scrolling through social media. Doug had on his reading glasses—the ones I had to *beg* him to wear—and was intently studying his tablet. Initially I assumed he was down a YouTube rabbit hole, watching grown men blow each other up with homemade explosives. But when I peeked over in curiosity, I discovered he was reading a *book*.

What kind of wife becomes suspicious of their husband when they choose to read?

When you've been married for as long as I have, you learn to live with your partner's habits that drive you bat-shit crazy. Things like burping, farting, cracking knuckles, picking your ass right in front of your partner's face—you try to *avoid* these obscene tasks in their company when you're young. And of course in due time, these courtesies go *right out* the window. Doug was *not* shy about doing all of these and more. It was like he *reveled* in his ability to smell his fingers after they'd been down his pants, counting on me to not say a damn thing about it.

The morning after I caught him reading, I decided to take an inventory of the changes I've noticed. I laughed to myself as I stared at the list. Because it was *long*, and it keeps getting longer. It's just as much about the things he *doesn't* do, than the things he *does*. Most of those gross habits have up and vanished, replaced with acts of kindness and empathy.

Angela, isn't this what you wanted? Why are you complaining? Shut up and say "Thank you", you ungrateful bitch.

The truth is, I *am* grateful. Sure, my birthday prank on Doug is going tits-up before my very eyes. But isn't this objectively *better*? I have pushed him for *years* to make changes for the sake of his health, and he has finally obliged me.

So what's the problem, you ask? There *isn't* one. *That's* the problem. But Doug *is* different, in ways that I can't understand or explain. When we're together, it often feels like I'm sitting next to a *completely* different person. A wolf in sheep's clothing. A *shapeshifter.*

Part V

As weeks roll on and Doug continues to perfect his body, more aspects of his life fall neatly into place. He just received a huge promotion at work after being stuck at the same level for years. His admirable climb up the corporate ladder resulted in a raise, annual bonuses, and company stock options.

I meet Doug at work today to see his new office and have lunch together. When I step off the elevator and onto his floor, I realize I have a lot of nervous energy swirling inside me. I'm not really sure why this is. I wipe my sweating palms against my brand new skirt and speculate what could be causing this tornado of unprompted anxiety. It finally hits me as I turn a corner, faced with the outside of Doug's office.

Could it be the secretary thing?

The company had given Doug his own executive assistant to help balance out his increased workload. Until now he's told me little about her, other than the fact that she exists.

My father was a company man for many years—loyal to a fault. As a little girl I admired his dedication. I would eventually learn that his loyalty didn't necessarily extend to every facet of his life. I don't think I'll ever scrub my brain of the memory where I once found pink panties in the backseat of his car—the pair that *obviously* didn't belong to my mother.

I remember holding them in my hand, studying them like I had never seen underwear before. It was just my dad and I, and he was driving us somewhere, although I can't remember where. I spent several minutes looking at the lingerie bottoms, running the soft lace through my fingers. When I began connecting the dots, I silently handed them to my dad. He accepted them without taking his eyes off the road. After studying what I'd given him for only a second, his expression went blank. He looked horrified and guilty, and I remember this making me feel the same way, like I wasn't suppose to find them.

"Are you going to tell mom?" he had asked, his voice quiet and shaky, eyes darting back and forth between the road and me in his rear-view mirror.

He said "Are you going to tell mom?"—not "Please don't tell mom". I shook my head silently, my 12-year-old brain not fully comprehending what I was agreeing to. He nodded his head, and we never spoke about it again.

So yeah, Doug's new secretary *could be* a 67-year-old chain-smoker named Delores. But my gut tells me otherwise, and I am right to believe it.

This little unforeseen spark of jealousy I feel is abrupt and unprecedented, and it only gets worse when I meet Julia for the first time. She smiles and introduces herself, and I'm forced to mask my rage over her overwhelming beauty. The company might as well have plucked her directly from a Victoria's Secret catalog, slapped a pencil skirt on her, and plopped her down in front of my husband's new office.

Her wavy chestnut hair has an unattainable shine to it, and frames a face that is both youthful and experienced. She wears a pair of bold-framed glasses that make her appear distinct yet still fuckable. But I somehow get the feeling that the men in the office don't spend much time looking at her eyewear. I size her up discreetly as she brings me a bottle of water. Her hourglass figure boasts a set of breasts that refuse to quit, and an ass that even I can't help but ogle.

I wipe more sweat from my palms as Julia and I make small talk. Doug is on the phone, pacing leisurely back and forth, concealed by the frosted glass of his office door. Julia asks me about Samantha and Rebecca, and says things like "awe" and "so sweet" in all the right places. She tells me that she wants kids someday, preferably a daughter, and a husband who brings home "all of the bacon". I choke as I try to stifle my laughter. She has just acutely described my life.

Bite your tongue, Angela. Blood in your mouth beats blood on the ground.

I take a deep breath when I regain my composure, and I wish Julia the best of luck in her quest to be the world's most fuckable housewife. Doug's office door finally swings open and he's standing in the doorway, peering at me with hungry eyes. At first I don't even recognize him. He's wearing a brand new tailored suit—one of many he treated himself to after his raise—and he motions for me to come inside.

I quietly lock the door as it closes behind me and I let Doug show me around his office. It's modestly sized and there isn't much to see, but it's impressive enough and it has a nice view of the city. He's telling me all about the new, larger accounts they've given him, and how the responsibility seems daunting yet manageable. I try to listen but my mind is still stuck *outside* his office, sitting next to the hot piece of ass that will be greeting my husband every morning.

More sharp twinges of jealousy cut into my side and I realize I have to do something about all of this bottled-up anxiety. An idea hits me and my lips curl into a devious grin, one that cuts Doug off mid-sentence. He looks at me with narrowed eyes and we're suddenly conversing in an unspoken language, just as we had done in our halcyon days.

I walk slowly toward him. My sudden prowl must be unnerving because he backs away and into the floor-to-ceiling glass windows that overlook downtown. I pull the hair tie from my ponytail and my hair falls down my shoulders. I'm feet away from him as he tries to speak.

"Ange, wh- what's going on?" he asks with a nervous giggle.

I put a finger to his lips and close the distance between us. "I think you know *exactly* what's going on," I say softly. I lean in close to whisper in his ear. "Don't worry, I locked the door."

My hand slides down the front of his freshly minted suit pants and I give his crotch a gentle squeeze. The nervousness in his grin fades when I press my lips against his. We kiss with a passion that was prominent when we were young and stupid, and I wonder why I'm doing this. I'm questioning where my motivations lie, and how much is fueled by this irrational jealousy I now feel over my husband.

I decide that the time for questions is over and I drop to my knees. I unbutton his slacks, then pull them and his boxer briefs down to his ankles. He's rock-hard as I take him in my mouth. I cup his balls with my hand, giving them a gentle tug as I bob my head back and forth.

His fingers tangle in my hair as he exhales soft moans of pleasure, and I have a sudden urge to increase his volume. I hold onto his hips and guide him deeper into my mouth, reveling in the control I have over him. His short, labored breaths and quivering legs make me feel triumphant, each of his thrusts filling me with victorious pride.

"I... Ange.. I'm gonna..." he stutters, but I refuse to relent. Instead, I pick up the pace, my cheeks hollowing as I take more and more of him down my throat.

His knees buckle as he finishes, one final gasp of ecstasy escaping him. His eyes are wide with lustful surprise, an expression I relish in and store away for later.

I plop myself down in Doug's executive leather chair, allowing him a moment to regain his composure and pull his pants back up. He thanks me for the "lovely surprise" and promises to return the favor. I tell him that (for once) I'm not worried about it, and I actually mean it. I no longer feel that nervous energy swirling inside me.

A few minutes later, Doug and I are walking out of his office hand-in-hand, and he tells Julia that he's going out to lunch. She says "Okay, Mr. Rivers, have a good lunch!" and as we walk toward the elevator I take one final look back over my shoulder. I wink at her and she flashes me an awkward smile in return.

I'm witnessing Doug step up and into the role of the ideal father and husband. Our lives rarely see a dull moment as weekends start to fill up with activities we previously didn't have the time or money for. By day we attend ball games, amusement parks, aquariums, and zoos. No expense is spared and our daughters are spoiled rotten. By night, Doug and I dine in upscale restaurants, attend Broadway plays (*not* mindless action movies), and afterwards he ravishes me with the sexual prowess of a Greek god. And I'm happy to report that we are no longer restricted to just *one* position. In fact, we fuck in *all* of the positions. Gone are the days of me soullessly grinding on top of him, fantasizing about someone else, and *praying* he doesn't finish before me.

Some days I do feel like this uptick in orgasms is going straight to my head. The line that separates what's real and not real blurs easily if I stare at it too long. Doug's transformation has been... *comprehensive*, with the rate of his shapeshifting increasing each day. The wrinkles and lines in his face smooth out. His eyes—the ones I looked into as we recited our wedding vows—are no longer his own. His touch is always gentle and passionate, yet void of any semblance to the "real Doug".

The night of his birthday, I had cast a penny into the wishing well, praying for the man of my dreams. And here he was, in the flesh. Doug is perfect in every sense of the word. I no longer feel like a footnote within his life, or even my own for that matter. I *am* his life. I no longer need to fantasize about better men—*sexier* men. I'm just as excited as the girls are when he arrives home each day. But when he takes me into his embrace, those sculpted arms holding me close, the heart that beats against my chest doesn't feel like the same one that captured my own.

Part VI

I'm propped up in bed and sifting through the latest pop-news gossip on my tablet. I look up when I hear a few random, staggered grunts from outside the bedroom. Doug is shuffling sideways down the hall, carrying the enlarged family portrait that hangs in our living room. After crossing the threshold, he lumbers over to my side of the bed and props up the enormous frame so I can see it.

"Ange, what's wrong with this picture?" he asks, his tone insinuating a pop-quiz rather than a genuine question.

I study the portrait for a moment. It's several years old, so Samantha and Rebecca were practically *babies* compared to how they look now. The Doug standing next to me wasn't *just* my husband 75 pounds heavier, he was a completely different man than who is currently holding the frame. The biggest shock is me. Somehow, I look *happy* in my posed position alongside my family.

"Um... it's *old*?" I guess.

Doug points an enthusiastic finger at me as if I'd just won The Price is Right. "Yes, *exactly*! What would you think about having an updated portrait taken? You know, since your *amazing* husband has dropped a few pounds, and *you* of course look just as stunning as ever. Plus, the girls have grown like *weeds* in the last couple of years!"

Under normal circumstances I'd *jump* at the opportunity to schedule a new family portrait. Except these *aren't* normal circumstances. The man in the photograph and the man holding it? They are *not* the same person, in *every* sense of the word. And I'm not thrilled about the idea of permanently commemorating that fact. However, since Doug *had* been well-behaved for the first family photo. I suppose it's only fair that I return the favor.

It's now a month later, and I'm watching Doug from the living room couch. His muscles flex and splay as he maneuvers the new framed portrait onto the wall hook. I'm concerned for the integrity of his t-shirt as his swollen build threatens the seams. Perhaps it'll *shred* off, "Hulk Hogan" style.

Oh brother...

The new family photo with its custom frame is obscenely large. It's at least twice as big, and three times more expensive than its predecessor. Doug, however, was all smiles when handing over the credit card to pay for it.

I'm still conflicted about Doug's seemingly impossible evolution—the one that only *I* seem to notice, for some reason. I know deep down that this isn't my husband. It *can't* be. The person standing before me exudes an aura of sophistication and gentleness that was foreign to the man I married.

Despite my hesitations, my primal instincts still surge with desire. I am overcome with an animalistic magnetism when I'm around him. Even now I can *feel* the wetness between my legs as I gaze at him, this romance novel love interest brought to life.

Doug and I stand side by side and marvel at the hung portrait in silence. He places a hand on my hip and pulls me close to him.

I instinctively rest my head on his hard, bulky shoulder, and a wave of melancholia crashes over me. The happy family on the wall stares back, a moment forever captured in time. It's a representation of our altogether *perfect* life, and yet so blatantly disingenuous.

"You are absolutely *stunning*, honey," Doug says, his tone reverent and reflective. "And the girls have *never* looked more beautiful. You have truly done an *amazing* job raising this family of ours."

"I look... *frigid*," I sneer. "I feel like I don't belong in this picture."

"*Hey*," Doug says, turning to face me, "you are the *backbone* of our family. Everything would fall apart if it wasn't for you. And I don't just mean that literally, babe. Because your posture is impeccable! Have you been taking your pilates to the next level?"

I wipe away an unexpected tear as my eyes roll from his mollycoddling. This newly developed technique of his—the ability to placate and diffuse tension—is just another tool in his belt that makes him the *best husband ever*. And I *fucking hate* it. Never in my life would I have predicted me complaining about Doug being *too* nice. Am I *completely* pathetic? Perhaps I'm a lunatic, masquerading in a skin-tight smile suit.

The portrait's been hanging for a week now, and tonight we have our old friends James and Darcy over for dinner. The four of us met in college and were tight-knit until Doug and I moved out to California. We lost touch for a number of years, but thanks to social media we were able to reconnect and passively keep up with each other's lives.

When they arrive, they *too* are blown away by Doug's metamorphosis. A never-ending slew of jokes ensue, citing their disbelief that *this* was the same doughy oaf from Biology 101.

I'm chatting with Darcy, catching up on lost time over our first bottle of white wine. I catch occasional glances of the men on our renovated deck. From my position in the kitchen I can see James watching over Doug as he sears several cuts of expensive red meat on our new grill. Every other minute they throw their heads back in laughter, undoubtedly reminiscing over old times.

"*So*, Doug's lost quite a bit of weight, yeah?" Darcy suggests, taking a sip of wine.

"Yep, he *sure* has!" My smile is wide and shit-eating, and I'm curious how well this manufactured enthusiasm is masking my contempt.

"I almost didn't recognize him when we arrived! You must be *so* proud of him and all the progress he's made."

"Oh, I am. It certainly was... *unexpected*!"

"Really? What do you mean?"

I pause for a moment and consider how I can best illustrate to Darcy the depth of this rabbit hole. I could simply shine a flashlight and let her imagination fill in the rest. *Or*, I could grab her by the shirt collar and drag her down to hell with me.

Fuck it.

I lean in toward Darcy and soften my tone. "To be completely honest? I got him the health club membership as a *joke*. I thought it'd be... *funny*."

Her mouth curls into a weak smile, eyes peering at me. "I don't understand. How is that a joke?"

"Oh, you know. Just to watch him struggle, and *finally* recognize that he had a weight problem. I suppose it sounded a lot better in my head."

Darcy's face shifts into an odd, quizzical look, as if I'd just delivered the world's most tasteless punchline. So I backtrack and mop up after my spilled the beans.

"*Thankfully* all of that blew up in my face! Because Doug *did* end up losing a bunch of weight. And now, things between us are... better than ever, I suppose."

I breathe a quiet sigh of relief as Darcy's expression retreats back to its rightfully tipsy state.

Now it's her turn to lean in, a sly grin forming on her face. "Ok, so I *have* to ask... how's the sex? I mean, it must be *fantastic*, right? I bet Doug has stamina for *days*."

Her question makes me cringe, and memories come flooding back from the last time Doug and I fucked (earlier this afternoon, *for those playing at home*). He's now the most gentle, caring, and assertive lover that any *rational* woman could only dream of. But it doesn't change the fact that it *literally* feels like having sex with a stranger.

I bite my lip anxiously, taking another glance outside at Doug and James. I'm praying for them to come in and break up this nonsensical conversation.

"Oh *come on*, Ange!" Darcy insists. "It's just us girls. Now come on and dish!"

Alright, bitch, you asked for it.

"Okay, *fine*," I say with a defeated grin. "Every single time we fuck now, Doug *always* goes down on me. And I'm not talking about a half-assed, 60-second 'wham-bam, thank you ma'am' either. He's down there for ten minutes, *minimum*. And when I come, I come *hard*. Last night, I squeezed his head so hard with my thighs that I thought it was going to explode like a watermelon."

Darcy chokes on her wine and spirals into a coughing fit. I reach for the bottle to fill up her glass and continue obliging my old friend without skipping a beat.

"Then, once I'm nice and wet, he *glides* into me with that *enormous* cock of his—it's somehow gotten *bigger* with the weight loss.

Did you know that's a thing? Anyways. For thirty minutes he fucks me like a prize-winning stallion. I'm telling you, Darcy, *porn stars* don't get fucked this good.

"Now, I know what you're thinking. 'Thirty minutes? *Really?*' Yes, really. And he *always* uses that time wisely. We've tried every position in the book. Doug has bent me into all sorts of crazy angles, all while touching places inside me I didn't even know *existed*. My husband has made a *contortionist* out of me, I tell you what. And it's only after I've had about five or six orgasms when Doug himself finally finishes. He would even suck it out of me if I asked him to clean up after himself."

Darcy stares back at me, frozen and mouth agape, with a mixed expression of shock, horror, and (*I'm guessing*) a bit of jealousy. I nod slowly, my eyes wide and confirming, and I take a long sip of wine. Doug and James walk though the back door in an act of perfect timing, carrying a large platter of grilled steaks.

"Mmm, smells *great*, babe!" I tell Doug enthusiastically as I gave him a peck on the cheek.

He kisses me back, but the enamored expression on his face fades as he catches sight of Darcy's stone-cold demeanor.

"Whoa, Darcy, are you okay? Looks like you've just seen a ghost!" Doug's tone is playful yet concerned.

A weak smile begins to spread across her face. "Oh- *yes*, I'm *so* sorry," she says, shaking her head, "Angela and I, we were just... um... talking about..."

"*You*," I finish. "We were just talking about *you*, honey, and how *amazing* you are."

I give Darcy a wink that says a thousand things all at once.

It says *"Yes, all of what I just told you is true"*.

It said *"Yes, my husband fucks me better than yours ever could"*.

It also says *"Darcy, please be careful what you wish for"*.

The four of us eat and drink long into the night, polishing off several bottles of wine and glasses of whiskey. When we all run out of things to talk about, the conversation naturally loops back around to Doug's *astonishing* weight-loss.

"You really do look amazing, Doug," James says. "I mean, you're more physically fit *now* than you were back in college!"

"Oh, *come on*," Doug replies bashfully with a friendly wave, "all that flattery is uncalled for, my friend. Besides, Angela here is the *real* hero. She's the one who got me the gift certificate in the first place! And she's been *so* supportive every step of the way. She and the girls are the best cheerleaders a man could ask for."

Our old friends gaze upon my husband and I with adoring eyes. Doug gives me *another* loving smooch, and I grin from ear to ear like a perfect, *obedient* Stepford Wife.

Secretly, though? I'm grabbing my steak knife and *lunge* across the table toward our friends. My arms outstretched, I clothesline them both to the floor. Then I'm carving their eyes out of their skulls, and even in this fantasy I can feel the warm blood spurting up onto my smiling face. I shove the eyeballs into their gaping mouths to muffle their obnoxious screaming. But even *that's* not enough to shut them up, so I drive the knife down into their hearts to be done with it.

Doug is frozen, watching all of this unfold in uncomprehending revulsion. And I think to myself, *what an asshole he is for believing he's blameless in this. How dare he be shocked over the monster he's created.*

So I come at him with the knife raised high like Norman Bates in the shower scene (or at the top of the staircase). He's so appalled at the sight of me and the spectacle I've created that he trips and falls when he backs away. Now I'm straddling him at the waist (*just like the good ole days, right?*) and I begin cutting off his face, just making a *real big* mess of things, right there in the middle of our dining room. And once it is only his bleeding, *gory* skull staring up at me, I toss his face skin aside and breathe a sigh of relief.

"Angela? Earth to *Angela!*" Doug's voice ushers me back into the real world, and I give them an apologetic smile.

"I'm sorry, guys," I say with a laugh, "I guess I zoned out for a second. What were we talking about?"

"Just how your husband is practically a new man, and is making us all look bad!" James says this and the three of them burst into idiotic, *ear-splitting* cackles.

"Oh, so you *agree*, then?" I ask James.

Still laughing, he gives me a quizzical look. "Wh-what do you mean?"

"That Doug is a new man."

Their collective laughter slowly fades as they recognize my seriousness.

"Do you agree, James, that Doug *really is* a new man?" I press further.

His eyes dart between Doug and Darcy, desperately searching for help. "Well, of *course*, in a... manner of speaking," he says with a nervous smile.

"Yeah, *relax* Ange," Darcy says, coming to her husband's rescue, "it's just a... figure of speech, you know?"

There's another brief spell of anxious laughter from the table as I continue to glare at them, unamused. I reach into my purse and pull out a wallet-sized version of our family portrait—the *old* one—and slam in on the table. The plates and glassware rattle in the dead silence I've manufactured.

"Then tell me *why*, James," I say through gritted teeth, "tell me why my husband in *this* photograph is a *completely* different person from the man in *that* photograph?" I point aggressively to the new portrait that hangs in our living room.

James and Darcy glare at Doug wide-eyed, hoping for some direction—or intervention. They are out of luck because my husband is *also* slack-jawed and at a loss for words.

I rise from my seat amidst this awkward silence, and march over to the new family portrait. I clumsily pluck it from the wall (Doug had made the handling of it look *so* effortless) and walk it back to the dining room. After propping it against the wall, I study it mockingly as if it were a provocative piece of art.

"Hey Ange?" Doug says, finally speaking up, "I think James and Darcy just wanted to point out that—"

"Point out *what*, Doug?" I ask, my tone dripping with unbridled resentment. "That I'm going *nuts*? That I'm only *imagining* things?"

Doug gets up from his seat and cautiously makes his way toward me. He resembles someone who's trying to corner and cage a wild animal.

"Honey, James and Darcy were *only* being polite, okay?" Doug says calmly. He then turns to the portrait and gestures at it, still wearing his award-winning smile. "I mean, just *look* at us in this portrait. We've *all* changed, the *four* of us!"

"No, *you've* changed, Doug," I declare, jabbing my bony index finger into his swollen, beefy chest. "What have they been doing to you in that health club, huh? What do they do while you're there? What do *you* do while you're there? *Tell me* what has happened to my husband!"

My frustrated screams reverberate off of every wall in our home. From the corners of my tear-soaked eyes, I see Darcy reaching under the table for her purse and James fumbling with his car keys. Any *rational* woman would apologize at this point, or at the very least excuse herself for upsetting the dinner party. But I *am* rational, and these fucking idiots *refuse* to admit the glaringly obvious.

James and Darcy have made their way to our foyer, and Doug's attention is anxiously ping-ponging between them and me. I shuffle off Doug's light grip on my shoulders and stomp over to the fireplace to grab one of the cast iron pokers.

"Alright, guys, it was great catching up!" I call out to our friends who standing in the doorway, frozen and horrified. "But before you go, you guys *really* should see my final act! Just in case you had *any* doubts about how *fucking bonkers* I really am!"

My husband dodges me as I charge back to the new family portrait, the poker held high in the air. I stand over the framed photo for a brief moment, recognizing it's beautiful and expensive frame. I glare at our two beautiful daughters in their matching outfits. I stare daggers at the man that is my husband but *not* my husband. Finally I meet the eyes of myself, remembering how on that day it took every ounce of energy within me to *force* that smile onto my face.

I come down on the portrait with the fireplace poker with all the power I have in my small, fueled-by-pilates frame. My first strike creates a spiderweb of cracked glass that spreads in all directions, distorting our perfect faces. My second strike results in a full shattering of the glass pane and I can feel shards crop up and nick my skin. The poker penetrates the shattered glass on the third strike. It tears a hole straight through the portrait *and* the drywall, and I have to tug *hard* on the iron poker to get it free.

Doug and our friends stare at me, transfixed, too horrified to make any movement. I can feel the weight of their worried eyes, but I don't dare look up to meet them. My sights are set solely on the dead ones that mock me behind the shattered glass. Aside from that fractured facade, my tantrum has only resulted in slicing open a large gap across my posed body. My face curls into an insidious grin, and I jerk back the poker and strike at it again. And then again. And again. And again. And suddenly I'm an unhinged Jack Torrance, hoping to cut down the poor, cowering Wendy.

When there is nothing left of our beautiful family but a mangled mess of splintered wood and broken glass, only then do I notice that James and Darcy have retreated to their car. I make my way to the foyer in a mad dash—the fireplace poker still clutched tightly in my right hand—and swing open the front door. I wave goodbye from our front porch as I glare at them like an insane person. Their headlights flick on and cast a large, ominous shadow of me against the brick facade of our home. And as our friends' car hurriedly backs out of our driveway, maniacal laughter erupts from deep within my chest to pierce the tranquil night air.

Part VII

It's hard to tell how much time has passed since my little... *outburst*—the one that concluded our reunion with James and Darcy in *spectacular* fashion. Weeks? Months, maybe? Who knows, and *who cares*. Not me, that's for sure.

It would've been *completely* understandable for Doug to scream in my face and tell me how *irrational* I behaved that night. If he wanted to call me a drunk or nutcase for causing a scene and destroying our new family portrait, he'd be well within his rights to do so. And if he were to drive off with Samantha and Rebecca, leaving me to stew in my own mess, no one—*especially* me—would blame him.

None of that happened, though, which made things even *worse*. It was like the elephant in the room had grown into a monster, devouring any sense of normalcy in my life. What is real and what isn't? I can no longer trust my own perception. The uncertainty has left me feeling lost and helpless.

I don't really have to worry about much these days, thanks to my new therapist who prescribes me pills. Between him and Doug, most of the burdens of everyday life have been *lifted* from these well-toned shoulders. We've also outsourced a lot of our menial errands and chores. Most days I don't even have to worry about shuttling the girls to and from school. We have a part-time nanny to take care of that, now. So now I am free to do a whole lot of fuck-all, every day, all day long.

The rushes of excitement that I once craved have become a *bore*, now that they occur on a daily basis. With yet *another* promotion and pay raise, Doug has officially reached a status that ensures none of us will want for anything. Our family has taken countless trips and vacations. Doug has fucked me more times—*and* in more places—than I can count. Exotic beaches, restrooms of exclusive bars and nightclubs, fitting rooms of high-end department stores; you name the place, and my husband has *probably* been inside me there.

The girls are at school, Doug is at work, and I am in the bathroom standing idly over the toilet. I'm staring at the prescription bottle in my hand with narrowed eyes, and I'm trying to decide if the pills inside are my enemy or my friend. It's been several days since I've last taken one of the little pink capsules, and I think I'm getting better. I can *feel* things again. My vision is clear like it was not long ago.

I shrug my shoulders, then turn the bottle upside down. The pills make little plinking sounds as they all hit the toilet water. A smile starts to grow on my face as I watch them spin around and around, disappearing through the drain to join the rest of the waste.

I'm sitting at the dining room table. The empty pill bottle is cradled loosely in my hand, and I'm staring at the impeccable patchwork that was done on the drywall. The hole that I had made there with the fireplace poker had been promptly filled in, leaving no signs of damage. This makes me laugh unexpectedly because, in a way, it's an accurate representation of what my life has become. There is no problem that can't be fixed. No hole that can't be patched up. There is no margin for error, because errors are no longer possible.

I feel the clouds parting in my brain in real time, and I can once more visualize my life with clarity. I walk to the kitchen to retrieve my purse. While I'm there I grab a pen, a few sheets of paper, and a plain white envelope, then return to my seat in the dining room.

I take my time with the letter, scratching out certain lines, making corrections along the way, until I'm happy with the final draft. I sign it with my name. Above it I struggle with the decision of whether to put "Sincerely" or "Love". As I wipe away a tear—my first since the night of our dinner party—I decide on the latter.

I take one final look at the old wallet-sized family portrait. I force back more tears as I run a finger down the faces of my daughters, and then Doug, and then myself. This was the family I had; the family I knew. But the girls are older now, still sweet and innocent, but not as they once were. And *Doug*... well, I don't think I need to explain my feelings there.

I kiss the photograph once before placing it in the center of the letter. I crease it into three folds, then stuff it into the envelope. After placing the letter on the kitchen counter where Doug can see, I walk into our bathroom and turn the shower on. I go to my closet and decide on an outfit while the water heats up. I get undressed and step into the steamy shower. I don't bother shampooing my hair, but I do masturbate one last time. When I do, I fantasize about Doug—the way he once *was*, before I went and fucked everything up.

I'm sitting in the driver's seat of our SUV, wearing my most expensive outfit, and I'm watching the garage fill up with CO_2 emissions. I start to feel tired, lightheaded, and for a moment I see a new life for our family. All of us are happy, myself included. I can't tell if this is us a year ago, several years ago, or maybe some multiverse variant of our family. But in the end it doesn't matter, because it's a world where our problems don't have immediate solutions. It's a life that's difficult, and complicated, and frustrating, and beautiful. Things in that world aren't perfect, and somehow that's just fine.

The music on the radio is muffled, incoherent. My grip on the steering wheel loosens, hands falling into my lap. I begin drifting off to sleep, my world slowly fading into black. But there's an abrupt, brilliant burst of light that forces my lids back open, and I am suddenly reborn. Everything is in slow motion as a man in a suit pulls me from the car. My last vision before falling asleep, cradled like a baby in my husband's arms, is the garage door closing, and I'm placed on top of a mountain of pillows.

As it turns out, I picked the *wrong day* to attempt a suicide.

Between going off my prescribed medication, and just losing my shit in general, I managed to get my days mixed up. Doug was only scheduled to work until noon that day, and he found me in the garage when he arrived home.

Just in the nick of time.

The whole incident was papered over nicely, to the point where only Doug and my therapist were aware of it. And honestly, that's probably for the best.

The therapist recommended an increased dosage of my medication. I thought about fighting it. I finally opened up to him about my thoughts on Doug's transformation. Until this recent re-evaluation, I had been a closed book on the matter. I was in no way interested in detailing my steady decline into insanity to this weird stranger. Most of all, I think I was afraid of telling the truth about why I had given Doug his birthday gift. There was no way of telling what might happen if I decided to pull on that particular thread.

So in the end I acquiesced. Aside from his birthday present being a practical joke, I told the therapist about everything. He didn't seem at all concerned about my perceptions of Doug's metamorphosis. I suppose it's kind of his job to say things like "No, I don't think you're crazy" and "Sure, believing that your husband is a shapeshifter is a completely rational response to his weight loss". After I spilled the beans, I'm honestly shocked they didn't toss me in the looney bin. So in a way, I'm grateful that all I got was more meds and a temporary suicide watch.

On the home-front, we sold our home, and that old SUV. We then upgraded to one of the nicest neighborhoods that northern California has to offer. Our new home—which is nothing short of a mansion—is still *thankfully* within a reasonable commuting distance for my therapist, Doug's job, and of course *New You*. Doug is happy. The girls are happy. And I'm...

As I sit in my shiny new car with its *luxurious* leather interior, I'd like to recount to you one last anecdote before I bid you farewell. It's a story that feels appropriate to tell for what I'm about to do. And don't worry, it's *not* what you think. I'm not going to try and off myself again.

Last week, I was pushing an empty shopping cart around the grocery store—which is kind of funny, considering that's where this whole thing started. And there was no particular reason for me to be there, since we now have people that take care of our shopping *for* us. But there I was anyway, a head full of air and a body full of pills, staring blankly at the seemingly *endless* isle of cereal.

Suddenly, I catch sight of a man who was picking out a box of Raisin Bran. There was nothing particularly special about this guy. In fact, one *could* make the argument that he was the most generic, boring-looking dude to ever be dreamt of in human history. He wore a khaki jacket, a pair of loose-fitting dad jeans that did absolutely *nothing* for his ass, and a generic polo shirt with a few minor stains. His facial hair was too long to be a sexy five o'clock shadow, and too short to be called a beard. His thinning hair was slicked to the side in a glorious combover. In every sense of the word, this man was *ordinary*.

And yet, I decided to *follow* him. For half an hour I observed this man as he plucked items from shelves. He shopped with the air of a dutiful husband, sometimes comparing an item to his paper grocery list, and then would ultimately place it in his cart. Or not.

Something *unexpected* began to happen to me in this curious state. For the first time in what felt like *ages*, I started to fantasize about this man. And although there was *nothing* sexual about him, I could *not* keep myself from imagining his thick, clumsy hands massaging my shoulders. I thought about how wonderfully ordinary his naked body might look as it writhed on top of me, *not really* pleasuring me with his average-sized penis. I smiled at the thought of how tired I might be at the end of a *long* day, and he would still hold out hope that I'd put out. And then I would sigh and tug my underwear down in an *almost* obligatory manner.

The irony of all this was—and *still is*—not lost on me. I'd like to think I've retained *some* level of self-awareness, which might explain why I ended up here in the first place: Sitting in my car, in the parking lot of the *New You* health club. My knuckles are white as I grip the steering wheel, watching the droves of unattainably attractive people move in and out of the building. In my clearest state of mind, I know that I am *nothing* like these people.

Me? I'm just a mom of two beautiful girls. A woman on the *wrong* side of 40, who does pilates alongside free YouTube videos. I'm just the wife of an insanely attractive husband who looks like he hopped off the front cover of the latest issue of GQ magazine. I'm just plain old Angela, who gets ketchup stains on her clothes and mows her front yard and tries to kill herself in the garage.

These people, walking in and out of the building with its shiny windows and freshly-painted facade, they all look so fucking *happy*. So happy, and so impeccable, and infallible.

And I think, *How dare they be so content, and proud, and blissfully unaware of what they're doing to their loved ones?*

Do they not know how their actions are affecting the people that care about them? And I also think that maybe I was right; maybe I *am* going insane.

I step out of my car and walk to the front of the building. Some asshole in a sleeveless shirt stands there to hold the door open for me. His smile is as blinding as the reflections off the building itself. I walk through the door without saying "thank you" and approach the receptionist at the front desk.

"Hi, can I help you?" She asks with a perfectly punchable smile.

And I say, "Yes, you can, actually. I'd like to fill out a membership application, please."

"Well, I guess this is growing up."
— BLINK-182, "DAMMIT," *DUDE RANCH* (1997)

"Hey, hey, hey, hey. Smoke weed every day."
— DR. DRE & SNOOP DOGG, "THE NEXT
EPISODE," *2001* (1999)

CHAPTER 5

Not If, But When

Part I

"Come on, Darko, answer the phone!"

I'm pacing around my apartment in a frantic haze, smartphone gripped tightly in hand. Each passing second is agony as my dealer's dial tone trills incessantly.

"Please, *dude*, pick up your damn phone!"

I feel like a complete mess. I *look* like a complete mess. My body, my hair, my shirt, they're all greasy with sweat, and not just because of the scorching, late-July heat. I'm still praying to the old gods and new that my dealer will pick up the phone any second.

"*Darko...* I *swear*, if you don't—"

The trilling of the line comes to an end, and the outgoing voicemail message kicks in. Darko's prerecorded stoner voice is not the one I want to hear right now.

"*Hey, you've reached the cellular device of Donnie 'Darko' Sullivan. I'm either busy doing other stuff or ignoring your call. Either way, feel free to leave me a message.*"

The tinny beep that follows is the final twist of the knife. "Hey Darko, it's Craig," I begin with a defeated sigh. "Look, it's an emergency. I just smoked my last bowl. Sorry for the late notice, dude, but if you could call me back soon I'd appreciate it. Thanks."

Damn. I really miss the days when you could slam a phone back in its cradle. How are you supposed to prove your anger when ending a call on a smartphone? Push really hard on the red circle? *So* stupid.

I plop down on my sofa and feel myself sink into the torn pleather cushions. My head is swimming, and not just because of the Skywalker OG Kush I just smoked. I can't remember the last time I was left without my "medicine". And that's not a joke, either. It might sound like one, me being a stoner and all. But I really can't recall when I accidentally let my supply run this low.

I'm what the cannabis community calls a "functional stoner". I have a salaried position at a thriving, agile company. My apartment is tastefully appointed by all things clearance from IKEA. I pay the note on my Toyota Prius on time every month. And yes, I enjoy smoking "the devil's lettuce" and getting higher than giraffe pussy.

But I'm not really thinking about work or my flimsy furniture right now. I've got my mind trained on Darko, hoping that any second now he'll return my call. It's partially—okay, *mostly*—my fault for waiting until the last second before requesting a refill. CVS automatically refills my medication. Would it be that big of an ask for my dealer to do the same?

His real name isn't Darko, by the way—it's Donnie, or Donald. He adopted "Darko" a while back because of that movie with Jake Gyllenhaal and the freaky looking rabbit. I think he watched it at just the right time in his life, and it ended up changing his perspective on... well, pretty much everything. He tries to get me to watch it with him whenever I pick up my ounce. I don't mind it, it's an interesting flick. But I'm more of a comedy guy, ya know? *Tropic Thunder*, *Pineapple Express*, *Step Brothers*. Now *those* are modern-day stoner classics.

A shock of excitement crackles through me when my phone vibrates. I tell myself that it *has* to be Darko, as if there's no other option. It's not him, though—it's *Jane*. My heart leaps again at the sight of her name in my notifications. I tap it right away to read her message.

> Hey Craig. I was hoping to come by your apartment later today. My laptop charger broke, and I could really use the spare one I accidentally left behind. If you could just set it outside your door, I think that'd be for the best. Thanks.

I resist the urge to chuck my phone at the wall—I've already destroyed *one* phone post-breakup. Jane gave me the "stanky boot" earlier this year, a month or two before the pandemic lockdown. *Excellent* timing, really.

At the start of our separation, she left a bunch of stuff at my apartment: Cosmetics, a hair straightener, a backpack, underwear, lotion. They were things she kept here when we were together, to make sleepovers easier. Over the last six weeks I've watched those items disappear, one by one. I barely batted an eye when the unimportant things went first. But now, inside the vacant dresser drawer, only one item remains. And after today, when the charger is gone, only the ghost of Jane will remain.

Fuck it. Maybe it's for the best.

After placing her charger in a plastic grocery bag and setting it outside my apartment as she requested, I tell myself things like "It's fine, no big deal" and "We're just taking a break, there's no need to panic." Even though everything is clearly *not* fine. I simply add it to the growing list of things I'm in denial of, ranking it right up there alongside "working from home."

What was supposed to be a pretty sweet, albeit *temporary*, situation is currently teaching me the true definition of "cabin fever."

Living alone and working from home is only cool if you're able to go out and socialize in your free time. However, when everything is closed and your girlfriend has broken up with you, it becomes a lonely and isolating experience. Being confined to my home has shown me that running out of weed and entertainment can turn into a special kind of torture, made worse by the fact that my dealer won't answer his phone.

My pot-induced haze has lifted and all of these conundrums seem to hit me all at once. How long will it take me to fall asleep tonight without the help of my little green friend? *Will I* sleep tonight? Surely it won't be *that* bad. Right?

Part II

My first night without the aid of cannabis *sucked*. Sleep was a *cock-tease* if there ever was one. Just as soon as that unmistakable drowsiness seemed to be settling in it would scramble away, cackling, giving me the middle finger. I retaliated against my insomnia in my own way—by beating my dick furiously. And thanks to that attempt at purposefully wearing myself out, I now know that angry masturbating is *not* a good color on me—even if I'm doing it in the name of sleep.

According to the data on my smartwatch I finally drifted off after 4 AM. However, my internal clock, the *true* asshole that it is, forced me awake only a few hours later. I reached for my phone, eyelids feeling like anvils, and I breathed a frustrated groan—nothing from Darko, nothing from Jane.

I've successfully dragged my limp body out of bed and put the coffee on. The way I shuffle around my apartment reminds me of *Weekend at Bernie's*, except I'm playing the role of the dead guy *and* the two dudes that have to hold him up. I open my front door to see that the bag with Jane's laptop charger is gone. *That's it, then.* No follow-up text saying "thanks" or "got it". I guess Jane really *wasn't* kidding when she asked for a clean break with no communication.

I was totally shocked when she asked for some time apart. It *seemed* like things were going so well. I had reached a dating checkpoint with Jane that far surpassed any from my previous relationships. We even said the "L" word to each other. But I suppose that ain't enough glue to hold things together.

The smell of freshly percolated coffee fills my tiny studio apartment as I maneuver to my desk, stepping through the ocean of clutter and dirty clothes along the way. I power on my work laptop and I begin checking emails, ignoring my eyelids that are threatening to slam shut like bank vault doors. Like any other given morning my inbox is replete with newly opened bug tickets, fires to put out, clients to call, and a handful of Zoom meetings that should undoubtedly be emails.

My morning wears on in a sluggish march, punctuated by the dull drone of workplace responsibilities and the incessant clattering of keyboard strokes. My thoughts constantly circle back to Darko like a moth to flame; I'm only checking my phone every 30 seconds or so. But he remains elusive as ever. No calls, no texts—*nothing*.

I have never felt more drained of ambition as I do in this moment. My lack of sleep has robbed me of any sense of self-preservation. I have no girlfriend, and no weed. *Everything* is shut down. Might as well be relegated to the mountains of Tibet, sentenced to live out a monotonous, sexless existence.

I *think* the clock on my computer monitor says "11:03 AM" when I sense my world start to go black. Holding my eyes open is an impossibility. I have officially given up fighting back sleep when there's a knock at my front door that snaps me back to reality. The sudden rapping sends adrenaline rushing into my system. *What if it's Darko?* He *could* be making a surprise house-call. Or maybe it's Jane. She's come back once more, because she's finally come to her senses and wants to get back together.

I'm wobbly on my feet as I saunter over to the front door. While half of my brain may still be in bed, the other half is like exploding firecrackers, excited at the possibilities. But the hope drains from me as I peer through the dirty peephole. Regrettably, it's not Darko *or* Jane on the other side but some dude wearing a mail carrier uniform.

"Delivery for Thompson," he says, bored and nonchalant as he hands over a small package.

I stare at it, confused and disappointed. Who could possibly be sending me something? I haven't ordered anything recently, I don't think.

Back inside my apartment I rip open the cardboard box to reveal... a giant bag of *weed*! It's an entire freezer bag full of luscious, *beautiful* bud. Holding the bag up close to my face, I marvel at the dark green cloves with little squiggles of purple. Peeling open the seal I take in the sweet and tangy smells, noting delightful hints of citrus.

There's a note inside the box.

Sorry I missed your call, dude. Let me make it up to you with this giant bag of herb! Enjoy, brother!

- Love, Darko

Oh Darko, you *beautiful bastard*! I just *knew* you'd come through!

Letting his note fall to the floor I pick up the bag of weed, holding it up proudly like a would-be king. I then upend the bag and let all the bud tumble out onto my face. I catch a few of the nugs in my mouth and chew on them with glorious fury. It's sticky and delicious, and I can't wait to put this in my pipe and smoke it.

A dog barking furiously outside my living room window jerks me awake. I scramble to wipe the drool off my cheek, realizing that it's almost noon and I have fallen asleep at my cluttered desk. The sunlight streams through the sheer curtains, casting a warm glow in the room. Outside, the incessant barking continues, accompanied by the distant sound of cars passing by. I stretch and yawn, feeling stiff from sleeping in an uncomfortable position.

There had been no generous care package containing the sweet medicine that I so *desperately* need. How cruel it was for my mind to play such games. What's odd, though, is I have this unmistakable taste of weed in my mouth. In my bizarre dream, I was eating it like some sort of ravenous freak. And now, I can actually *taste it* on my tongue.

I take a sip of my now-cold coffee to rid the lingering tang. Wincing, I can't tell which of the two is worse. Setting the mug down, I glance at my monitor and notice a slew of notifications, with coworkers trying to reach me. My brain is still partially trapped inside dreamland as I draft generic responses to each one.

Just before dinner I decide to try Darko again. *Just in case.* But it's the same thing—voicemail. Fucking *voicemail*. What kind of dealer doesn't answer his fucking phone? What kind of half-assed business model is that? How are you supposed to fulfill your customers' orders when you're off the grid?

A lightning bolt of guilt shoots through me as I consider a possibility: what if Darko's got Covid? What if he's laid up in bed or knocking on death's door? There's no vaccine for this thing yet, so there's no telling what he could be going through right now.

I toss my phone on the counter and rub my temples. *Christ on a cracker*, what the *fuck* am I gonna do? I *could* make a trip to the drug store and buy all of their melatonin gummies. Is it possible to overdose on Unisom?

Part III

I'm lounging on the couch in the living room, mindlessly staring at a box of stuff my dad just dropped off. It's starting to hit me just how much this whole "social distancing" thing sucks. The mundane routine of each day is wearing on me, and not *only* because I ran out of weed. I barely sleep, and when I do it's nothing but nightmares. Entertainment options like Netflix and video games, while objectively abundant, have become boring as hell. And the absence of Jane has never felt more real. So when my pops mentioned he had some things to bring by, I was genuinely excited for some company and to see a friendly face—*any* face, really.

To my dismay, however, he dropped it on my welcome mat, knocked on my door, and ran back to his car like a friggin' UPS courier. I don't blame him, though. He's got a few of the pre-existing conditions the news is going on about—the ones that supposedly put you at a higher risk for contracting Covid, *and* having a terrible time with it. And ever since my mom passed he's been more cautious about his health. So, yeah, I was sad that I didn't get to see him and give him a hug, but I suppose safety *does* come first.

Rifling through the box's contents makes me feel both better *and* worse, discovering most of the items once belonged to my mom. Many are gifts I gave her throughout the years, now making their way back to me. Instead of reminiscing on all the memories tied up in each item, I consider how *cruel* it is that I have to sift through this box in the first place. *It was never supposed to be this way.* They weren't meant to return to me like some boomerang of sadness. She was supposed to hold onto these forever.

My mind suddenly makes a hard left turn, showing me a vision of what it'd look like if I dumped this entire box in the garbage. I feel a tightening in my chest as the scene plays out in my head. The satisfaction that my actions bring are far removed from what they *should* be. In my mind's eye I'm grinning like a fool, inexplicably happy about my dead mother's things now sitting in a crumpled heap at the bottom of a dumpster.

I swallow past the lump in my throat, my heart thudding erratically, and attempt to force out *all* thoughts, both good and bad. *This is only a side-effect of your lack of sleep.* Leaning back against the torn upholstery of my couch I feel the heaviness of my eyelids. They're like anvils, begging to be closed. Do I oblige them, allowing myself a quick nap before returning to work? *Sure.* What could be the harm?

"What do we have *here*?" a familiar voice asks.

My eyes ease back open and I discover my mother sitting on the opposite side of the couch. A smile curls her lips as she rummages through the box, reuniting with the fond memories associated with each knick-knack. Her eyes glint with a remarkable shimmer when she picks up a black portfolio, containing several drawings I did in my college art class.

She opens it and leafs through the preserved artwork, taking her time with each piece. "I remember *this one...*" she says with a widening smile. My mom holds up the portfolio to show me the self-portrait I drew for her in Drawing II class. "You were *so proud* to give it to me," she continues, "but not as proud as I was to receive it."

"*Mom...* w-what are you *doing* here?" I ask with a confused smile. I notice that she's wearing her favorite dress—the one she was buried in.

"Oh, I just thought I'd stop by for a quick visit," she replies, meeting my gaze briefly. "I know how much you've been missing your father, *and* Janey. I always liked her. Such a *sweet* girl."

I open and close my mouth several times, a thousand questions dangling on my tongue, begging to be answered. The crippling anxiety that was coursing through me not long ago has dissolved, replaced by a calm, reassuring serenity. Because somehow my *mom* is here, sitting on my couch, talking to me as if it were just an ordinary day.

"How... did you know about me and Jane, and that I was bummed about dad?" I finally manage, shifting on the couch to face her.

"I'm *dead*, dear—*remember*?" she replies, reaching the final page in the portfolio.

Placing it neatly back inside the box, she then takes out a framed photograph that makes her eyes go wide with excitement. My stomach performs somersaults, my own smile widening at this seemingly impossible reincarnation of my deceased mother. She glows like a ray of hope under the afternoon sunshine that peeks through the window.

"Oh *look*, sweetie!" she exclaims, holding up the photo of us at Disney World. "It's us, standing in front of that big silver ball!"

"At Epcot, yeah," I chuckle, rubbing my neck, trying to brush off how fucking *weird* this all is.

"I remember like it was yesterday. *'The happiest place on earth'.*" She grips the frame with both hands and purses her lips, making the same face she always did whenever she got all sentimental.

Mom continues rummaging through the lost-and-found items, intermittently cooing and smiling at every other thing she stumbles upon. I watch her in awe, while feelings of love and nostalgia pummel me like white water rapids. I try to remind myself that this isn't real—it *can't* be real. Because mom died more than a year ago. Fucking cancer.

My parents booked that trip to Disney World under the guise of one final blowout, before I shuffled off to college and subsequently the rest of my life. What they *didn't* tell me was that mom had been recently diagnosed with a rare form of cancer. And although she fought the good fight, prolonging her life for another year or so with the chemo, the disease had spread too quickly to beat. So that trip had secretly meant to serve as a moment for dad and I to look back on, after mom had... well, you know.

"Hey, mom? Did you ever have insomnia, or nightmares?"

The fondness fades from her face and she glances up at me, concern in her eyes. "Sometimes. The cancer treatment would often give me *horrible* dreams." A sly grin suddenly reappears on her face. "They were few and far between, though, thanks to *you*, my beautiful son. I was never big on grass until the treatments started. But once I started smoking, to ease the pain and the nausea, it was a *lifesaver!*"

"*Mom*, I told you, no one calls it 'grass' anymore," I chuckle. "*Shit*, even 'Marijuana' is on its way out the door."

"It *is?*" she asks, genuinely concerned.

I shrug my shoulders. "Kind of." I close my eyes and shake my head, wondering how—and *why*—I'm having this conversation.

Currently she's juggling an array of memorabilia in her arms; gifts and trinkets that were given to her long ago, now being cherished once more. She studies them with such intensity and reverence, as if she may never see them again. And in a way I suppose that's true.

"I know you've been struggling lately, Craig," she begins, placing the items back in the box one by one. "Everything you're going through—the pandemic, Jane, your sleepless nights, the isolation—it's all just *too much*." She's emptied her arms of memories, now turning to look me in the eye. "You don't have to be strong *all* the time," she continues. "It's *okay* to be vulnerable and scared. But life will never *not* throw challenges at you, so it's your responsibility to learn how to catch them. To wrestle them to the ground and show 'em who's boss."

She takes me into her arms and holds me like I'm a little kid again. It takes everything I have to not burst into tears. My mom runs her long fingers through my greasy, unwashed hair as she makes shushing noises, lulling me like a baby.

Another question suddenly pops into my head, one that I am dying to ask. I try to pull away from her but it's *difficult* for some reason. Her grip on me tightens to the point that it's actually uncomfortable. I don't want to say anything, afraid that I'll hurt her feelings—she's probably just as sad as I am, having to say goodbye.

A foul stench wafts into my nostrils, like bags of garbage baking under the heat of our current August sun. It's horrendous enough to make my eyes water and stomach churn. I catch sight of my mother's arms, the flesh now a sickly yellow that hangs loosely from her bones. Bruises and black rot also form, spreading outward like the disease that took her from this world.

"You'll *always* be my sweet little boy..." she whispers. Her voice, once sweet as honey, is now coarse and strained, creaking like the hinges of an old door.

I instinctually shove her off of me, finally breaking the uncomfortable bond between us. Her wicked witch style cackles echo violently in my head. My eyes widen at the sight of my mom's face. Her's are gone, replaced by discolored cotton balls that protrude from the sockets of her skull. Her sunken cheeks are all too reminiscent of those final days in the hospital bed.

She reaches her bony arms out to me, joints creaking as if they haven't moved in years. "Come, give mommy a *big kiss!*" Her raspy voice smells like rot and decay as she inches closer. I'm frozen in place, petrified by this impossible circumstance.

Her tongue, a dehydrated piece of jerky, comes out from between her lips and dances around like a serpent. "Come now, *Craigy*. Let mommy make it *all better...*"

I struggle to open my mouth, desperate to release the scream trapped in my throat. With a burst of adrenaline, I lunge off the couch but my footing falters on the shag carpet. She's slithering towards me with a toothless smile, her nonexistent eyes gleaming with madness. In a panic, I back myself into a corner as she closes in on me. I kick at her using all my strength, but my foot sinks into her decaying face like quicksand. My cries for help reverberate off the walls as I try to make sense of this creature. This is not my mother, not the kind and loving figure I knew. Fear consumes me as I realize she is no longer human, but a terrifying being that wants to harm me.

Suddenly I'm awake and upright, *screaming* on my couch. My chest is heaving and I'm drenched with sweat. The box full of mom's stuff is still next to me—my mom, thankfully, *isn't*. It wasn't real. It was only a nightmare. A horrifying, heart-pounding nightmare.

I make my way to the bathroom and splash cold water on my face. After several minutes my breathing returns to normal. The line that separates my reality from the otherwise *terrifying* is now more clear and defined. And yet, the mental image of my deceased mother still lingers like a heavy fog. *This was not how I wanted to spend my lunch break.*

Part IV

Fingers tapping, I flick through webpage after webpage—each one a rabbit hole of half-truths and hearsay about cannabis withdrawal. It's like they're speaking directly to me, detailing nightmare fuel that matches my own twisted nocturnal experiences. Sure, the whole world's gone haywire with this Covid mess, but these dreams? They're something else, man.

"Vivid dreams common in cannabis withdrawal"—one headline blares at me from the screen. My bloodshot eyes scan the blocky text as if salvation lies within those digital lines. And even though the article itself doesn't offer much in the way of treatment, I still feel instantly validated knowing I'm not alone. I lean back in my chair, the fabric creaking under the weight of my unrest. With every click, every scroll, I'm hunting for that one magic bullet, that gem of wisdom that'll snap me out of this hellish loop of insomnia.

"What should I do about cannabis withdrawal symptoms?"—asks a user of one of the many weed subreddits. It's no surprise that unhelpful comments like "keep smoking, bro" and "withdrawal symptoms are for quitters" have the most upvotes. It's good to know that in these uncertain times, amidst a global pandemic, the mouth-breathers of the internet have managed to retain their sense of humor. I guess it's my fault for thinking any support could be found in the cesspools of the web.

"*Fucking trolls,*" I mutter to myself, shaking my head. I push forward, continuing my search for answers, trying to keep a positive outlook on things. An unexpected burst of laughter escapes me as I stumble across an article from HighTimes.com titled "So You Had to Give Up the Ganja. Now What?"

I totally get that taking mental health advice from a weed website might sound like a bad idea, but who could resist with a headline like that? The article, fairly comprehensive, starts out by explaining what you can expect from your dope detox in the days and weeks ahead. It then follows up with preventative measures and unavoidable pitfalls.

The author of the article cites several therapists and doctors who have weighed in with their knowledge of the detox process. Although there are a few minor differences in each of their own "objective, scientific truths," there *is* a common denominator to be found. This happens to line up perfectly with what I've experienced personally: restless nights, waking nightmares, and irritability—just to name a few.

Again I feel vindicated, seeing that my insomnia and bad dreams are to be expected. That reassurance is short-lived, however, as I skip down to the "Treatments" section of the article. I deflate at the realization that the few existing options don't apply to me.

The weaning method—which is what they recommend to *prevent* the symptoms of withdrawal—is out by default. You can't wean yourself off of weed if one day you have a stash, and the next you don't. The crowning glory of this shit-show is at the very end, when they discuss how long you can expect these side effects to last: two *fucking* weeks.

I stare dumbfounded at the computer monitor, rubbing my eyes just to make sure I'm seeing clearly. How on earth could it be two weeks, when I've been struggling with nightmares for over a *month* now? It just doesn't make any fucking sense!

Scrolling to the bottom of the article I read through the comments, hoping I find *one person* who's in the same boat as me. "Come on, *come on!*" I mumble aloud, searching for that single kindred spirit. All I find, however, are happy, educated cannabis smokers who are thankful for the article's information.

My blood starts to boil and, just as quickly as I welcomed it with open arms, I turn against the unhelpful blogpost like a rabid dog. *This is such a load of bullshit.* I lean back in my desk chair, exhausted yet too wired to fall asleep, and close my eyes. Endless headlines flicker behind my lids like a news ticker at 10x speed:

"Study Finds Strong Link Between Insomnia and Increased Anxiety Levels"

"Anxiety from Sleepless Nights May Lead to Crippling Depression"

"Depression and Lack of Rest Leads to Spontaneous Death."

"You are Worthless, and Jane Never Loved You, Anyway."

"Darko is Purposefully Ignoring Your Phone Calls. And He is Fucking Jane!"

"*Goddamnit!*" I scream out, leaping from my chair. *There has got to be some way out of this*, I think to myself, pacing my apartment. The increased tension has my shoulders and back all tied up in knots. My white-knuckled fists are like granite. I strike out suddenly, punching a hole in my living room wall. *If one is good, more must be better.* I thrust the other fist out for good measure, clearing a second divot in the half-inch drywall.

I've heard that when your body surges with adrenaline you can experience a delay in pain. I assume that, based on my two throbbing fists, that science goes out the window when your sleep-deprived brain is working on a fraction of its normal capacity.

"*Fuck me!*" I shriek through gritted teeth. I resist the urge to go for the hat trick, deciding instead to check out the damage I've done to myself. *I need a damn ice pack.* Stumbling my way through the living room, I do my best to avoid the garbage that litters the floor. A tangle of USB cords snatches my footing, however, and brings me crashing down to the carpet. Why *not* add some more bruising and carpet burn to the mix?

I breathe a sigh of relief when I finally make it to the freezer—*and* in one piece, I might add. The blast of cold air as I open the door is a shock to my agitated system. The ease that the ice pack brings to my fists of fury is nothing short of exceptional. After a few deep breaths I make my way back to the living room, plopping myself onto the sofa with a grunt.

With half-lidded eyes I glare at my Jimi Hendrix poster. "There must be some kind of way outta here..." I say to no one, my voice a mix of defeat and defiance. Each article, each shared experience from strangers on the net—it's all part of the puzzle, right? At least, that's what I keep telling myself. But as the sun dips lower, casting long shadows across the room, a creeping urgency settles in my gut. This can't go on. Something's *got* to give.

Part V

It's 11 PM and, as per the instructions of the *High Times* article, *all* distractions have been eliminated. My phone is docked on its charger *outside* of my bedroom. The television is off. Even the moon, full and glorious, doesn't stand a chance against the blinds and blackout curtains. So, now it is only me and my thoughts. *Lucky me.*

I spent the remainder of the evening nursing my swollen hands with ice packs and ibuprofen. I'm sure I can expect more dull, throbbing pain to greet me in the morning. Against my better judgment I tried calling Darko again, only to be greeted with—yep, you guessed it—his *voicemail*. His *full* voicemail, actually. Talk about adding insult to injury.

The pressure to get a full eight hours isn't nearly as high, tomorrow being Saturday and all. So I stayed up late, playing video games and binging The Office, waiting patiently for my eyelids to grow heavy. I actually got *giddy* when I noticed my first yawn around 10:30 PM.

So here I am, listening to the distant sound of cars whooshing by on the highway. My upstairs neighbors are out on their balcony. Their chatter is muffled, which is just as well. If I could hear what they were saying, it would only be another distraction from me falling asleep.

Just as I feel my lids start to close, I hear a low rumbling sound from the corner of my bedroom. It's reminiscent of a clothes dryer, and I initially dismiss it as such. But then a strange clicking noise accompanies the grumbling, and what little semblance of sleep I felt creeping in is now gone.

What the fuck is that? I ask myself, irritated. It kind of sounds like someone modified a geiger counter to detect supernatural phenomena. It sounds like when kids used to put playing cards in the spokes of their bicycle tires. It sounds like... *breathing*. But not *natural* breathing, from something with human lungs.

I've decided that this is a lost cause, and my lack of distractions has ironically become a distraction. When I sit up in bed, about to throw the sheets off so I can grab my phone, I find that I'm actually frozen in place. My eyes are locked onto the corner of my bedroom, where the ominous plinking still persists. The room is dark with all of the shades drawn, but not as dark as the shadow that looms in the corner.

It's a tall, lanky figure that could almost be the shadow of a man. In fact, that's exactly what I presume it to be at first. But you need *light* in order to cast a shadow, and I've done too good of a job at making my bedroom pitch black.

"H-hello?" I call out, feeling all sorts of ridiculous for doing so. It doesn't answer—doesn't move. It only stands there, stoic, motionless. "*Hello?*" I ask again, thinking that maybe it didn't hear me the first time.

You're being an idiot, Craig, I tell myself. *You're sleep-deprived, and angry, and sexually frustrated. And that's why you are—*

"Hello, Craig," a deep voice says. "Having trouble sleeping?" It could be coming from the corner of my room; it could be coming from inside my head—it's hard to tell. And, yeah, my asshole is now *officially* clenched in a tight pucker. But I also can't help but find some humor in the tone of the disembodied voice. It sounds like what you'd expect from one of those voice modulators that can make you sound like Satan.

"W-what do you want?" I ask the shadow thing that may or may not be there.

"What do you *think* I want, Craig? I want to sit on your face..."

A nervous chuckle escapes me. "Wait, *really*?"

There's a low hitching in its voice that *sounds* like a chortle. But is it laughing *with* me, or *at* me?

The shadow finally begins to move, making inhuman sucking sounds as it morphs and changes form. I'm frozen in bed as I watch this unfold, feeling like a kid who's been paid a visit by a shapeshifting boogeyman.

The figure's evolution slowly comes to a stop. "Isn't that what you *want*, Craig? Don't you want me? Haven't you *missed* me?" The voice is eerily familiar.

"*Jane*?" I whisper, my body *trembling* with excitement.

The shadow figure takes a jerking step forward. One of its long, lanky arms reaches up to caress its neck and begins to moan. "Oh *Craig*, how I've *missed* you..." it says in a sultry voice that's reminiscent of Jane's.

I bring my palms up to my face, rubbing my eyes. I then shake my head to clear away the notion of what's happening—because I *know* it's not real. It *can't* be real.

"*Fuck off*," I say, crossing my arms over my chest, stern in my resolve. "You are *not* Jane." My words to this entity are a declaration of truth, the vision of my decrepit mother still firmly planted in my mind.

"How many times have I *told you*, Craigy? You can't keep running from your feelings. One day you will have to put down the weed and face facts..."

My eyebrows furrow in bewilderment as I try to make sense of the shadowy figure's words. The more it speaks, the more it sounds exactly like my ex-girlfriend. My rational mind knows that this is not real, but I can feel my grasp on reality slipping, unsure if I can discern truth from fantasy.

Just as I open my mouth to respond, the figure begins to spasm, transitioning into a *new* physical form. It grows in height, the silhouette of Jane's long, flowing hair turning into thick dreadlocks.

"Don't listen to that bitch, *man*," the new voice says, also uncannily familiar. "*She* don't know what you *need*. *I* know what you need, brother."

"D-Darko?"

"That's *right*... Sorry I haven't texted you back. I've been *real* busy. But I'm here now, and I come bearing *gifts*..."

"W-what *kind* of gifts?" I ask cautiously, my voice trembling.

"Oh, I think you know the gifts I'm referring to..." the Darko voice replies.

A great, unchecked temptation courses through me. My head *swims*, heart ballooning at the notion of having weed in my system again. But I steel my nerves, reminding myself that this *isn't real*. This is a *dream*, just as the zombified version of my mother had been a dream.

"Get lost, dude," I demand. "I know for a *fact* that you don't have any weed."

The shadow of Darko starts to chuckle, its voice shifting several octaves, back to its low, eery grumble. "That's where you're *wrong*... *dude*. *Now*, open wide and take your *medicine*..."

A gaping maw opens up in its head, somehow even *darker* than the rest of its silhouetted body. Objects of varying size begin to tumble out, floating through the air like underwater pool toys, inching closer and closer to my face.

I can feel my nerves of steel start to weaken; my resolve wearing thin. Suddenly I'm cemented to the bed, arms and legs like boat anchors. I jerk my head from side to side, the familiar looking objects now close enough that I can *smell* them.

Monstrously oversized nuggets of cannabis, some the size of small melons, hover menacingly in front of my face. My mouth is forced open with a sharp crack and I scream in agony, my jaw stretching to its limit. But my cries of protest fall on deaf ears as the drugs inch closer, now inevitable. As I struggle against this cruel violation, I try once more to convince myself it's just a nightmare. But the terror gripping me is so intense that even that small comfort slips away

I can taste the tangy flavor of the buds as they brush my lips. Arms pinned at my sides, I use the tip of my tongue like a pool cue to bat them away. But even my tongue is now immobilized and I am stuck watching as the softball-sized nuggets find their way into my mouth. I don't understand how something this big can possibly fit, but they do.

The sticky buds scratch my throat as they're forced down, courtesy of some evil magic casted out by the Darko shape. I try to breathe through my nose, praying I can bear this force-feeding until it's over. One by one I can *feel* them drop down into my stomach, a sensation akin to—*I'm assuming*—swallowing a pine cone.

The shadow figure is smiling and laughing while the buds pour freely from his gullet. I try to curse him, but all that comes out is a jumbled slew of vowels. My only reassurance in this hellish nightmare is knowing that, sooner or later, I *have* to wake up.

The nuggets have *finally* tapered off from the shadow's black maw. I ready myself for the final jump scare, the one that always wakes the protagonist from their dream. But it doesn't come. I swallow the rest of the cannabis nugs, my throat scratching like sandpaper. And shadow Darko, the shapeshifter, the malevolent entity that is the antithesis of my weed dealer, fades away.

A long-awaited scream erupts from my lungs, jolting me awake. My voice, coarse and loud, echoes off the walls of my bedroom as I shoot straight up in bed. The sheets are twisted around my limbs.

My heart races like it's trying to escape my chest, each beat a drum of panic. I've sweated so much that it looks as though I've pissed the bed.

"*Jesus...*" I mumble, voice hoarse. "What the fuck was that?"

Darkness still consumes my room, but I see that everything has returned to normal. I have agency over my own body. No supernatural shadow figure lurks in the corner. I shove damp hair from my forehead, trying to steady the earthquake in my hands.

"*Got* to get a fucking *grip*..." I say, but even as the words leave my mouth, they sound hollow, empty. Like they're disappearing into the same void where my calm used to live.

It's time for a change, I demand of myself as I lay back down in bed. *Change starts tomorrow, damnit.*

Part VI

I blink awake, unaware of the time of day. It's Saturday, I know *that* for certain. The light from the window feels like a punch to the face as I flick open the blinds. Despite last night's horrific nightmare, I've clearly gotten a decent amount of sleep. My mouth is desert-dry and nasty, with faint notes of cannabis clinging to my tongue. I try not to linger on the possibility of my bad dreams following me into reality.

I make my way to the kitchen, eager to brew what's sure to be the first of several pots of coffee. As I scoop the grounds, my final thoughts from last night echo in my ears: *It's time for a change.* It was no longer an option—it was a *necessity*. This isn't sustainable, what's happening to me. I simply cannot go on living like this: nightmares every single night, and sometimes during the day. Restless sleep, when I'm lucky enough to get any. Living alone, isolated from the entire world. No girlfriend. No dealer. I can tell... my tipping point is just around the corner.

While the coffee percolates, I scan the absolute shit-show condition that my apartment's in. Old pizza boxes stacked by the front door. Dirty clothes I've stripped off, too lazy to walk them to the washing machine. Countless records, CDs, and movies I've taken off the shelves. Candy wrappers. Coke cans. Bags of popcorn. *God, this is fucking disgusting.* How the hell did I let it get like this?

Some mild comic relief presents itself when I'm reminded of the holes I punched yesterday. I look down at my hands, noting the pain relievers and ice therapy I opted for last night had actually helped. Just for good measure I utter another "fuck you" to the tangle of cords that tripped me up in the first place.

I can't do anything about Darko not answering my calls. And I can't do anything abut Jane dumping my ass for reasons I've yet to understand. But I can sure as hell clean up this fucking pigsty. So I pour my coffee, put on some tunes, and get to work.

Ridding my apartment of all the garbage is a job best suited for a team dressed in hazmat suits. Neatly putting away all of my belongings is a task more fitting for Marie Kondo. But I find a way to make it all work with just myself—not like I have much choice in the matter.

I began by filling several large garbage bags with trash from *just* my living room. As I did so, I performed some quick mental math, searching for a date when I let this all go to hell. While it's true I've never been the *cleanest* guy on the planet, I am in *no way* the dirtiest. After racking my brain for a good 20 minutes or so I finally pinpointed the last time I did a decent deep-clean of my apartment: It was about five months ago—when Jane dumped me.

My penchant for sloppy living was *not* the reason she dumped me, although I'll admit that it probably didn't help. I'm sure you're familiar with that classic breakup line, "It's not you, it's me." Who isn't? It's an excuse as old as Mother Earth and Father Time. Except, that *wasn't* the excuse Jane used. In fact, it was just the opposite. And to make matters worse, she was all *nice* about it.

I wanted so desperately to be pissed off that she was leaving me. I wanted to shout and throw things. I wanted her to argue and scream back at me, just to make the whole ordeal a much bigger mess than it needed to be. But I couldn't do *any* of that. That would be like picking a fight with the Dalai Lama. Leave it to Jane to wield the proper tact when breaking up with someone.

Despite its unfortunate ending, the majority of our relationship was nothing short of stellar. At least, that's what I remember, looking back with those infamous rose-tinted glasses. It wasn't *always* holding hands and frolicking through meadows. But she got me, and I got her.

Jane was—*is*—a strong, independent, self-possessed woman; a genuine joy to be around. And anyone who says different is a fucking liar. With a heart of gold and a bubbly personality that was as sweet as apple pie, I didn't think I could ever achieve a higher standard. Her career as a Special Education teacher was just the tip of the iceberg when it came to her altruistic, Hufflepuff ways. She wasn't happy unless she was actively enriching others' lives.

Despite her kind and sweet demeanor, it was impossible to imagine just how much of a *freak* she was in bed. A twenty minute, passion-fueled fuck session with Jane would wear me out to the point that I wouldn't even *need* my nightly bong hit. And it wasn't *just* about the quality of the sex—which was *mind-blowing*—but also the sheer quantity. We fucked so often that my jerk-off numbers took an *astonishing* nosedive. I didn't mind this at *all*, though; beating my meat paled in comparison to having her ride my cock like Annie Oakley.

Simply put, we couldn't get enough of each other. The electric chemistry between us made every moment feel like a roller coaster ride, and I wouldn't have had it any other way.

Our solid connection extended *beyond* the bedroom, of course. Although our personality types differed, they were complimentary in all the ways that mattered. Jane was the kind-hearted, generous type, who stopped at nothing to appease those she cared about. Meanwhile, I spent most of my time wrapped up in my own drama. I enjoyed diving into the fictional worlds of comic books and video games, knowing they'd always be better than whatever was happening in real life. Hell, standing next to Jane I probably looked like some crazed, self-absorbed hedonist.

She never seemed to mind my introverted nature, or the stark juxtaposition of our two personalities. In fact, on numerous occasions she told me how much she admired my independence. However, she *also* told me it was possible to be self-involved and *still* not take care of yourself. It didn't make sense then, and it doesn't make a whole lot of sense now. Yet *another* reason why our relationship ultimately went tits-up.

Yesterday's deep-clean was so thorough, so successful, that it took several laps of walking throughout my apartment to appreciate it all. Hands on hips I surveyed my hard work proudly, like a dad admiring his freshly mown lawn—minus the grass-stained New Balances and jean shorts. Slices of light from the warm glow of the sunset scatter across my *vacuumed* carpet. I can actually *walk* from my kitchen to the living room without putting my life in danger. And thanks to Home Depot's online ordering and curbside delivery, I even managed to spackle where I fisted the drywall!

Fuck, did I feel accomplished. It was an amazing feeling. And you know what else? I was *damn* tired. And not just the kind of exhaustion that comes from a criminal lack of sleep. It was the kind where I shut down completely the second my head hit the pillow.

Because yesterday's cleaning frenzy was so successful, resulting in a night devoid of bad dreams, I decide to tackle *another* intimidating project: my bedroom closet. Not unlike the rest of my apartment, the cleanliness of the small walk-in has been neglected for quite some time now.

Almost immediately I uncover a pair of shorts I totally forgot I owned. The bad news? They don't fit. And these aren't some shorts that I've held onto since high school. No, I bought these *last year*. Stripping them off is worse than wriggling out of a diver's wetsuit. The lost-and-found shorts are so tight that, when I finally get them off, they take my boxer briefs with them.

Standing naked in front of my full-length mirror I assess the damage of the last several months. Everyone on Facebook seems to be putting on weight because of the pandemic. It's just an inevitability when there's not much else to do but sit on your ass and eat snacks. And if that's *all* it was, I'd be slightly less ashamed. But the truth is, my nutritional health has been in a downward spiral since Jane.

I tried to play it cool when it first went down, acting nonplussed about the whole thing. It felt good for a while, pretending that the breakup was amicable; I was *almost* able to convince myself that was the case. The tears did come eventually—about two weeks later, when I realized how amazing the sex had been, and how I took it for granted.

It wasn't *just* about the sex, of course. It was the way Jane's hand fit neatly in mine, like they were cast from the same mold. I felt safe when I was with her, like nothing could ever go wrong. It was her smile, and the way she'd look at me. There were times when she would wake up before me, her long, auburn hair splayed across the pillow. She'd lay there patiently, sometimes for an hour or more, just *waiting* for me. And the first thing I'd see when I finally woke was *her*, smiling back at me with that big, toothy grin of hers.

Now, I wake up to *dog shit*—metaphorically speaking. And the proverbial cherry on top is that I've gotten *fat* from the crippling loneliness. Can you believe I actually made my own fried Twinkies? I mean, how disgusting can you get? And it wasn't just once, either; I made them *several* times! I didn't know that the Twinkies had to be frozen beforehand, and the recipe took some tinkering before I got it just right. So, by the time I made one *correctly*, I was so fucking sick of fried Twinkies that I couldn't even enjoy them.

In the mirror's reflection I catch sight of another relic from my past—my running shoes. Two pairs, actually. One from high school that I have *refused* to give up, and a second that's never seen the light of day. Jane and I would often bicker about my insistence on holding onto the tattered pair. So, when she proposed a new pair was in order, the compromise was that I'd spring for some, but I'd also get to keep the old pair.

I had always enjoyed running for some casual exercise, but I *really* took it up a notch when Jane and I got serious. When we became exclusive, the sex was *on*. And she was in terrific shape, which meant that *I* needed to be, as well. It was paramount that my stamina matched hers—a fool's errand, if there ever was one. But when the sex came to a spectacular halt—as well as the rest of our relationship—the need for looking after my physical health fell by the wayside.

So, here I am: an amorphous blob of my former, more attractive self. Say what you will about that Buffalo Bill character from *Silence of the Lambs*, but at least he had the confidence to dance naked in front of the mirror. I quickly throw on some clothes that fit, set both pairs of running shoes aside, and continue my closet purge.

Several hours and five large trash bags later I am *finally* done organizing my wardrobe. And just as yesterday's garbage purge had released a bucket-full of serotonin, as did today's task, too. I'm *still* not the radiant ball of energy I'd like to be, however. Because, under these fat-guy clothes, I'm still a fat loser who hasn't been laid in almost six months. But considering my original plan for the weekend was to sit on my ass, watch movies, and masturbate, I think I've accomplished a lot. And because I have daylight to spare, I've decided to dust off those old running shoes and go for a jog.

Part VII

A pivotal moment rests in my hands, both literally and figuratively. It's been *two months* since that horrific nightmare—the one in which the shapeshifter force-fed me genetically modified weed nuggets. Two months, since I decided to clean my apartment. Since I said "enough is enough" and started exercising again. And now here I stand, eight short weeks later, with my old running shoes cradled delicately in my hands.

It's bizarre how much can change in such a short amount of time. And how small changes can feel so monumental. So often, I've discovered, you only need but *one* domino to fall, before the rest follow suit.

I went out jogging that afternoon, just along the dirt trail that surrounds my apartment complex, wearing my high school running shoes. It was a *short* run, if I'm being honest. Between the rolling hills and my flabby gut, I couldn't handle much more than twenty minutes. The southern heat bore down, relentless; the unbearable humidity like a hot blanket of death. But I did the thing, and I was damn proud of myself for it. And that night, I slept like a baby.

This period of transformation hasn't *always* been sunshine and rainbow-shitting unicorns. There have still been plenty of sleepless nights, or nights when my sleep is laced with nightmares. These instances tend to leave me a shell of my normal self, at least for a day or two. Sometimes I think it's a miracle that I haven't been fired yet, considering the amount of times I've drifted off at my desk. My saving grace—if you want to call it that—is that I'm not the only one that's afraid of losing their job.

The pandemic, which only seems to be getting worse, has been a threat to everyone and everything. If it's not busy killing folks, it's robbing people of their jobs. And while there are talks of a vaccine, it sounds more theoretical than anything at this point. The Covid virus is like a moving target that they can't quite nail down.

Discussions have been had about going back into the office, where *extreme* precautions would be taken. But aside from the company spending a shit-load of rent money on a building we're not even using, there's not much motivation to get back inside our brick-and-mortar location. Thanks to advancements in technology, working remotely has never been so easy, and commuting to an actual office building has never seemed so pointless.

I *did* finally hear back from Darko, which had been quite the surprise—*and* disappointment. As soon as Covid got serious he drove down to Florida to be with the rest of his family. As it turns out, things are a bit more lax there than they are compared to the rest of the country. And it wasn't even anything serious, the reason why he didn't return my calls or texts. He dropped his phone in the fucking *ocean*. How idiotic is that? And because he's paranoid as hell he didn't have *any* of his contacts or data backed up to the cloud. So he had to go through a half-dozen level of friends in order to finally reach me. All that to say there was *nothing* he could do about supplying me with weed.

And then there's *Jane*. I've actually been thinking about her a lot lately. Not really sure why, either. It's hard to tell if I miss her, or if it's something more than that. As I mentioned before, I initially embraced my newfound freedom when she gave me the stanky boot back in February. That autonomy felt good for a *minute*, thinking about all the possibilities that the single life meant. But as it turned out, those were only self-inflicted scales I had firmly lodged over my own eyes.

I think that's why the exercise has had such a positive impact on my day-to-day living. Sometimes it feels like I'm literally *running* from my demons; running to keep the fucked up thoughts at bay. So that I can actually sleep at night. And it *works*, for the most part. The catch is I can't stop—can't slow down. If I do, shapeshifters might get me.

They definitely didn't catch up to me today, I can tell you that much. In fact, I ran so hard, and so fast, that I tore holes through *both* of my shoes; The damage had made them unwearable, and I had to take them off and *walk* home. I'm sure I was quite the sight for those driving past me.

What's perhaps the funniest thing about the whole ordeal? The implications of finally wearing through my old runners hadn't dawned on me until I walked through my front door, my endorphins finally mellowing out. A relic from my past, one that I've clung to for arguably *far* too long, is ready to be retired. But am I even capable of tossing them in the garbage? It seems silly to keep them around. Sure, they were old and dirty before, but they were perfectly functional shoes. Now, whether I like it or not, it's high time to put these ancient memories to rest.

I open the lid to my garbage can and toss them in without much ceremony. It feels... *wrong* to lay them to rest with last night's spaghetti and this morning's coffee grounds, but I do. *Ashes to ashes, dust to dust.*

I consider the weight of all this as I lean against the kitchen counter, drinking the rest of the water from my run. Normally after a jog I feel light as a feather. And if it's an especially good workout, I can even feel *invincible*. But something about throwing out my shoes has got me in a funk. Like a heavy weight sits on my chest, one that I'm not yet strong enough to lift. Because of that I need to get creative on how I could possibly remove it.

I've cut down on things like screen time and video games, opting for the hardbacks that've been collecting dust on my bookshelf. That said, I'm not against flipping on the tube from time to time. There's only so much exercising and reading a guy can do, before you say "fuck it" and rewatch The Office, front to back, for the hundredth time.

I down the rest of my water and start digging in the freezer, realizing that I've managed to work up quite an appetite. The pickings are slim so I move to the fridge, only to be presented with more of the same. I *really* don't want to mask up and go grocery shopping this late in the day, and I also don't want to spoil my hot streak by ordering a pizza—as delicious as it sounds. So I move back to the freezer, pushing things from side to side, even taking things out, to make sure I haven't overlooked a gem of some sort. And as it turns out, that's *exactly* what I've done.

A small container with a crumpled up baggie inside is shoved all the way to the back of the freezer. I stare at it with unparalleled fascination, like it's some foreign object from outer space. I don't have much Tupperware in my house, and this surely isn't a piece that I own. My intrigue and curiosity rise at an alarming rate as I pop the top and break the seal on the baggie. *What are you?*

I dump the baggie's contents into my palm and my eyes go wide. I know what it is, but my mind refuses to accept it. The room starts to spin, and suddenly I *must* sit down. I'm a little uneasy on my feet, but thankfully I don't have to navigate through piles of clutter in order to reach my couch safely.

In my hands I hold a small handful of edibles that have been sitting in my freezer for who knows how long.

A few short chuckles escape me at first, my brain still comprehending what I've found. Those chuckles evolve slowly into a continuous laugh. They crescendo into a full-on *cackle*, not unlike every mad scientist who stopped at nothing to accomplish their work.

"Holy... fucking... *shit*," I cry, wiping the tears from my eyes. I'm in complete shock, denial overriding every other thought in my brain. *This can't be real. This has to be a dream.*

It's been a while since my last lucid nightmare, so while it's unlikely that this is the case, I still pinch myself for good measure. "Gah, *fuck*!" I exclaim as I nick myself a little *too* hard. The pain is made temporary, however, thanks to my lord and savior—*weed*, in the form of gummy edibles.

My racing heart is practically thudding against my ribcage as I try to decide how I want to handle this situation. Only a minute ago I was deciding, with my limited options, what to have for dinner. And now it feels as if I'm worlds away from such pedestrian decisions. *Where did the edibles come from? Had Darko given them to me?* I vaguely remember him offering me a sample a long time ago. And, because I'm not a *total* idiot, I graciously accepted his generous contribution to the "Keep Craig High" fund.

Before I can even decide how I'm going to divvy up the four square gummies, one of them is already making its way to my lips. I put it on my tongue, its sour notes and citrus an explosion of flavor in my mouth, and I chew. I eat it reverently like I've just accepted the body of Christ—if the son of God just happened to be a pot farmer. *Damn, now that's a church I could get behind.*

Uncontrollable giddiness is bubbling up inside me, begging to be let out. I do a little dance on my way back to the freezer, replacing the gummies from whence they came. This is a moment I've anticipated for *months* now, and even though the small supply of edibles will surely come to an end, I can't help but live in the moment.

I am going to enjoy the fuck out of this, I think to myself. It's been so long since I've enjoyed the mellow high's that cannabis offers that I draw a blank on what to do next. Should I listen to music? Play video games? Maybe I should order that pizza, after all.

Music. Yes, music sounds like an *amazing* idea.

I opt for a vinyl record in lieu of a Spotify playlist, dropping the needle on a Neil Young 45. All that's left to do is plop down on my couch, put my feet up, and wait for the good times to roll.

The edible, I'm noticing, has a strange aftertaste. The bitterness of the sugar has worn off, leaving me with the lingering notes of the gummy itself. *Strange*, it doesn't really *taste* like weed. All of my prior experiences with edibles had bolstered that familiar cannabis tang. This gummy, on the other hand, was far more *earthy* than tart. In fact, it kind of tasted like...

Oh fuck...

Oh no...

I- I don't think those were *weed* edibles—they were *psilocybin* edibles. Magic *fucking* mushrooms. I am so *fucked*.

Part VIII

Things are slow, now; slow and heavy. But also, very *light*. It kind of feels like I've got no bones. Does that make sense? No? Well, you would if you were me right now. An hour into this mushroom trip, and I am *feeling* things.

I remember coming to terms with my predicament. I think that was maybe... fifteen minutes ago? I *was* pretty panicked about it because, historically speaking, mushrooms and I don't mix well together. They have a tendency to... how should I say this... open the floodgates on *all the feelings*. But I've decided that I am *not* going to let that happen this time. Also, why does it look like the trees are alive?

I'm going for a nice walk. That was my most *recent* brilliant idea. Except, I couldn't find my shoes. Not my old running shoes, no. I threw those away, because they were basically flip-flops. I'm talking about my everyday casual shoes, my slip-on Vans. Couldn't find them *anywhere*. You know what I *did* find, though? The pair that Jane forced me to buy.

They had that familiar new-shoe stiffness when I slipped my feet into them. Only wearing them once outside of the store, that had been enough for me to decide my old running shoes were a better fit.

Wait... you don't think that's the reason why she broke up with me, do you? Because I didn't wear the new running shoes? The ones that she, herself, bought? No. No, that's idiotic. Who would dump someone over shoes? Also, why do I suddenly feel like Gumby?

I'm currently trekking through the dirt trails that encompass my apartment complex. I wonder how Jane would feel, knowing what had become of her investment. Shoes relegated to the recesses of my closet, only to be unearthed several months later *after* she's gone. And now they're spending a mushroom trip with me.

I remember her face in the shoe store, though. It was lit up like the night sky on the Fourth of July. It was odd seeing her so happy over a new pair of runners, especially since they weren't even hers. There was this distinct twinge of resentment I felt in my chest, like she was *happy* that she got her way. Standing at the cash register, watching Jane fork over her credit card, it suddenly didn't feel like the "compromise" we agreed on. Maybe *that's* why I shoved them into the back of my closet, where I could conveniently forget about them.

I'm almost certain I'm speaking aloud. Now that the words are out of my mind and into the open, they *do* seem absurd. But the trees and shrubs that line either side of me, their branches are reaching out as if to pull me into their world. Maybe I should just let them? *Shit.* What's keeping me here?

While it's true that my life has improved in the past few months, I can't help but wonder if *I* have truly changed. My nights are no longer plagued with constant nightmares, and I have taken more responsibility for my well-being and surroundings. I've learned to accept the things beyond my control and adapt to those within my power. But maybe I *should* just leave and join the forest people; they wouldn't do things like force me to buy new shoes or abandon me for not caring for myself.

"You have it in you to be a *great* man, Craig," Jane had said, gripping my hands reassuringly. "I truly believe that. I believe in *you*. But... I don't think you can become the person you need to be while I'm around."

"Are you saying that you're holding me down?" I asked. She shook her head, wiping tears away from her freckled, porcelain cheeks. "What, then? Am I holding *you* down? I don't get it!"

"I *know* you don't, Craig. That's what makes this so difficult. One day, though, you *will* understand."

I had stared at her with unmatched incredulity. She was right, I *didn't* get it. Like, at *all*. I remember her using all kinds of metaphors that described our situation—the state in which our relationship had wandered into. None of those made any sense, either. I only recall being pissed off that she couldn't just be straight with me. That she had to put it in ways that might help me understand. That was Jane, all right—*always* had to be helpful, and kind. Even while she was busy breaking my fucking heart, she had the resolve to be gracious, merciful. *Fucking Hufflepuffs.*

"You wouldn't leave me, would you?" I ask a random oak tree as I hug its thick trunk. The contact feels nice, especially with the warm evening sun against my back. Gone are the days of the blistering southern heat, replaced by the ideal temperatures of October.

"I wouldn't leave you Craig. I couldn't. I'm a tree, after all!"

"Oak tree? Is that *you* talking? How are you doing that?" I back up, studying the tall, brown monster with wide eyes. I stroke its bark like the fur of a dog.

"I'm not just a source of oxygen, Craig. I can do many other things!"

"L-like what?"

"Well, what can't I do? I can be a home for birds, and owls, and squirrels. I can provide shade on a hot, summer day. I give you beautiful leaves in the Fall. And if you must chop me down, I can be used as firewood to keep you warm."

"Wow, oak tree," I say breathlessly, "you're so... versatile. I guess I've never thought about—"

"I can also tell you how much of an idiot you're being right now," oak tree interrupts.

I furrow my brow, feeling called out. "*Hey*, I'm tripping balls right now. Be nice. I thought you were supposed to be my friend? Friends don't call each other 'idiots'."

"Are you done wallowing, Craig? Because I'd like to continue, if that's alright with you."

"Be my guest..." I shrug, taken aback by oak tree's assertion.

Oak tree grumbles for a few moments, acting like some weird combination of an Ent from the Lord of the Rings, and the grandpa from the Princess Bride.

"*When Jane dumped you, it was for good reason,*" oak tree continues. "*You had fallen subject to an impossibly difficult circumstance. Your mother had passed away, and it took you a long time to make peace with that. For over a year you thought you might wake up one day to discover it had all been a dream. But Craig, we cannot learn and grow as people if we're too busy holding on to the past.*"

My face scrunches in frustration and anger. "What do *you* know about it, oak tree?" I demand. "You don't know me, or my life, or my *family*. Do you know what it's like to have your mom *ripped* from your world? *Do you?*"

"*I know what it's like to be firmly planted into the ground, and be forced to watch many things around you wilt away. But guess what, Craig? Life has a way of circling back around—of blooming once more. But you'll never find those rejuvenated opportunities if you're busy with your head down.*"

I open and close my mouth several times, trying to find the right words. But oak tree has me stumped. *Pun intended?* In lieu of a cohesive response I blow a raspberry at oak tree instead. "Enough of your 'Gandalf wisdom,' oak tree. Can't you just let me ride out the rest of this unsolicited mushroom trip in peace?"

"*Oh, you know I can't do that, Craig. WE can't do that—not anymore. It's time to face facts, son.*"

"Oh yeah? And what facts are those?"

Oak tree grumbles again, more frustrated than ever. "*Have you not been listening this whole time? Jane dumped you for your own good, Craig. She was the only one who could see that you needed to be on your own. So that you could spread your wings and learn to fly.*"

Once more I'm at a loss for words. I fall to the ground, crumpled like a bag of bones at the altar of oak tree. "Why does this have to be so hard? I thought I was doing *good*, oak tree? I cleaned my apartment! I've lost fifteen pounds! I have made *significant* improvements! Have I not?"

"And you'll have plenty more improvements to make, Craig. You are on the right track, but there's work to be done yet. And you know what else? There are people out there who believe in you, who pick up the slack when you can't believe in yourself. Your work colleagues. Your father. Jane."

"*Psh*... Okay, oak tree. I think your logic is *seriously* flawed. I don't think—"

"She still loves you, you know?"

The peaceful stillness of the forest is suspended only by the gentle chittering of bugs and birds. The warm rays of the sun are slowly sinking below the horizon, painting the sky a vibrant hue of sherbert ice cream. My heart flutters with excitement and my body feels weightless, as if I could be lifted from the forest floor at any moment. I can almost imagine being carried away by the gentle breeze, dancing among the leaves and dandelion fluff like a whimsical sprite.

"How could you know that..." I demand. "How *could* Jane love me? I'm a *mess*."

"Not anymore," oak tree replies, tall and wise. *"You are now a mess who's working to get better. You've already taken the necessary steps toward improvement. Toward enriching your life. When your mother died, you buried yourself in weed and video games. You convinced yourself that, as long as you couldn't feel those bad feelings, they didn't really exist. And when you ran out of weed, you were forced to reconcile with the fact that those disparaging thoughts and feelings never truly went away. And just look at how far you've come, in only two month's time. You should be proud of yourself."*

I'm once again struck silent, words failing me. If I'm being honest, oak tree is a bit of a dick—and quite possibly a narcissist—but he's also very wise. It's just too bad I have to hear this from a tree, instead of having some sort of profound revelation like they do in movies and books.

"I *am* proud of myself," I say softly. "I *have* made a lot of improvements, and I'm sure I'll make a lot more in the future." I nod my head enthusiastically, jazzing myself up. "Can't always be a stick in the mud. Got to be more upbeat, and positive."

"*Of course. And you will, indeed, find more ways to enrich your life,*" oak tree replies. "*You'll also continue to make mistakes. And bad things will still happen to you, things that will be out of your control.*"

"I can face those down, too," I chime in, eager. There's now a light at the end of this dark tunnel I've been traversing for the last few years. That light, it's only the size of a pinhole, but it's there, and it's getting brighter. "Hey, oak tree? Do you think I'll have to give up weed *entirely*? I know I've found ways to make do without it, but I don't know if I could ever swear it off completely."

Silence from oak tree. My boneless form begins to tremble at the thought of him leaving me, my question unanswered. But then he grumbles back to life. "*I think you will be able to answer that for yourself, dear boy.*"

A sudden congregation of sounds erupt all at once in my head: roots slithering in the earth, swaying of tree branches, rustling of leaves. I consider calling out to oak tree, to question if this is him I'm hearing, but I think I know better by now.

I continue to lay in the dirt, unaware of how much time is passing. I bear witness to the vibrant sky, full of oranges and pinks and reds, transitioning into a deep, dark blue. As beautiful as this all is, though, I can't help but think I'd be much more comfortable on my living room couch.

I'm a bit wobbly as I rise to my feet, but I manage. I pat the trunk of the large tree that had kept me company for who knows how long. "Thank you, oak tree," I whisper, still tripping my ass off. "I hope you know how much you've helped me, today."

As I make my way back to my apartment, the world around me swirls in a dizzying kaleidoscope of colors and shapes. The starry night sky above is reminiscent of Van Gogh's "The Starry Night," with its deep blues and vibrant stars. It's been hours since I ingested that shroom edible, but its effects still linger, adding a dreamlike quality to everything I see. Perhaps I stood up too quickly, or maybe the psilocybin was just taking its time fully absorbing into my blood-stream. Either way, I can feel myself teetering on the edge of con-sciousness, my senses overwhelmed by the surrealness of it all. A wave of dizziness washes over me, threatening to pull me under into a hazy slumber.

Not too much farther, now, I tell myself, watching my apartment building come into my limited view. *Just need to walk a little more. And as soon as you're through that door, you can crash on the couch all you want. But right now you need to keep your head up and your legs moving.*

The trail evens out and I'm back on solid ground, surrounded by apartment buildings. There's something about them that feels dis-tant and unfamiliar, yet also recognizable. I know which building is mine, which door leads to my apartment. But at the same time, it's as if I'm disconnected from this world and this life. It's like my soul is separating from my physical body, leaving behind an old existence and rushing toward a new one.

My vision is dark around the edges as my hand grasps the knob to my apartment door. I pause for a moment, thanking the shining stars above that I made it back in one piece. This is the last thought that runs through my mind before—

Part IX

It's bright the next morning—or perhaps afternoon—when I finally wake up. I slept on the *couch* last night, and I'm not really sure why. In fact, I don't really remember much after stepping foot into my apartment. It's not so much that I blacked out, and am now suffering from extreme memory loss; I don't think that's even a symptom of psilocybin. It's more so that my brain feels like it was puréed in a blender, then poured back into my skull. I'm hoping that coffee helps.

I absentmindedly watch the dark brown liquid percolate into the pot, my thoughts transfixed on the events from the day before—or what I can recall of them. They're forming—*reforming*—in real time. I remember mistaking the edibles for cannabis gummies. I remember hiking the trail that surrounds my apartment complex, possibly making friends with a tall oak tree.

My mind is racing, trying to piece together the events of last night, when suddenly there's a loud knock at my door. My heart stops and my body freezes in fear as my eyes widen with dread. Who could it be? I haven't ordered anything recently and I'm not expecting any visitors or care packages. It couldn't be a postal carrier or Amazon delivery, so that leaves me with a sinking feeling in my stomach. Is it another tenant, one that I bothered last night by accident? Or worse, could I still be dreaming, and the evil shapeshifter has returned once more? My thoughts are interrupted by the persistent knocking, each rap sending chills down my spine. I never imagined my peaceful time alone with nature could lead to such a terrifying situation.

My mind is blank as I approach the front door, my hand reaching out to grasp the doorknob. Without bothering to check through the peephole, I twist the knob and pull open the door. My heart almost stops dead in my chest when I see her standing on the other side of the threshold. The girl with fiery red hair, her vibrant locks cascading over her shoulders, is unmistakable even with a mask obscuring half of her face. Her green eyes, wide like saucers, lock onto mine in shock at this serendipitous encounter. Facing each other for what feels like an eternity, I try to make sense of this surreal moment.

"*Jane...*" Her name is a whisper as it finally leaves my lips. "What are you—"

"Hold that thought!" she blurts out, her words slightly muffled by the mask. She reaches into her purse and pulls out one of those thermometers that looks like a child's toy gun. I stand stoically, still in shock that she's here, as she points the temp taker at my head. A few seconds later it sounds off with a couple beeps. "Okay, all good!" Jane says, putting it back in her purse. "Can I come in?"

I continue staring at her, deciding if this is real life or some cruel joke my mind is playing on me. Perhaps the psilocybin hasn't worn off yet and I'm *still* tripping. Is that even possible? Is Jane a hallucination? Ultimately I decide that, either way, it would be rude to leave her standing in my doorway.

"Um, of course," I reply, my voice shaking. I hold my hand out, inviting her inside.

She slips her mask off her face and holds it in her hand as she turns back to me. The sight of her, freckles and all, causes a massive fluttering of butterflies in my stomach. Half of my brain is still trying to process that she's actually here in my apartment, while the other half is falling in love all over again.

"Your place looks *great*," she says, her lush lips parting in a grin that sends me into overdrive. She whips her head back at me, a look of suspicion forming on her face. "You didn't hire a *maid*, did you?"

"Nope, this is *all me*. I almost broke my neck a few months ago, trying to navigate my way through the ocean of clutter. When that happened I finally decided it was time to clean."

"*Hm...*" she begins, head wobbling side to side, mouth curling into a teasing grin. "Not *terrible*, as far as excuses go." We share the smallest, most innocuous of laughs that feel like the heavens opening up, declaring eternal sunshine for all.

The coffee maker gurgles the last of the water, reminding me of the pot I brewed. "Do you, um... would you like some coffee?"

After considering the question for a moment Jane nods her head enthusiastically. "I'd love a cup!"

Jane takes a seat on the couch while I make for the kitchen, grabbing two mugs from the cupboard. My hand actually trembles as I pour the coffee, again struck with the terrifying thought that this could all be a dream. It would be a cruel twist of fate, but not at all uncharacteristic, considering the circumstances. But when some of the hot coffee accidentally splashes on my hand, I'm reminded that this is *very* real.

"So, how have you been faring with the world shutting down and everything?" I ask as I take a seat next to Jane, handing her a mug of coffee.

"I've been *okay*, all things considered. I still have a job... for *now*. It's nice that remote learning was an option for schools, so kids wouldn't fall behind. But it's kind of difficult to teach special education over zoom. So, while the paychecks are still coming in, it's still scary not knowing what the future holds."

"Man, I can only imagine," I reply, shaking my head. "I'm sure things will work out, though. Chaos in your world is *always* short-lived."

Jane's smile, although optimistic and her own, bears a hint of defeat. "Yeah. We'll see." She winks at me, sending currents of electricity throughout my entire body. "What about you? *Obviously* you've found ways to occupy your time." She glances around once more at my tidy living room.

I chuckle, rubbing the back of my neck nervously. I'm trying to decide how to properly open up about the last few months of my life *without* sounding like an insane person. Do I tell her about running out of weed and the sleepless nights that followed? What about the nightmares that felt so incredibly real? How do you inform your ex-girlfriend—the one you haven't seen in over six months—that you hit rock bottom, and are still in the process of climbing out of the hole.

"*Well...*" I begin, rubbing my palms together, "as you're aware, the pandemic made *quick* work of eliminating pretty much all fun activities. Which meant that all that was left for me to do was finally clean this trash heap."

"*And* play video games and binge-watch The Office on repeat?" she teased.

I attempt a smile, knowing this was just a friendly and teasing jab between us. But it also hit a little too close to home, reminding me of what led to our breakup in the first place. Sensing a sudden moon shift, Jane's smile also starts to fade. Her eyes again dart around my apartment—possibly for the sake of avoiding eye contact—sipping quietly at her coffee.

The uncomfortable silence becoming too much, I decide to speak up. "*So...* what brings you by?"

Jane whips her head at me, her face wrinkled in amused confusion. "*Really?*" she replied, as if it should be painfully obvious. "I'm here because of that strange voicemail you left me last night."

My look of uncertainty holds steady for several moments. It then shifts slowly into a horrified, wide-eyed realization. Resurrected memories swirl around in my brain. Events, originally presumed as bizarre dreams, suddenly turn out to be real life.

"I... called you last night," I say slowly, my response not *quite* a question.

Jane's lips curled into an *I know something you don't know* grin. "I guess I'm not *too* surprised you don't remember," she smirked, her voice bubbling into laughter. "You sounded high as *balls*."

I'm piecing together the puzzle in real time, still trying to play catch-up. "Um, *yeah*, I guess I *was*," I chuckle. "But it's not what you think! I actually haven't smoked weed in close to three months."

My admission, spoken aloud, carries a weight and vulnerability that I hadn't fully realized until now. For so long, it had been my closely guarded secret, hidden away from the world. But now, the truth is out in the open, exposed for all to see—for *Jane* to see. It feels like standing naked in front of a crowd, my innermost thoughts and struggles laid bare for judgment. I am strangely exposed and vulnerable, but also relieved to no longer carry this burden alone.

Jane peers at me through narrowed eyes, her lips pressed firmly together. She was always good at figuring me out; calling me on my bullshit, for better or for worse. "Why do I have a hard time believing you?"

"Because I'd never give up weed on my own," I shrug. "I ran out, and Donnie went AWOL. And that, as they say, was that."

"So, what was up with that phone call, then? The tell-all voicemail?" She let out a chuckle, tucking her hair behind her ears. "You went on *forever* about this wise, old oak tree who apparently gave you 'stellar advice'." More memories come flooding back. "Apparently, he 'showed you the way,' whatever *that* means. *Do you* know what it means?"

I drag both hands down my face, letting out an exasperated sigh, as fantasy and reality are finally separated in my head. "Um, *yeah*, I think I do," I admit, taking a deep breath, readying myself for a conversation—*the* conversation—that's been a long-time coming. Shifting on the couch to face Jane I look up in her eyes, resisting the deeply-ingrained urge to take her hands in mine. "I've been through some... *significant* changes these last few months, Jane."

My stunningly gorgeous ex-girlfriend nods her head, smiling, gently urging me to continue. I return with my own awkward grin, my mind racing to figure out the next words to say. Because, for a talk that I've been *aching* to have, it's almost infuriating how dumb-struck I am.

"There's... a *lot* that I need to catch you up on, Jane," I begin, wringing my hands together, "so I apologize if any of this sounds... disjointed. And in case that *does* happen, and this goes off the rails like I think it might, I want to come right out and say it. You were *right*."

With the words officially out in the open I take a deep, shaky breath of air, and push forward.

"And *I* know that *you* know that you were right—about pretty much everything. Ever since my mom died I've been burying myself in weed, comics, and video games—whatever I can find, just so I don't have to *feel* anything. I thought that, if I didn't give myself the chance to be sad, I could eventually out-maneuver those feelings. Which I realize now is idiotic."

With a gentle smile, Jane reaches across the worn couch to take one of my hands in her own. The warmth and comfort of her touch sends a sudden rush of adrenaline through me, causing my heart to beat faster and my thoughts to become jumbled. Memories flood my mind as I try to focus on the present moment with her.

"You were *right* to leave me," I continue. "It was something you had to do. At the time I didn't—*couldn't*—understand that. Couldn't understand *why*. And... I don't think I was *supposed* to. I mean, that was probably the whole point, right? I had to learn how to face the demons I'd been repressing, and I couldn't do that with you around. You would've tried to hold my hand and guide me through it, but *you* knew it wouldn't have worked."

Now feeling like I'm on a roll, I gather the courage to recount the events of the last few months. Beginning with the day I ran out of weed, calling Darko in a mad frenzy, I describe in great detail the sleepless nights and waking nightmares. With little shame I share my experience with the shapeshifting entity. How it taunted me, taking the form of her and then Darko, ultimately force-feeding me cannabis nuggets. I tell her about dreaming of my mother, and how it went from a beautiful illusion to a horrific nightmare.

She had to hold back laughter at several moments, like when I hit rock bottom and punched several holes in my wall. And when I stood naked in front of the mirror, faced with the neglect of my physical health. When I tell her about opting for my old running shoes over the pair she bought me, her eyes justifiably roll like ball bearings. And even though I only began to use the new pair because the old ones finally fell apart, a prideful glint strikes her eyes, noting my choice to throw them in the garbage.

We both laugh uncontrollably over mistaking the psilocybin edibles for cannabis, and the subsequent trip that followed. The events of returning to my apartment and calling Jane were *still* a little foggy, but I ran with it anyway, assuming it was all a part of my mind's healing process.

By the time I was finished, both of my hands were cradled in hers. Her deep, emerald eyes now steadily locked onto mine, a million and one emotions rush through me like white-water rapids. I resist the urge to speak up again, hoping that she'll take the lead. And yet I'm worried about where things could go from here.

This is a moment I've literally dreamt about since we broke up. Having her in my apartment, alone and to myself, not in a group gathering so as to provide a buffer, it's all too surreal. I'm reminded again of all those times where I had trouble discerning fantasy from real life, and a gnawing feeling in my gut wants to tell me that this is just another one of those instances. But my mental health has experienced too many improvements to believe that could be the case here.

Jane's lips tighten, appearing to search for the right words to say; the proper response to this profound evolution that sits in front of her. Her grip on my hands tightens ever so slightly, tethering me back to reality, reminding me of the here and now. "Wow. That was certainly more than what I was expecting. And to think, I almost deleted your voicemail last night, sight unseen."

We share a chuckle, one that seems to break up a bit of the tension that's formed between us. "Well, I'm glad you didn't," I reply, giving her hands a gentle squeeze. "I know that might sound weird, seeing as I have little recollection of calling you in the first place. But it did lead you here, back to me. Something that I've wanted desperately for so long, now. So, I'm sorry you had to come over and listen to all this craziness. I'm sure it wasn't your intention to see—"

"Craig, *stop*," Jane blurts out, her voice trembling with emotion. Her hands are clenched into tight fists at her sides, her eyes shining with unshed tears. "Do you have any idea how many sleepless nights *I've* had, too, since our last conversation? How many times I've replayed it in my head, searching for ways I could have done or said something differently? Wondering if I was too demanding or not understanding enough." She takes a deep breath, trying to steady herself. The weight of our past arguments and unresolved issues hangs heavy in the air between us.

"For *months*, Craig. I thought I had lost my chance. That I had lost you, forever. I wanted you to learn how to leave your nest—learn to fly. But half the time I ended up worrying that I let go of you too soon. And then out of the blue, you call me sounding more fucked up than I've ever heard you, and I just... I couldn't *not* come. I had to make sure you were all right. I had to know that the Craig I knew, the one who was there for me when I needed him most, wasn't gone."

Her admission catches me off guard, and I'm rendered speechless. Memories of our past together flood my mind, each one like a book flipping open. I remember the day we met, at a house party that neither of us had wanted to go to. I remember the first time we kissed, the electricity in the air so palpable that it had taken my breath away. Our first date together, our first kiss. It was like Jane had been the one that life had just been waiting to drop into my lap. And then, before I knew it, my mom was gone, and Jane had been there to pick up the pieces, to help make the pain bearable. All of these images and more flood my mind, each one searing themselves into my mind like a brand.

"Babe, it's *okay*," I reply softly. My old pet name for Jane falls too easily off my tongue. "You *don't* have to backpedal and take responsibility for problems that weren't your own. *I* was the one who needed to change, *not* you."

Jane's widening eyes blink slowly, staring at me as if I'm someone she's never met before. Her trembling lips then form a smile, igniting an excitement within me. "I- I'm *sorry*," she says finally. "Some habits die hard, I guess."

"I think I understand that more than most, now." We share another laugh, one that sends waves of relief throughout my entire body. It's both foreign and familiar in equal measures. It's been so long since I've felt a comfort like this, but I remember the warmth fondly.

An awkward silence settles heavily in the air between us, as I desperately search for the right words to say. I've bared my soul and confessed to all of my shortcomings, leaving myself vulnerable and exposed. Sweat prickles at the nape of my neck, having recounted to Jane the innumerable hours I've spent working to improve myself. I desperately want to show her just how far I've come, how I've been through hell and back, trying to get better.

As the words leave my mouth, I immediately regret asking. The question hangs in the air, heavy with a sense of dread. I know I shouldn't pry, but I can't help but wonder if there is someone else. My voice betrays my anxiety as I tentatively ask, "So, have you... been spending time with anyone else?" It feels like I'm bracing myself for a blow, unsure if I really want to hear the answer.

Jane's lips part in a furtive grin. "No, *definitely* not," she laughs. "A global pandemic, I'm *assuming*, is probably not the best time to find someone new. So, whenever those *lustful* urges escalate to a tipping point, I only have to break out my 'pleasure chest' of sex toys and *boom*, I'm taken care of!"

My eyes go wide, stomach fluttering at the thought of Jane, *naked*, masturbating with one of her vibrators. It plays out like some perverted fantasy in my mind. I can envision her long limbs sprawled across the bed, wavy red hair tousled, perfect breasts heaving slowly with each labored breath. A thin layer of sweat forms across her fair skin as she bites her lip, allowing her toy to perform the work I so desperately want to do again. Her free hand grips the bedsheets, preparing for the big finale. And even if it's *not* true—it is *my* fantasy, after all—I imagine her moaning my name as she reaches orgasm.

I shake the thought away and clear my throat. Shifting my position on the couch, I attempt to conceal the massive erection that's formed in my pants.

"You still with me, *Craigy*?" Jane smirks. "Has it been *that* long for you, too?"

The aim to hide my bulge had been blundering and transparent, my ex-girlfriend too quick-witted for her own good.

I lick my lips then take a sip of my cold coffee, my throat dry like sandpaper. "*Maybe*..." I reply sheepishly. "I *have* been doing my fair share of wanking—speaking of things that never change."

Jane throws her head back, laughing. Whether it's *at* me or *with* me is entirely up for debate. Our openness concerning our sexuality, while admittedly awkward in this context, still feels comfortable and familiar. Just like old times.

"So, there's *really* been no one else?" I ask again, craving confirmation.

She shakes her head vehemently. "Absolutely *not*. Besides, I've been kind of... *waiting*."

My brow furrows, face scrunched in confusion. "Waiting? For *what*, exactly?"

"For *you*, silly."

"For *me*?" I ask, incredulous, laughing nervously. "I don't understand. Why would—"

"I *knew* that this day would come eventually, Craig. Honestly? I'm a little surprised you haven't figured that out yet. *Especially* considering all of these significant changes you've made, that have led to a better, more meaningful life."

I can only shrug, mulling over her words that *sound* flattering but only add to my confusion. "I guess I just assumed that that door was closed. Even if I *did* get better, it didn't really make sense that you'd want me back. And that's not me trying to throw myself a pity party, or some lame attempt at collecting sympathy from you, either. Just... the facts."

I pull away gently from her grasp, a sudden urge to reinforce my independence bubbling up inside me. The immediate sensation of not feeling her hands in mine tugs at my emotions, chilling my bones like a biting wind. Becoming more tactile by the second, I *try* to bat away this suffocating notion that I need her in my life again.

I had successfully convinced myself that getting back together with Jane was just a pipe dream, never to become a reality. But now that she's sitting in front of me, I can't help but think there's something much larger at play. Is this what an existential crisis looks like?

The question remains, what *truly* led me here? And did it even matter? Do I deserve another shot at her love? Would any of this have happened if Darko hadn't absconded to Florida? My transformation into a better man, according to Jane, had been less of a theory, and more of an inevitability. Not a matter of *if*, but *when*.

A sudden lightning strike of clarity erupts in my head, shattering all of these meaningless questions and hypotheticals. Because right now, there is only *one* question left to answer; one query that deserves resolution over all others. And that question is—

"Is that something you'd want to do?" Jane asks through a hopeful smile. "Try again, I mean. You and I, together again."

My eyes widen at her words. They sound strange, and seemingly impossible. Jane persists, reaching over to take hold of my stilled hands. I watch as she does so, then meet her eyes. Something inside me *bursts*, and the waterworks start to flow. "I love you, Jane. Of *course* I want to try again."

The words roll off my tongue like the easiest test question I've ever had to answer. My steeled nerves tense and release, buzzing electric at another chance at love.

A familiar feeling of disdain flickers through me, as if waiting for Jane to revert back to her dark, shapeshifting form that once tormented my nightmares. I half expect her to say *"I got you"* and then disappear into the darkness, laughing with twisted pleasure.

Before those terrible thoughts have a chance to take root, Jane *lunges* across the couch with a fierce determination, pressing her soft lips firmly to mine. Wasting *no time*, our tongues dance the familiar, passionate tango we enjoyed long ago. The taste of her is an exceptional sweetness. Her auburn hair falls like feathers against my face. Its freeing scent fills me up with memories, and then reminds me there are now plenty more to make.

Jane settles perfectly into my arms, our bodies pressed together in a tangled mess of limbs and desire. It's almost as if she had never left at all. With every touch, she sets off an explosion of sensations that leave me dizzy with pleasure. The way she makes me feel, how she lifts me up, it's better than any high I could imagine. I want her. I *need* her. I can't get enough.

"I have *one more* important question to ask you," Jane whispers softly, her lips inches from mine. She pulls away, just far enough to reach for her purse. Reaching in she produces a small tin of mints, although it doesn't rattle like it might if it was full. She lifts the lid and my eyes grow wide with what's inside. "Will you accept this peace offering?" she asks, her lips spreading in a grin.

Jane takes one of the pre-rolled joints out of the tin and hands it to me. I accept it, turning it over with my fingers, admiring it with a renewed sense of reverence.

"All right..." I say, smiling, suspicious. "Now I *know* I'm dreaming."

The world out there is dangerous and ambivalent. Unknown variables linger around every darkened corner, just waiting for you to let your guard down. We *all* have fears, whether they're as universal as death, or as personal as the demons that haunt your dreams. The trick is to make *peace* with those evils; face them down, head-on. Let them know you won't stand for their fuckery. And if all else fails? Smoke a joint, make love, and brace for impact.

"Civilization is like a thin layer of ice upon a deep ocean of chaos and darkness."

— **WERNER HERZOG**

CHAPTER 6

The Hat Trick

Part I

Mark's pickup truck slowly came to a stop outside the dark, abandoned house. He parked behind two other cars that were already there, both of which he immediately recognized. Directly in front of him was John's Mazda, and after that Will's Camaro.

Mark wasn't a police officer or a cadet in training, but tonight he felt like one, responding to a random distress call. Approximately 30 minutes earlier, he had received a strange text from his friend Will that included this house's address. Little information had been given in the group text, other than Will's request for them to hurry.

Mark's heart began stuttering in his chest as he closed the door of his truck and slowly made his way up the cracked path. He had a weird sense of déjà vu as he observed his surroundings, noticing the overgrown lawn that was mostly weeds, the picket fence with its chipped paint.

He was halfway to the dilapidated house's front door when John emerged from the dark interior. Spilling out onto the front porch, grasping onto one of the railings for support, John was silent, his face a ghostly white. Mark felt a shiver crawl up his spine, knowing immediately that something was terribly wrong here.

"H-hey man, what's going on?" Mark asked, brow furrowed. "Is Will inside?"

John acted as if he wanted to respond, and even went as far as opening his mouth to speak. But when he did, all that came out was a long slew of vomit. This wasn't a *total* surprise to Mark, as they had both just come from the same end-of-summer party that had a seemingly endless supply of beer kegs.

"Whoa, dude..." Mark chuckled, picking up the pace to the front porch. "If I'd have known you were *this* drunk, I would've insisted we both take—"

"It-it's not the booze..." John muttered, a long line of drool seeping from his bottom lip. His puking had momentarily subsided, and he wiped at his face with the back of his jacket sleeve. He then slowly narrowed his watering eyes at Mark and shook his head.

Mark began to make his way up the dilapidated porch steps, noting the groans of the rotting wood. He patted John's shoulder as he passed him. He was about to cross the threshold of the front door when John grabbed him by the wrist.

"D-don't..." he said weakly.

Mark froze in the doorway. He turned back to John, his face as pale as moonlight, eyes glazed over with a horrible sadness. John slowly shook his head again. He tried to say "don't" once more, only getting as far as the first syllable before an encore of puking ensued over the front porch railing.

Mark turned back and, eschewing his friend's advice, stepped into the black, dilapidated house. The inside was deathly quiet. The old hardwood floors creaked under his feet with each step. Inside the foyer was a staircase leading up to the second floor. To his right was the dining room, which wrapped around to adjoining rooms, finally ending with the living room and foyer.

"Will?" Mark called out, his voice echoing through the darkness. "Hey man, you here?"

He considered going upstairs, but decided to clear the downstairs area first. His father's words of wisdom played in his mind as he cautiously stepped through each room. His father, a long-standing sheriff of Crestwood, had never been short of imparting unsolicited policing advice to his kids. This usually went *double* for Mark, being the oldest of his siblings.

Mark carefully inspected the dining room, the den, and the kitchen. He stood in the doorway of where the kitchen met the living room, hands on hips, eyeing his surroundings. From his perspective he saw the shadow of John sitting on the front stoop. His arms were crossed and propped up on his knees, his head bowed solemnly.

Is he crying? Mark thought to himself. He wrestled with his deepening confusion, perplexed by John's catatonic state, as well as his own inability to find anything—including Will.

Just then he heard a third car pull up outside—undoubtedly Gus, the last guy in their group text. Mark stepped through the dark living room, heading toward the front door to greet him when he tripped over something.

"Ah, *fuck*," he said through gritted teeth after tumbling to the floor. After dusting himself off he reached into his pocket and pulled out his phone. He used it to shine a light on the mystery object he had fallen over.

It was their friend, Will, lying face-up on the floor. Only, that wasn't *completely* right. Mark tried to hold his phone steady, keeping the light trained on his friend's motionless body as he crawled toward it.

"*Will?*" Mark whimpered. He continued crawling toward him when there was no response. He was about to shake his friend awake when he realized what he was looking at—Will had only *appeared* to be lying face-up. In reality his head had been turned—no, *forced*—backward. His eyes bulged from their sockets, bones protruding from his broken neck.

Mark refused to accept what he was looking at. There was no *way* that this was his best friend, Will. He had spoken with him earlier that day at football practice. How the hell was it possible for him to be alive and well one second, and have his head jerked around 180 degrees the next? Furthermore, who could do something like this?

Mark felt a wave of panic wash over him like an unwelcome guest. He attempted to regulate his breathing, to no avail. He finally understood why John had been as pale as a ghost when he first saw him. In desperation, he shook John's unmoving body, hoping—*praying*—for some miraculous revival. Because the reality before him, however finite, was impossible to accept.

Gus had made his way down the walkway and up the stairs to the front door. His footsteps were heavy, and the wooden planks of the porch creaked loudly under his massive linebacker's frame. And although Gus had the grace of a drunkard, Mark hardly registered his appearance in the doorway.

"What... the *fuck*..." Gus muttered. He had taken his own phone out and turned the flashlight on.

"He was like that when I got here," John called out from the front porch, his voice weary. Easing himself to his feet, holding onto the wall for support, he reluctantly made his way back inside. He *had* been crying, both from the drinking and the discovery of his friend's body. Sniffing, he wiped at his eyes with his palms.

"Who did this to him?" Mark asked, still kneeling next to their teammate.

"His text said he was here with Ben," Gus chimed in. "There's no way th-that *he* could have done this. Is there?"

The three high school seniors remained in silence, engulfed in the blackness of the living room. They were afraid to look at one another, afraid to look at their dead friend, speechless on what to say next. How could you even begin to think about what should be done next, when you're too busy still trying to accept the past?

Suddenly, all three of their phones chimed at once, interrupting their collective trance. Mark, now feeling as if he too might be sick, checked his phone. After blinking back nausea-induced tears, he read an unrecognized number that had somehow joined their group text thread. Mark knew, despite his grief, that the privacy settings wouldn't allow a foreign number to join a text thread without permission; they had to be *invited*. Yet, here it was regardless.

> Good evening, gentlemen. I'm sorry you all had to find Will this way—it wasn't my intention to leave him like this. But he made his choices, and they unfortunately had fatal consequences.

"Is...is this *Ben*?" Mark asked, as if his two friends might know the answer. He was about to follow it up with something like, *Sorry, guys, that was a bit of a dumbass question*, but then another text came through.

> Mark, last season a transfer student to Crestwood High threatened your position as first-string wide receiver. In order to ensure that didn't happen, you and a few teammates jumped him after practice one day and shattered his left ankle.

The three football players traded worried glances. This wasn't news to John or Gus. In fact, they were two of the players that helped Mark administer that injury.

Another text came through.

> John, you have cheated most of your way through high school. This has not only allowed you to keep your position on the football team, but qualify you for numerous scholarships next fall. And when the teachers refuse to negotiate with the coaches, you pay them off with daddy's "hush" money.

"Who the fuck does this guy think he is, *Jigsaw*?" John questioned, his voice cracking.

A third message displayed in the thread.

> Gus, you have sold drugs to underclassmen on numerous occasions. This wouldn't be particularly heinous, if a few of those students hadn't died because the drugs contained lethal amounts of fentanyl. And since you knew about the stepped-on narcotics, that also makes you a piece of shit.

Mark and John snapped their heads at Gus.

"*What?*" Gus asked, incredulous. "Fucking *everything* has fentanyl in it, these days. I couldn't take that big of a hit."

Although this was a revelation for Mark and John, they were less concerned about chastising Gus at that moment. They were more interested in figuring out who this mystery person was that had joined their group thread—and somehow knew intimate secrets about them all.

The room's silence was sliced by Mark's angry, labored breaths. After staring daggers into space for several moments, he began searching for a number in his contacts.

"Mark, what are you doing?" John asked cautiously.

"Calling my dad," Mark replied, his voice low and stern.

It wasn't a terrible idea, getting Deputy Alan Thompson involved. The police would eventually have to be notified of Will's body. But, did it have to be right then?

"Not yet," John commanded. Mark set his phone down, shooting his friend a confused look.

"Dude... we *have* to call this in. It's... it's Will's..." His voice broke, rendering him unable to finish. He gritted his teeth as he choked back tears for his fallen, mangled friend.

John, finally able to stand on his own, stepped slowly into the darkness of the living room. "I know," he agreed mournfully, placing his hand on Mark's shoulder. "And we *will* call it in. But right now, the three of us have more *pressing* matters to tend to."

Part II

"I cannot *wait* to kick this little piece of shit's teeth in," Mark muttered angrily.

It was the first line of dialogue spoken between them since they had piled into his truck. All three of them had been too shocked to speak; to think, or feel any valid emotion. They had no clue what to expect when they each responded to their friend Will's distress text. John had thought it was maybe Will playing a practical joke. Mark assumed that, despite his friend's urgency, there had been no *real* cause for concern. But it turned out there had been.

"You *really* think it was Ben who did that?" Gus asked from the backseat.

"Who the hell else could it be?" John replied, irritation heavy in his voice. "Will said in his text that he was at that house, with Ben, and that he had gone off his rocker."

"But, Ben has always seemed so... harmless," Gus added. "I'm just saying. He's not a big dude. I doubt he could bring himself to snap a chicken's neck, let alone..." He trailed off, suddenly too nauseated to finish the thought.

"Maybe you sold him some tainted drugs," Mark jabbed. "Did you start mixing PCP into your cocaine?"

"Dude, shut the fuck up," Gus shot back. "I am not the one who's on trial here."

There was a beat of awkward silence between them, ultimately interrupted by another three-way chime between their smartphones.

"What does it say?" Mark asked, unable to reach his phone. "Is it *him* again?"

"Um, yeah," John replied uneasily. "It's a video..."

John tapped the play button and held his phone out. The video depicted the same living room of the old, abandoned house. Two figures wrestled with one another, fighting and throwing punches. It was at first difficult to make out any details, but as the video progressed they were able to confirm that one of the two was, in fact, their friend Will. At one point, when Will and his adversary had risen from the floor, the lights began to flicker and the unknown figure disappeared. There were several seconds of pitch black video footage, accompanied by rage-filled screams in Will's voice.

"Come out!" Will shrieked. "Come back and fight me like a man!"

Mark, John, and Gus continued watching with bated breath. When the lights in the video flicked back on, the shadow figure had once again appeared in front of Will. It was much closer to him, and although the darkness still consumed most of the room, the three could finally discern that it was Ben.

The final seconds of the video were like watching a movie where the ending had already been spoiled: despite knowing the outcome, they still *needed* to witness the events unfold. Ben muttered something incoherent to Will. And then, with inhuman strength and speed, Ben grabbed Will's head and twisted it around. The splintering and cracking of Will's neck was gut-wrenching to their ears.

All three of them screamed as they watched this happen. Mark, captivated by the video, had to swerve his truck to avoid careening into a ditch. Unbeknownst to him, a police cruiser parked on the side of the highway had clocked not only Mark's reckless driving, but his speeding as well.

"Oh my *fucking fuck!*" John exclaimed. He tossed his phone onto the dashboard then lowered his head into his hands.

"That *was* Ben, wasn't it?" Mark demanded.

"I think so," Gus added. "He looked *jacked*, though. And how the fuck did he do that? I didn't even think it was possible to—"

Gus was cut off suddenly by the need to vomit again. He rolled down the window and began violently retching. Mark and John traded glances, hoping their friend's sickness wouldn't cause a chain reaction.

"I think we need to reconsider our strategy," John admitted, shaking his head. He turned to face his friend in the driver's seat. "Mark, I've changed my mind—you were right. I think you need to call your dad."

Mark scoffed loudly over the vomiting in the backseat. "Are you fucking *kidding* me? Absolutely not. We stick to the plan."

"*Mark!* We are *clearly* out of our depth here!"

"Dude, *relax*. There's three of us and only one of him. I don't care how fast or strong he got over the summer. All we need is for *Gus* to get a hold of him, then it's lights-out."

John rolled his eyes and threw up his hands. "Great. So we're just going to go to his house, drag him onto the front lawn and beat him to death in front of his parents?"

Mark was unresponsive. An eerie, awkward silence had fallen over the truck's cab. So quiet, in fact, that John and Gus— no longer puking—could hear their friend's white-knuckled grip tightening against the steering wheel.

"Admit it, dude!" John continued. "We need to call this in, before anyone else gets hurt.

Mark opened his mouth to respond. but was cut off by the sirens and flashing lights behind them. "Fuck me," he muttered angrily.

He caught a glance at his speedometer before slamming down on the brake pedal; he had been doing 90 in a 50 mile per hour zone.

"Great, now we're *really* fucked," John said, shaking his head.

"Chill the fuck out," Mark sneered, pulling his truck to the side of the highway. "My dad's the deputy, *remember*? This cop's gonna take one look at my information and then let us go—*if* he doesn't recognize me, first."

As the truck came to a stop, John craned his neck to look out the side view mirror. Mark had another flash of rage when he noticed his friend still looked uneasy.

"What's your *deal*?" Mark asked him.

"The cop's windshield wipers are going," John replied cautiously. "It's not raining outside..."

Gus cleared his throat from the backseat. "Yeah, that's, um, *my* fault. I think I puked on his windshield."

"Oh great, now we're really, *really* fucked!" John exclaimed, throwing his hands up.

"I said *relax*," Mark said low through gritted teeth. "If it comes up, I'll tell him Gus ate some bad Mexican food."

"Good evening. Do you know why I pulled you over?" Officer Karen Mitchell stood next to the driver's side door, addressing Mark, a hand not too far away from her holstered firearm.

"Yes ma'am," Mark nodded. "I was driving over the speed limit. Also, I swerved once, maybe twice, because I thought I saw something in the road, so you may have also stopped me for reckless driving." Thanks to his father, Mark knew what the officer both wanted *and* needed to hear. He was also proud of how he was able to admit to all of this in a way that was both respectable *and* cohesive, given his inebriated state. "But here's the thing, officer," Mark continued, "I'm not sure if—"

"License and registration, please," Officer Mitchell interrupted.

Mark rolled his eyes—*after* turning away from the officer—and reached into the glove compartment for his documentation. He handed it over with a polite grin.

"Have you boys been drinking tonight?" Officer Mitchell asked.

"No, officer," they lied.

"*Really*? That's interesting, because I have vomit chunks on the windshield of my cruiser that says otherwise."

"Oh, um, yeah that was me, officer," Gus chimed in from the backseat, holding his hand up. "I'm *really* sorry about that. I guess that's the last time I eat Taco Bell after midnight."

The three boys laughed—even Gus, wincing and holding his still-aching gut. Officer Mitchell, however, remained stoic, her eyes bouncing suspiciously between them. She took Mark's documentation as he handed it over, and was walking back to her cruiser before he could say another word.

Several minutes later—much longer than the three of them would have preferred—Officer Mitchell returned, carrying a metal clipboard with a traffic citation attached to it.

"You were *correct*, Mr. Thompson," she began, addressing Mark as if he had just won a radio giveaway. "I am citing you for *both* of those instances you mentioned. And I am going to have to ask each of you to perform a breathalyzer test, as well."

Mark felt his blood heat to a boil in a dangerously short period of time. He took a deep breath to try and calm himself down, even managing to loosen his grip on the steering wheel. "Is that *really* necessary, officer? Did you happen to see who my—"

"I know who your father is, Mr. Thompson. I'm not an idiot. He's my *boss*, remember? And being the kid of a Deputy does *not* absolve you of the proper punishment for neglecting the rules of the road. Now please, I'll ask you to step out of the vehicle first."

Mark's grip tightened again, his teeth grinding to prevent flying off the handle. "*Okay,*" he began softly. "Can you at least—"

"Step out of the car *right now*, Mr. Thompson," the officer demanded once more. Her voice had lost all leniency, as well as patience.

Mark's fury had quickly dissolved into sheer embarrassment. He felt as if he'd just been scolded by a teacher for pulling a classmate's hair during recess. He opened his mouth to speak again, but then reconsidered. Guilty or not, he knew that anything he'd say or do at this point would only result in more trouble for him and his friends.

Part III

Around 2 AM, almost an hour after their traffic stop, Mark, John, and Gus were ushered into the holding cell at the Crestwood County Police Station, courtesy of Officer Mitchell. All three seniors had failed their sobriety tests, leaving Mitchell with no other choice but to cuff the boys and bring them into the station.

"You're gonna fucking regret this!" Mark shouted as he was shoved into the steel cage with his friends. "I cannot *wait* to watch my dad fire your ass!"

"Save your threats, Mr. Thompson," Officer Mitchell grinned, sliding the heavy cell door closed with a loud *thunk*. "I hardly think that doing my job warrants termination. As for your father, you can talk it over with him when he gets here."

"Oh, believe me, I *will!*" Mark shot her a mocking glance before turning to face his friends. They were already sitting on the long, metal bench, looking sick and morose. "Thanks for having my back, guys!"

John and Gus both looked at each other and shrugged.

"She's a *cop*, dude," John whispered. "You have leverage with your dad. *We* don't."

Gus only nodded, his forlorn gaze fixed upon the cell floor. Mark stared daggers at his two friends, making it glaringly obvious how disappointed he was in them. After a moment he took a seat next to John.

Several minutes of silence went by as the three mulled over the events that had recently unfolded. They had all begun to sober up, and the crushing reality of their friend's death was settling in. Will's gruesome demise was still a shocking mystery. *How could Ben do such a thing? How could that have been Ben in the video?* The way he moved, how he seemed to shift with the shadows and lights, it all looked so disturbing—so... *unnatural.*

Officer Mitchell sat at the desk just outside their holding cell; she had begun the futile act of filling out the paperwork for the boys' "arrest". She regretfully understood that, once her boss arrived, all of this would go in the shredder. Mark, John, and Gus would then get a slap on the wrist, and the worst punishment they'd receive would be some grounding from their respective parents.

Despite the futility, Mitchell kept a satisfied smile on her face. Sticking wasted, irresponsible teenagers in the drunk tank had become one of her favorite past-times since joining the force. Most third-shift officers saw it as glorified babysitting, courtesy of the taxpayers' hard-earned money. Mitchell, however, recognized it as a genuine opportunity to keep little shits like these from killing innocent kids.

"What if we tell her about Will?" Gus proposed in a whisper. "I mean, we *have* to report it anyway, right? And when we do, maybe that'll take some of the heat off us."

"That's *stupid*," John replied flatly, his arms crossed tightly over his chest.

"No, actually, that *could* work," Mark said, a grin growing across his face. "We tell her about responding to Will's text, and how we found him in that house."

Mark took a deep breath, then stood up and made his way to the barred holding cell door. He whistled at Officer Mitchell who sat at her desk, scribbling diligently across a stack of forms. She appeared to be lost in her own little world.

Mark cleared his throat when she didn't answer. "Excuse me, officer?" he began with a faux sweetness. "Hypothetically speaking, what would you say if I told you that earlier tonight we found our friend dead in an abandoned house?"

"I'd say that you have a very poor taste in humor," Mitchell replied, eyes fixed on her paperwork.

"But it's true! That's actually *why* I was speeding to begin with. We were heading *here*, to the station, to report it!"

"Why wouldn't you just call it in, Mr. Thompson? That's what *normal* people do when they stumble across a murder scene."

Mark breathed a frustrated huff, then looked over his shoulder at his two friends. They only shrugged their shoulders, offering no helpful suggestions. This prompted another grunt from Mark as he rolled his eyes, strengthening his grip against the cell door bars. The trio was once more at a dead end.

Mark's head hung low, his eyelids growing heavy. The smartphone video of his friend's death played on an unforgiving loop in the darkness of his mind. No matter how hard he tried to push it away, the image of Will's violently twisted head kept resurfacing.

The "how" was what Mark struggled with the most. Variables such as the "why" and the "what" were still mysteries, but at a glance much easier to solve. Ben had been forever jealous of the friendships

Will had outside of their own. So it was no surprise that those feelings had escalated into an inevitable rage. And to answer the "what", Mark only needed to reference the memory firmly lodged in his brain.

But *how* Ben had possessed enough strength to perform the "Exorcist twist" on his best friend was beyond Mark's understanding. In fact, right up until he discovered Will's body, he didn't even know it was humanly possible to accomplish such a feat—even if Ben did show significant gains over the summer. *No.* This type of fatality was reserved strictly for horror movies.

"*Psst...*" Gus called from the bench. Mark turned to look at him, a disappointed frown etched into his features. Gus got up and shuffled silently toward the barred door. He cupped his hand over Mark's ear and whispered an idea to him. Mark's eyes widened, shining bright with renewed hope.

"What if I told you I had *proof*?" he asked Officer Mitchell. A sly grin creased his lips when her writing came to a stop.

"You have *proof* of your dead friend?" she asked, still not looking up. "What kind of proof would that be, Mr. Thompson?" Her tone, while exhausted, carried the faintest hint of curiosity.

Mark nodded and gestured to the pile of smartphones on her desk. "You can check my phone. Some *psychopath* classmate of ours sent us a video earlier, where he *murdered* our friend, Will. He's been taunting us all night." Mark had become so caught up in the exhilaration of the yarn he was spinning that he suddenly lost track of what was true and what wasn't. "In fact, I think he might be after *us*, now! Holy *shit*, Mitchell, I didn't even think of that! What if he tries to come here, to the station?"

After a moment of contemplation, Mitchell let out an exasperated sigh. "Well, I have to hand it to you, Mr. Thompson, you certainly have an active imagination. But have you forgotten where you live? This is *Crestwood*. No one gets murdered here." She let out a huff that was deeply lined with sarcasm. "I mean, *shit*. Do you guys *really* think we didn't know about that kegger the seniors were throwing tonight? It's a small town, boys, and word travels fast."

"Come *on*, officer!" Mark pleaded. "What do you have to lose? It's less than 60 seconds of your time. I'll give you the passcode for my phone, and then you can watch the video and see for yourself!"

"Yeah, come on, officer. Just watch it and see!" John exclaimed, coming to Mark's aid. "If we're wrong, you can add it to the list of our offenses. But if we're *right*... can you imagine what this could do for your career in law enforcement?"

Mitchell placed her pen down on the stack of papers and rose slowly to her feet. Hands in pockets she sauntered over to the holding cell. "Let me get this straight..." she began. "You three discovered your *dead* friend in an abandoned house. You then *fled* the scene, in lieu of calling 911. And now you're trying to *barter* with me, using supposed footage of the event, sent to you from a random number?"

Hearing it phrased this way, Mark suddenly understood that his earlier proposition sounded eerily close to bribery. But it was too late to back down; he had said what he said. Now it was up to Officer Mitchell to make the call.

"I've got to hand it to you, guys," Mitchell laughed. "You all have surely kept me entertained this evening." She peered at each of them carefully for several moments, smirking as she did so. And even though everything they had told the officer was true, the boys did their best to appear sober and trustworthy. "*Fine*," Mitchell sighed after a long examination. "What's the passcode?"

Mark gave her the passcode to unlock his phone, then directed her to the group chat with the video. She watched it in silence from her desk, while the boys returned to the metal bench. They bowed their heads as they listened passively to the audio, quietly remembering their fallen comrade, the horrific scene replaying in their heads.

Mark felt renewed rage fill his body. Everything about this night had felt so surreal, so *fake*, that he couldn't adequately process the information. He *knew* that his best friend Will was dead. He had watched it happen with his own two eyes—had *found* his lifeless body in that dark, abandoned house. Yet still, he couldn't fully wrap his mind around the fact that Will was gone.

Officer Mitchell had reached the end of the video. She played it again, and then once more, turning the volume all the way up. Her eyes widened further each time she replayed it. After the third time she glared blankly at the phone. Mark could tell she was mulling it over, and *hopefully* making strides toward taking them seriously.

She turned her head slowly to the three boys in the holding cell. "If this turns out to be a joke... some sort of sick *prank*... I can guarantee that you boys will be a lot more *fucked* than you currently are."

"I *promise* you, officer... it's real," Mark said softly, sincerity in his voice. "I wish it wasn't. That's... that's my *friend* in that video. And he's..." Mark couldn't bring himself to finish. He gritted his teeth as he forced back tears.

Officer Mitchell breathed a sigh of defeat, then reached for the radio strapped to her shoulder. She called out to one of the on-duty police officers, giving them the address of the abandoned house, telling them to proceed with mild caution.

She was about to set Mark's phone back down on her desk, returning to her paperwork, when it chimed with an incoming message. She tapped on it and read the message as if it were her own phone.

"Hey!" Mark yelled, concerned. "Is that a new text in the group chat? Is it from that asshole with the unknown number?"

Officer Mitchell didn't respond right away. She read over the brief message several times, her face contorting in profound confusion. Soon her feet were carrying her to the holding cell. She slowly looked up from the phone, her face pale and ghostly, and met the eyes of Mark, John, and Gus. She held the phone out to them so they could read the message.

The three boys had their faces pressed to the bars, reading the latest text from who'd they come to believe as Ben. The simple message, comprised of only two words, struck a cold fear in their hearts:

> You're next...

"'You're next'?" Mark read aloud. "What the fuck is *that* supposed to mean?"

Before anyone had a chance to offer an opinion, all of the lights inside the police station began to flicker. All four individuals looked up to the ceiling, watching the flashing bulbs with wide, skeptical eyes.

Gus pushed his bulky body forward against the bars. "Please, officer!" he pleaded. "You have to let us out! This is *exactly* what happened in the video!"

Officer Mitchell stumbled backward, surprised by Gus's sudden begging. Her eyes bounced back and forth between her detainees and the lights above, grasping for anything that'd explain these strange occurrences. Although the cell phone video *looked* real, she couldn't yet discount that it wasn't just some homemade horror movie. The responding officer to the abandoned house would ultimately confirm the reality of the situation. However, things at the station were escalating at a rate that was making her annoyed and uncomfortable in equal measures.

"R-relax, it's probably just a... power shortage or something," Mitchell proposed sternly. It was an odd coincidence, the station lights flickering at the same time they had read the message. But she refused to allow her detainees to dupe her into letting them out of the drunk tank.

The overhead lights strobed for several more seconds, before cutting off completely. Encompassed in total, breathtaking darkness, a surreal quiet fell over the station. Each person waited, their skin prickling with anticipation, hoping that the lights would come back on.

"*Officer?*" John said, his voice quavering. "I think you better let us out of here." It wasn't a request, or a demand—it was a *plea*.

Mitchell's trembling hand reached for her radio. "This is Officer Mitchell. I am currently at the station, where we have just lost power, *over*." Her breaths were heavy as they cut through the silence. There was a pronounced *click* as she undid the clasp on her firearm holster.

A familiar voice responded to her call for aid within seconds. "*Officer Mitchell, this is Deputy Thompson. I am en route to the station. ETA less than 10 minutes. Over.*"

The four of them breathed a collective sigh of relief, comforted by the sound of a familiar voice. Their surroundings were still enveloped in shadow, but the flickering lights offered a glimmer of hope and provided some solace against the oppressive void. They all looked up hopefully, keeping an eye on the pulsating fluorescents and silently wishing for them to stay on.

The lights in the police station erupted with life, and another sigh was shared—Officer Mitchell included. "Thank *God*..." she muttered, snapping the clasp back on her holster.

Part IV

Mark, John, and Gus began loosening their grip on the bars of the cell door. Weak smiles curled their lips, relieved that the strange phenomenon was only a result of average, rolling blackouts during the hot summer months.

Officer Karen Mitchell, however, was *not* smiling. She was backing away slowly from the cell door, eyes wide and unbelieving. Her hand trembled as it once more reached for the radio pinned to her shoulder.

"Officer Mitchell?" John asked, his concern closely mirroring her own. "Is... everything *okay*?"

The officer's voice caught in her throat as she tried to speak. Her terrified gaze was fixated on something behind the three high school seniors, a look of horror etched into her features. The three boys turned slowly to face what had struck so much fear into Mitchell. High in the corner, where the walls met the ceiling, was *Ben*, crouching like a spider. His eyes were wide open and staring unblinkingly at them. His body was twisted and contorted into an unnatural position, as if he were an amorphous shape made up of limbs.

The four of them jumped when Ben started to *untie* himself. His arms and legs snapped into their anatomically correct position a little at a time. The gut-wrenching sounds they made were like broken bones being snapped back into place. His skin was like twisting silicone as it smoothed out.

Officer Mitchell had backed up all the way to her desk. Mark, John, and Gus were pressed as far against the barred cell door as they could get. Their jaws were slack, hearts beating impossibly fast, as they watched Ben unfurl into his final form and then drop to the floor of the cell.

Ben rose against the back wall, hands at his sides, eyes narrowed at them. His lips curled into a hideous and evil grin. He stood motionless for what felt like an eternity, a wax representation of himself.

Mitchell's radio crackled to life. *"Officer Mitchell, this is Deputy Thompson. ETA five minutes. Over."*

Thompson's transmission did little to ease their collective tension. Five minutes *seemed* objectively reasonable, but in that moment it sounded more like a death sentence.

Ben's eyes darted between the three boys for a moment before he flinched. *"Boo!"* he exclaimed, shooting his arms out toward them. He clapped his hands and cackled as they all gasped, huddling together like terrified children. "Oh *man*, that was *hilarious*! You should have seen your faces."

"Wh-what the *fuck*?" Mark whispered, his voice trembling. "How... how did you... *why* did you—"

"Kill Will?" Ben interrupted. "I told you earlier, I didn't *want* to. Will had every opportunity to walk away unharmed, but he chose to fight me." He sighed heavily and shrugged. "I guess some people just don't know when to fold 'em."

Gus was the first to strike, charging quickly and suddenly. He barreled toward Ben like a freight train, fully intent on pushing Ben *through* the brick wall behind him. His movements were surprisingly agile despite his size.

Ben reacted with break-neck speed, as if he *knew* Gus would be the first to attack. He held up a hand, *freezing* Gus in place, then thrust his other hand outward like a battering ram. Mark and John winced as they were misted with a warm, crimson liquid. Slowly opening their eyes they noticed that Ben had punched a hole *clear through* their friend's chest.

Gus collapsed to the floor with a *thud*. Blood spread out in all directions from underneath his lifeless body. Red droplets fell from

Ben's arm that was caked in gore. John was transfixed by the hole in Gus's back, as well as the rate at which all of this had escalated. Mark glared at Ben, an equal blend of horror, revulsion, and hatred coursing through his veins.

"*What the fuck...*" Mark whispered.

Ben had opened his mouth to respond but he clocked Officer Marshall steadily reaching for her radio. He held up his index finger and, smirking, made a *tsk tsk* gesture.

Terror had seized Marshall, not unlike it had the boys. She still somehow found the resolve to make the call. "I need all available units and emergency services to the Millhaven Police Station, ASAP! I repeat, we have—"

Her distress call was cut off when a sudden force gripped her throat. She had taken her eyes off the apparition in the holding cell only for a second. It was, however, long enough for him to disappear in a plume of black smoke, reappearing mere inches from her. Ben's impossibly strong grip was tight as he lifted Officer Marshall off the ground. She kicked her feet frantically as one hand reached for her sidearm. She had no idea if this person—this *thing*—was immune to bullets, but it wasn't going to stop her from trying.

"You are *pure*, officer," Ben said in a low growl. "My business is not with you tonight."

Officer Marshall suddenly went limp in his grasp. Ben dropped her to the floor like a weighted rag doll, then turned to face his last two victims, still locked inside the steel cage. Mark and John backed away slowly from the cell door, their feet sliding through their friend's pooling blood.

"Come on, man, you don't have to do this!" John pleaded.

"Y- *yeah*..." Mark agreed, "whatever beef you had with Will, that's between you guys. We didn't do *anything* to you!"

Ben's lips spread apart in another devilish grin as he stepped slowly toward the cell door. "I *would* be a fool to act this way over some harmless bullying, wouldn't I?"

Mark and John could only shrug, offering a weak, terrified smile.

"But this isn't *just* about me," Ben continued. "This is about *everyone*. All of the defenseless students you three have tortured over the years? They deserve... *retribution*."

Ben walked right up to the holding cell door and passed straight through it to the other side, rejoining the captives. Mark and John were once more trapped inside the steel cage with this supernatural version of Ben.

"Oh *fuck!*" John cried out, shocked by this impossible act of physics. Ben's reappearance had jarred him to the point where he began *tripping* over Gus's blood. He scrambled to catch his balance, his arms flailing like windsocks. When he finally fell backward, his neck made a chilling *crack* as it connected with the edge of the metal bench.

Mark steadied himself, terrified to break eye contact with Ben. He wanted—*needed*—to check on his fallen friend, but had a sinking feeling that it was too late to save him. His feelings of self-preservation and fear formed a perfect cocktail that turned his hands into fists.

Mark stood his ground, hardening his face as well as his posture. If tonight would be the end, he would go down swinging. "Let's do this, *asshole*," he said through gritted teeth.

"*Hopefully* you're a better dance partner than your friends were," Ben taunted.

Mark let out a battle cry as he descended upon Ben. His fists were a barrage of hammers as they struck the face and body of the apparition. Hope shot through him like lightning at the feeling of his

290 DAVID T DASSAU

knuckles against *real* meat. He huffed and panted like Rocky Balboa in the final round, blinded by sheer will and determination.

Ben held up his forearms, protecting himself from Mark's ravenous pummeling. He gritted his teeth and let out primal grunts, pretending to be weakened by the onslaught when in reality he was enjoying every moment of it. Behind his determined expression, a sly smile played on his lips. Mark wanted a fight and Ben was more than happy to oblige, relishing in the brutal exchange of blows as they both fought for dominance.

Rage burned through Mark's veins, fueling the relentless pounding of his iron fists into Ben's crumpled body. Each blow felt like sweet revenge, a release from years of pent-up aggression. As blood and sweat splattered against the steel bars of the cell, Mark reveled in the power pulsating through him. He had shed his former self and emerged as a ferocious warrior, destined to be crowned as the infamous "King Ghost-Slayer". No longer vying for popularity or fame, he now sought only vengeance and glory in this brutal battle.

Mark's prideful grin widened at the sound of a car door slamming shut just outside the station. His father's concerned voice rang out loudly from Officer Mitchell's radio, confirming his arrival. And soon he would witness Mark arise victorious against an actual *ghost*.

Suddenly, he was only punching air. He blinked away the sweat from his eyes and noticed that Ben had once more shape-shifted into a plume of black smoke. "Get back here!" he screamed. "Fight me, you fucking *coward*!"

Deputy Thompson threw open the front door of the police station and sprinted toward the back room. He rounded the corner just in time to witness the biggest, most insane bloodbath he'd ever seen. Officer Mitchell lay on the floor, *thankfully* only unconscious—he noted the gentle expanding of her chest. Those in the holding cell, however, were not as lucky. Through the blood and gore, he recognized the two bodies as his son's friends.

Center stage to this carnage was his son, Mark. A strange, black cloud was circling him like his own personal tornado. It whistled faintly, wicking red droplets all across the holding cell like sideways rain.

Deputy Thompson watched stoically as mini funnels started branching off the tornado and slithered into Mark's orifices. His son's body convulsed from the unsolicited intrusion, somehow managing to stay upright in spite of the blood his feet danced across.

The convulsions finally ceased once the ominous black cloud disappeared fully into Mark. Deputy Thompson took this as the right moment to finally approach his eldest.

"S-*son*?" Thompson asked weakly. "W-what the hell *happened* here?"

Mark's expression turned from blank to twisted as his father's words sank in. His eyes widened, the whites bloodshot and bulging like a cornered animal. Suddenly, Mark's head snapped back and his eyes rolled up, revealing a swirling vortex of dark charcoal black. The Deputy stumbled back, gasping in shock at the transformation taking place before him.

Mark's jaw snapped open, forming a horrible, gaping maw. "*There is no more Mark... Deputy Thompson.*" said the deep, sinister growl. The voice that had spoken to him was not that of his son's. It was, Thompson thought, not of this earth at *all*.

What he had stumbled into was a scene straight out of a horror picture. He wanted to believe that this was all just a dream—a *nightmare* he'd soon wake up from. He would stumble out of bed, meander down the hallway, and find his son sprawled across his bed, fast asleep. But this... was *no* dream.

Thompson gathered his remaining courage and planted himself tall and firm. "Who *are* you?" he asked, steadying his voice. "What have you done with my boy?"

A guttural laugh escaped Mark's throat. "It's not what I've done, but what I *will* do that should frighten you."

Thompson quickly unholstered his service revolver and pointed it directly at his son. He knew that it was beyond ludicrous, and he would never intentionally fire at his son, regardless of the circumstances. But in the moment it was all he could think to do.

"You let him go, you evil piece of *shit*," Thompson sneered. "You let him go, or I'm gonna—"

"*Oh, Deputy...*" the voice interrupted. "*You have no jurisdiction here...*" Mark's jaw remained open, immobile, as the words that were not his own continued to spill out. "*You are, however, a respectable man. One who is worthy of a proper goodbye.*"

Mark's body suddenly reanimated with natural life. He charged the cell door upon recognizing his father. "Dad!" he exclaimed, his wide eyes clear, no longer saturated with darkness.

Deputy Thompson made no effort to respond. Instead he rushed over to the desk, stepping over Officer Mitchell, and grabbed the large ring of keys. He knew which one opened the holding cell door—it was a key that had seen much use during his tenure as an officer and deputy. But his eyes had welled with tears of relief at the sound of his son's natural voice, making it difficult to see.

"*Dad*?" Mark said again, cautiously. "Dad, I... I don't feel so good..."

Thompson looked up from the set of keys, noticing his son's ghostly white complexion. He wiped the tears away with his shirt sleeve and *scrambled* to find the correct key.

Mark saw the room begin to rotate and thought he was going to vomit. It was more than nausea, however—it was *Ben*. Instead of bile, a blood-curdling scream escaped his throat. It echoed loudly throughout the entire station. His father, startled, dropped the keys to the floor. The sound of distant sirens, barely audible over Mark's painful wails, brought no relief to either of them.

There was a lot that Mark wanted to say to his father, somehow knowing he only had seconds to live. There was so much to say, so much to do, so much to apologize for. But all he could do... was *scream*.

"It's okay, son! It's going to be alright!" Deputy Thompson crouched to retrieve the set of keys. But when he stood up he found himself stumbling backward, his eyes wide with terror.

Mark's face, once a sickly pale, was now blackening. Cracks formed and spread like spiderwebs, as if molten lava was bubbling just beneath the skin's surface. Mark's screeches crescendoed, culminating with his body *bursting* like a meat-filled balloon. Deputy Alan Thompson was thrown backward by the sheer force of the explosion.

Stumbling to the ground, he watched in dumbfounded horror as little pieces of his son splattered against every surface of the holding cell. The trajectory of the mangled skin and bones painted his white undershirt a dark, crimson red.

Deputy Thompson, his heart pounding out an erratic rhythm, remained motionless amidst the macabre ruin of his world. His mind refused to accept the gruesome tableau before him, pieces of what was once his flesh and blood now fragmenting the very essence of his reality. The station, once a haven of order and safety, had been transformed into a chamber of nightmares.

The distant sirens grew louder, piercing through the veil of shock that had descended upon him. They carried with them the promise of aid, yet Thompson knew no amount of help could reverse what had transpired. The malevolent force that had infiltrated and shattered their lives was beyond human power to combat. And somewhere in the shadows of his terror-stricken thoughts, he realized that this was just the beginning.

As he struggled to his feet, a low hum began to resonate within the walls of the station—a sound that seemed unearthly in its timbre. Then came a chilling whisper that danced across the chaotic remnants of flesh and bone: "Vengeance... is *unfulfilled*..." The disembodied voice slithered like a serpent finding its way back into darkness, leaving an icy trail of dread upon Thompson's soul.

Just then another voice, more human than the last, spoke up. "What the *fuck* happened?" Officer Mitchell said groggily. She folded herself into a sitting position next to her Deputy. When she finally caught sight of Mark's disappearing act, her hand shot to her mouth, stifling a scream.

"What *happened*?" Deputy Thompson said sorrowfully. "I think... there's a *ghost* in Crestwood..."

Afterword

I'd like to congratulate you on reaching the end of this collection! I'd also like to congratulate myself, because if you stuck around long enough to read all six of these stories, obviously I did something right. I do hope you enjoyed at least a *few* of the collected works. It was quite the eclectic array of stories which employed many different themes of suspense and horror. So, I can more than understand if you loved one but hated another. Even *I* have my personal favorites, which I know is a shameful act akin to having a favorite child. But I can't help it! That's just the nature of storytelling: sometimes you simply want to tell a spooky tale, and then there are times where that tale comes from a more raw, visceral place.

"A Ghost in Crestwood" is a great example of the latter. When I set out to write it, I wanted it to be a cathartic experience more than anything; whether the reader found it truly scary had always been secondary. I know this might not make sense from a marketing standpoint, but I am a man with a history of going against the grain just to prove a point.

Friends can come into our lives—often in the most serendipitous of ways—and stay with us for a lifetime. They enrich our very existence and help make our own personal journeys all the better. If you're lucky you may have one or two of these. And the most wonderful aspect about these relationships is the person could be anything from a spouse to a plutonic life partner. Isn't it great when you abandon the archaic rules of friendship? I sure think so!

And then there are also friends are only meant to come into our lives for a short while. This opposite side of the coin can be difficult to accept—I know it was for me. To this day I *still* struggle with the acceptance of friendships that ended way too soon. But sometimes you lose touch (or purposefully end a relationship) because it is simply not working.

I had this one friend when I was younger, who came into my life much like a Trojan Horse. I was incredibly shy at the time so naturally I was horrible at making friends. When this guy hopped off his wooden steed and invited himself in, I was more than happy to have him. In many ways he really helped me to come out of my shell and learn how to talk to other kids. So, regardless of how things played out between us, I still owe him a debt of gratitude for that.

And then one day he opened the hidden hatch of that horse and a war ensued. Because I hadn't many friends at that point in my life, it took a long time for me to learn that the ways this kid treated me were not how friends were supposed to treat each other. In fact, it wasn't until perhaps ten years later when I made this discovery. And with that discovery came both the good and bad. The *good* was that I *did* finally make that connection. The *bad* was that the revelation felt a little too late. It felt a lot like coming up with the perfect clapback to an argument you had with someone five years ago.

Writing "A Ghost in Crestwood" was my attempt to work through a lot of those conflicting feelings I had unhealthily held on to for too long. Sure, it may not be the most suspenseful or scary tale in this collection, but it allowed me an opportunity to process a lot of those long-buried feelings.

I think there's a bit of all of us in the characters of Will and Ben. Just as we have the ability to be amazing to each other, we can just as easily treat people like absolute shit. This is a big reason why there is no clear "good guy" protagonist in the story. Yes, Will did have a disturbing history of treating Ben like crap... but did he deserve to *die*? And while Ben did get his revenge against Will—the person who for so long masqueraded as a friend—was acquiring supernatural abilities in order to carry out said revenge truly justifiable? I'll let *you*, dear reader, be the judge of that.

"The Last Stall on the Left" is a great example of simply wanting to spook the reader (did it work?). I wanted it to be a nod to the spooky tales that shaped my childhood—think Goosebumps and Scary Stories to Tell in the Dark. Those Stephen Gammell illustrations really did a number on us, didn't they? After wrapping up a hefty 20,000+ word novella that was "A Ghost in Crestwood," I wanted to dive into something shorter, something that could be written in the span of a single weekend. The result was this story, which blends a touch of humor with a classic scare.

In crafting the protagonist, Tim, I wanted to explore the irrational fears we all have, focusing on his phobia of using public restrooms. The third-person perspective allowed me to have a bit of fun with his character, almost poking fun at his fear while still rooting for his success. The idea was to let Tim triumph in the end, but not without a good scare for both him and the reader.

One thing that I believe is worth mentioning is the unwavering support that Tim receives from the people around him. His therapist of course is a helpful aid along his journey to overcoming his fear of the toilet monster. And not to diminish the work she does with him, but I think the *real* hero in this story is Tim's wife, Cynthia. If you have someone in your life that has stuck by your side, someone who is willing to put up or even *help you* with your weird quirks, you know *exactly* how amazing it feels to have that kind of support.

At its core, this story is a reminder that we all have our own quirky fears, and that's just another thing that makes us human.

If I had to choose a favorite from this collection, "I Fucking Hate Cannibals" would be it. This story took the longest to write, and every step of the process was a wild ride. When I set out to write it,

I imagined Stranger Things, Evil Dead, and Shaun of the Dead colliding in a bloody, chaotic harmony. It's a blend of heavy metal, the hysteria of the "Satanic Panic," and the campiness of 1980s horror movies—a combination that I couldn't resist exploring.

The writing process, however, was anything but straightforward. Every time I sat down to work on it, I'd come up with some grand new idea that would completely derail everything I had written up to that point. I was constantly going back and forth on whether to make it a short story, a novella, or even a full-length novel. Eventually, I settled on a novella, only to have one of my "Constant Editors" read it and tell me it needed to be a full novel! That feedback drove me nuts, but it also affirmed that I was onto something special.

What makes "I Fucking Hate Cannibals" so dear to me are the characters, Ronnie and Maddie. They are very much stand-in's for one of my closest and longest friendships, and writing their dynamic was a joy. I hope you enjoyed spending time with them as much as I did because this won't be the last you see of them (wink wink).

What happens when your deepest desires come true? What do you do when your wildest fantasies become reality—only to have that reality turn into a waking nightmare? These questions were at the heart of "I've Created a Monster." But as I delved deeper into Angela's psyche, the story evolved into something much more than an exploration of the age-old adage, "be careful what you wish for."

My life has been profoundly shaped by strong, resilient women—my wife and mom being two of the most significant influences. As a married man, I wanted to explore the other side of marriage, especially the sacrifices that women are often forced to make. While I've been fortunate to find fulfillment in my career and hobbies, my wife has dedicated the past eight years to being a stay-at-home mom to our two autistic children. I've watched as she willingly relinquished much of her personal identity to meet the needs of our kids, without complaint or hesitation.

Witnessing this selflessness was both heartbreaking and awe-inspiring. It deepened my respect and admiration for my wife and all the women who endure similar trials. Through this story, I sought to echo the struggles and sacrifices that so many women face daily, often without recognition.

Perhaps my favorite aspect of "I've Created a Monster" is how the reader follows Angela as she descends further into madness while her husband, Doug, transforms into a peak specimen. It's a classic case of the "unreliable narrator," where the reader must decide if Angela *truly* believes that Doug is becoming a different person, and if that is in the physical or metaphorical sense.

As a man, I know I can never fully understand what it's like to be Angela: a woman in a world filled with impossible expectations. But this story is my tribute to the women who move mountains for the people they love, expecting nothing in return.

"Not If, But When" is a fun combination of two separate instances in my life that I decided to mash together and make into a novella.

If you talk to any frequent cannabis user and ask them what happens when they quit cold-turkey, they might tell you about a slew of horrific nightmares. This was exactly the case for me a few years ago. Immediately when I went off weed I began having intense dreams and nightmares, as if my brain was making up for lost time. But the pendulum had swung so violently in the opposite direction that it became a problem for a few weeks, leading me to believe that I might not ever sleep again.

The second true-life account was when I tried psilocybin mushrooms for the first time, which did happen during the Covid pandemic. I definitely had my reservations about mushrooms and the effect they might have on me, but I was willing to give a smaller dose a try. The experience in turn opened my mind—temporarily and permanently—in ways I'm unsure could've happened otherwise. And I'd like to think that my trip had a lot of influence in this short story. Granted, I didn't do anything as crazy as Craig did, such as mistake an oak tree for a talking ent. However, at a time when it was difficult to remain positive about anything, it helped me take stock of everything in my life that I had to be thankful for.

So, in an effort to make light of the former of these two experiences, and repurpose the latter, I decided to inject rough translations of them into Craig's story. And the result ended up being something I was really happy with.

There are a lot of downbeats in these collected works, with a few of the stories that end on sour notes—it *is* horror, after all. But I wanted at least one that concluded where "the guy got the girl"—literally. I also really enjoyed this tale and Craig's journey because it doesn't follow a lot of traditional horror beats. I know this means that some of y'all probably didn't like it—or perhaps *hated* it—but I wanted to tell a story of a man who has a revelatory experience by means that many of us can relate to. And then have those experiences lead to a happy conclusion that involves Jane coming back into his life.

Although "The Hat Trick" is a direct sequel to "A Ghost in Crestwood," it didn't start out that way. What's cool about the story is that it *can* work on its own if it needs to. It's not dependent on the reader being aware of prior events—but it does help.

"The Hat Trick" mirrors many of the same concepts as its predecessor, particularly the notion that there isn't a clear "good guy" to root for. I didn't set out to make Mark, John, and Gus unsympathetic to the point where the reader felt that the three high schoolers "deserved" their bloody punishments. Instead, I was more interested in detailing how dirty revenge can be.

Revenge always has an agenda, and Ben's agenda in this continuation is to clean up the loose ends in the wake his mess he made with Will. This not only leads to an even *bigger* mess, but also sets the stage for a major problem in Crestwood. Will we see a continuation of this (or any other) storyline in future volumes of *A Home for Wicked Thoughts*? I guess we'll see, won't we?

Until next time, take good care of yourself and those that you love. And remember that it's okay to be scared. Because without fear, there would be no bravery.

David T. Dassau is a writer and software developer based in Nashville, Tennessee. When he's not crafting code or penning stories, David enjoys a variety of creative and leisure pursuits. He is an avid podcaster and a devoted fan of pop-punk music, often found at concerts soaking in the energy of live performances. A lover of all things horror, David also delights in watching scary movies, always on the lookout for the next great thrill.

David cherishes his time with his family, which includes his wife, Lindsay, their two children, Charlie and Erin, and their loyal dog, Harvey. Whether he's exploring the latest tech trends, attending a local concert, or simply enjoying a movie night at home, David's passion for storytelling and the joy of shared experiences are at the heart of everything he does.

Printed in the USA
CPSIA information can be obtained
at www.ICGtesting.com
CBHW030832011124
16733CB00022B/532